JOSIE'S GIFT

A Novel by
Donald Smith

xulon
PRESS
MID-AMERICA CHRISTIAN UNIVERSITY
C.E. BROWN LIBRARY
3500 S.W. 119TH ST.
OKLAHOMA CITY, OK 73170

Copyright © 2011 by Donald Smith

Josie's Gift
by Donald Smith

Printed in the United States of America

ISBN 9781613793558

All rights reserved solely by the author. The author guarantees all contents are original and do not infringe upon the legal rights of any other person or work. No part of this book may be reproduced in any form without the permission of the author. The views expressed in this book are not necessarily those of the publisher.

Unless otherwise indicated, Bible quotations are taken from The HOLY BIBLE, TODAY'S NEW INTERNATIONAL VERSION, TNIV. Copyright © 2001, 2005 by International Bible Society. Used by permission of International Bible Society.

"TNIV" and "TODAY'S NEW INTERNATIONAL VERSION" are trademarks registered in the United States Patent and Trademark Office by International Bible Society.

Some brief quotations and references to Scripture are from the New Jerusalem Bible (NJB) copyright 1985 by Darton, Longman & Todd, Ltd. And Doubleday a division of Bantam Doubleday Dell Publishing Group, Inc. All rights reserved.

www.xulonpress.com

ACKNOWLEDGEMENTS

My heartfelt thanks to Diana Zertuche, of Del Rio Texas, herself a Catholic Sephardic Jew for getting me hooked on the research into Sephardic Jewish families, names, customs, and history. I also want to recognize my longtime good friend and fellow counseling practitioner, David Loberg, who is a practicing Messianic Jew living in Houston. Dave was always willing to patiently answer my questions. Dave read the manuscript and offered important corrections and suggestions. He also wrote the Preface. I want to recognize the Baruch Hashem Assembly in Del Rio, Texas. I want to also recognize the Congregation Beth Messiah in Houston, Texas. Both Baruch Hashem Assembly and Congregation Beth Messiah have welcomed my wife Anita and me at the times when we visited and were blessed by their services. Finally, to my wife, Anita who has Sephardic ancestry on both sides of her family, for her encouragement and love that helped me to keep going in this project.

I want to thank, Lisa Sue Bell, my daughter and Dianne Smith who were kind enough to read the manuscript and offer many corrections.

DEDICATION

This book is dedicated to all of my Jewish brothers and sisters who have found their true Messiah in Yeshua. On a day known only to God, we shall all, Jew and Gentile alike, be one in Yeshua and share together in His glory. Shalom!

To my wife, Anita

FORWARD

Messianic Judaism in the twenty first century is not unlike Messianic Judaism in the first century. In the first century, the first believers were mostly Jewish along with a few Gentiles. By the third century there was a split between the Jews and Gentiles that has lasted for about seventeen hundred years. Because of the way the Jews were treated by the church, they rejected the Gentile ways of faith and the Christian Christ/Messiah until the last century. However, through those centuries there has been a remnant of Jews who have not rejected Yeshua/Jesus as their Messiah.

With this backdrop Josie's Gift begins as a story of a typical teenage girl rebelling against the godly Messianic faith of her ancestors and into an evil, sinful world. When Josie's chosen life takes a sharp "left turn", God places a caring community of believers where she needs them to help her put together the mess she has made of her life.

Unlike the Messianic community of the first century, today most believers are in Christian churches filled with Gentile believers and some Jews who have accepted Jesus as their Messiah. This is where Josie finds herself. It is in the loving atmosphere that a gift from God, prophesied by her grandfather years earlier begins to be unwrapped.

When evil enters lives it brings with it heartache and pain, not only to the individuals directly involved, but to parents and friends and many whose lives they touch. Josie's parents are such. They are Messianic Jews with a godly heritage. Their lives exemplify what God intended for His followers to show the world, first to their family, and then to their community and beyond.

When Josie lets God into her life, things don't magically become wonderful. On the contrary, they become challenging, but nothing that trust in an Almighty God is not capable of overcoming. As Josie grows in her faith, the challenges grow with it. She finds that she is never alone in these challenges. She has her faith community and always God is ever present.

Josie's story is the story of many lives. The details of each one are different. Any of us could be one of them. The outcomes will depend on the choices that are made and the people to whom we choose to listen. God has given everyone a gift. We don't have to bear the penalty of our bad choices; God and a community of believers who have gone before us are willing to walk with us through the consequences and into a new life.

David T. Loberg, MS, LBSW
Houston, Texas

PROLOGUE

Josefa Ruth Blandón, was born in Churchill, Texas, into a family of Sephardic (Spanish) Jewish Believers, the daughter of Moisés and Ruth Blandón. She has two older brothers, Josef and Israel. Her childhood was a happy one but was divided between a Christian faith and the ancient Jewish traditions of her parents and grandparents. As a child she had great difficulty understanding her being Jewish and at the same time, Messianic. She reveled in the Jewish celebrations along with the Davidic dancing, but felt guilty for it. Other children often made fun of her family and called them *Judeos* (Jews) and *matadores de Cristo* (killers of Christ). A childhood trauma sets her onto a path of rebellion against her family, her faith, and her ethnicity.

Josie's Jewish ancestors originated hundreds of years ago in Spain, probably driven there when the Romans burned Jerusalem or perhaps hundreds of years later when the Islamic armies pushed into Palestine. For generations after Spanish Queen Isabela's edict of expulsion in 1492, which banished all Jews from the Iberian Peninsula, Blandón ancestors along with thousands of other Jews, were hounded and jailed by the Inquisition. Their properties were confiscated and many who refused Christian baptism were burned at the stake. Tens of thousands of Sephardic Jews fled to

New Spain (Mexico and South America) where, free from the close scrutiny of the church, they again prospered.

Two hundred years after their arrival in New Spain, several Blandón ancestral family members were tried by the Mexico City Inquisition for being Judaizers, and were subsequently imprisoned and burned at the stake. Ultimately, the Blandón family remnants converted to Catholicism by forced baptism, and were known as *Conversos* (new Christians). As persecution continued and the situation became more intolerable for them, they fled north with a company of *conquistadores* to Santa Fe, New Mexico, where they joined with other Sephardim. There, they walked a fine line between being Jews and being Christians. Openly they practiced Christianity, but covertly and behind darkly curtained windows they practiced many of their Jewish traditions and holidays hoping they were free of the prying eyes of the Church.

Eventually the inquisition followed them into New Mexico and the persecution once again continued. The *Conversos* were forced into secret groups and carefully concealed their Jewish practices until the inquisition died and officially ended in 1820. They came to be known as Crypto Jews or hidden Jews. Even after the inquisitions ended, they were rejected by ethnic and religious Jews and were subjected to great suspicion by Catholics. They literally walked in a religious "no man's land". Over the next two hundred years, Christian faith and practices gradually came to dominate their lives, and many of their Jewish traditions were lost to time and marriage outside their Jewish kin.

The Blandón family was among numerous small groups who, though *Conversos,* clung tenaciously to their Jewish traditions. Marriages were often arranged between second or third cousins in order to preserve the Sephardic identity. Josie's parents, Moisés and Ruth, were second cousins. Some of the Blandón family ancestors, while in New Mexico, responded to Protestant Missionaries from the United States,

Josie's Gift

who brought bibles to the western frontier, and converted from Catholic to Protestant faiths, notably Methodist and Presbyterian, but others continued as Catholics. The bibles were coveted because they contained the Old Testament books so revered by Jews. Moisés and Ruth Blandón's ancestors were among the former who converted to Protestantism. One of Moisés great uncles became an ordained Methodist evangelist and pastor.

After the War Between the States, the Blandón ancestors migrated from New Mexico into Texas. For the most part they held to their Jewish traditions and some of the language, but all, including Moisés and Ruth were Spanish speaking, not learning English until they entered public or private schools. As years passed, with each succeeding generation, except for many foods, rituals, and important prayers and expressions, more and more of the Hebrew language and culture became integrated into the lives and language of the border areas.

As time went on, some *Converso* families found each other and banded together in communities. Today, they call themselves Believers (see Acts 5:14 etc.) and Messianic Jews rather than Christians, so as to maintain an identity with their Jewish roots. Gradually, the rituals and practices began to resurface and they established congregations (synagogues) of Jewish believers. Josie's family benefited from the fellowship of a few other Jewish believers in Churchill, Texas. The group was too small to form a Synagogue so like the early Jewish believers in Jerusalem, they continued in their Christian practices on Sundays, and at home with the few Messianic families they knew, on Shabbat (Saturday/Sabbath), they practiced many of their Jewish traditions which had been passed on from one generation to the next (see Acts 2:46; 3:1; 5:20, 21, 42, etc.). Josie's childhood enjoyed a rich heritage of Christian and Jewish tradition, though seemingly contradictory and difficult for a small child to comprehend.

The Blandón name was a real name, and may be to this day. It was picked from lists of *autos de fe* from early Mexico City Inquisition archives, so as to make the story more authentic. Though the name is real, the family depicted is completely fictitious—a product of the author's imagination, and resemblance to any person of Blandón ancestry, living or dead is purely coincidental. Many of the events portrayed are based upon historical facts, but no intention is made to judge those events as being right or wrong. Some names of places, such as Rock City, Churchill, and Littleville, are fictitious. Others such as San Antonio and El Paso are real.

It is my earnest prayer that this book will not only be informative but will also be a blessing to your life. Should you wish to contact the author, you may do so at, P.O. Box 949, Brackettville, Texas 78832, or email at donald3112@sbcglobal.net.

May the God of Abraham, Isaac and Jacob; the Father of our Lord Yeshua, bless you and keep you for all time.
Donald E. Smith

*Who has gone up to heaven and come down?
Whose hands have gathered up the wind?
Who has wrapped up the waters in a cloak?
Who has established all the ends of the earth?
What is his name and what is the name of his son?
Surely you know!
(Proverbs 30:4)*

*Baruch Ata Adonai Elohainu Melech HaOlam,
SheHakol Barah Lichvodo
(You are blessed, Lord our God, the sovereign
of the world, the creator of man.
(Sheva Barachot, the First Blessing)*

CHAPTER ONE

It was dark when they pulled up beside a gas pump at a convenience store near Lancaster, Texas. Roger got out and filled the car with gas. When he was finished, he leaned through the window and spoke pointedly to Josie. "Put Stevie in the back seat; then get over here in the driver's seat. Keep the engine running and be ready to move fast when I get back."

"What're you going to do, Roger?" Josie asked with a worried tone in her voice.

"Just do as I say," he commanded. "We need some money!"

Roger looked around, opened the driver's door, reached under the seat, pulled out a pistol, and stuffed it under his belt in the small of his back. He pulled his shirt down to hide the gun and nervously looked around as he headed into the store.

Following Roger's instructions, Josie started the car and waited. She anxiously looked into the store through the glass door. Suddenly, through her open window, she heard two shots in quick succession followed by Roger running out toward the car. He hurriedly slid in through the passenger door and breathlessly commanded, "Get moving Josie! Fast! Go!"

Josie pushed hard on the accelerator; the tires spun and screeched as she steered the car away from the gas pumps and into the street. Roger looked back to see if anyone had followed. When he turned to look forward in their direction of travel, he saw flashing red lights and heard a siren heading toward them. "Slow down," he shouted. "At the next street, turn right and keep going." Roger anxiously watched as the police car passed them, heading toward the convenience store.

They drove for ten or fifteen minutes with Roger looking back every minute or so to see if anyone was following. There was nothing, and they blended into the traffic. "When you see an alley we can drive into, go for it and park," Roger commanded.

Josie did as she was told. When she stopped, Roger quickly got out and ran around the car to the driver's side. "Get to the other side Josie." He opened the door, slid in and pushed her to the passenger seat. "There's some stuff to eat and drink in that sack," He said, pointing to the floor. "We gotta get as far away from here as we can without attracting any attention."

They drove until nearly midnight with Stevie sleeping soundly in the back seat. Josie was trying to sleep leaning her head on the passenger door. Roger saw a sign, "ROCK CITY - ONE MILE". He drove through the city, and was heading out of town when he noticed several cheap motels and a strip mall across the highway from a river. On the outskirts of town and about a half-mile from the nearest lights he saw an elevated area overlooking the river. He turned off the car lights and pulled over. A plan formed in his mind.

"Look, Baby, we gotta ditch this car and hole up for a few days. I got 'nough money ta take care of us for awhile."

"What'll we do?" Josie asked.

Roger looked around. The highway was deserted and the moisture in the air was forming a cool blanket of fog. He got out of the car and walked around to the high bank of the river, then got back into the car.

"OK, here's what we're gonna do! We'll push the car off this bank and into the river. Nobody'll see it there. Quick, get Stevie and our stuff outta the car. You and Stevie hide over there, across the road in those bushes. Take our stuff with you."

They worked quickly. When everything was secured in the bushes, Roger maneuvered the car so they could push it forward and get it over the embankment. When he and Josie tried to push it, the car was too heavy, and the ground too uneven. Roger looked around and found a large rock.

"What are you going to do with that," Josie asked.

"Go across the road; hide with Stevie and our stuff and just watch." As soon as Roger saw her safe in the bushes, he put the rock on the accelerator and put the car in gear. He jumped out and rolled out of the way as the car roared forward and down the embankment. It disappeared into the muddy water, a gusher of steam rising from the hot engine.

Roger ran across the road. "Are you all right?"

"We're OK," she answered.

"OK, take Stevie and a sack of clothes and start walking back in the direction of town. It's not very far. There's a motel at the edge of town on the right. When you get there, check in and wait for me. Leave your door open so I'll know which room you're in. I'll bring the rest of our stuff. Here's some money; pay for two nights. We'll get some sleep and then make some plans."

"What if the motel clerk asks questions? I'll have to tell him there're three of us."

"Just tell him your husband had to go to the all-night supermarket down the street and he'll be back in a little while."

It was several hours before Roger showed up at the motel, and Josie was getting worried.

"What were you doing for so long?" She asked doubtfully.

Roger looked at her, disgusted with her question. "Look, I had stuff to do, OK?"

Looking at the sack in his hand, she asked, "What kind of stuff, Roger?"

"Just stuff, OK? Get off my back and quit askin' questions." He was yelling now.

"I gotta know! Was it another holdup?" Josie yelled.

"None of yer business, Josie. I can do what I want, OK? Now leave me alone."

Roger peeled the top of the sack down revealing a bottle of liquor. He quickly unscrewed the top and took a long drink of the amber liquid straight out of the bottle. He let out a long, loud sigh, set the bottle on the table and wiped his mouth with the back of his hand.

"I gotta know something Roger. Did you shoot someone back there in Lancaster at the convenience store? I heard two shots!"

"Shut up Josie! Just shut up!" Roger yelled.

"I need to know Roger!" She screamed. "Did you shoot somebody?"

Roger glared at her. "Damn it, Josie, shut up—shut up," he yelled.

"Did you?" she screamed again.

This time Roger just glared and said nothing. He raised his arm and walked in her direction. She tried to avoid him, but there was nowhere to go. She knew what was coming and put her arms up to protect her face. His fist connected to the side of her head. With his other hand he slapped her hard. She was bleeding when she fell onto the bed.

He put a knee into her abdomen and pushed, got down close to her face, and yelled. "I've told ya a thousand times, don't question me. This is what happens when ya do!"

Josie's Gift

Josie lay on the bed sobbing. Stevie ran to the closet and hid himself. He knew his dad would turn on him if he so much as said a word. Roger picked up the door key, the bottle of liquor, whirled, stomped out the door, and left in a flurry of curses.

Josie cried herself to sleep. As the sun came up, she awoke with severe cramps in her abdomen. She looked around. Roger was on the other bed sleeping off a drunk. She yelled for Stevie and heard a whimper. When she opened the closet door he was curled up in the corner behind the clothes.

As the cramps grew worse she collapsed on the floor. She could feel blood on her legs so she crawled to the bathroom. Holding onto the sink she managed to pull herself up. Looking in the mirror she was horrified at what she saw; one eye was swelled and turning black; blood was crusted on her face. She quickly shut the door and dropped her jeans and underwear to her ankles. Blood was all over her jeans and her underwear. She sat down on the toilet and put her head on her arm on the sink to her left. Her heart was racing. The last thing she remembered was the room spinning. Her blood pressure dropped precipitously, and she fell to the floor.

Stevie cautiously opened the door and peered inside. He yelled at his mom but she didn't respond. He ran to his dad and shook him as hard as he could. "Daddy, Daddy, wake up! Mama's sick!"

Roger slowly opened his eyes and rubbed them to try to get his head cleared.

Stevie repeated, "Mama's sick!"

"Where?" Roger asked.

"In the bathroom," Stevie yelled.

Roger finally got himself up and stumbled in the direction of the bathroom. "Oh hell!" he exclaimed when he saw Josie on the floor in the pool of blood.

Josie was white as a sheet and barely breathing. He tried to get her up, but she didn't respond. He left her lying on the floor and went to Stevie. "Wait here Stevie," he commanded. "I'll be right back."

Roger ran out the door and toward the super market. In the parking lot he quickly went from one car to another looking for one that someone forgot to lock. Finally he found one. Within minutes he was inside, had found an extra set of keys under the floor mat, started the motor and had the car headed back to the motel. As quick as he could, he got Stevie's and his clothes into a bag and into the car.

"Stay in the car till I get back," he commanded Stevie.

"But, what about Mama?" Stevie cried.

"She'll be OK. They're going to take her to the hospital and we'll see her there."

Roger ran to the motel office where he confronted the clerk. "My wife's sick. Call an ambulance."

As the clerk picked up the phone and dialed 9-1-1, Roger ran out the door and back to the car. He peeled out of the parking lot, and with the tires screeching, headed down the road and away from the motel. He knew when the EMS saw the bruises and blood they would be looking for him. He couldn't afford to get caught. A man was dead at the convenience store in Lancaster, and he knew he would face life in prison and maybe the death penalty.

Stevie was crying uncontrollably, and Roger was yelling at him, trying to convince him that his mama was going to be OK. When he wouldn't quit crying, Roger leaned over the seat and hit him with the back of his hand. "Shut up, damn it…shut up!"

There was another cheap motel on the other side of town and Roger pulled in. "Stay in the car, Stevie," he angrily commanded. "I'm going to get us another room.

Stevie did as he was told, and Roger went into the office to check in. "I'll be here two nights; maybe more," he breathlessly told the clerk.

The clerk looked at Roger and then out at the car where he could see Stevie watching what was going on. The clerk sighed, "OK, that'll be twenty dollars a night for the three of you." He assumed that Roger had a wife.

"No, just me and the kid. My wife's sick; I had to get her to the hospital. She'll be there for a few days."

"Oh," the clerk replied still looking dubious. "I'm very sorry; I hope she recovers quickly. That'll still be twenty dollars each night."

Roger decided not to argue about the price. "She's in good hands. Thanks for your concern."

"Here's yer keys—room 14 down at the end," he said, motioning with his hand the way to go.

Roger took the keys; returned to the car and started the engine. He turned around and headed to the end of the wing of rooms until he saw number 14. He got Stevie out and unlocked the door. The room smelled like a combination of stale food and smoke. Stevie found the TV and turned it on as Roger brought everything they had in from the car.

Roger knew it would only be a matter of time before the police discovered the car. He devised a plan. He turned to Stevie. "Daddy's got to go out for a little while; you stay here and watch TV. Don't leave the room or open the door for anything or anyone. Is that clear?"

Stevie nodded at the familiar instructions.

Roger drove to a car wash not far away and washed the car thoroughly. He used a wet cloth from the motel to wipe everything clean on the inside. He didn't want any of his fingerprints found on anything. He carefully got every little scrap of paper and looked for small toys Stevie might have left. When he was satisfied, he put on a pair of gloves, drove to a shopping center parking lot, threw the keys on the driver's seat, and locked the doors with the door lock button. He then closed the driver's door and walked calmly away. For all his trouble cleaning the car, he didn't think even once about cleaning the motel room where he'd left Josie.

He found a supermarket and bought some food for himself and Stevie. Then he found a liquor store, bought himself a bottle and started walking back to the motel.

In the meantime the EMS and the police arrived at the motel where Roger left Josie. The manager opened the door and let them inside. From the door they could see blood leading to the bathroom and Josie's feet near the doorway where she collapsed. The technicians quickly got on their knees beside Josie and began looking her over for signs of trauma and at the same time checking for vital signs. All Josie had on was her blouse. Her jeans and underwear were still pulled down around her ankles.

One of the technicians wore a two way radio on her belt with a microphone pinned to her shoulder strap. She quickly keyed the microphone and began to describe the scene to someone in the Emergency Department at the hospital. A doctor responded and gave some instructions. After they got Josie hooked up to a portable machine that monitored blood pressure, oxygen, and heart rate, they began to transmit the data to the ER doctor, who quickly responded with specific instructions for intravenous fluid and an injection to try to stabilize her blood pressure. He also wanted them to collect what they could from the toilet for lab testing. The IV was started. A police officer took pictures of the scene. They got her onto the stretcher, into the ambulance, and on the way to the hospital. All of this took no more than a few minutes.

At the hospital, the doctors and nurses worked quickly. She was still in a coma but the bleeding had stopped. The contents of the toilet collected in a sterile plastic bottle, were sent to the lab for examination and testing. The doctor ordered three units of blood then turned to the EMS technicians and asked questions. Police detective, Randall Sandoval was there to listen.

The technicians described the scene as best they could. "It looked like the woman had a miscarriage. The police at the scene took her purse and a few other things with them for their own investigation. There was a considerable amount of blood on the floor where she collapsed and we could clearly see marks on her face and her abdomen where it appeared she'd been beaten."

Detective Sandoval spoke up. "I brought her driver's license identification along." Handing it to an attendant he continued, "This is all we have at the moment. You can copy this for your records here, but we'll need to keep the original. The clerk at the motel said she was there with her husband and a little boy, maybe five or six years old. He also said that the husband was the one who had him call EMS, but the man left right after that. The clerk said he just assumed that the guy was going to the hospital. We have a good description of him and the car and good fingerprints from the room, all of which are being checked out in our database. If anyone comes in asking about her, you call us immediately. It looks to me like she was beaten and this could turn into a crime."

"Doctor," one of the nurses called out with urgency in her voice. "Her blood pressure is going down again. There must be some internal bleeding."

The doctor ordered her to radiology for an abdominal MRI scan.

The EMS technicians got their equipment together and left. Detective Sandoval stayed near the ER. He wanted to see if Josie's husband would show up.

The doctor hurried to Radiology, where he quickly scanned the pictures coming from the MRI. "Looks like we have some bleeding near the left kidney. Get her into the operating room and get hold of the surgeon on call; we'll need to open her up and deal with the damage."

As the surgeon was scrubbing, he discussed the situation with the ER doctor. "It looks like the blow to her abdomen was severe enough to cause a tear in a blood vessel near her kidney."

"Yeah, we'll know as soon as you get her opened up. Let's hope you can keep enough blood in her till you can get that vessel repaired."

The nurse in charge of the OR interrupted, "Doctor, we don't have anyone to sign permission for surgery. Do we go ahead?"

"We have to go ahead," the surgeon replied. "At this point it's a matter of life and death. We'll deal with the consequences later, if there are any," the surgeon added.

At the conclusion of four hours of surgery, the team relaxed. They were satisfied the bleeder had been stopped. Josie's blood pressure was now stable and the blood transfusion was terminated. "Let's go talk to the detective," the surgeon suggested.

Detective Sandoval was still waiting around the ER, and the ER doctor joined him when the surgeon came down the hallway.

"Any word on the woman's husband, Detective?" The ER doctor asked.

"We've got the husband ID'd from the fingerprints at the motel; name's Roger Brown and he's got a record of, among other things, family violence. We'll have a blow up of his driver's license photo to leave here with your staff. Right now he's our prime suspect. I left my card with the information desk with instructions to call me immediately if he or anyone else shows up and asks about her."

The surgeon described the damage as the detective took some notes. "We believe her life was seriously endangered by the beating which caused the torn blood vessel. We also believe that the amount of time she lay on the bathroom floor could have made death more certain. It's a miracle she survived."

"How do you think the blood vessel got damaged?" Sandoval asked.

"Well," the surgeon replied. "From the severe bruising on her abdomen, we believe she could have been hit with a fist or kicked with a foot or a knee. We took some pictures in the OR. The blow to her abdomen was hard enough to compress her internal tissues and organs to the extent that the blood vessel was stretched and it sustained a small tear where it was attached to her back. She lost a lot of blood before she was brought in here. We had to give her a total of five units before things were finally under control."

"Yeah," Sandoval replied. "From the blood clotting on the bathroom floor and her clothes, we figure she was laying there unattended for at least two to three hours. We'll have info from our lab on all that within a few hours. Whoever did this, we'll find him!"

"That's good," the surgeon replied. "We're transferring her to ICU, and the people there have orders that she is to have no visitors until I sign the order. We'll keep her in an induced coma at least for two or three days and watch her for any signs of internal bleeding. That'll give our patch time to heal enough to take her off the coma-inducing drug. Then we'll wake her up and call you if she's strong enough to talk."

Sandoval held out his hand to shake hands with both doctors. "Thanks to both of you for all you've done. Keep in touch! OK?" He turned and walked toward the door.

Two days later, Sandoval returned to the hospital. He was shown into the ICU where the doctor who was in charge of Josie's case was on duty. "Well, Doc," he said. "Did you find out anything from the tissue and stuff the EMS techs recovered from the scene where Josie Brown was found?"

"The stuff recovered from the toilet was a fetus that appeared to be about six weeks into gestation. It looked normal and healthy until Josie's body spontaneously aborted it, probably as a result of the beating. It also appeared she'd had one or more prior abortions, and they could also have contributed to her failure to carry to term. Let's walk over to her bed and see if she's awake and up to talking yet. What do you have?"

"We found a car in a local shopping center parking lot. It had been reported stolen the same night Josie was beaten so we figure there might be a connection."

The conversation was interrupted by their arrival at Josie's cubicle.

Sandoval continued. "As I was saying, we had the car detailed and dusted, but Brown had wiped it pretty clean. He missed one spot on the inside of the glove compartment door where we recovered a single print. It's going through the data base right now. We also discovered a car at the bottom of the river just outside of town. It fits the description of the car involved in a hold-up over in Lancaster in Scott County. The convenience store clerk was shot and killed in that one. The car is being detailed for anything that might be significant. There were no witnesses to the robbery and killing, but the security camera got a pretty good shot. It looks like Roger Brown so everything we have here is beginning to connect. The only thing we worry about now is the kid with Brown and of course Josie here. She's the only person who can connect the dots for sure, and Roger is certainly capable of trying to eliminate her."

"OK, the doctor replied. "What do we need to do here?"

"We're going to send a couple of our plain clothes guys down here to keep an eye out for a few days."

"OK," said the doctor. "Josie will need to be transferred to a floor in another day or two. I'll still be in charge of her case so you can communicate with me. Have your guy identify himself with the info desk and with the nurse in charge of ICU when he gets here. When she's transferred, we'll let him know."

"Oh, by the way, could we get a tissue sample from the fetus for a DNA check?" Sandoval asked.

"Sure, the doctor responded. "Let me call the lab, and you can go right on up. They'll have it ready for you."

"Thanks. Look for one of our guys around here this evening. His name is Smith. They call him Smitty. I'll be back in another couple of days. Just call me if she wakes up or if anything develops." Sandoval turned and left.

CHAPTER TWO

Roger was reluctant to go out, so he spent most of his time in the motel watching TV and drinking. He shaved and cropped his hair as best he could so as to change his appearance. He bought a baseball cap, a new pair of jeans and a shirt. He could pull the cap down enough that it would shadow his eyes. He figured his new look would help him blend into a crowd wherever he needed to go.

A few times he took Stevie with him when he walked to the grocery store for food. After two days of hiding in the motel, he decided he needed to find out what he could about Josie. He cringed at the thought that she could identify him and connect him to the shooting in Lancaster. There was only one hospital in town, so he figured she'd be there since there were no reports of suspicious deaths on TV. He decided the evening would be best, close to dark.

"Look Stevie, I gotta go check on Mama at the hospital. You can't go."

"Why, Daddy. I want to see my Mama!" He began to whimper and cry.

"They don't let little kids in the hospital, Stevie so you'll just have to stay here."

"But Daddy, I'm afraid." His crying got louder.

"Shut up, ya hear! Shut—up!" Roger yelled, emphasizing each word.

Stevie bounced onto the bed and buried his head in the pillows.

Roger bent over him and turned him face up. "Listen to me," he commanded as he shook him. "I'm going to lock the door when I leave. Don't open it for anyone or for any reason! Don't even stick your head out! There's plenty to eat and you can watch TV. I'll be back soon. Do you understand?"

Stevie was silent except for his whimpering.

"Stevie," Roger yelled. "Do—you—understand what I'm telling you?"

"But Daddy, I'm scared!"

"Just do as I tell you! Is that clear?" Roger walked out and locked the door behind him.

Roger's cell phone rang just as he closed the door. He looked at the screen and noted the number. His heart beat faster and he felt sweaty. "Yeah, what's up," Roger said.

A hoarse voice with a Spanish accent spoke, "You listenin' Brown?"

"Yeah I'm listening."

"Tomorrow morning after ten o'clock, go to the motel office and ask the clerk for a message. He'll give you a sealed envelope. Your instructions will be in it."

"Okay, ten o'clock," Roger answered.

"Listen Brown, you bin makin' too many mistakes lately. We know about the clerk in Lancaster. NO more mistakes Brown, is that clear? You owe us big time!" The hoarse voice said.

Roger hung up the phone. The call made him edgy, he needed a drink but knew he couldn't take any chances.

At a fast, steady walk, it took Roger twenty minutes to get to the hospital. Street lights were beginning to come on and cast an eerie glow through the moist evening air. The front entrance to the hospital was well lit as were the few smaller doors he could see. He decided to walk around outside a little while and find some of the other entrances. He made careful mental notes of every exit and entrance door. He noted the ones leading directly to staircases.

He walked back to the front entrance and walked inside. He found the wall-mounted directory and studied it. A cheerful voice to his side startled him. "May I help you," she said.

Roger turned, "Uh...no Ma'am!" He thought better of his remark and added, "Actually I'm looking for the ICU; my...uh...sister's there." Roger had no idea where Josie might be but figured to start there. The hostess pointed down the hall.

"What's your sister's name? I can look her up and tell you if she's...."

Before she could finish her sentence, Roger turned and quickly walked in the direction of the ICU.

When he found the ICU, there was a waiting room just outside the big doors that opened and closed automatically. He read the signs about the hours and rules for visitors. He decided to sit in the waiting room and read magazines just to see who went in and out. Before long a clean cut man in casual clothes with a brown leather jacket and brown cowboy hat walked into the waiting room and looked around. Roger eyed him cautiously. The man in turn seemed to study him.

Roger's heart sped up and he felt very nervous. *"This guy's a cop,"* he said to himself.

The man sat down across from him and began to read, periodically looking up and glancing at him. Roger tried to anticipate the glances and was careful not to meet the man's eyes. After about ten minutes, the man got up and went toward the buttons on the wall that opened the big doors. The doors opened and he glanced back at Roger who by this time was getting very uncomfortable.

Josie's Gift

Roger kept his eyes in the magazine he was reading. As soon as the doors shut, he got up and hurried out of the waiting room and went back to the front entrance. He glanced back every few minutes to see if the man had followed him. *"So far, so good,"* he thought.

Just as he was walking down the driveway toward the parking area, he saw the same man walk out of the front entrance and look around. Roger froze and tried to blend into the shadows of the bushes nearby. The man pulled his jacket back and got a two-way radio from his belt. Roger could see him talking to someone and looking around at the same time. As soon as the man went back inside, he rushed back toward the motel.

When he was safe at the motel, Roger felt a sense of security, at least temporarily. *"But,"* he thought. *"What if that cop recognized me?"*

It was late and he was tired, not just from the walk, but from the fear of being found. He got Stevie ready for bed and collapsed. *"Tomorrow,"* he thought. *"I've got to make a new plan."* He reached for his bottle of liquor and drank until he fell asleep.

The next morning Josie was beginning to stabilize, and they took her off the critical list. The doctor decided to bring her out of the coma and transfer her to a regular patient room on the third floor. By the time they were ready for the transfer, she was waking up, and Detectives Sandoval and Smith showed up.

Sandoval addressed the Charge Nurse. "Was there anyone in here last night that looked suspicious or was looking for Josie Brown?"

"No sir. The duty nurse last night didn't say anything this morning."

"Smitty here thinks he may have seen Roger Brown in the waiting room last night around nineteen hundred hours.

Thanks," Sandoval said as they turned to follow Josie's bed to third floor.

After Josie was settled, the doctor examined her surgical site and spoke to the nurse. "Everything is looking good. Looks like her blood pressure and oxygen levels are good, and her heart is strong. No sign of infection. Temperature and breathing okay?"

"Yes, Doctor!"

The doctor bent down over Josie. In a very soft and kindly tone he spoke. "Missus Brown, how are you feeling?"

Josie just looked around through half-opened eyelids. "Where am I?" She asked in a hoarse whisper?

"You're in the hospital," the doctor replied. "You've been a very sick girl!"

Suddenly Josie panicked. "Where's Stevie, my son? And where's my husband?"

The doctor put his hands on her shoulders so she couldn't bolt upright. "We don't know the answers to those questions, Missus Brown—but we're trying to find out."

Josie looked puzzled.

"Why don't you just try to relax for a little while, and I'll be back. The nursing aide is going to stay here in the room with you until you're fully awake."

The doctor left the room and stopped to talk to Sandoval. "Not yet, Detective, she's not quite fully awake. It's going to take another hour or two before she's ready for company. The nursing aide is going to stay with her 'til I get back. Why don't you guys go have a cup of coffee? I'll go to the cafeteria and get you when I'm ready to come back here."

"Thanks Doc!"

The two detectives passed the time drinking coffee and talking cop talk. Two and a half hours later the doctor showed up. "Let's go up to Missus Brown's room and see if she feels like talking."

Josie's Gift

When they got to the room, the doctor went to her. Josie's eyes were sunken; she still had a black eye, her face was drawn she looked very sad. Her skin was beginning to show a little color.

"Missus Brown, I need to talk with you for a little while and ask you some questions. Do you understand?" His voice was soft and kind.

Josie turned her head to him and nodded. Her eyes beaded up with tears. "Is my son all right?"

The doctor looked at the detectives and then back to Josie. "There've been no police reports so we assume that he's okay."

After a short pause the doctor continued. "I notice your name is Josefa. That's a very pretty name. Do you have a nickname?"

"Josie," she said through her tears.

"Okay Josie, I'm going to raise the head of your bed up slightly. You may feel a little pain from the site of your surgery."

The doctor pushed a button, the bed whirred, and Josie's head lifted slowly to a slight angle. She grimaced when she felt the skin and muscle in her back stretch a little.

"Are you okay?" The doctor asked again.

"Yes," she said in a barely audible voice.

"Okay," the doctor said. "Just relax. You were brought in here by ambulance almost three days ago. You were unconscious and have been asleep ever since."

"What happened?" She asked, surprised.

"Well, to tell you the truth, we don't know the exact details. We do know that somebody beat you pretty severely." The Doctor stopped and looked for signs of recollection in Josie's eyes. "Do you remember anything about that night Josie?"

"I...uh...I'm not sure."

The doctor continued. "You were six weeks pregnant. Did you know you were pregnant?"

"I...uh suspected it," she said slowly.

The doctor took her hand and continued. "The beating caused a very small tear in a blood vessel near your left kidney, and you also had a miscarriage. You lost a lot of blood, and it appeared to the EMS that you had passed out on the bathroom floor. When you arrived here, you were immediately taken to surgery. We've kept you in a coma for the last few days just to give your torn blood vessel time to heal."

The doctor paused then continued. "Josie, I can't emphasize enough that it was a miracle you survived. God has graciously given you a beautiful gift—another chance at life."

He paused again to give her time to absorb what he was saying. "I'm sorry to bring more bad news, but your uterus was damaged by one or more abortions in your past. That, plus the severe bruising in your abdomen, is probably what caused you to miscarry. It's not likely that you will ever be able to bear children, and you should have a hysterectomy sometime in the near future."

The doctor paused, still holding her hand. Josie's eyes flooded with tears, and she squeezed his hand to let him know she understood. "There're a couple of detectives here, and they'd like to talk to you. Do you feel like you can answer their questions?"

Josie nodded affirmatively. "I'll try," she whispered.

Sandoval sat down next to the bed. "Hi, Josie. I'm Detective Sandoval. Most people just call me 'Sandy'." Pointing to the other man, he continued. "This is Detective Smith, and most people call him 'Smitty'."

Josie looked at both detectives. She held out her hand and in a weak voice said, "Hello."

Sandy looked deep into her eyes. He could see the sadness and the pain—something about her drew his heart to

Josie's Gift

her. He began the questions. His voice was soft and kind. "Did your husband, Roger Brown beat you at the motel four nights ago?"

"Yes," She said and quickly added, "But he's not a bad man. It's just that when he drinks and when I don't do what he tells me or when I argue with him, he gets angry. It's really my own fault. I know I could keep it from happening if I tried hard enough."

"So, is this something that happens often?" Sandy asked.

Josie looked away and tried to change the subject. "He's really a good husband and a good father to Stevie. Most of the time we're very happy, but it's just that when he drinks..." Her thoughts trailed off, and she looked from one to the other, then to the doctor who broke the silence.

"Maybe it's time to get some rest." He suggested.

The doctor and detectives turned to leave.

"Wait!" She said tearfully. "Will you find Stevie for me? Please?"

"We'll find him Josie, I promise you," Sandy answered as he brought his index finger up and caught a tear dropping from his eye.

Roger knew he had to move on. After the close encounter with the cop at the ICU, he knew it was only a matter of time. He had a plan, but first he needed a car. Leaving Stevie at the motel he walked to the mall parking lot and found an unlocked car. He soon it had running and moving in the direction of the motel. He quickly got his and Stevie's things together and into the back seat. He looked at his watch and walked to the motel office.

"You got a message for me?" He asked the clerk.

"Yeah," the clerk said and handed him an envelope. "It was in the mail slot before I got up and into the office this morning."

Josie's Gift

Roger walked back to the room and opened it. He gasped! The envelope had a picture that appeared to have been clipped from a magazine. It showed a close-up view of a traffic light and the green light was on. "Holy sh*#*!" Roger exclaimed. He knew exactly what the lights meant. Under his breath he said, "I'm marked. They've got a green light on me. I gotta get outta here and away from this city, now!" Roger got into the car and as he backed out, he looked around to see if he was being watched. "*Clear,*" he thought to himself.

"Am I going to see my Mama?" Stevie asked as they drove in the direction of the hospital.

"Yeah, sure," Roger answered without thinking.

Stevie perked up. "Is she all right Daddy?" he asked.

"Yeah, she's all right."

"Will we be there soon?" Stevie asked.

Roger was becoming agitated. "Just shut up, will ya? I gotta think right now!"

In spite of Roger's harshness, Stevie seemed jubilant at the prospect of seeing his mom. He began to quietly sing a little song she had taught him.

Roger pulled into the hospital parking lot and found a space in the shadows of some trees. It was getting dark and he hoped he wouldn't be noticed.

At the same time Detective Sandoval walked out of the hospital entrance and found a place in the shadows where he could watch the parking lot and the entrance. He saw the car pull into the parking space away from all the other cars. He saw a man and a little boy get out of the car and walk toward the entrance. It looked like Roger Brown and Stevie. Not wanting to alarm the little boy, Sandy waited and watched. Within minutes, another car drove in and slowly moved behind Roger's car, briefly stopped and then moved on. Sandy made note of the car and where it parked.

Josie's Gift

Roger walked into the front entrance and looked around. He found a part of the waiting area that was out of the way and where he didn't think he would be noticed. He figured he could leave Stevie there and sooner or later someone would find him. By that time he planned to be alone and far away. He picked out a spot near a television set that was tuned to a station running cartoons. There were a few other children there also.

"Sit right here Stevie. I'm going to get Mama and I'll be right back," Roger commanded.

Roger watched from a distance and made sure Stevie was not going to follow him, then he walked back to the front entrance and out the door. He looked around; all looked quiet, so he walked back to the car. He was just about to open the door and slide inside when he heard a man's voice.

"Police, Roger, don't move."

Roger reached for the gun in his waistband when he felt another hand on his.

"I wouldn't do that if I were you, Mister Brown. Get down on the ground and spread 'em."

Roger quickly assessed his situation. He made a split-second decision that was a big mistake. He swung around, and with all his strength, hit Smitty with the back of his hand. When Smitty went down; Roger reached for his gun. At the same instant, he saw Sandy's gun coming down on his head. He heard a loud cracking noise from inside his head, and everything went black as he crumpled to the ground.

"You okay, Smitty?" Sandy asked.

Smitty rubbed the side of his head. "Yeah, I'm okay."

Sandy rolled Roger over onto his stomach and brought his two arms around to his back. He quickly placed handcuffs on his wrists and another pair on his ankles. "That oughta keep him out of trouble," Sandy grumbled.

The two detectives dragged Roger to his feet. By this time he was beginning to come back to consciousness. Sandy turned him toward Smitty. "Are you listenin Brown?" Sandy yelled.

"Yeah," Roger mumbled. As his head began to clear, he was thinking about the green light.

Smitty got right into Roger's face and read him his rights in a louder than normal voice. "You have the right to remain silent. Anything you say can and will be used against you. You have the right to an attorney."

"Yeah, I want an attorney" Roger yelled.

"We'll get you one when we get downtown," Smitty yelled back.

Roger remained silent; his bloodshot eyes were full of hate—inside, his emotions were boiling, like a dormant volcano pushing to come to the surface. He had one thing on his mind, to escape and if he had to kill somebody, so be it. He twisted and turned trying to loosen the handcuffs. Finally he gave up. His only hope was to get out on bail. He felt sure his business associates would get him an attorney and get him out; but he thought of the empty envelope. *"Maybe I'm wrong,"* he said to himself. *"Surely they'll get me out of this—they've done it before and they don't want me to finger them!"*

Just then a car came around the corner, tires screetching, heading straight for them. Sandy pushed Smitty and Roger away and rolled onto the ground. Shots were fired from the car and it sped away. Sandy slowly got up, his gun ready. "You two okay," he asked.

"Yeah, we're okay Sandy," Smitty replied. "Looks like some of Roger's buddies decided to interrupt our party."

Sandy turned to Roger who was white as a sheet, "Looks like someone had you marked, Mister Brown."

The two detectives dragged Roger to their car and pushed him into the back seat. Both men were breathing hard from

Josie's Gift

the exertion. "Call for backup, Smitty. When they get here take 'im and book him. I'll go see to the kid. In the meantime, watch for that car just in case Brown's friends decide to show up again to finish the job."

Sandy walked into the hospital front entrance and spoke to the clerk at the information desk. She pointed to the side room where Sandy saw some children and adults. He walked in and looked around. He saw one boy sitting by himself without any adult nearby. "That must be Stevie," he thought.

He walked toward Stevie and sat down in the chair next to him. "Hi, Stevie."

Stevie was startled by the voice. He turned around and looked at Sandy, "How'd you know my name?"

"Oh, a little bird whispered to me a few minutes ago," Sandy replied smiling.

"I'm waiting for my Daddy to get my mama so we can go home to the motel," Stevie volunteered.

"Well," Sandy said. "I'll bet you're very anxious to see your mama, that right?"

Stevie smiled and nodded his head, yes.

"I'll tell you what Stevie," Sandy continued. "I think I could pull some strings here and get you right into the room to see your mama. Would you like that?"

Stevie was jubilant. "Let's go!" He said as he jumped up out of his chair.

Sandy took his hand and started walking. "Tell you what," he said. "I know a place right down that hall over there that sells ice cream. How about we eat some ice cream and get acquainted."

"Okay," Stevie said excitedly as he tugged on Sandy's arm.

Sandy paid for the ice cream and they found a place to sit. "Tell me something, Stevie! How old are you."

Stevie thought for a few moments, looked at his fingers and replied, "Six."

Sandy smiled, "That's interesting! I have a grandson who's six years old!"

Stevie looked into Sandy's eyes. "C'n I play with him? I'd like to play with him! What's his name?"

"His name's David, but we call him Davie. He goes to kindergarten. Do you go to school, Stevie?"

Stevie looked surprised. "No, but I'd like to...I'd like to have some other kids to play with!" His tone of voice evidenced his disappointment.

"Don't you ever get to play with other kids?" Sandy asked.

"Naw," Stevie said, looking at the floor. "All I ever get to do is watch television. We're always movin, an I don't never get to know any kids."

Sandy decided to ask Stevie if he knew anything about his mother's beating. "Stevie, I want you to think real hard about what happened between your mom and dad four nights ago. Can you remember?"

Stevie looked at the floor and then up at Sandy as if trying to decide if he really wanted to remember anything about that night. He paused for several minutes during which Sandy remained expectantly quiet. Finally he spoke almost inaudibly. "Yes," he said. "I remember!"

"Can you tell me what happened?" Sandy asked.

Stevie thought a few moments and then slowly began. "My daddy left us at the motel and went to get us all somethin' ta eat. When he was gone a long time, my mama got worried. When he got back, him and my mama got into a big fight about him bein' gone so long. He was drinkin' and they got to arguin' real loud."

"What did you do?" Sandy interrupted.

"I went to the closet and shut the door. I went to sleep in there and when I woke up, I went to the bathroom and I saw my mama layin' there and lots o' blood on the floor."

"Then what did you do, Stevie?" Sandy asked.

Josie's Gift

"My daddy was sleepin' so I woke 'im up, an' he went into the bathroom. I heard him say some bad words."

Sandy took a few bites of his ice cream, waiting patiently for Stevie to continue.

"My daddy an' me went to the car. We stopped at the office and then left real fast. He said they were goin' to take my mama to the hospital an' we'd see her there."

"Did you see your daddy beat your mama?" Sandy asked.

"Naaw, I didn't see it, but I heard it."

"Did it happen pretty often? I mean that your daddy and mommy got into fights."

Stevie looked up at Sandy. He began to cry very softly. Sandy decided he'd heard enough for now. "You're a brave little boy, Stevie."

Sandy almost had tears in his eyes as he got up from the table and took Stevie's hand. He just looked down at this frightened child for several long moments. Then he squatted down to Stevie's level and took him in his arms and held him very close. "From now on," he whispered, everything's going to be all right. Your daddy's never going to beat your mama anymore and you're not going to have to hide in the closet anymore!"

Sandy and Stevie walked slowly in the direction of the elevator. "Push the number three button, Stevie," Sandy said when they got on. Stevie stood very close to his new friend as the elevator door closed and they felt themselves going up.

On the third floor, they stepped off the elevator and started down the hall. A nurse smiled when she saw them. The doctor was in the hallway waiting. "Stevie, this is Doctor Johnson; Doctor Johnson, this is Stevie."

Dr. Johnson stooped down to Stevie's level and took the little hand that was held out to him. "I'm very pleased to meet you, Stevie." He looked up at Sandy with an approving nod.

"Can I see my mama now?" Stevie asked in an anxious tone.

"First I need to explain something to you," Doctor Johnson said. "Your mama's been hurt pretty bad, and she's had some surgery. That means we cut her open to fix the place where some blood was coming from. Right now she's kinda weak and has some bruises on her face so she doesn't look very pretty. In spite of all that, she's doing just fine, and she's anxious to see you. You ready?"

Stevie looked worried, but didn't wait for the others to walk into the room.

Josie began to cry the instant she saw Stevie coming through the door. She stretched her hand out to the side of the bed and waited. Stevie rushed to her and took her hand. She grimaced as she pulled him to her. She put her other arm around him and hugged him with the kind of hug that didn't want to let go.

"Oh, Stevie; Stevie. I'm so glad to see you! I love you so much!" she said through her sobs.

"I love you too, mama," he said as he kissed her bruised face.

The nurse had tears in her eyes as she brought a chair close to the bed. "Here, Stevie," she said. "Here's a chair for you to sit on."

Josie looked up at Sandy who was standing at the foot of the bed. "Roger?" She whispered.

"Later Josie," Sandy whispered. "Smitty and I'll be back in a little while."

Sandy stepped out to the hallway where Smitty waited. "I contacted the Family Services," Smitty said. "One of their people'll be here in a few minutes."

"Good," Sandy replied. "Let's go get a cup of coffee!"

"I'll tell the nurse," Smitty said.

As they sipped their coffee, the two detectives were quiet, each thinking about the events of the day and about Roger Brown.

"Brown safely away?" Sandy asked.

"Yeah, we booked him and locked him up. As soon as the paper work gets here on that store clerk he murdered, we'll have enough to keep him out of trouble for a long time," Smitty replied. "You know they're gonna want to extradite him and try him in Lancaster, don't you?"

"Yeah," Sandy replied. "We've got two counts of grand theft auto here, but that won't trump a murder charge. I'd sure like to try him here."

"Maybe we can get the District Attorney to work out a deal with Judge Jacobson to move the trial here. He can always claim Brown won't get a fair trial over there. Besides we're still in the same Judicial District. By the way, look what we found in the car." Smitty showed Sandy an envelope and a picture of a traffic light that they put into a plastic bag. "It hasn't been dusted yet so best to not open the bag."

Sandy looked carefully at the bag's contents, then turned to Smitty. "You know what this means?"

"Yeah, Roger's been working for somebody and he's screwed up. They've marked him."

"That probably explains the attempt to eliminate him in the parking lot a while ago."

At that moment a pleasant female voice interrupted. "What're two cops doin' here drinkin' coffee? Aren't you two supposed to be out there lookin' for bad guys," she said with a laugh and a noticeable southern drawl, waving her arms toward the street as she spoke.

Both men stood up. "Hi, Bev," Sandy said with a big smile. He pulled out a chair for her to sit with them. "Want some coffee?"

"If Ah drink any more coffee, Ah'll have to take up residence in the bathroom," She said with a chuckle.

"What's goin' on in your world?" Smitty asked.

"Thank God things have slowed down a bit," she said. "Now what's this about a little boy you big strong guys have in custody?"

Sandy and Smitty both laughed. Sandy spoke. "Yeah we got a kid, and we need to figure out what can be done with him 'til his mom's out of the hospital. His dad's in jail right now on charges of auto theft and soon to be murder. Kid's name's Stevie Brown."

"So how long's his mom goin' to be here?" Bev asked.

"We don't really know just yet, but probably at least another week or so," Sandy answered.

Bev thought for a moment. She looked at both men then spoke. "Well, probably be best in a foster home. Whatta you think?" She looked directly at Sandy, knowing from past experience what he was going to suggest.

"Well," he began. "I thought maybe you could fix it so me and Joann could take care of him for a while. We're takin' care of Davie during the day while Jean and Sam are workin'. Stevie'd have somebody to play with, and besides we could take him to kindergarten with Davie."

Bev smiled. "You know what Ah think, Sandy?" She paused then continued with a chuckle. "You'd take in every stray kid in town if you could." She paused again, looking into Sandy's expectant eyes. "Yeah, Sandy. Ah'll have the paper work for ya in the mornin'. I hereby remand Stevie Brown into your custody until further notice."

Bev got up from her chair, and both men stood. As she turned to leave, she chuckled and said, "You two stay out of trouble, ya heah. Have a good evenin'!"

"You too, Bev," both men said in unison.

"OKay," Sandy said. "Let's tell the nurse we're leavin'. We'll go down to headquarters and make up our report. I gotta call Jo and tell her we're gonna have a guest for a few days. Then I'll be back up here for Stevie. We're gonna have a few more questions for Josie when she's able to talk."

CHAPTER THREE

When Sandy returned to the hospital, it was nearly daylight. Josie was sleeping very peacefully, and Stevie was asleep in the chair beside the bed. Instead of waking them, Sandy decided to go to the cafeteria for breakfast and give Josie and Stevie time to wake up.

When he got back to the room, the aides were taking breakfast around to the patients. Stevie was awake and rubbing his eyes. A nurse was tending Josie's incision and the intravenous bottles and bags hanging beside her bed. Stevie stared in wide-eyed wonder as he saw what was going on. In spite of all the activity of the previous night he was perky and ready to eat. The nurse handed him a washcloth and towel with instructions to go into the bathroom, use the toilet and then wash up. He smiled and readily obeyed. It seemed his life was once more in perfect order. He didn't once question anybody about his dad. When he finished, he sat in the chair and he and his mama had breakfast together. Sandy just watched admiringly.

"Detective," the Nurse said when they finished eating. "Would you mind taking Stevie out of the room for a walk so we can get Josie up and bathed?"

"Sure," Sandy answered cheerfully. "C'mon Stevie, let's go for a walk."

Stevie reached for Sandy's hand, and they walked out and down the hall to the elevator. "Push number one, Stevie."

Down they went to the lobby area. When the door opened, Stevie pulled on Sandy's hand and led him out. "Can we go outside, Mister Sandy?"

Sandy smiled, "Sure, let's go!"

The outside air was fresh and cool; the sun was bright and rising in the cloudless sky. They walked silently for awhile just taking in the fresh newness of the day.

Stevie waved his arms around, "Isn't God just wonderful, Mister Sandy?"

"Yes, he sure is!" Sandy paused. "So, you know something about God, Stevie?"

"Yeah! My mama reads to me sometimes from a holy book. It has stuff in it all about God. I think she calls it her 'salms or something like that. She says her daddy used to read it to her all the time. Whenever she reads, she cries 'cause it reminds her of her daddy and mama."

"So, that's your grandpa and grandma. Have you ever met them?" Sandy asked.

"No, I ain' never met 'em, but mama says someday we're goin' to visit 'em. I know I love 'em already 'cause I know my mama loves 'em." Stevie paused then looked up at Sandy with a big grin.

"Mister Sandy, do you carry a gun? A real gun?"

"Yes, I do Stevie. I'm a cop and all cops have to carry guns."

Stevie was thinking and finally said, "My daddy carries a gun, but he's not a cop."

Sandy chuckled, "Yeah, I know. I met your daddy last night, and he was carrying a gun." Sandy paused and then continued in a very serious tone. "Stevie, we had to take your daddy to jail last night. He stole some cars, and he beat up your mama."

Stevie's serious answer surprised him. "Yeah, I know he's in jail. He's always doin' bad things an' I knowed he'd git in jail." Then he smiled a big smile, "C'n we go back to the room and see mama now?"

"Sure thing. Let's go; I brought some clean clothes for you to wear."

When they got back to the hospital room, Josie had been up for a short walk and was sitting in the chair. Stevie ran to her and hugged her. Sandy watched, then spoke. "How're you feeling Josie?"

"I'm doing good, I guess," was the hesitant reply.

Just at that time Bev from Family Services walked into the room. She was smiling and cheerful. The first thing she did was walk over to Stevie, stoop down and hold out her hand. "Hi, I'm Missus Rowland, and you must be Stevie."

Stevie held out his hand. "Hi, Missus Rowland!"

Bev then turned to Josie and introduced herself. "I'm real sorry for what happened to you, Josie. Let me explain what's going on and why I'm here. Last evening your husband left Stevie downstairs in a waiting room. He apparently had no intention of coming back to pick him up or of coming for you. Detectives Sandoval and Smith took him into custody in the parking lot just as he was about to leave. They called my department because a child was involved whose mother was hospitalized and father in jail." She could see the worried look in Josie's eyes.

"Don't worry Missus Brown. We'll take care of Stevie until you can get back on your feet and are ready to leave the hospital and care for him by yourself." She grinned and looked at Sandy. "Instead of getting a foster home for him, Detective Sandoval wants to take him to his home where he and his wife Joann can take care of him. They have a grandson Stevie's age so he'll have someone to play with. I've already signed the paperwork to make it happen. All we need is your signature."

Josie was still worried. "But—will I get him back?"

"Yes you will certainly get him back—that is, unless the court says otherwise, and I don't expect that to happen." Bev laid a paper in front of Josie to sign; then patiently waited. She knew what Josie was thinking and how worried she must be.

Bev spoke, "Sandy, would you take Stevie out for a short walk down the hallway?"

"Sure Bev!" Sandy reached for Stevie's hand. Stevie had a worried look and was reluctant to leave his mama.

As soon as the door shut behind Sandy and Stevie, Bev spoke to Josie. Her voice and her face showed she was serious. "Josie, I must be honest with you. Your husband, Roger Brown, allegedly murdered a store clerk and is accused of several counts of auto theft. I know from experience that the District Attorney's office is going to want to talk to you, and you may be implicated as an accomplice with your husband. I also know from experience that he will require you to remain in Rock City until the investigation is completed, and you are either cleared or charged. Now, Sandy and Joann are wonderful Christian people. You can trust them completely to care for Stevie until the court decides what's going to happen."

Tears came to Josie's eyes as she looked at the paper. "Can I talk to Sandy now?"

"Sure Josie. I'll get him back to the room."

Josie looked up at Sandy. "You'll take good care of him, won't you?"

"You can count on it Josie, and either Joann or I will bring him back to visit you every evening. I'll get him enrolled in the kindergarten where Davie goes. He's going to be just fine!"

Bev interrupted. "Josie, Sandy knows very well that if you don't sign these papers, the court will make the decision for you. That decision may not be to your liking. It would be far better for you, and for Stevie, if you do this willingly."

Josie looked at Bev, then at Sandy. She was sobbing when she looked at Stevie who immediately rushed into her arms. "Stevie will you go with Detective Sandy and live with him for a few days 'til Mommy gets well?"

Stevie nodded that he would.

Josie signed the papers, and Stevie walked away with Sandy. Bev stayed behind to comfort Josie and to answer any questions she might have.

Josie was healing well, but she was having trouble walking. What originally was expected to be one week, turned into three weeks of therapy, and the progress was slow. Either Sandy or Joann and Stevie came in to visit every evening. Stevie stayed in the hospital room with his mom while Sandy drove to the station and did his daily report. The nurses were falling in love with Stevie, who loved to play little games with them. He seemed to have an innate outgoing personality that quickly made friends with everybody.

Bev visited as well, and she and Josie discussed the future. She was up front with her about the prospects of Family Services having to monitor how things turned out, and that there was always the possibility that she could lose custody if there was any hint of trouble.

Josie knew she had to make some plans because it was inevitable that she would have to leave the hospital soon. It seemed she had picked up the habit of scheming from the years with Roger. A plan began to form in her mind.

"Hi, Jenny, this is Josie. Remember me from when we met at the Laundromat several weeks ago."

On the other end of the line, Jenny thought a few moments then answered. "Yeah sure, Josie. I remember. You in trouble or somethin'?"

"I'm in the hospital, Jenny, and I need some help. Can you come over here?"

"What room?"

"Room number is 310."

"Okay, Josie, I'll get there as soon as I can."

An hour later, Jenny walked into the room. Josie was sitting in the chair. "Hey Girl, you don't look so good! What happened?"

Josie told her the whole story, including that Roger was in Jail. There's an unexplainable bond that quickly evolves between street people, not only because of a commonality of circumstances but even more from a commonality of experiences. Jenny hugged Josie and said, "I'm here for you, Josie. What do you need?"

"Well," Josie replied. "In another day or two I'll be discharged from this place and I need a place ta stay for awhile." She paused, then quickly added, "Just for a little while—you know, 'til I c'n get back on my feet."

"And, Stevie! Where's he at?"

Josie paused and tried to avoid eye contact. "He's uh... uh...staying with a foster family."

"Yeah, I understand" Jenny said. "Okay, I'll get some things taken care of and make plans to get you out of here."

"Maybe you could get me a room close to you?"

"You got any money," Jenny asked.

"Yeah, I've got 'nough for a little while, I think. They uh...gave me what Roger had when he was picked up."

"Okay, it'll prob'ly cost twenty a night for the two of you—that's as cheap as you c'n git. But, if you sweet talk the manager, you might get it a little cheaper, you bein' without work and all. Call me when you're ready!"

Josie felt better about her situation. She really didn't want to stay with Sandy and Joann. It just wouldn't be comfortable. They weren't her kind of people.

Josie's Gift

Sandy was upset when he learned of Josie's plans. "Josie, it isn't the best thing for you to do—believe me I know what's out there. And you've got to think of Stevie."

"Another thing," Bev added. "You've got to think about every possibility. If you make one misstep we'll have to take Stevie away from you."

"Look," Josie argued. "I've got to make my own way now, and I need to see that Roger has a lawyer and gets a fair trial. I need to see him—he's my husband and I love him, and I know he loves me and Stevie."

"Let me put it to you straight," Bev said. "I have the authority to take Stevie away from you right now! Do you understand? I could leave this room with him and there wouldn't be anything you could do about it."

Josie was beginning to get emotional. "Please...please! You've got to believe me—you've got to trust me. I know what I'm doing."

Bev breathed a deep sigh and looked at Sandy, whose face was like a stone. Finally she spoke, "Okay Josie, you have my card, and you have Sandy's card. If anything—and I mean anything, comes up you give one of us a call."

"Josie smiled. "I appreciate everything you guys have done for me and Stevie, but right now it's time for me to look out for myself."

Sandy stepped to the bedside. "Josie, I want you to know that when Smitty and I arrested Roger in the parking lot, somebody was watching. They fired some shots in an attempt to kill Roger. These are very dangerous people. You have to consider that they may come looking for you!"

Josie looked down at her lap. Her voice was hushed and thoughtful. "I understand and I'll be careful."

Sandy and Bev looked at each other, then turned toward the door. "Anything, Josie! You hear? Anything!" They walked out of the room and took the elevator to the lobby.

53

When they got to the parking lot, Sandy turned to Bev, "Whatta you think. Bev?" he asked.

"I don't have a good feeling about this one, Sandy! I guess for the time being, we've done all we can do. See ya in court!"

Josie signed herself out of the hospital and with Stevie, waited in the lobby for Jenny. Jenny arrived and helped her into the passenger seat of the '99 green Buick she was driving. Stevie got in the back seat and buckled himself up. "You get the clothes I asked for?" Josie asked.

"Yeah, I got what I could. It's all used but in good shape."
"Josie smiled. "Great, let's go home!"

They arrived at the Sundown Motel and got things put away in Josie's room. Jenny shared what she had for a cold lunch. Each of the rooms had a small kitchen with a refrigerator and stove. There was a supermarket within walking distance where she could get some food.

"You two take care of yourselves now," Jenny said. "I need to get some sleep. Got some customers coming around this evening."

"Don't worry Jenny! Thanks for bailing me out!" She turned to Stevie. "Whatta ya say we walk over to the store and lay in some food, Stevie?" Stevie took her hand and they left for the supermarket.

By the next day, things were beginning to get back to normal. Stevie spent most of his time watching TV. Josie went to the office and asked the clerk for directions to the County Court House and Jail. The clerk got out a city map and showed her where things were in relation to the motel. Josie traced the distance with her finger, noting just where to turn and how far it would be. She decided it was too far to walk and asked Jenny to borrow her car. Jenny agreed to the car and also to watch Stevie for her.

Josie's Gift

Josie parked in the jail parking lot and looked for the front door. A sign beside the door had instructions for gaining entrance. She pushed a button, and an attendant came. He slid a small door open at eye level, and she stated her business. "I would like to visit with Roger Brown—he's my husband."

"You got a picture ID with ya?"

"Yes, Sir!"

"Wait a minute while I check the status of your husband," the voice on the inside said.

Josie heard a loud buzzer, several clicks, and a voice from a small speaker told her to enter. She pushed the door open and walked in.

A man behind a desk spoke, "Be right with ya! Sit down over there." He picked up a phone, punched two buttons and spoke to someone else.

Before long a guard appeared with a clipboard and some papers for her to sign. She signed them, and the guard led the way to a waiting room that had steel bars over the windows and a steel mesh divider separating the room into two halves. She sat down in a chair on one side of the divider. The guard told her to wait.

After a few minutes, a door opened on the other side of the divider, and Roger appeared. His eyes narrowed, and for several long moments he just looked at Josie. His hair was growing out again and he hadn't shaved in a long time. "Whatta ya doin here, Josie?" The tone of his voice was brittle and expressed the anger Josie saw in his face.

"I'm here," Josie said in an equally angry voice, "because I love you. You're my husband! I wanted to see you!" Her voice got gentler. "I've been laid up in the hospital for three weeks, or I'd been here sooner."

Roger leaned close to the divider. His eyes were cold and piercing. His voice softened a little. "Ya don't need ta be here Josie. There's nothin' you c'n do for me."

"The District Attorney's investigator came to the hospital to question me. He asked me about the clerk over in Lancaster and about the stolen cars." She smiled and looked into his eyes for approval. She continued, "I told him you didn't murder that clerk, and that I didn't know anything about the stolen cars."

Roger smiled a somewhat sinister smile, more of a smirk. His voice had a little laugh. "Ha, so—you lied! You think he believed you?"

"I don't know. I told him what a good man you are and what a good dad you are to Stevie. Please Roger! I believe in you—you can beat this. You're good at talking your way out of things."

They both sat quietly. It seemed there was nothing more to say, her overtures to Roger were rebuffed. Josie felt betrayed and alone.

A voice behind her said, "Time's up Ma'am. Ya only git ten minutes. Let's go."

"I love you Roger," she said as she was led out of the room.

Instead of being led out to the front door, she was led to a room where a man was waiting for her. "Missus Brown, I'm Will Brent, investigator for the District Attorney's Office, we met in the hospital."

Josie looked at him. "Yeah, I remember!"

Brent continued. "The papers you signed here clearly stated that your visit would be monitored. Did you forget there was a guard in the room with you when you talked to your husband?"

Not wanting her eyes to betray what she was thinking, Josie quickly looked down at the floor. "I uh...don't know what you're talking about!"

"Missus Brown, do you know that lying to a criminal investigator is an offense and that you could be charged, along with your husband, in the murder over in Lancaster? I believe you know more than you're willing to tell us." Brent paused and looked intently at Josie. "On the other hand," he said in a kinder tone. "If you cooperate with us and tell the truth, you could get away with probation. I believe you really didn't have anything to do with the murder or the auto thefts, but it won't look good for you in court if you lie. You could get a lengthy jail sentence and lose your son to state custody."

Josie began to cry. "Will I have to testify?"

"I'm sure the defense will not want you on the stand but I can assure you that the prosecutor will call you to testify. What I'd like to do at this point is take a sworn statement from you. That may keep you from having to testify personally, but your statement will be entered into evidence."

"So...now what?" She asked, resigned to this change in fate.

"I'll need you to come over to the court house across the street. We'll take your statement and then you can go. You will, however, have to remain in Rock City 'til this is all cleared up. That means staying here 'til both the trial and the sentencing are concluded. Are you willing?"

Josie looked up at Brent. She felt like a caged bird. She knew if she didn't cooperate she faced jail time and would lose Stevie. She thought of what Bev had said. "Okay Mister Brent, let's go!"

After the interview, Will Brent walked with her back to Jenny's car in the jail parking lot. She was feeling depressed and guilty—like she'd betrayed Roger. She felt strongly that she should be trying to protect him, but the thought of losing Stevie was overwhelming, so she had chosen to cooperate with the investigator. It was either Roger or Stevie, and she chose Stevie. Will opened the door for her and she got in. "Missus Brown, I sincerely hope this all ends well for you. If you have any questions don't hesitate to call. Here's my card."

Josie took the card and drove toward the motel.

CHAPTER FOUR

The Bailiff looked at his watch then quickly stepped to a door on the south side of the courtroom. He announced in a loud voice, "All rise."

The district courtroom in Rock City was paneled and finished in dark walnut wood, richly finished and polished. In spite of the sun shining brightly in through the tall windows on two sides, the room had a dark and serious atmosphere. The subdued light caused a very cold chill to hover over the proceedings.

The room suddenly got quiet as District Judge Brian Jacobsen walked into the court, up to the bench, and took his seat. He looked from side to side focusing on the two tables where the prosecution and the defense sat.

The Jury filed in and took their seats. Judge Jacobsen shuffled the papers in front of him, adjusted his glasses, looked around again then announced, "The defendant will please rise!"

Roger Brown and his attorney, Michael Sheffley, stood and faced the bench.

Roger was tall—about six feet two—thin, with a long skinny neck and pronounced Adam's apple. He was dressed in street clothes for the trial but his hands and feet were shackled. His hair was a dirty blonde and somewhat disheveled, giving him a look of having just gotten out of bed. He was twenty-nine years old and his pale body reflected years of alcohol and drug use. Roger would have been a handsome man if he had taken better care of himself.

The courtroom was buzzing with muffled voices. With her hands cupped against her face, Josie Brown sat crying softly in the front row of spectator seats. Josie, as she was known to everyone, was a very pretty young woman, but her recent near-death experience in the hospital, the stress of the trial, and Roger's jail time had taken a toll on her appearance. Her eyes were sunken in their sockets, her eyelids drooped, and she looked sad as if she hadn't slept well in some time. Her clothes were wrinkled and looked like they were previously owned. Her face was pale and drawn.

In a stern and serious tone of voice, the Judge addressed Roger. "Mr. Brown, you have been accused of murder in the first degree and tried by a jury of your peers. Do you want to make a statement before the verdict is read?"

Roger looked at the Jury then back at the Judge. In a defiant move, he sneered and squinted his eyes, but said nothing. Michael Sheffley shuffled his feet and looked down at the floor. Roger turned his head to look at his wife; he smiled faintly, one corner of his lips turned up.

Josie mouthed the words, "*I love you*," then buried her face in her hands once again.

Sitting in the last row of seats Reverend Isabelle Jefferson watched. She had been in the courtroom for the entire three days of the trial. Judge Jacobsen had asked her to be there, knowing Josie would need a friend when the trial was over.

Isabelle was a handsome African American woman of thirty-seven and not married. She was tall and thin, wearing a dark skirt hemmed below her knees with a white blouse and dark matching jacket. Her clerical collar identified her as a member of the clergy, and her warm smile and friendly expression marked her as genuine and caring.

"Josie is an attractive young woman perhaps twenty-two or twenty-three years old," Isabelle thought to herself as she had watched her throughout the trial. *"How could such a beautiful young woman with bright possibilities for a good future take up with a killer and get tangled up in such a mess?"* She sighed—she had seen this scenario played out many times in the years she had been pastor of the Lighted Way Ministries, an inner city mission ministering to people on the street. Before the verdict was read, she quietly moved forward to Josie's right side.

Judge Jacobsen looked at the Jury then spoke. "Members of the jury, have you reached a verdict?"

The jury foreman stood, "We have, your Honor!" He handed the bailiff an envelope which in turn was handed to the judge, who opened it.

The judge took out the paper inside, unfolded it and scanned the words. He spoke again to the jury, "Members of the jury are you agreed, one and all, that this is your verdict?"

"It is Your Honor," answered the foreman.

The judge handed the slip of paper back to the bailiff, who handed it to the jury foreman.

Josie put her face on the rail in front of her and sobbed openly.

The Judge addressed Roger. "Mr. Brown, please face the jury."

The foreman of the jury read the findings. "Your Honor, in the charge of murder in the first degree, the jury finds Roger Brown…," he paused, moving his eyes from Roger to Josie then back to Roger. "Guilty!"

There was a collective gasp, and the courtroom erupted into noisy conversation. The family of Roger's victim wept loudly, some even lifting their hands skyward and thanking God for justice.

Josie screamed. Isabelle put her arms around her as the judge pounded his gavel.

Josie's Gift

When there was a semblance of quiet, he announced that there would be a sentencing hearing in one week. He turned to the bailiff and spoke.

"Bailiff, get this killer out of my court!"

Roger was led out still wearing the shackles he had worn when he arrived from the county jail. Josie screamed again and reached her arms out over the rail toward Roger.

"Reverend Jefferson," the judge said in a more kindly tone. "You will take Mrs. Brown to your shelter and see that she and her son are cared for. She is hereby remanded into your custody until further notice!"

Isabelle looked at the Judge. "Yes Your Honor," she said.

The bailiff went to where Isabelle and Josie were still standing. "Reverend Jefferson," he said. "Take Mrs. Brown into the Judge's conference room where you can talk for a while in private. The judge will have some papers for you."

Isabelle led Josie to a room behind the judge's office. News media were gathering nearby. Before they could ask their questions, Isabelle quickly ushered Josie inside and shut the door. She pulled out a chair from the big table and invited Josie to sit down. As soon as she was seated, she put her head in her arms on the table top and continued to weep. Isabelle sat beside her quietly, with her arm around her shoulder.

After five or six minutes, Josie quit crying. Through teary eyes she looked at Isabelle. "Who are you?" she asked in a somewhat defiant tone.

"Hi Josie," Isabelle said. "My name is Isabelle Jefferson. I'm a pastor, and Judge Jacobsen has asked me to be here to be your friend."

Josie looked at Isabelle but said nothing. Through teary eyes, she looked around. Isabelle handed her a box of tissues and waited. Josie finally spoke; she was defiant. "I don't need any friends; just leave me alone!"

Josie's Gift

The door opened slowly, and the judge appeared. He looked at Isabelle, who nodded. He sat down on the other side of Josie, turned toward her and spoke.

"Mrs. Brown, do you understand the nature of the proceedings of this court over the past three days?"

Josie nodded affirmatively.

Judge Jacobsen continued. "I must tell you that there's potential evidence that may implicate you in some of the criminal actions of your husband. The District attorney is going to review all the facts and decide whether to charge you with anything."

Josie looked at the judge—tears again filled her eyes. "But...but, I have a son, and I need to take care of him! Can't you just leave me alone?"

"I know your situation," the judge replied. "I've asked the DA to take his time so there will be nothing in the immediate future. However it will be necessary for you to stay here in Rock City until the decision is made."

Josie interrupted, "I don't want to stay here. I hate it here, and besides there's nothing for me here now."

"Where would you go, Josie?" Isabelle asked.

"Anywhere! Just not here. I'll find something!"

"Mrs. Brown, I'm sorry, but I can't let you do that. But, I'll tell you what, you can either go to jail on a charge of accessory to murder or go with Reverend Jefferson. It's your choice!" The judge sounded decisive.

"What will happen to my son Stevie?"

"If you choose to go to jail, I'm afraid he'll have to be remanded into the custody of State Family Services and will live for the time being, or perhaps permanently, in a foster home. If you choose to go with Reverend Jefferson and agree to stay there, then Stevie can go with you."

Josie lowered her head. "All right I'll go with Reverend Jefferson," She said quietly, almost in a whisper.

Josie's Gift

The judge spoke again. "For now you're in my charge. I've signed papers that will, for the time being, put you into the custody of Reverend Jefferson and the Lighted Way Ministries. They will take care of you and your son."

The judge rose from his seat, and before turning to leave, handed some papers to Isabelle. Then he took Josie's hand. "God bless you, Josie. I hope and pray for the sake of your son, this whole thing will be straightened out soon."

Josie Looked at the judge and then at Isabelle. "So, what now?" she asked.

Isabelle took Josie's hand. "Let's make a plan," she said. "Where're you living? We'll need to pick up your things and your son. The two of you will be living with us at the mission."

Josie looked down at the floor, obviously embarrassed. "We've...been living at the Sundown Motel. I left Stevie, my son, with a neighbor next door."

Isabelle took a deep breath and tried not to look shocked or disappointed, nor did she speak what was on her mind. The Sundown was a cheap motel not far from the mission. Its customers were mostly poor transients. Some of the rooms were permanently rented by prostitutes. There was a lot of gang and criminal activity in the area. She hoped Stevie was safe.

"I know the place, Josie. Let's go get you moved to a new home."

"On the way out of the court house, news media people were waiting near the steps. Seeing Isabelle and Josie, they hurried to meet them, their questions coming in a gusher. Isabelle spoke in a loud preacher voice that everyone could hear. "Please, one question at a time!" She held tight to Josie's hand.

"Missus Brown, did you expect the guilty verdict from the jury?" One of them asked.

Josie looked tired and distracted. "I...I didn't...uh know...uh what to expect?"

Another question, "Missus Brown, were you present when your husband killed the store clerk in Lancaster?"

Isabelle spoke up. "I'm sorry, that question cannot be addressed due to an ongoing investigation!"

"Does that ongoing investigation involve Missus Brown?"

Again Isabelle, spoke. "Missus Brown cannot address that question."

"Missus Brown, does your son know about his father being convicted of killing someone?"

Josie began to cry. She wanted to run as fast as she could away from these people who were harassing her. "NO," she shouted. "He does not know. Get away from me—all of you—get away."

Isabelle squeezed her hand and led her away amid cameras clicking and TV cameras rolling. They rushed across the sidewalk and to the street. They stopped momentarily and then continued to the parking lot as the news hawks relentlessly pursued them hoping for more of a story.

The Sundown was on the opposite side of town from the court house. Isabelle tried to make conversation on the way, but Josie just stared out the side window and remained silent for the whole trip. The unforgiving actions of the media were crushing in on her mind.

"What number, Josie?" Isabelle asked as they neared the motel.

Josie was silent, then as if she was awakened from a deep sleep she spoke, "Uh, what'd you say?"

"What's your room number?"

"Oh, ten," Josie replied. "Right over there," she pointed to Isabelle's left.

Josie's Gift

Isabelle parked the car and got out. Josie walked toward the door, and before she could get the key into the lock, a child's voice yelled, "Mama." Stevie ran into the arms of his mother. Josie and her son held each other as if they were the last human beings they would ever see. Josie's tears were contagious, and Stevie was soon in tears though he didn't know why.

"What's the matter, Mama?" He asked.

Josie released him and looked into his eyes. "Your... uh...your Daddy's guilty of killing somebody."

"I know, Mama. I know he killed somebody, but don't worry; we'll be okay!"

Isabelle breathed a sigh of relief that Stevie was safe. She bent down to his level, "You must be Stevie. I've heard a lot of nice things about you."

Stevie wiped his tears on his sleeves and beamed as he took Isabelle's hand that was extended in his direction. "Are you one of my mama's friends?" He said with excitement.

"Yes, I am, Stevie."

Stevie looked Isabelle up and down and then with his eyes on her clerical collar, "Are you a preacher?" He asked.

"Yes, I am," Isabelle replied, somewhat amused.

Stevie was quiet for a few moments then he blurted out, "Mama's never had a preacher for a friend."

"Well she's got one now! In fact you and your mama are going to come and live with me and some of my friends for a while."

"Will there be some kids for me to play with?"

"Yes, Stevie, there're other kids there for you to play with."

Suddenly Isabelle became aware of another woman close by. She turned in the direction of the door next to Josie's room. Josie swallowed and turned to speak.

"Barbie, this here's Reverend Isabelle Jefferson."

"Hi, Barbie!" Isabelle put out her hand.

Barbie was silent for a few moments. She felt awkward and somewhat embarrassed, not knowing quite what to say to a preacher. She chewed on a wad of gum and sipped on a can of soda. She looked uncomfortable in her skin tight clothes.

Isabelle recognized Barbie's discomfort. She smiled warmly and gave her a card with her phone number and a scripture verse on it. "I'm very pleased to meet you, Barbie. I work at the mission over on Third Street. If you ever need a friend and need a place to stay, you're always welcome."

Barbie smiled and seemed genuinely pleased with Isabelle's attention.

Isabelle turned in the direction of a high pitched and somewhat screechy voice a couple of doors away. "Hi, Isabelle," she hollered. "Whatcha doin' in this neighborhood?"

Isabelle smiled and hurried in the direction of the voice. "Hi, Jenny."

She took Jenny's hands and pulled her into a warm embrace. "It's so good to see you again Jenny!"

Jenny glanced at the others with a sheepish look on her face. Barbie and Josie smiled, trying to hide their amusement with Jenny's obvious embarrassment.

Isabelle took over the conversation. "Jenny and I are friends from way back, aren't we Jenny? Say, would you girls like to help us get Josie and Stevie packed up and ready to move to the mission?"

They all went to Josie's room and pitched in to help. Isabelle was surprised at how little there was to pack. Several worn out suitcases held everything that Josie and Stevie had to their names. Josie took one last look around the room, walked out and shut the door behind her. She felt as though a bridge to something in her past was gone. It left her a little sad. She hugged Barbie and Jenny and said a teary good bye.

"If ya ever need ta work, ya know where ta come," Barbie said.

At the mission, Isabelle got someone to look after Stevie and to find some other kids he could be friends with. Then she helped Josie to unpack her things and put them away. Isabelle showed Josie where the showers and bathrooms were located then sat down to talk.

"Do you have any money Josie?"

"Only a few dollars."

"Anything over five dollars, I need you to give to me for safe keeping. While this is a Christian mission, sometimes things like money have a way of 'walking off'. I'll give it back to you as you need it for personal stuff, and we'll keep an accounting of every dollar."

Josie smiled, but she was suspicious. She got out her purse and hesitantly handed a roll of bills to Isabelle, who carefully counted it, gave five dollars back and wrote down the remainder amount.

"This is quite a bit of money, Josie. Did you have a job?"

Josie looked at the floor. "I...uh...I turned a few tricks for Barbie and Jenny when they couldn't uh...perform."

Isabelle wasn't surprised. She knew the neighborhood well, and she knew what the girls did for money to pay their expenses. She sighed and put her arm around Josie's shoulder. "Sometimes things are pretty tough, Josie, and we do what we have to do."

Josie looked into Isabelle's eyes. She saw love and understanding—something she hadn't seen since she last saw her mother. In a barely audible voice Josie said, "Thank you, Isabelle. Thank you for not being judgmental. Yes, I... uhm...did what I had to do—and I hate myself for it." She burst into tears.

The door opened slowly and a woman poked her head inside. "Is it okay if I come in Isabelle?"

"Come on in, Darlene."

"Hi, you must be Josie. I'm Darlene."

"Where's Stevie?" Josie asked looking at both women.

Darlene responded. "He's having a good time downstairs with my two boys."

Isabelle looked at Josie. "Darlene is one of our residents here. She gives her time to helping women like you who are struggling to get adjusted." She smiled and continued, "When I found her she was living at the Sundown too."

Josie brightened. "Do you know the girls there?"

"No, not any more. All the girls I knew are uh...gone now."

"Gone?" Josie asked.

"Yeah, two of 'em moved on and two of 'em are uh... uhm...dead—murdered. That's when I made the decision to take Reverend Isabelle's invitation to come here."

"So, how'd they die?" Josie asked.

Darlene looked at Isabelle, who nodded. "They were both killed for holding out money from their pimp. Both stabbed and cut up bad."

Josie swallowed hard; feeling a bit overwhelmed with everything, she asked, "Can I be alone for a while? I need time to think!"

"Sure, Josie," Isabelle responded. "Darlene is your buddy while you're here. She'll come for you when it's time for chapel and supper."

"Chapel?"

Darlene took over the conversation and Isabelle left the room. "We all go to chapel for a short worship before supper."

"Do I have to go? I don't think God will want to see me."

Darlene smiled, "God loves you, Josie, no matter what. I'll come for you when it's time, and we'll go together."

Darlene turned to leave, but Josie spoke again. "Does Reverend Isabelle preach at the chapel services?"

"Sometimes," Darlene answered. This evening though it's going to be a very special guest. His name is Father Jeremy Jamison—he's the chaplain at State Prison. He comes here quite a lot to visit and minister to some former inmates. His uncle was Father Willie Weldon, who was Chaplain at State Prison when Isabelle's father was an inmate there. It's quite an awesome story. If you ask her, she'll tell it to you some time" (See *Beyond These Walls: A Future and a Hope;* by the author).

CHAPTER FIVE

Josie was in a deep sleep when she heard Darlene's voice. At first it sounded like someone far away. Then she heard it again, "Hey, Girl, I gotta git you up for chapel and for dinner." She took Josie's hand and helped her up.

"You startled me, Darlene."

"Sorry, Girl. I didn't mean to startle you, but we gotta git goin'." She sat down on the bed beside Josie who was now sitting up. "You were deep inta somethin' there, that's fer sure.!"

"I was thinkin' 'bout me and Roger an'..." She looked down. "Just give me a minute, okay. Where's Stevie?"

"He's just fine. He's downstairs playing and having a good time. He sure is a sweet kid, but I guess you know that!"

Josie got up, straightened up her clothes and then went to the bathroom to wash her face and hands." She emerged looking a little more relaxed.

Darlene led Josie downstairs and showed her around the facility. They found Stevie with some other children. Stevie and Darlene's boys joined them, and they went into the chapel to find seats. It was obvious from their clothes and mannerisms, the people in the chapel were from the street. As they did with all new people who came to the Mission, they looked Josie and Stevie over as they walked down the aisle. Josie felt a slight tug at her heart, wondering how many of them might be facing similar threats from the courts as she was facing. About a third of the crowd was women, many of them with children from babies up to teenagers. Some of the mothers looked to be teenagers themselves. She wondered how many of them had made the same kinds of choices she had made with Roger.

She and Darlene and the boys sat down quietly. Someone began to play softly on a piano to set a mood for worship. Someone else got up on stage, sat down by the piano and began to play the guitar. It all brought back memories that were buried deep in the back of her consciousness for at least seven years. This little chapel was similar to the church she remembered from her childhood, and the atmosphere seemed the same as she remembered it—holy, and she thought she could feel a spiritual presence. There was some whispered chatter among the street people in the crowd, but it was respectful. There were a few men and women who were obviously dressed differently, and she guessed they were volunteers from local churches who were there to help.

As the music continued, Isabelle walked in; tall and stately and with a wide smile. Father Jeremy followed. Isabelle began to sing and move her arms as if directing a choir. Without hesitation the music picked up in volume and tempo, and Isabelle continued singing; her voice rich and powerful. The crowd stood to their feet and began to clap. Some waved their hands in the air and lifted their eyes as if to heaven. This was nothing like she remembered from her childhood, but she felt a definite presence of God. A lump began to grow in her throat and tears formed in her eyes. For a single moment, she felt as if she was the only person in the building, and she wondered if God was saying something directly to her.

When the music was over, everybody clapped and sat down. Josie thought to herself, *"How strange to be clapping in church."*

Isabelle walked to the podium to introduce the guest preacher. Pointing to Father Jeremy, she began. "This man needs no introduction this evening. Many of you have seen him before..."

Someone in the back interrupted, "Yeah when Ah wuz in prison. Ya'll listen cuz he knows jes how you feel." Everybody laughed and clapped again.

Josie couldn't believe how relaxed everybody was. This seemed to be a place where everybody was the same, and nobody was better than anybody else. She smiled...she felt welcomed...she felt good to be here.

Father Jeremy walked to the podium. "Some of you here who have been around for many years, not only know me from prison, but you also remember my uncle, Father Willie Weldon. I am almighty glad to be here with you and to see you again. You are my friends and I love you, each and every one."

Some in the audience shouted, "Yeah...Yeah." There was more clapping. Josie could tell that this man was loved by all.

Father Jeremy lifted his hands skyward and prayed; then he began to preach, animating every word with his arms. "Tonight I'm here to do just one thing—tell you about my good friend, Jesus. He's the one who'll calm your fears and heal your sorrows. He'll patch up your life and help you get onto the right track." He paused and looked around, "Looks like some of you missed that train!" There were more yells from the audience, agreeing with him and more clapping. Some laughed.

Father Jeremy continued. "Don't you worry none Jesus is patient—he'll wait for you to hit bottom if necessary." Then his voice changed; he pleaded, "You don't need to hit bottom; that's a dangerous place to be. You come to Jesus now before the bottom comes right up to hit you on your backside. Now, it's going to be time to eat in a little while, but I know there are some of you here who need healing for your soul and healing for your body. We're going to sing now, and I'm going to wait here in front with Reverend Isabelle. You come on up here, and we'll pray for you. You can go to supper a new man or woman. Some of you are teenagers, and you need Jesus too."

They all began to sing with gusto and clap to the beat. A few walked up to talk to Father Jeremy and Reverend Isabelle. Josie watched with interest as they laid their hands on each one of them and talked to each one individually and prayed for them. Once in a while someone collapsed on the floor. When that happened, they let them lay and went on to the next person. All the while the singing and worship continued. Many were shouting, "Praise the Lord," and "Amen".

Josie thought she heard some strange sounds and looked over at Darlene. She had her hands raised toward heaven and her eyes were closed. She was singing softly in a very strange language. This was something she'd never seen or heard and wondered what her mother, and especially her dad, would think of it.

In spite of the strangeness of it all, she didn't feel uncomfortable—that is until she thought she heard a voice whisper in her ear. It was scratchy but syrupy sweet, "You don't belong here!" The voice said. "You need to buy a big knife and take it to Roger to help him escape from that jail cell! You do love him don't you? You owe him that because he's your husband. That'll make up for the things you told the District Attorney's office."

Josie cautiously looked around; nobody was there and there was no person to go with the voice. She shivered and suddenly felt cold and afraid. Again the voice spoke. This time it was cold and icy, "Leave this place, you have no business here. These people don't care about you. Isabelle took your money didn't she? All they care about is your money!"

Darlene noticed Josie's turmoil. She was shaking almost violently. "NOooo!" She shouted. Darlene grabbed her as she was about to collapse onto the floor. Josie was breathing hard and fast as if she were running for her life. Father Jeremy and Reverend Isabelle made their way to where she was sitting—she was moaning and gasping for breath. Someone else grabbed Stevie and lifted him up and held him in his arms.

Father Jeremy took hold of her hand and began to pray. Reverend Isabelle put her hand on Father's shoulder and prayed in her own way. Gradually Josie began to come back to reality and calm down. Father helped her up and sat her in the chair. He sat down beside her and began to talk to her in a very soothing voice, telling her that everything was all right and that Jesus was in control.

"What happened, Josie?" Isabelle asked.

Josie told her about the voice and what it had said. Isabelle looked at Father who nodded. They both knew where the voice had come from, and they knew what must be done. "That was the Devil talking to you, Josie!" Isabelle said. "His job is to rob and steal and even kill. He doesn't want you to be happy and above all he doesn't want you to know Jesus in a personal way. He's trying to block you from having healing come to your life."

Josie looked bewildered. She had never heard such talk and didn't understand it at all.

"Josie," Father Jeremy said. "Isabelle and I are going to lay our hands on you and we're going to say some pretty strong words to the Devil. We're going to command him, in Jesus Name, to leave you alone. Is that okay?"

Josie nodded; her eyes were full of tears, and her throat had a big lump that felt like it could come right up and out of her mouth. She saw people watching and she felt self-conscious.

Father took a small crucifix out of his pocket and opened Josie's hand. "Here," he said. "Take this. Isabelle will teach you about it and how to use it against the Devil." With that He put his hands on her head; Isabelle's hands joined his, and they began to pray in perfect agreement. "Father in the Name of our Lord Jesus Christ, fill Josie with your peace; and by your Holy Spirit give her understanding. By the blood of our Lord Jesus, we command Satan, the Devil, to leave her alone and, with all his evil followers, go back to the pit from whence they came. By your authority, we direct her angels to guard her life and her soul night and day as long as she lives. AMEN!"

Josie slumped into Isabelle's arms. It was like a dream, all warm and comfortable there wrapped in Isabelle's love. She looked into Father Jeremy's eyes, "Thank you," she whispered. She reached out and hugged him. Finally, she looked up at Stevie, who was quietly crying, not knowing or understanding what was going on, but sensing that his mother had undergone something deeply emotional. She reached out and took him from the stranger's arms. "Oh Stevie, everything's going to be all right now, I promise! Jesus is going to help us."

Others from the little crowd came to encourage her in their own way—some even dared to hug her. Most were unkempt and wore old clothes and carried everything they owned in bags of various sorts. A few even smelled bad, but this night all was right in Josie's life, and she hugged them back.

Next morning when it was time for breakfast, Darlene came to her room and led her downstairs. They went to the chapel and sat quietly for a little while. Darlene read her Bible and seemed to be praying. Others were coming and going and doing the same thing. Josie sat with Stevie and tried to understand what was going on. Finally Darlene explained it to her. "This is what we call our morning devotions, Josie. We come here and quietly read and pray to get the day started. Those of us who live here all have chores to do before and after breakfast. Some will be helping in the kitchen. Everybody who stays here for any length of time is assigned to duties either in the kitchen or in cleaning and repairing the buildings or just helping others with counseling and encouragement. Sometime today, you'll be talking to Isabelle, who will ask you where you'd like to help out."

"I don't have a Bible, Darlene, and I really don't know how to pray."

"We have plenty of Gideon Bibles around here and you can have one. We have some Bible classes and stuff like that where you can learn about the Bible and how to pray. We want you to grow in the Lord while you are here. And, by the way, there are organized activities for the kids that Stevie will enjoy."

Josie hugged Darlene and thanked her for everything but she was silently bearing a huge cross that weighed down her mind and emotions. Part of her was somewhere else all the time. Hardly a moment went by that she didn't think of Roger. She was his wife—she missed him and wanted to be near him. She never thought of the beatings or the bad times—she only thought of the good times. It was a delusional kind of existence.

Soon after breakfast, Isabelle came to Josie's room. Josie was just finishing making up hers and Stevie's beds and getting the few clothes they had put away in the dresser. Isabelle poked her head inside and spoke, "Can I come in Josie?"

"Hi Isabelle! Come on in."

"I've got several things we need to discuss; one is Roger." Isabelle carefully watched the expression on Josie's face.

Josie frowned and looked at the floor. "Okay, what do we need to discuss about Roger?"

"Well, they've postponed the sentencing phase of the trial for another week. Michael Sheffley, Roger's attorney, wants some extra time to prepare for his presentation. Will Brent, from the District Attorney's office, told me that Sheffley plans to put you on the stand as a character witness. He's trying to get a lighter sentence for Roger. Will told me that the DA is going for the death penalty, and Sheffley wants a life sentence with possibility of parole in twenty years."

Josie looked worried and began to cry. "What should I do?"

"You'll have to decide if you will testify on Roger's behalf. The DA can get you out of testifying if you can convince him that you will be a hostile witness. What...uh, what do you think you'll say if you do testify?"

Josie thought for a few minutes. Her words interspersed with her sobs, "I'd tell them...what a wonderful father he is...and how much I love him. I'd tell them...what a wonderful person he is—he has so much potential, and...I just know I can help him change."

Isabelle spoke in a soft and understanding tone. "You have strong feelings for him don't you? In spite of everything, you really love him. I know how you feel Josie—not because I've experienced what you have; but because there've been many women just like you who've come to this mission. Like you, they loved and tried—they wanted so much for the man they loved to change. They suffered and cried just like you're doing now, and they found peace and healing here with others like themselves and with finding the One, Jesus, who is the healer of all hurts and broken hearts."

Josie got control of her tears, but was still absorbed in her own pain. "I need to be there for him, Isabelle! I need to go to the jail and talk to him." She paused, "Will you take me over to the jail so I can see him before the punishment part?"

Isabelle thought for a few moments. "Yeah, Josie! I'll take you over...on one condition."

"What's that?"

Isabelle looked Josie directly in the eye, "On the condition that I go into the visiting room with you, and I get to talk to Roger too, okay?"

"Yeah," Josie said. "Yeah, I think that would be nice. I think Roger would like to meet you so he kinda knows where I'm at, an what I'm doin'."

"Okay, I'll let you know as soon as I know exactly when the sentencing's going to be. Oh, and by the way, I talked to Detective Sandoval; he asked about you and Stevie and told me to give you his and Joann's love."

Josie looked surprised. "He's so busy an all, I didn't think he would remember."

"He's keeping tabs on you, Josie. He wants the best for you and Stevie. He also told me that if you needed anything to let him know."

Josie was touched. "Him and his wife are wonderful folks. I think they loved Stevie like he was their own grandson."

"One more thing, Josie; you need a few days to get used to the mission life then you need to start sharing some of the work. Carla's making the schedule for next week. What do you think you'd like to do as far as work here is concerned? We have inside work like kitchen and housekeeping or outside work like lawn and gardening."

"I don't know...maybe doing the cleaning or laundry. Would that work?"

"That'll work, I'll let Carla know. Darlene is your little guardian angel here, and she'll help you get acquainted and to get started when it's your turn. In the meantime we have opportunities here that you should take advantage of. Mind you—we can't force you into anything; but you should attend the women's Bible study group. It meets every day; Darlene'll show you the place. We also have educational

Josie's Gift

opportunities...like G.E.D. classes so you can finish your high school education."

"How'd you know I never finished high school?"

Isabelle laughed. "Honey, I looked at your age and I looked at Stevie's age and I know you been on the run for a long time. It just all came together."

Isabelle's voice turned serious. She took Josie's hand in hers. "Honey, how'd you get into this mess anyway?"

Josie looked down at the floor. She was silent and seemed to ignore Isabelle's question. She remembered her mother's voice. The words played in her mind as if her mom were saying them at this moment.

"You're what?" Her mom asked.

"Please don't be mad at me and don't tell Papa." Josie pleaded.

One word expressed her shock and surprise as Ruth responded to her daughter. *"Pregnant? How could you? You're only sixteen!"*

Josie's tears begged for her mom's understanding, but all her words came out wrong. *"But Mama, it was an accident... I didn't mean to get pregnant."*

"Getting pregnant is never an accident Josie," Ruth said, her anger rising. "It's a choice! When you choose to have sex, you choose the possibility of getting pregnant! And you expect me not to be mad? How could you? We had dreams and hopes! We had plans for college! Yes, I'm more than mad...I'm very angry!"

Josie was sobbing. Trying to placate her mom, she continued, "Mama, listen to me...please listen. It'll be okay. Roger says he loves me, and he wants me to move in with him. We can make it. I know we can. Just give it a chance."

Ruth's anger was beginning to turn to sorrow and now into pity. Her mind was racing but she tried to sound loving and civil. She had tears in her eyes as she looked directly into Josie's eyes.

Josie remembered her mother's tears and the utter and complete disappointment in her eyes.

"What do you mean, make it? Roger doesn't even work. He's twenty-two and has never held down a full time job. He refuses to go back to school. He's a loser Josie. When he had sex with you he committed a crime...do you realize that?"

"Mama, you don't know him like I do. You're being judgmental. I believe in him. He has big plans. Inside, he's a wonderful person."

"No, Honey," Ruth said trying to sound more loving. "He's an ugly frog who thinks he's a handsome prince. He's a loser, and I'm not being judgmental...I'm just being truthful. Getting pregnant was your first bad decision. Moving in with Roger will be the second bad decision. There aren't enough kisses in the whole world to turn that frog into a handsome prince. You and I will talk to Papa, and he will talk to Roger and to the police. We can handle your pregnancy, but not with Roger as a part of your life."

Josie was devastated. She had hopes and dreams for her relationship with Roger. She knew he was experimenting with drugs, but she'd surely be the princess who would transform him from the ugly frog into a handsome prince. She felt so important when Roger told her how much he needed her. He talked openly about his bad habits, but he kept telling her she was the only one who could change him. When things got bad and even violent, he begged her to stay with him. With her he could make it. He promised. Then the unplanned pregnancy...Roger wanted her to get an abortion, but she refused.

She and Roger ran away together. She lied about her age, and they married in another state.

"Josie, are you okay, Honey?"

Josie looked into Isabelle's eyes. She saw love and understanding. She told the story to Isabelle. When she finished, she laughed aloud at her immaturity. "I wonder, Isabelle; what I would do if the same situation came up again."

Isabelle laughed and hugged Josie. "I hope that opportunity never comes around again. I'll leave you to Darlene now, and I'll let you know about goin' to the jail."

CHAPTER SIX

Josie was reading her new Gideon Bible in the chapel. This was a new experience for her, and she had many questions she wanted to ask the women's Bible study group. Isabelle came down the aisle and quietly sat beside her.

"How's it going, Josie? Are you learning anything?"

"I'm learning I don't know a thing about this Bible!" She answered.

Isabelle rose from her seat and took Josie's hand. "Let's go out into the hallway where we can talk."

"I got word from Will Brent that Roger's sentencing will be next Tuesday at nine in the morning. Today is Thursday, and this afternoon would be a good time to go visit Roger. I have a light schedule so we can leave here around three. Would that be Okay with you?"

Josie thought for a few moments, "This is kinda sudden but I guess that's how these things are. Yeah, I'll be ready."

Isabelle turned and started to leave.

"Isabelle…thanks; thanks a lot. I really do want to see Roger, but I'm not sure what I want to say."

Isabelle took Josie's hand and pointed to the chapel, "Go back in there. Just sit and meditate and ask God what you need to say — not what you want to say."

Josie sat quietly, other ideas began to intrude on her meditation...ideas she didn't like. *"Could I smuggle a knife into the jail? Could I do something to help him escape? What can I say when I'm on the witness stand that would help Roger not get the death penalty?"* She fingered the little crucifix hanging around her neck and like a fresh breath she had a feeling of peace. *"I'll cross that bridge when I get there. Besides, Isabelle will be there with me."* She said to herself.

Isabelle came to Josie's room right at three. Josie was ready but nervous about seeing Roger. Sensing her feelings, Isabelle took her hand and invited her to pray. "Heavenly Father," Isabelle began; "We pray for Roger, for his soul—that he will hear your voice and feel your love. Go with us and lead us step by step to the jail and fill our hearts and minds with love for Roger and tell us how to minister to his need. In Jesus name we pray, AMEN."

It was nearly three-thirty when they arrived at the jail. Isabelle pushed the button to call the attendant. The little door slid open, and eyes peered out and immediately recognized Isabelle.

"Hi, Reverend Isabelle, give me a few seconds to get to my desk and open the door for you."

There followed a loud buzzer and several clicks signaling the door was unlocked. They pushed the door open and walked inside. "Hi, Jim!" Isabelle greeted the attendant and thrust her hand in his direction. "It's good to see you again."

"Who ya need ta see?" Jim asked.

Motioning to Josie, she answered, "Jim, this is Josie Brown, wife of Roger Brown, and we'd like to visit with Roger for a few minutes."

Jim showed a apprehensive look and picked up the phone to speak to someone on the inside. Turning back to Isabelle and Josie, he spoke again. "Roger's been causin' a lot of trouble lately, and they've had to isolate him from the other prisoners—for his own safety as much as anything."

"Oh... what kind of trouble?" Isabelle asked.

"Mostly taunting the guards and some other prisoners. He's started several fights and had to be subdued by force." Jim replied.

Isabelle looked at Josie. She looked worried and lowered her eyes to the floor. "You okay Josie?" Isabelle asked.

Without raising her eyes, she quietly answered almost in a whisper. "Yeah, I'm okay." But, she was on the verge of tears.

Isabelle put her hand on her shoulder, "It'll be okay—God is here with us!"

A man with a clipboard opened a locked door on the other side of the room and walked to Isabelle. "Nice to see you Reverend, you know the procedure!" He laughed and handed the clipboard to Isabelle.

"Nice to see you too, Tom!" After signing her name, she handed the clipboard to Josie and showed her where to sign her name.

"Follow me," Tom said.

They were led through the locked door and into the room where Josie had visited Roger over a week ago. Both women sat in chairs near the steel divider; Tom stood behind them near the door. In a few minutes a door opened in the space opposite the steel divider and Roger was led in. This time he was in handcuffs and ankle shackles. The guard accompanying him stood behind him near the door.

Roger tried to turn away, but his guard commanded him to sit next to the divider. He twisted his mouth into a sneer—his eyes were filled with hate. "Why'd ya come back here Josie? Yer thu reason I'm in here! If it hadn't been fer you... we'd still be tagether. I don't want ta see ya no more, ya hear!" Roger was yelling and swinging his arms. "Git outta here, Josie!"

Josie was sobbing uncontrollably. The guard walked to where Roger was sitting and tried to calm him down. Roger swung his handcuffed hands at the guard who stepped back just in time to avoid getting hit. The guard called for backup, and two other guards appeared within moments.

Isabelle tried to calm Roger. She spoke softly and calmly to him. "Roger, we're here to help you. I'm Reverend Isabelle Jefferson, pastor of the Lighted Way Ministries. Josie's living with us temporarily. She still loves you Roger, and just wants to encourage you."

Roger was still agitated and angry. "I don't care—git her outta here—I don't want to hear about it. I don't care about you either so leave me alone!"

"I have a message for you from God, Roger." Isabelle said softly.

"I don't need no messages from God," Roger screamed. "I don't care about him, I don't care about you, and you can all go to hell and take Josie with you!"

Isabelle continued calmly with a tone of voice that reflected her love and God's love. "It doesn't do anything to diminish God's love just because you reject him and reject me and your wife. In spite of all your anger and the crimes you've committed, God still loves you and wants to heal your broken heart and save your soul!"

Roger just looked at her—his eyes full of hate and evil. He got up from the chair and started ranting and raving about her and about Josie and about God. The three guards quickly subdued him and led him out the way he came in.

The guard who stood at the door with Isabelle and Josie came to where they were sitting. He took Josie's hand and gently lifted her out of her chair. Isabelle got up to stand beside her. Josie was confused and couldn't understand Roger's attitude. She had felt all along that Roger would be glad to see her.

"I'm very sorry ma'am," the guard said. "He's getting more and more uncontrollable."

Isabelle looked into Josie's eyes. "You've seen him this way before, haven't you Josie?"

Josie was choking on her sobs. She nodded in the affirmative but didn't say anything.

"Was he like this when he beat you?" Isabelle asked.

Josie looked up. "Yes," she said, almost in a whisper.

Isabelle put her arms around Josie and pulled her into a strong embrace. "God loves you, Josie; and you won't ever have to face that again. Roger's where he belongs, but take comfort in knowing that God still loves him."

"But how can we reach him?" Josie sobbed.

"We have a man named Martin Green who was a friend of my father's in State Prison. He lives at the mission and is part of our Prison Ministry. He's now an ordained minister and is in charge of the men's division, just like Carla's in charge of the women's division. Martin and his volunteers will be praying for Roger and you, and I will also pray for him. Let's bow our heads and say a prayer right now."

Speaking to the guard, she asked, "Will you join us, Tom?"

"Yes, ma'am," Tom answered, a little embarrassed.

"Heavenly Father," Isabelle prayed. "Let your love and peace flood this jail where so much evil is represented in the deeds of men whom you love. We pray for Roger, and Lord we simply leave him in your hands though we know the choice is his. AMEN"

The guard led them back to the outer office where Jim waited. "Well," Jim said. "How'd it go?"

"He's pretty agitated, Jim," Isabelle answered. "We prayed for him and that's about all we can do!"

Jim turned his attention to Josie. "Miz Brown, I just want you to know that we're doing the best we can do here. In spite of his anger and tirades, Roger's being treated as humanely as possible. But, please understand that we have to do what we have to do." He smiled and shook her hand. "It'd probably be best if you didn't come back." He added as an afterthought.

Josie was depressed when she left the jail and in spite of encouragement from Darlene and Isabelle, she remained very sad and distant for the next several days. When Tuesday came around, Josie seemed to be in better spirits. Just knowing that another part of this awful saga would be over, put her mind a little more at ease.

Isabelle saw her at breakfast. "Good morning Josie; you look like you're feeling better today."

"Yeah," Josie replied. "I feel relieved to know that today it will be over—at least I'll know Roger's fate. I hope they don't ask me to testify on his behalf though—I don't think I could handle it."

"Don't you worry, Josie, Darlene and I will be there with you, and God will be there. We're all praying for a miracle, and I have the feeling they won't call you for testimony— but you never can tell. We're prepared anyway it goes."

In the car on the way to the courthouse nobody spoke. They parked and walked in the direction of the courthouse. Darlene leaned over and whispered to Isabelle, "I don't have a good feeling Isabelle. It's like something is wrong—bad wrong."

"Me too Darlene. All we can do is pray, and keep our eyes and ears open."

On the courthouse steps there was a crowd of TV and newspaper reporters waiting for word from inside. Microphone stands were set up near the street for news conferences later. Isabelle smiled at everybody as she, Josie and Darlene made their way up the steps.

The courtroom was full because Judge Jacobson had scheduled several sentencing cases for the same day. Before they went into the courtroom, Will Brent told Isabelle that

Roger's case would be third on the list. "You can all go get a cup of coffee if you like, Isabelle," he said looking from one to the other of the three women.

Isabelle looked at Josie. She shook her head, "I think I'd rather sit in there and watch what goes on."

There were three empty chairs Will had saved for them on the left end of the first row of the section on the right of the room. A three-foot high railing separated them from the tables with the attorneys. The three women made their way in and sat down. Soon the bailiff walked in and in a loud voice proclaimed Judge Jacobson's court was in session. The first two cases were rather simple cases of burglary, and the proceedings consisted of brief statements from the defendants and their victims, and the judge handing out appropriate jail or probation sentences.

In the meantime a sheriff's deputy was given the task of walking Roger from the jail across the street to the court house and into a holding room in the basement below the ground floor. His hands and ankles were shackled so it was slow going. Roger was sullen and angry; his emotions were busy hijacking his rational thinking. He scanned his surroundings carefully. His brain was at work scheming and trying to think of some way to escape. As he sat in the holding room, he thought of a plan. It was risky, but he felt like he had nothing to lose at this point.

After the deputy left the room, Roger hobbled over to the door and stood against the wall where he would be hidden behind the door when the deputy opened it. As soon as the door opened and the deputy walked in, Roger put his shoulder against the door and shoved it closed. In the same quick motion he swung the heavy handcuffs at the deputy's head. They connected with a sickening sound of steel on bone, and the deputy went down on the floor, blood running from a wound on his head. Roger was immediately on top of him swinging the handcuffs over and over until blood was also coming from the injuries on the deputy's face and he lay still on the floor.

Roger rolled him over onto his back and fished along his belt for the keys to the handcuffs and ankle shackles. He quickly located them and unlocked both. "Free at last," he moaned as he pulled the deputy's Glock automatic 40-caliber pistol from the holster and then filled his pockets with two extra magazines. Roger's heart was beating at a panic rate, and he was sweating profusely.

He opened the door slowly and looked around. Nobody in sight; and the stairs were to his left. It took him only seconds bounding up the stairs to reach the third floor. As he turned toward the court room he met a surprised and wide-eyed bailiff who started to draw his pistol. Roger fired, and the bailiff went down holding his abdomen. Roger burst through the court room door, shooting as he went. He first turned toward the judge and fired a shot that hit the Judge who fell behind his bench. Everyone in the room was screaming and diving for cover. It was pandemonium. Roger aimed at the prosecutor and fired. The prosecutor fell, wounded in the left shoulder.

Josie stood up screaming, "Roger, no...please, Roger don't do this."

Isabelle stood up to pull her down behind the railing. At the same moment Roger swung the gun in their direction and fired again. Isabelle spun around to her left and fell down onto the floor, bleeding. Sirens were blaring as police answered the emergency calls.

As he was pushing a new magazine into the pistol, suddenly a male voice, loud and clear shouted, "Police, Roger—drop your gun, NOW! Drop it Roger!"

Roger turned toward the voice and saw Detective Sandoval standing in the doorway. His heart was pumping hard and fast. His forehead was shedding big drops of sweat, and his hands were trembling. Now in his brain everything was happening in slow motion; his body was full of adrenaline, and his perception was dulled by rage.

He looked to the voice and saw a Glock automatic pistol like the one he was holding pointed straight at him. On the side of the pistol he saw a tiny bright red light. In a moment of indecision, he lowered his head and saw the tiny red dot in the middle of his chest. As he swung his gun toward the voice with the gun, Sandoval fired. Roger felt like someone had hit him in the chest with a sledge hammer; he groaned and stumbled backward but didn't lose his footing. He brought his gun up again. He was screaming curses, and frothy blood was running from his mouth and nose. The red dot was still there, but now it was blurry; the dot moved to his forehead. His eyes were seeing double. He felt incredible pain in his chest. He started to pull the trigger, but Sandoval fired again; the explosion echoed inside Roger's head. A small round black hole appeared on his forehead. His head snapped backward then forward as his body crumpled to the floor. He was dead on his feet even before he began to fall.

Detective Sandoval holstered his pistol and walked to where Roger fell. He knelt down and looked into the eyes that were wide open and staring at the ceiling. He shook his head in disgust, picked up the gun Roger was using and put it into a plastic bag. Emergency Medical Personnel were bursting through the door. "Don't bother with this one," Sandy said. "He's dead. Crime scene investigators will be here in a few minutes and will tend to things. They'll need the body to take pictures and gather evidence."

Then he turned and shouted to the people still in the courtroom. "Ladies and gentlemen you are safe; the gunman has been eliminated. Please stay right where you are and keep the doorways clear for Emergency Services personnel. Within a few minutes there will be uniformed officers here to talk to all of you and take some statements."

Josie's Gift

Sandy ran over to where Josie was kneeling beside Isabelle. She was sobbing uncontrollably. "Please, Isabelle... please don't die. Please, dear God, don't let her die." Sandy reached down and pulled her up and half dragged her out of the way so that the medical personnel could get to Isabelle. He held Josie in his arms and talked to her softly like a dad would talk to his broken hearted daughter.

"They're taking care of her Josie. There's nothing you can do now."

"Is she dead, Sandy?"

"I don't think so, Josie, but she's in bad shape." His tone changed, "Josie, listen to me," Sandy spoke as if to emphasize something; "The bullet that hit Isabelle was intended for you...remember that. Roger wanted to kill you—Isabelle stood up and stepped to you to pull you back down behind the railing. It looked like the bullet hit her in the left shoulder. As soon as they take her to the ambulance, you and Darlene can follow her to the hospital. Here's her purse...she'll need her ID and insurance cards. I'm sure her car keys are in there too. Right now it's very important for you to be able to think clearly. I've got to stay and assist CSI and then go to the station to make out a report." He laughed, "Ha...I'll be on desk duty for awhile because of the shooting. They have to do an internal investigation. There'll be uniformed officers at the hospital—they'll take your statements there. I'll join you there later."

"You're not in trouble are you?" Darlene asked.

"No, no trouble. I'll go down to the hospital as soon as I get my report done." He looked at his watch, "Probably a couple of hours."

"What about Roger?" Josie asked through tears rolling down her cheeks and sobs that choked her words. With her arms outstretched, she started to walk to where he was lying but Sandy grabbed her arm and pulled her back.

"Don't go over there, Josie—you won't like what you see. He's dead, and there's nothing you can do. Police crime scene investigators will be here shortly, and they'll take care of the body. In a few days they'll need you at the morgue to claim his remains."

"But I don't have any money to take care of him," she cried.

"You tell 'em at the morgue you don't have money for burial, and they'll arrange things with the county. I'll be there to help you out, and Darlene will also be there so don't you worry."

Josie looked at Sandy. How can I ever thank you and repay you for all you've done for me and Stevie?"

"You take time to thank God, Josie. It is He who spared your life today, and He works in mysterious ways. He loves you and sent Joann and me to be there when you needed someone. God has a wonderful plan for your life. I'll see you in a couple of hours. They're taking Isabelle out now so you two better get going."

The reporters and cameras were everywhere trying to get statements and interviews. One of them spotted Josie and Darlene and the gurney bearing Isabelle. Running beside them, the reporters' shouted their questions. Josie was confused and still crying. Darlene asked for patience and promised interviews at the hospital. Just then Sandy walked up and went to one of the microphones to make a statement. All the reporters followed him.

Josie and Darlene walked beside the gurney taking Isabelle to the ambulance. They didn't leave her side 'til the gurney was pushed in and the back doors shut. "C'mon, Girl," Darlene said. "We gotta get a move on."

They arrived at the hospital about the same time as the ambulance and followed the gurney inside. A nurse told them where they could wait.

"Nurse," Josie said. "I have her driver's license and ID cards here when you need them!"

"Oh, okay, follow me!" The nurse said.

When they got to the door of the emergency room, two uniformed police officers were standing by the double doors. Darlene and Josie were handed off to another person who had a clipboard and began asking questions. The uniformed officers listened and took notes as they related everything they could remember, including the circumstances of the shooting. As soon as the questioning was finished, they were told to go to the waiting room down the hall. Before they left, Darlene talked to one of the police officers about the other victims.

"Josie, I'll go get us some hot chocolate. You want anything else?" Darlene asked.

"Hot chocolate will be fine Darlene, nothing else." Josie answered.

When Darlene returned, they sat and talked.

"The officer told me that there were five people shot, including Isabelle. The judge is in critical condition, as is the sheriff's deputy. The others are extremely serious, but will be okay in time. They're all going to have to have extensive surgery. They've got several surgeons on their way to the hospital right now."

"When will we get to see Isabelle?" Josie asked.

"Not 'til she's out of surgery and in the recovery room. Even then she won't be able to talk. We'll just be there by her side and pray."

Josie was silent and stared at the floor. The awful scene at the courthouse was just beginning to sink into her mind. "Darlene, Sandy told me Roger intended to kill me when he hit Isabelle instead. I feel really bad about that. I'm the one who's supposed to be in there instead of Isabelle—I wish it was me."

Darlene turned and looked at Josie. "Remember Josie, how Jesus was nailed to the cross for our sin? It was really us who deserved to be on that cross, not him. He was and is the perfect Son of God and didn't deserve that pain and suffering and death. Jesus even told his disciples that there is no greater love than when one person gives her life willingly for another." Darlene paused. "Isabelle is that kind of person. She's not going to die—thank God—but she willingly risked death to save you. That's truly an awesome thing, isn't it?" When Darlene finished talking, she had tears in her eyes.

Josie too, had tears in her eyes; tears of shame, tears of guilt, tears of thankfulness, tears of loss, and tears for Roger. It was only now that the full impact of Roger's actions and his tragic death began to sink in. She couldn't get the picture of Roger's lifeless body lying on the floor out of her mind. She felt anger and deep, deep sadness.

"Darlene, did Sandy **have** to kill Roger today?"

Darlene just looked deep into Josie's eyes. She could see pain and knew there was a broken heart inside—not just because Roger was dead, but because of all the failures and unfulfilled dreams she had nurtured and all the broken promises that had never been fulfilled. Now, there were no more dreams, no more hopes, and no more plans that would include Roger. She would never realize her dream of turning him into a handsome prince.

"Yes, Josie," Darlene answered. "Sandy did what he had to do...to save his own life and the lives of many others who might have died in the rampage. If Sandy had not done what he did, Roger would've kept on shooting and many others would have been wounded or killed."

Josie didn't comment; she laid her head on Darlene's shoulder and closed her eyes. Darlene closed her eyes too and both fell into a shallow sleep.

When Josie awoke, she could see the sun getting low in the sky out through the tall windows. There was an eerie

Josie's Gift

glow as if God, even in the midst of this tragedy, was again looking down on his creation and saying, "It is good!" As Darlene opened her eyes, a nurse was walking down the hallway toward them. By now, families of the other victims had gathered. A few reporters and cameras were also there and waiting. "The surgeons will be down to talk to you in a few moments," The nurse announced.

When the surgeons arrived, one of them announced, "Judge Jacobson and Deputy Goldman are still in surgery. As soon as we know anything about their conditions the surgeons will be down and talk to you."

One of the surgeons asked for family of Isabelle Jefferson. Darlene and Josie stepped forward where they huddled with the doctor. "She has no family, Doctor. She's the Pastor at Lighted Way Ministries. We're her friends and the mission is her only family."

The doctor smiled. "Then I suppose you're going to tell me she has a lot of people praying for her."

"She sure does!" Josie and Darlene said almost in unison.

Still smiling, the doctor continued. "Well, you keep up the praying. At this point she's stable and resting comfortably. We had to remove the bullet and clean out the deep wound and sew up some torn tissue inside. We also had to have an orthopedic surgeon repair a fracture and put some tendon back together. She lost quite a bit of blood, but the bullet missed a couple of critical arteries and veins as well as her lung. We're going to keep her asleep until tomorrow just to make sure everything is okay. She's strong and in good health. Now, I suggest you two go on back to the mission and let everyone know how things are going." As an afterthought he said, "And keep on praying!"

"Can we go to her bedside and pray for her right now?" Darlene asked.

"Sure," he said. "Follow me!"

After they prayed at Isabelle's bedside, they went back to the waiting room to talk to the other families who were still waiting there. Josie was astonished at Darlene's willingness and ability to speak to each family. She gave some words of comfort and prayed a short prayer for each family and the victims before they left. By the time they were walking toward the outer doors it was dark and reporters were waiting.

Speaking to Josie, one of them asked, "Are you Missus Brown, the wife of Roger Brown?"

"Yes," Josie said, as tears formed in her eyes. Cameras snapped pictures, and a TV crew stepped in.

"Missus Brown, I understand you're not from Rock City. Where did you live before you came here?"

"I uh...lived over in Churchill. My parents and some other family still live there."

"Missus Brown, why did you and Mister Brown come to Rock City?"

Josie's eyes narrowed and tears were running down her cheeks. She screamed, "He was accused of committing a crime in Lancaster. We...uh he was running, and this is where we ended up. Now, leave me alone!"

The media persisted. "Missus Brown, were you involved in your husband's crime spree?"

Just then Will Brent stepped in front of the camera. "Ladies and Gentlemen, I'm Will Brent, from the District Attorney's office. There'll be no more questions now as this case is still under investigation. The DA's office and the Police Department will put out a joint statement in several hours and will hold a formal news conference regarding the court house shooting sometime tomorrow. Thank you all." Will, ushered Darlene and Josie through the crowd and to the front door.

On the way out, they met Detective Sandoval on his way in. "Thanks, Will, looks like you got here at just the right time." Turning to Darlene, "How's Isabelle doin'?" he asked.

Darlene told him everything the doctor had said.

"Are the uniformed officers still there? I need to talk to them for awhile."

"They're still there, Sandy," Darlene answered.

"Okay, I'll see you tomorrow. Oh, and don't make any statements to the news media. We'll handle all of that from either mine or Mister Brent's offices." Sandy turned and continued into the hospital.

Josie was sobbing hysterically. Darlene held her close as they moved toward the car.

CHAPTER SEVEN

Back at the Mission, an around-the-clock vigil was quickly organized to pray for Isabelle. In spite of their exhaustion, Darlene and Josie each took a turn in the chapel that night. Stevie was fast asleep when Josie got to the room. One of the volunteers was asleep in the chair beside Stevie's bed. "Thank you Sarah," Josie said as the two women hugged.

Josie lay awake for a long time reliving the day's events. She couldn't get the images of Roger dying so violently out of her mind. She could still see the twisted, distorted expression on his face, the narrowed eyes, the hate...as he aimed his gun directly at her. She remembered screaming and looking into those eyes...it was like looking into a black, empty well. She could still feel Isabelle crumple into her arms as she fell...see the blood staining Isabelle's blouse as it seeped into her left sleeve, and ran down to her hand. It was a nightmare.

She kept thinking of all she and Roger had been through in the seven plus years they had been together. Things seemed pretty good at first, but as time went by, Roger became more violent and desperate. He became so possessive and jealous of her that he would never allow her to go anywhere without him. She dared not ever look toward another man; she couldn't even give him the impression that she was looking at other girls and women...or think about making friends with them. Except for Stevie, it became a lonely existence.

In spite of all the heartbreak, she never gave up hope that she could help him change but the harder she tried, the worse he became. She had been with Roger, and yet so alone for so long, that even now, among friends she felt uncomfortable — like it was something she shouldn't be doing.

Finally she lapsed into a fitful and shallow sleep. In a dream she thought she heard her own voice crying, *"Mama, Mama!"* She saw her mother reaching out to her and running toward her. Awakening with a start, she sat up and saw Stevie at the side of her bed.

"Mama, Mama," he cried. "Are you okay? I heard you crying and woke up."

Josie had to clear her head. Her face was wet, and she knew she had been crying. Leaning over to Stevie, she hung her legs over the side of the bed and gathered him into her arms. "Yes, my darling... yes, I'm all right."

Josie held her son until he was asleep, then gently picked him up and laid him back in his bed. She pulled the covers over him and knelt beside the bed. For a long time, she prayed and looked at him, her eyes going over every little feature of his beautiful face. Suddenly it dawned on her; this was her future now...Stevie was her hope...he would be what Roger was never capable of becoming. She looked up and thanked God for this little miracle and for her survival, and for the first time, she realized how close she had been to the precipice of death. She felt at peace. *"The Father is merciful and good,"* she whispered to herself.

Josie dozed for two hours, when Darlene walked quietly into the room and touched her. "It's time for you to be in the chapel, Josie," she whispered.

"Okay, I'm ready. See you in the morning."

Josie found it difficult to stay on her knees for an hour and to keep her mind on Isabelle. Periodically when her mind strayed, she prayed the Lord's Prayer she'd learned as a child in her Sunday school classes. At other times she recited some Psalms she remembered from her father. In the hour she was there, she learned something about disciplining her mind. When her hour was finished, Carla took her place and the prayer went on for Isabelle's healing and recovery.

As Josie made her way back to the room, it unexpectedly hit her—she had to talk to Stevie about Roger's death. *"What will I say? How can I help a six-year old child understand and accept the violent death of his father? Take it one step at a time, Girl,"* she told herself.

It was nearly five in the morning, and she didn't want to go back to bed, so she decided to stay awake, read her Bible and meditate. It was so quiet and peaceful. Yesterday seemed almost like it had been a bad dream—like it had happened lifetimes ago.

At about seven, she heard Stevie stirring in his bed. He sat up and looked around. Josie met his gaze and got up from her chair and went to his bed.

"Is it time to get up, Mama?" he asked.

"Yes, Stevie it's time to get up. Go to the bathroom, use the toilet and wash up. I have your clothes out for you."

Stevie did as he was told. When he was dressed, he sat on his bed. "Mama, what happened at the court house yesterday? They been sayin' that Reverend Isabelle was hurt bad an's in the hospital."

Josie was surprised at what Stevie said. "How did you know that, Stevie?"

"It wuz on TV, an they also said my daddy wuz the one that shot her."

Josie had to quickly collect her thoughts—she just looked into Stevie's eyes, searching for what his little mind was thinking. She pulled him to her in a tight hug. Finally

Josie's Gift

she pushed him away at arm's length and looked straight into his eyes.

"Yes, it was your daddy who shot Reverend Isabelle—and he shot some other people too." She thought better of trying to tell him that his daddy had tried to shoot her, but shot Isabelle instead.

She continued with tears welling up in her eyes. "Your daddy's dead, Stevie. Detective Sandoval had to shoot him before he could shoot any more people." Stevie's reaction surprised her.

Stevie had tears in his eyes; he clenched his fists, his eyes narrowed, his mouth turned down and quivered. His voice was angry, "I wished I'da killed 'im!"

"No Stevie," Josie said. "You don't mean that."

"Yes I mean it, Mama—an' I'm glad he's dead! Now he won't beat you anymore!"

Josie pulled her little boy with the big thoughts to her again. She said nothing and just held him in a loving embrace for several minutes. Finally, she pushed him from her to arm's length, and breathed a prayer of thanksgiving to God. "Let's go to breakfast!"

Stevie smiled, took her hand and started to lead her out the door. He turned to her, looked up, smiled, and said, "Don't worry, Mama, I'll take care of you. Nobody will ever beat you again!"

Josie's heart swelled with pride. "I'm glad I've got you to take care of me, Stevie!"

After breakfast and as soon as their assigned chores were finished, Darlene, Josie and Carla hurried back to the hospital. They were allowed into the critical care unit for only long enough to pray. Isabelle lay very still, breathing regularly with the help of a machine. She was hooked up to all kinds of tubes and monitors. In spite of it all, she looked very peaceful.

Carla spoke quietly to Josie, "They say people in this condition can hear what's going on even though they can't speak or even move."

Josie got close, and with tears in her eyes, took Isabelle's hand in hers and leaned down to Isabelle's ear. "Isabelle, I don't know quite what to say, except thank you for saving my life. Thank God you were there—I love you, Isabelle and we're...that is me and Carla and Darlene and everybody at the mission is praying for you."

Out of her purse Darlene took a small bottle of oil, opened it, and put a drop on her finger. With the oil, she made the sign of the cross on Isabelle's forehead. "May the Lord bless you Isabelle, and may He add length to your days and put smiles in your heart; and may He bring complete healing to your body."

Isabelle's finger moved, and she squeezed Josie's hand ever so slightly. "Thank you Isabelle," Josie said, "We'll be back later."

The three women headed for the hallway and in the direction of the elevator. When the elevator opened, Will Brent stepped off. He tipped his hat, "Hi Ladies." Turning to Josie, "Uh Missus Brown, could we talk for a few minutes?"

Josie looked at Darlene and Carla. "We'll see you downstairs," Carla said.

Brent took off his hat and held it in front of him. "I'm very sorry about your husband, Ma'am. Uh... could we maybe get a cup of coffee and talk?"

"Sure, Mister Brent!" Josie replied.

They walked to the elevator. When the door opened, Brent motioned for Josie to go first. When they reached the ground floor, he again motioned for Josie to exit first. When they got to the cafeteria, he motioned Josie to a seat. "What do you like in your coffee?"

"Just sugar, please."

Brent returned with the coffee. He sat quietly stirring the liquid for several minutes.

Josie was becoming uncomfortable. "Uh...what do we need to talk about?"

Brent looked at her and for a few seconds, his thoughts were not about business. *"She's a very attractive young woman,"* he thought to himself.

"Mister Brent!" Josie said.

"Oh, yes. Uh...the thing is, Missus Brown..." Showing his embarrassment, he interrupted himself. "...could we get on a first name basis? The mister and missus stuff seems kind of stiff and awkward."

"Sure, Will," she said.

"We're trying to clear up this whole thing about Roger and his past. The District Attorney wants an autopsy on Mister Brown, uh...Roger. There's the possibility of brain problems like maybe tumors, or drugs...or even the possibility of fetal alcohol syndrome."

"Fetal...what?" Josie questioned.

"Well, that happens when someone's mother uses alcohol during her pregnancy. Children, who are affected grow up and sometimes act very much like Roger when they're young adults. It's almost as if they don't have a conscience and they don't seem to care how other people feel. The medical examiner thinks she can see some tell-tale facial features. On the other hand, brain tumors can also be at fault. We have to explore all the possibilities before we can make a final report on Roger's actions. We'd like to have your approval to go ahead with the autopsy." He paused, "...actually we can go ahead without approval but we think it would be best if you cooperate."

"Sure," Josie answered, "Whatever you need!"

"One more thing," Brent said. "How well do you know Roger's family?"

Josie looked thoughtfully into her coffee cup. "Actually, when I stop and think about it, I didn't know them well at all. I only met them one time. I know that sounds crazy; married for seven years and only meeting them one time."

"Sounds like you two did a lot of running. Do you know if there was a lot of alcohol consumed in the home?" Will asked.

Josie thought for a few seconds. "Not really. But the one time I met them, they were both drinking wine but not drunk."

"The Medical Examiner would like to talk to them and get a family history, and a health history on Roger, if that's possible. Do you know where they live?"

"I know where they used to live, if that'll help," Josie answered. "They used to live in Churchill, clear over on the east end of the state. That's where I'm from too."

Will was busy writing notes. He looked up. "Okay, we'll try to track them down. Just out of curiosity, when was the last time you were back in Churchill and visited your family."

Josie was embarrassed at the question. "Not since I ran away with Roger, maybe seven years ago. My father probably disowned me, and I know my mom was very upset. I'm not at all sure if I'm even welcome anymore."

"Forgive me for getting into this—but, do you ever think about them?"

Josie was almost in tears. "Yes...I do think about them. Stevie, my son, has never met them. Someday, we'll go back and I want him to know them."

"Why don't you go back home now, you don't have Roger to worry about?"

"I'd uh...I'd rather not talk about that part of my life just yet," Josie said flatly. "I uh...I'm just not ready to go home."

"Okay," Will said, "I understand."

"Thank you," Josie responded coldly.

"Look, Josie I'm sorry I have to bring all this up. I really want to get you cleared of any potential charges as soon as possible. I'm going to need to question you a lot more over the next several days. Would you rather do that at the Mission or perhaps at my office? It would probably be best at my office because there'll be others there as well as recording equipment."

"Can I think on that?" Josie asked.

"Sure, I'll be in touch. Oh, and by the way, I need a complete history of yours and Roger's traveling from the day you were married. You could help expedite things if you'd write down a time line of where you were and when since leaving Churchill. There're investigators from other counties who are interested in talking to you and may be with me when I question you."

Josie was getting agitated. "And, what if I don't want to talk to them?"

"Look Josie," Will said pointedly, "I'm trying to make this as easy as possible. If you don't cooperate, they can file with Judge Jacobson to have you moved to another county, and put you under oath there, and hold you for their own investigations. Believe me...it would be best if we can get things cleared up from here where I can help you out."

Will moved his chair back and got up from the table. "Let me walk you back out to the waiting room near the entrance where Darlene and Carla are waiting, okay?"

Josie got up from the table as Will held her chair. She looked at him and smiled. *"He's trying to be kind and polite,"* she said to herself giving him the benefit of her doubts.

Before they parted at the waiting room, Josie asked one more question. "Can Darlene be with me when all these questions are asked?"

"Sure Josie, whatever you need. It's going to be an ordeal for you, and you'll need support. I promise you we'll get it all cleared up as soon as we can. The court will appoint an attorney for you who will also be there." He tipped his hat and left her with Darlene and Carla.

"Wow!" Carla exclaimed, looking in Will's direction. "What was that all about? You're not in trouble are you?"

Looking at the two women in front of her, Josie answered, "You two, and Isabelle are my dearest friends. At this moment only Isabelle knows about this."

"Knows what?" Carla asked.

"The truth is I was with Roger some of the times when he committed crimes, like armed robbery, and auto theft. They have to question me about those incidents and determine whether I was just there or if I was an actual accomplice. When he shot the store clerk in Lancaster, I was driving the car—the getaway car, you might say. I really didn't know what was going on, but I was there, and I was driving. So…"

"So…you're implicated, and might be considered an accessory, right?" Darlene asked.

"Yeah…yeah, I guess that's right," Josie answered.

"Josie," Carla said, "I've known Will Brent for a long time. He's a straight up guy, and he's honest, but he also has great respect for the law. And, he expects to uphold the law. If he says he'll help you—you can depend on it. He'll get to the truth. When he questions you, don't hold back a thing—be totally honest because if he finds out that you're lying, well—even if he likes you, he'll see that you get what you deserve."

Josie cringed at the thought, and wondered if Carla actually thought she would lie to Will. "Darlene, I asked him if you could be there when he questions me. He said you could be there. He also said I can have a court appointed attorney present. Will you come with me?"

"Sure, Josie! I'll be there."

CHAPTER EIGHT

"Moisés!" Ruth's voice expressed a sense of urgency. "What is it Mama," Moisés answered.

Ruth looked at her husband. "My mind has been on Josie all day. And now, look at the TV news. It's Josie!" Ruth said almost screaming.

Moisés turned his attention to the TV. "Oh my God, Mama; Roger has killed somebody!"

"She has been on my mind all day and now this!" Ruth burst into tears.

"So—we both think about her a lot." He took his wife's hand. "For seven years...not a day goes by that I do not think about her. I miss her more than I can tell you."

"This is different, Moisés!"

"And how is it different Mamma?"

"I had a dream last night. I saw her, and she was calling me. She was crying, and I ran to her with my arms open to receive her—and then...then, she was not there. She just disappeared. Now look what has happened."

"Ah, my Love—you and your dreams! How often have you had dreams, and then nothing comes of it?"

"Doesn't God sometimes speak to us through dreams? Doesn't He sometimes tell us something important?" Ruth asked.

Moisés thought for a few minutes. Then he looked into her eyes, "You are right my Love, God speaks to his people, and sometimes in the form of dreams. Many times our people have been led by the dreams of the great prophets. So, what do you think this dream of yours means?"

"I think she needs us Papa. Now she is in some great trouble, and she needs us!"

"She ran from us, and we did not know where to find her, Mama." Moisés' voice was rising and his eyes flashed anger, "We did not know where she was, because that...that... **animal** took her away from us. If he was here now I would **kill** him. With my bare hands, I would kill him. He does not deserve to live. I wish it had been me who killed him."

"And would you forgive your daughter if she was here right now?"

Moisés looked at his wife—he shook his head as if giving up the fight—as if he was drained of his fatherhood, of his energy. With tears forming in his eyes, he spoke very softly; "Yes, Mama...yes of course I would forgive."

"We must pray for her Papa!"

"We always pray for her my Love!"

"But, this is different—this is very urgent. There is danger, and there is trouble. I know it!" Ruth said. "When she was a little girl, whenever she was in trouble or danger of some kind, she would come running to me, and I would open my arms to receive her. She would fall into my arms and cry. Yes...I remember that!"

"Then, my Love, we shall pray." Moisés reached for his *talit* (prayer shawl). He kissed it and chanted the following blessing:

Baruch ata Adonai Elohenu Malech
HaOlam asher kidshanu
Bemetzvatov vesivenu lehitatef bat talit.

*(Blessed are you LORD our God King of
the Universe who has sanctified us
With your commandments and commanded
us to wrap ourselves in prayer)*

He carefully placed it over his head and shoulders. He then stretched out his arms and raised them to heaven. Ruth pulled her shawl up over head. In a deep and powerful voice he chanted his prayer as he would sing a song. This form of prayer was family custom for many generations.

"Blessed be the Name of ADONAI our GOD,
Blessed be His holy and righteous Name,
Blessed is He who made the heavens, and all that is in the earth,
Blessed is He who delivered us from our enemies and gave us a land for our dwelling,
Blessed be His Name.
GOD of our Fathers, remember us in our time of need,
Remember our only daughter,
As you gave to Sarah a son in her old age,
As you delivered Ruth in the time of her widowhood,
As you brought solace to Hannah and fruit to her womb,
So deliver our daughter and preserve her life,
Bring her to us once more. AMEN"

Then Ruth prayed. "LORD of heaven and earth, in the Name of JESHUA Mashiach, may our only daughter find peace, and promise of deliverance from her enemies. In the Name of the Father, the Son, and the Holy Spirit. AMEN"

After they prayed, they sat down and resumed their conversation. "It was a very sad day when she left, Mama. I was very angry, and now I regret that anger. I wish I could see her, and tell her how much I love her."

"Yes Papa, I was heartbroken. It seemed all of our hopes and dreams were dashed to pieces, like a piece of china dropped on the floor. But..." and Ruth's mood brightened, "...she is coming back to us; I know it—I can feel it."

The memory of that day, seven long and agonizing years ago, came flooding into Ruth's mind like a rushing river that couldn't be stopped.

"You're what?" She remembered screaming.

"Please don't be mad at me and don't tell Papa." Josie responded.

One word expressed the shock and surprise as Ruth responded to her daughter. *"Pregnant? How could you? You're only sixteen."*

Josie's tears begged for her mom's understanding, but all the words came out wrong. *"But Mama, it was just a mistake—an accident, I didn't mean to get pregnant."*

"Getting pregnant is never a mistake or an accident Josie," Ruth said angrily. *"It's a choice. When you choose to have sex, you choose the possibility of getting pregnant. And you expect me not to be mad? How could you? We had dreams and hopes for you—we had plans for college. Yes, I'm very angry!"*

Josie was sobbing. Trying to placate her mom, she continued, *"Mama, listen to me—it'll be ok! Roger says he loves me, and he wants me to move in with him—we can make it—I know we can—just give it a chance!"*

Ruth's anger was beginning to turn to sorrow, and now into pity. Her mind was racing, but she tried to sound loving and civil. She had tears as she looked directly into Josie's eyes.

"What do you mean, make it? Roger doesn't even work— he's twenty-two and has never held down a full time job! He refuses to go back to school! He's a loser Josie! When he had sex with you, he committed a crime because you are underage!"

"Mama, *you don't know him like I do! You're being judgmental—I believe in him—he has big plans. Inside, he's a wonderful person, and he needs me to help him get his life together. He tells me I'm the only one who can make him change!"*

"No, Honey," Ruth said in a softer tone. *"He's an ugly frog who thinks he's a prince. He's a loser and I'm not being judgmental—I'm just being truthful. Getting pregnant was the first bad decision—moving in with Roger will be the second bad decision. There aren't enough kisses in the whole world to turn this frog into a handsome prince. No!! You and I will talk to Papa, and Papa will talk to Roger—and to the police. We can handle your pregnancy, but not with Roger as a part of your life. A very wise man once said, 'A longing fulfilled is sweet to the soul, but fools detest turning from evil. (Proverbs 13:19)'."*

Moisés and Ruth refused to give their consent to marriage, so one day Josie and Roger ran away together in a stolen car. She lied about her age and they married in the State of Oklahoma.

Ruth's reverie was interrupted by the door bell. She looked at Moisés, and then went to the door. After a few minutes, Moisés heard loud voices, and went to investigate. He was taken completely by surprise when he saw Roger's parents, John and Doris Brown talking to Ruth. Their voices were loud and threatening.

Moisés quickly placed himself between his wife and the Browns. He was an imposing figure, more than six feet tall, well muscled from years of working at the mill. His forehead was prominent and his eyes dark, and piercing. His hands were bigger than most men's, and abundantly calloused.

"Señor Brown, please—you are welcome in my home if you come in peace." Moisés gestured toward the living room. At the same time his eyes never left Brown, who was very agitated and angry.

Brown brought his arm up in a threatening gesture. Moisés grabbed Brown's wrist in a vice-like grip while the arm was still mid-air. Brown was cursing, and called Moisés and Ruth numerous unflattering names. Then he hurled his attack at Josie, and cursed her as well.

"Moisés, Roger is dead and it's Josie's fault—she put him up to it." Brown wrested his arm from Moisés' grip and swung his fist at Moisés' face. Moisés swung his own fist, which collided in mid-air with Brown's forearm. Brown grabbed his injured hand, and screamed in pain. Both Ruth and Doris were screaming at the top of their lungs at each other.

A neighbor heard the commotion and came running to see what was happening. His wife had already called police who were on their way. John Brown continued his cursing and loud accusations and by this time, Doris Brown was joining in with curses and accusations of her own. "Those goddamned Mexican Jews," she screamed.

"Señor Brown, I am very sorry—I did not know your son was dead until I saw it on TV just this evening. Please forgive me for my impatience."

In spite of Moisés' condolence, Brown continued to curse and yell.

The police cruiser arrived within seconds, and both officers exited the car. John Brown started to run away toward his own car, but didn't make it before one of the officers tackled him. Pinning him on the ground, the officer attempted to put handcuffs on Brown's wrists, but he wrestled free, and got to his feet swinging at the officer. Doris Brown also began to assault the officer from behind. The second officer ran to assist his partner with his tear gas spray in his hand. Both Browns were sprayed—they both doubled over and began to cough—their eyes stung, and watered so bad they couldn't see. With both John and Doris subdued, and in handcuffs, they were dragged to the police car and pushed inside.

As one of the officers walked to the house to talk to Moisés and Ruth, his partner was calling in on the radio to report their situation. John Brown got his feet up against the steel barrier separating the front seat and the rear seat of the police car. He kicked violently, trying to push the barrier loose from its mountings. Unsuccessful, he turned in his seat, and began kicking the side window. The officer called for backup. Within minutes a second police car pulled up, and the officers were running to the scene. By this time, Brown had broken out the side window and cut both his legs. He was bleeding profusely.

Emergency Medical Services was alerted and on site in minutes. In the meantime, the four officers managed to get Brown out of the police car and face down on the grass, but not without a violent struggle in which one of the officers sustained a cut on the side of his face.

The EMS technicians treated Brown's legs as best they could, with wrappings to keep them clean and to stop the bleeding. The cuts were not deep, but would require stitches. Not wanting to transport Brown in the ambulance because of his agitated state of mind, the officers shackled his ankles, and made him lay on the grass, hoping he would calm down. They kept in constant contact with the Emergency Room doctor. One of the officers resumed his attempt to talk to Moisés and Ruth.

The officer extended his hand toward Moisés, and introduced himself as Officer Brand. "And, I am Moisés Blandón, and this is my wife Ruth." The two men shook hands, and the officer tipped his hat to Ruth.

"Please come inside Officer," Moisés invited.

"Thank you Mister Blandón."

Moisés motioned to a chair; Brand sat down and took out his note pad. Moisés and Ruth sat opposite him on the sofa.

"Mister Blandón, in your own words; describe for me what happened here tonight."

Moisés described the scene and told of their daughter and the Brown's son who was now dead. "That is all we know, Officer," Moisés replied. "Why they attacked us? You must ask them! I'm sure it had something to do with their son, Roger Brown, whom they said was dead, and they said it was our daughter, Josie's fault."

"Did Mister Brown or you begin the fight?"

"At first everything was just verbal, but then Mister Brown got physical, and I responded to protect myself and my wife." Moisés demonstrated his defensive actions.

"Thank you Mister Blandón. We may ask you for a sworn statement later on, after we decide what charges to file. I'll get back to you as soon as I know something. We've got to get Mister Brown to the hospital and Missus Brown to the police station."

"Officer, it appears that Josie is in Rock City at this time. She and Roger ran away and got married seven years ago, and we haven't seen or heard from them since. As soon as you find out more about Roger's death, will you please call us?"

"I will do that." Officer Brand tipped his hat to Ruth, "Good night; we'll be in touch."

Moisés and Ruth walked back to their favorite chairs and for a long time, just stared at each other, neither giving words to their thoughts. Adrenaline was still pumping through Moisés' body, and it took some time for him to calm down. Finally, Moisés broke the silence. "You are right, My Love. She is in trouble and needs us—we know she is in Rock City, but we do not know where. We must have patience and trust ADONAI for her care."

For three days Moisés and Ruth waited. Each time the phone rang, one of them lifted the receiver with anticipation, but it was always one of their sons, or one of their friends who called just to be sure they were all right. Finally, on the afternoon of the third day, Officer Brand's voice was on the other end of the line. "Mister Blandón, I'd like to visit with you—may I go to your house right now?"

"Certainly, Officer—we've been waiting for your call."

"They have some news, Mama," Moisés said to his wife.

"Good news or bad news, Moisés?"

"Officer Brand is coming right over, and we will hear it from him!"

Within thirty minutes, Officer Brand was at the door and Moisés opened it before he could push the doorbell button. "Come in, Officer!" Moisés said. "You are welcome to our home."

"Well, we have some news," Brand said, as he took his note pad out of his shirt pocket. "It seems that Roger shot and killed a store clerk in Lancaster, and the police caught up with him and Josie in Rock City. Did you know they have a child?"

"Josie was pregnant when she left us so we assumed she did have a child," Ruth replied.

Moisés and Ruth looked at each other with happy anticipation, and a silent message of love passed between them. The thought of a grandchild from Josie was good news.

"Information we have from our contact in Rock City, is that Roger was convicted of first degree murder, and was to appear at a sentencing hearing. He was in a holding cell in the basement of the court house when he overpowered a sheriff's deputy, got his gun, and ran upstairs to the courtroom, where he went berserk and started shooting. Several people were shot including the judge who is critical but expected to live. Roger was shot and killed by a Detective Sandoval who was on the scene."

"And Josie?" Ruth anxiously asked.

"No word on her, except that she was not injured in the pandemonium."

"Do they know where she is?" Moisés asked.

"No, but our contact did give me a couple of names and phone numbers that you can call. One is Detective Sandoval, who is the main investigator on the case, and the other is a guy named Will Brent, who works with the district attorney's office as an investigator. Here are their numbers." Brand handed a card to Moisés.

Moisés eyes were misty and he sniffled, "Thank you Officer."

"One more thing," Brand said. "We need to know if you plan to press charges against the Browns."

Moisés looked at Ruth. He looked at the floor for a few seconds. "No Officer, we will not press charges. They will have to face charges for fighting with the police. They are suffering enough over the loss of their son. No matter how bad a person Roger was, they still loved him."

"That's thoughtful of you Mister Blandón, but we still consider them to be dangerous. I suggest you be sure to secure your home and be careful when you answer the door. They will be facing charges, but in all likelihood will be released on a bond pending a hearing and trial." Brand tipped his hat, "Good afternoon, Folks. If you need anything more, here's my card."

Moisés nodded and showed Brand to the door. The two men shook hands, and Officer Brand walked to his car.

CHAPTER NINE

Josie was about to finish her chores, when Carla called her to the phone. "Hi Josie, this is Will Brent. Can you come to my office for some preliminary questioning this afternoon?" Will's voice was friendly and relaxed.

"What time?"

"I've set aside a block of time from two o'clock on. Do you need someone to pick you up?"

"Yeah that'd probably be best—Carla will go with me."

"Good, that'll be fine. Judge Jim Bryant, who's filling in for Judge Jacobson, has appointed a public defender to represent you as your attorney. Her name is Sheila Langdon, and she'll be there to pick you up at exactly two o'clock. I'll see you when you get here!"

Josie was disappointed. "Will! I thought you would pick us up!"

"My boss...the DA, felt like it would be best if Sheila picked you up. That way nobody could say there was any conflict of interest."

"Conflict of interest?"

"Umm...uh yeah. I'll explain it when this is all over. Just don't worry, Josie, It's going to be okay!"

Sheila picked up Josie and Darlene at exactly two o'clock. She got out of the car and introduced herself, then drove them to Will's office. Conversation was light and relaxed. "You feeling okay about this investigation, Josie?" She asked.

"I'm a little nervous, Sheila."

"That's pretty normal. Just remember, no one's trying to convict you of anything—we just want the truth about Roger's criminal history, and how you might have been involved. If we're going to clear you of any complicity in any of it, we must have the truth. Mister Brent will be asking some pretty pointed questions—but, just relax, take your time, take a deep breath and tell the truth. If there's anything out of order in the questioning or if there's anything that might lead you to incriminate yourself, I'll be stepping in."

"Will Detective Sandoval be there?"

"It's normal procedure to have the lead investigator from the Police Department in on the questioning as part of the overall investigation, but I don't expect it to be Detective Sandoval."

"Why?" Josie asked, her voice expressing disappointment.

"Detective Sandoval has grown quite fond of you and your son, Josie. It would probably be considered a conflict of interest for him to be in on this. He would be uh...biased."

When they arrived at the office, they were ushered into a room with a large oval table and padded chairs. Will followed them into the room—his appearance and his actions indicated that today he was all business. He put on an air of aloofness as he shook hands with everybody present, and directed them to specific seats around the table. Josie and her attorney were on one side facing Will. Before he began the questioning, he gestured to the person sitting beside him and introduced him as Sergeant Jim Bunning, the Police Department representative. He then introduced the person who was operating the electronic recording equipment. He then introduced police officers from counties where they believed Roger may have committed crimes. He looked

Josie's Gift

directly at Josie, and then at Sheila, and said that normal procedure would be followed, and the session would be videotaped. He asked Sheila if there were any objections. Sheila indicated that there were none.

Josie kept looking at Will for some indication that he noticed her as a friend and not just someone to question. But Will was all business, and didn't show it if he noticed her searching look.

He began. "Missus Brown for the record please, state your full name, and your current place of residence."

Josie paused. In her mind she was saying, *"Will Brent, I don't think I like you anymore!"*

"Missus Brown?"

"I'm sorry **Mister** Brent. My name is Josefa Ruth Blandón Brown. I live temporarily at the Lighted Way Ministries, two-thirty-three West Third Street, in Rock City."

"What is your age?"

"I am twenty-two years old."

"And, you have a son?"

"Yes, his name is Steven."

"Where did you live when you met Roger Brown?"

"At that time I was living with my parents in Churchill."

"And how old were you at that time...uh when you first met Roger Brown?"

"I was fifteen years old when I met Roger."

"And what attracted you to..."

Before he finished the question, Sheila interrupted, "Mister Brent, I don't think that question is relevant to the investigation—I object."

"I apologize, Missus Brown. We'll disregard that question." Will took a breath, and paused looking over his notes. "Uh...how old were you when you and Roger Brown got married?"

"I was uh...sixteen, and I was pregnant. Roger was twenty-three."

"So...he was seven years older than you, is that correct?"

"Yes, that is correct. I thought I was in love with him."

"What kind of person was he...uh...back then?"

Josie began to weep almost silently—her tears dropped on the table. She looked up at Will as if to say, "This hurts!"

Will wanted in the worst possible way to hold her hand, and tell her it was going to be okay, but he had to continue—in spite of Josie's pain, he had to continue. He breathed a silent prayer for Josie. "Would you like a glass of water or juice, Jo...uh Missus Brown?"

"Thank you, water will be fine."

Will, nodded to the recording person who shut off the equipment. He then got up, and went to the water fountain, and brought water for everyone.

Darlene had her arm around Josie, and Sheila was holding her hand.

Will motioned for all to return to their seats so the questioning could continue. "Missus Brown, I just want you to know that everything we're asking is important to this case, and Miss Langdon will see that we don't get off track. Just to make things a little more relaxed, I'm going to ask Sergeant Bunning to continue with the questioning.

Sergeant Bunning looked at Josie, "Missus Brown, what kind of person was Roger Brown at the time you got pregnant?"

"Well...umm...he was handsome, he was attentive, and he told me over and over how much he loved me and how much he needed me."

Bunning smiled, "Kind of swept you off your feet, as the saying goes, huh?"

"I guess so, I thought he was the greatest boy, uh...man in the world. It really made me feel good that he was so dependent on me!"

"At that time, did you know about his being in trouble with the Law? Did you know he had a record of drug use and sales?"

Josie hung her head in embarrassment. "Yes, I knew about those things. He kept telling me that he would change, and I believed him. He told me that I was the only one who could help him change."

Bunning showed her an envelope. "We found this envelope in the car Roger was driving when he was arrested. Have you ever seen this envelope or one like it?"

Josie looked at it and at the picture inside. "No...nothing, like that."

"Do you know what that picture means?"

"No...what does it mean?"

"Apparently, Roger was a 'courier' for one of the Mexican drug gangs. We believe he was connected to a very powerful cartel called The Federation. The picture indicates he was marked—they intended to send an assassin and have him murdered. They almost succeeded the night he was arrested."

"Why would they want him dead?" Josie asked.

Bunning thought for a few seconds before answering. "Because...he made one too many mistakes."

Josie looked down at the floor. "I never suspected," she said in a whispered tone.

"Did he attempt to keep you isolated from your friends, and did he ask you at any time, to do anything that was against the law? Like use drugs—or handle large sums of money—or package drugs for sale!"

"He didn't want me messing around with any of my friends, but he said that was for my own good because they would try to come between us. He never asked me to do anything illegal, like buy drugs for him, or use drugs with him. In fact one time when I wanted to smoke pot with him, he got real angry, and threatened to beat me. I cried a lot, and he told me it was only because he loved me so much that he would beat me to keep me from smoking pot. It was for my own good. I never saw any of the money. If he had all that money, why'd he need to hold up convenience stores?"

"Maybe he was spending it on his own habits. Or maybe he just enjoyed the thrill of committing crimes and getting away. How about your parents, did he ever at any time try to convince you that he loved you more than they did, and did he ever want you to do things they didn't want you to do?"

Josie thought for several seconds. "Yeah, I suppose he did. I had to sneak out, because they didn't like him, and forbade me to see him. He told me we had to have sex, because he wanted me to have his baby. I was excited about that—having his baby that is—not necessarily about sex. I knew that was a sin, but by that time, I didn't seem to care anymore—you know, about sin, and morality, and all that."

"Mister Brent, I have several questions I would like to ask."

"Proceed with your questions, Miss Langdon."

"Missus Brown, it seems to me, that Roger was positioning himself in your life so as to have a lot of control over you—did it seem that way to you?"

"No, not at the time, it didn't. I was convinced that it was all for my own good, and that he really loved me."

"And now?" Sheila asked.

"I don't know what to think now. It's all such a blur, like it was a bad dream or something!"

Sheila continued her questions. "Were you close to your mother?"

"Yes, we were close most of the time. Like every other teenager I thought she was pretty overbearing and strict. She was very religious."

"What was her reaction when you told her you were pregnant?"

"She was very angry, and told me how disappointed she was. I told her Roger wanted to marry me, and we wanted to live together. Then she started in on Roger and told me what a loser he was. She said he was just an ugly frog, and there weren't enough kisses in the whole world to turn him into a handsome prince. She said that we...that is, me, and her, and Papa could handle me being pregnant, but not with Roger in the picture, and under no circumstances would they give me permission to marry him."

"Then what did you do?"

"I stashed some clothes and personal stuff in a secret place, and met Roger after school, and we took off."

"No more questions at this time," Sheila said.

Bunning began to ask the questions again. "Missus Brown, did you know that the car Roger was driving when he picked you up was stolen?"

Josie looked surprised. "No, I didn't know that!"

"Didn't it occur to you to ask where the car had come from?"

"I just figured it was from his parents. They always had two or three cars around. No! It didn't occur to me that I should ask."

"Was Roger working at the time? Was he going to college, or getting any kind of education?"

"I don't know!"

"And you never asked?"

"Look, I was a 15-year old kid when we met—Roger always had money—we had fun! Why would I ask?"

"When you and Roger were on the run, where did you stay? In shelters, motels? Where?"

"Mostly cheap motels—sometimes just camped out in the car!"

"When was the first time you began to suspect Roger might be committing a crime?"

"I don't know...umm...probably a couple of months before the birth of my son. I noticed he would leave the motel, and come in drunk, or he would come back with a bottle, and drink all night. Sometimes he would show up with a car. I began to wonder!"

"Did you think about going to the police or anything like that?"

She laughed, "I was too busy being sick and thinking about my baby to be bothered with anything else. I just thought if Roger was getting us food and all—that was what was important. I was so uncomfortable and sick that I didn't care."

Sheila interjected, "Where was your son born?"

"He was born in Stephenville."

"Is that why you named him Steven?"

"Yes, except that I spelled it different. Actually I wanted to name him Stefan, which would have been more Jewish. I knew Papa would have approved, but Roger insisted it be Steven."

"So, you're Jewish?"

"Ethnically yes, by religion no! I guess I'm Christian—Methodist by baptism. But my family observes a lot of old Jewish traditions, and they tell me my ancestors were Jews from Spain."

Will looked at her and nodded. "That's very interesting, Jo...uh Missus Brown. I need to ask you about Roger's beatings. During the last episode, he beat you severely, enough that you miscarried and were in the hospital for several weeks, is that correct?"

"Yes!"

"When did he first begin to get violent toward you?"

"It seemed that Roger was always mad at someone or something. Before Stevie was born, he yelled at me a lot, but never got physical. He always said it was for my own good—that I had a lot to learn."

"When was the first time he got physical and hit you?"

"It was right after Stevie was born. I stayed in the hospital for two days, and they released me. Roger picked me and Stevie up at the hospital. I noticed he had a different car. When we got to the motel, I asked him where he got the car. He slapped me real hard, and it knocked me down onto the bed. I almost dropped the baby. He told me never to ask about things like that again. I figured he stole the car, and it bothered me some."

"Did the violence continue and did it get worse?"

"It got a lot worse. He was real jealous of the time I had to give to the baby, and he resented having to spend money on formula, and diapers, and baby clothes. Everything that went wrong, he blamed on me or the baby. He started drinking more too, and the more he drank, the more violent he got. It got to where I was afraid for my life. I had to do everything he told me to do, and didn't dare question anything."

"Did you ever wonder where he was getting money?"

"I did—but I couldn't question it. One time when I did, he beat me pretty bad—both my eyes were black and he made me stay inside for a week. Sometimes he said he had to meet somebody to get paid for something or other, and he would go out and be gone for several hours."

"Mister Brent, I have a few more questions if I may," Sheila said.

"Go ahead Miss Langdon."

"Missus Brown, I think it would seem to everyone in this room that you should have left Roger a long time ago. Why didn't you?"

"I couldn't!"

"What do you mean, you couldn't?"

"Well, for one thing, Roger told me if I ever left him, he would find me, and kill both me and Stevie. For another thing, every time he beat me, he would sober up, and promise never to do it again. Then for several days he would be the sweetest person you'd ever want to meet. He begged me to stay with him and always told me that he couldn't make it without me. I was his every reason for living. I felt like I was special, and that I could change him. I thought I could see another person inside of him, someone who was kind, and gentle, and sweet—and who would make me totally happy."

"Missus Brown, did you know that Roger owned a gun and carried it with him most of the time?"

"Yes, I knew!"

"Did he ever leave it around the motel room when he went out?"

"No, he always took it with him."

"Before he shot the store clerk in Lancaster, were you aware of him ever shooting anyone else at any time?"

"No!"

"Did you ever accompany him at any time when he stole a car, or when he held up a store, or when he did anything else illegal?"

"No! He made me stay in the motel, or in the car."

"But you were present when he shot the clerk in Lancaster, is that correct?"

"No!! I was in the car out by the gas pumps. He told me to put Stevie in the back seat, and to sit in the driver's seat and wait. I couldn't see inside the store, and didn't know what was going on. I heard two shots, and saw Roger come running out to the car. He jumped into the car, and yelled at me to drive fast. I did!"

"Were you afraid at that time?"

"Yes, I was very afraid. I was crying, and he made me stop the car as soon as it was safe, then he drove. We got to Rock City where he ditched the car in the river. You know the rest!"

The room got quiet. Brent looked at Sheila, and then at Bunning. "Any more questions?"

"Not at this point Bunning answered."

Will then turned the questioning over to the officers from the other counties. They asked very specific questions and Josie responded as honestly as she could. She either wasn't aware of most of the incidents or was not present with Roger when he committed the alleged offenses.

"Just one more question," Sheila said. "Will this case be turned over to the grand jury?"

"That'll be up to the D.A.," Brent answered. "After he looks at all the evidence, and has a chance to talk to Sergeant Bunning and me, he'll make a decision."

Will nodded at the person who was recording the session. He was unhooking equipment and gathering it up to leave the room. After the recording person left the room, Sheila asked Josie and Darlene to sit out in the waiting area and get a cup of coffee. After they left, she turned to Will, "Can the three of us talk a while off the record?"

"Sure Sheila. That okay with you, Sergeant?"

"Fine with me!" Turning his attention to Sheila, "What's on yer mind?"

Sheila looked at both men. "I know both of you men, and I trust your judgment. What do you think is the likelihood of this going to a grand jury?"

Bunning was the first to speak. "Personally, I don't think there's a case here. I'd hate to be the one to have to come up with evidence of complicity. Everything at this point is circumstantial." He looked at Will.

"I agree, however, the D.A. may see things a lot differently than any of us. Everything hangs or falls on the circumstances at Lancaster, and whether he thinks Josie was complicit. We will all be studying the video tape from the convenience store. It may also depend on the lab results from the medical examiner. We won't have any of that for another couple of weeks. Sheila, keep Josie as hopeful as possible, but don't hold out the possibility that she won't be charged. At this point anything is possible."

"What'll you recommend to your boss Will?"

"When I'm asked, I plan to recommend no charges be filed. I don't think she was a consenting accomplice."

Sheila picked up Josie and Darlene in the waiting room. "How about we find a quiet place, and have some dinner—on me?"

Darlene took Josie's hand, "Yes!! I'm ready."

Josie looked worried. "Do you think they believed me, Sheila?"

"Did you tell the truth, Josie?"

"Yes!"

"Then I think they believed you!"

After dinner, Sheila suggested they go to the hospital and visit Isabelle. Darlene and Josie agreed—they were both anxious to see how she was doing.

"Do you know Isabelle, Sheila?" Josie asked.

"Oh yes!" she laughed. "Everybody in Rock City knows Isabelle. I've defended numerous transients at the mission who were in trouble and facing charges of various sorts. I've also helped the mission at times with their own legal matters."

"What kind of legal matters did the mission have?" Josie asked.

Sheila looked at Darlene. "Well—and Darlene will remember this one. The National Civil Liberties Consortium filed a suit one time because Isabelle required people who came to the mission to attend religious services before they were fed, and especially if they were staying overnight."

"Why would they do that?"

"I remember that one for sure!" Darlene interjected. "The NCLC claimed that the mission was getting some funding from the city, and that since it was government money, it could not be used for any religious purposes."

Sheila continued. "Since the mission could not afford to defend against the suit I volunteered to do it *gratis*."

"What does that mean?" Josie asked.

"That means I did it for free."

"How'd it turn out?"

"Well, it was interesting. I met with the City Attorney, and we worked out a deal. The City would cease to provide funding that was undesignated, that is, money that just went into the general fund. Instead, the City would provide a specified amount of money per person for designated services, like meals, lodging, and education. All we had to do was to provide the city with the name of each person at the mission each day, and periodically, the City would write us a check for the value of the services. All that the City required of the mission was for us to provide meals for those people, provide a bed for them, and provide educational opportunities. The judge—by the way it was Judge Jacobson—approved the settlement. In the ruling, he said the mission provided a valuable service to the city, which the city could not provide, that the services were necessary for the public good, and that beyond food, lodging and education, we could do anything we wanted to do. Case dismissed!! The judge adamantly declared that he was not going to allow the mission to be shut down for the sake of somebody's political correctness agenda!"

When the three women got to the hospital, Isabelle was awake, and they had her bed rolled up so she was in a semi-sitting position. She smiled when they walked in the room.

"Sheila, I'm so glad to see you," she said in a barely audible voice. "It's been a long time!"

Sheila leaned over the bed, gently gave Isabelle a hug and kissed her cheek. "You're lookin' good, Woman!" She declared. Looking at a walker with a safety belt, she continued. "They've had you up and walkin' a little, haven't they."

Josie's Gift

Isabelle nodded and then turned her attention to Darlene and Josie. Both women gave her a gentle hug and kissed her on the cheek. Josie lingered a little longer.

"We've been praying for you Isabelle. This's all new to me, but I'm learning to pray and read my Bible. You and Stevie have given me the reasons I need to pray."

"Sandy was here a while ago and had some questions for his investigation. He told me what had been going on." Looking at Josie, "So, you've been under the microscope! Did it go okay with the interrogation?"

"It went just fine Isabelle."

Looking at Sheila, she quipped, "Well, you've got the best attorney in town on your side."

"So I'm learning." Josie paused. "Isabelle—how is it that here I am—a nobody, and I'm in as much trouble as anybody could be in, and I'm in the middle of the most wonderful people in the world!" She looked around and made eye contact with Darlene and Sheila and back to Isabelle, "…and I have to ask myself; **Why me?**"

Darlene looked at Isabelle, then turned to Josie and answered the question. "It's simply because God loves you, and He has a wonderful plan for your life. And, in His infinite wisdom and grace He brought the right people into your life—people who will nurture you, and teach you, and love you, and protect you, and take care of your needs when you are destitute. All He asks in return is that you turn your life over to Him, spend your days worshipping Him, and serve Him by loving others."

Isabelle reached her one good hand out to Josie; "Honey, God blesses us with people like you every day, and gives us the opportunity to play some part in His plan for their lives. That's what Lighted Way Ministries is all about—that's God's plan for us."

"Have they said how long you'll be here?" Darlene asked.

"Tomorrow I start the heavy duty physical therapy stuff. I have to learn to use this arm all over again." Isabelle smiled and giggled, "I'll be outta this place before you know it. Now, you all gather round this bed and let's have us a prayer meetin'—then ya'll go on 'bout your business."

CHAPTER TEN

The next morning at the mission, Carla answered the phone. "Hi, Carla, this is Sandy. Is Josie around there, and may I speak to her, please?"

"Hold on, Sandy, I'll get her for you."

Josie picked up the phone. "Hi, Sandy! What's up?"

"The medical examiner needs you to go down to the morgue."

Josie gasped, "Oh my God—I don't know if I can do that, Sandy!"

"I'm sorry, Josie, but this is something that has to be done! I'll pick you up in thirty minutes."

When Josie got off the phone, she was white as a sheet... at least as much as her olive skin allowed. She slowly turned to Carla.

"What's the matter, Josie? You look like you've seen a ghost."

Josie just looked at her. "Worse than that, Carla! I have to go to the morgue—I'm sure it's something about Roger's body." She began to cry and fell into Carla's arms. "I don't know how much more of this I can take, Carla. I feel like I want to crawl into a hole and die. It hurts—it hurts really awful and, I don't want to deal with it!" She sobbed.

"Is Sandy going to pick you up?"

"Yes, in thirty minutes."

"Okay, get hold of yourself—go upstairs and wash your face. I'll get Darlene to go with you."

By the time Josie got back downstairs, Darlene was waiting. She took her by the arm, "You okay, Girl?"

Josie's eyes were bloodshot and red...it was obvious she had been crying. When Sandy arrived, he took one look at her, and took her hand. "Be strong Josie...you'll make it through this, just like you made it through all the rest of this tragedy!"

When they arrived at the morgue, Sandy led the way to the medical examiner's office. The place looked like it was made of stainless steel and tile. Everything was cold including the temperature, and it smelled like chemicals. Josie shivered.

Sandy introduced Doctor Trumbel to Josie and Darlene. The doctor immediately directed them to sit in the available chairs. She addressed Josie in a kind and gentle manner. It was obvious she'd done this many times. "I know this is difficult for you, Missus Brown, but we have some formalities we must take care of. First of all, we need to know what arrangements you've made for the disposition of Mister Brown's remains."

Josie looked at Sandy. He nodded, encouraging her to tell Doctor Trumbel about her circumstances.

"Doctor, I'm embarrassed about this, but I have no money, no job, and no possible way to pay the expenses for my husband." In her own ears, her words sounded so cold and hollow, as if she was detached and talking from another world. It was surreal.

Doctor Trumbel was fully understanding of Josie's situation. "You needn't be embarrassed, Missus Brown—this happens frequently. What we do in such circumstances, is to turn everything over to Valley Funeral Home. The county has a contract with them and will take care of the expense.

During the autopsy procedure, we uh...had to remove some of the organs for tissue studies. They were replaced in the corpse, and the complete body will be cremated. Then the ashes will be given to you, and you can do whatever you like with them. I gave copies of the autopsy report to Detective Sandoval and to Will Brent at the DA's Office. Just for your information, we found no evidence of tumors in any of the key sites in the brain. However, I did find several lesions in the left prefrontal cortex. This coupled with some abnormalities in the amygdala, which is the brain's emotional center, could help to explain Mister Brown's periodic episodes of rage. You see, his prefrontal cortex processes emotional signals from the amygdala, and then controls his responses."

"Does that mean Roger couldn't help himself—that he couldn't control his anger and rage?" Josie asked.

"No, it doesn't mean that at all, Missus Brown. But it does mean that it may have been more difficult for him as an adult than for others without those markers. Mostly, it probably means he was born with more sensitive tendencies toward normal anger stimulating situations, and developmentally, he never found a need to control his reactions. In all likelihood his parents probably allowed him to get by with a lot of behavior that should have been brought under control, even as a small child. Developmentally, he was having 'temper tantrums' all his life. As he grew older and bigger, things became more violent."

Josie said nothing and just looked at Doctor Trumbel. She didn't understand what the doctor was telling her, but she didn't want to ask any more questions. Her throat was getting a big lump, and tears were welling up in her eyes. Everyone sat in silence. Darlene put her arm around her, to let her know she was there. Inside, Josie's feelings were churning, and her stomach felt like it was going to turn upside down. "*A couple of weeks ago,*" she thought. "*Roger was a living person—now they were all talking about him like he was just a...a thing—devoid of life and humanity."* She gulped and put her hands to her mouth; "Where's the restroom?" She choked.

Doctor Trumbel quickly reached for a stainless steel pan from the counter behind her, took hold of Josie, and led her out of the room. No sooner had the door closed, than Darlene and Sandy could hear her violent retching, coughing, and choking. Sandy nodded for Darlene to go help Doctor Trumbel. Sandy's feelings were churning over and over—tears welled up in his eyes as he heard Josie retching, over... and over, and over...until there was nothing but choking and gasping. He prayed out loud to God for mercy and healing for this little girl he had come to love—this child who had been cheated out of her most precious years—this fragile wisp of a woman who didn't deserve the hell and the suffering she was facing. He felt guilty for killing Roger but at the same time, was glad he was gone forever.

Soon everything grew quiet, and a few minutes later, Doctor Trumbel, Darlene and Josie walked back into the room. Sandy stood up, and with all his being he wanted to take Josie into his arms and hold her. He wanted to comfort her as a dad would do—but he was a cop and obligated to be professional.

"Missus Brown, if everything meets with your approval, you can sign the paperwork now, or if you prefer, you may come back another time," Doctor Trumbel suggested.

Josie was deep in thought. *"Seven years ago, we were happy and carefree. That first day when we ran away, we laughed and played—rolled in the grass and gazed at the moon. When he held me in his arms, I felt safe, like there was nothing in the world to worry about anymore—nothing would ever come between us. When we made love, we did it with complete abandon. We told each other our secrets, and then we laughed some more. We even laughed at our own silliness. Why had all the fun ended? Why did it all turn to*

Josie's Gift

yelling and eventually to beatings? Was I being punished by Roger for having a baby?"

"Missus Brown! Are you all right? Would you rather sign the papers at another time?"

Josie looked around. For a moment she had forgotten where she was and why she was there. "Oh! Uh, yes! I want to sign them now!" She was emphatic about doing it now.

Doctor Trumbel pushed the papers toward her and explained what they were and then showed her where to sign.

As soon as Josie signed the papers, she looked at Doctor Trumbel. "Would it be possible—that is, could I please see my husband before we leave?"

"Missus Brown, I wouldn't advise it. He looks very bad after the shooting, and our dissections. We normally don't show the body in situations like this."

"Please," she screamed. "I want to see him—I need to see him!"

Doctor Trumbel looked at Sandy. He nodded. "Okay, follow me," she instructed.

They entered a large room that smelled even stronger of chemicals. It was spotlessly clean and shiny. There were stainless steel sinks, tools, hoses, bright lights, scales and several examining tables scattered around the room. "Wait here!" Doctor Trumbel said. She turned and went to an enormous heavy door and opened it. White frosty air gushed from the cooler. She soon returned, pulling a table with a body covered with a large white sheet. There was a tag hanging from the big toe of the right foot. She brought the table to where Josie, Darlene and Sandy were waiting. "Are you sure you want to see this, Missus Brown?"

"Yes!" Josie covered her mouth and gasped as Doctor Trumbel slowly pulled the sheet back away from the head and chest. Josie's mind and emotions were churning—this couldn't be Roger—but it was Roger. She gasped a second time. The long brownish-blonde hair lay lifeless on the table under him, his lips were pale and slightly open; his eyes were looking straight up at the ceiling. Josie began screaming and beating her fists against his hollow, lifeless form. "Why did you want to kill me?" She was screaming. "Why did you want me to die? I did everything you wanted from me—why—why—why?" She turned to Sandy, almost fainted, and fell into his arms. "Why?" she whimpered. "Why did it have to end this way?"

Doctor Trumbel covered Roger's body, and slowly pushed the table back into the cooler. Sandy and Darlene, one on either side of Josie, gently walked her toward the door. Josie sobbed and choked, and then sobbed some more. "Why?" She kept mumbling.

Doctor Trumbel sympathetically watched them leave. She knew in her heart what Josie hoped for was some closure, but she could also sense that closure did not come. *"These are wounds that will not heal for a very long, long time, perhaps a lifetime,"* she thought to herself.

Back at the mission, Josie went straight to her room and shut the door. "Please Darlene, I need to be alone."

"I understand, Girl. I'll knock on your door when it's time for chapel and supper. Stevie's going to want to know what's been going on. Think about what you'll tell him." Darlene thought if she could get Josie to thinking about Stevie, she'd get her mind off herself, but she also needed space to grieve.

As ugly as things were with Roger, he was her husband, and they lived together for seven long years...she had to grieve. A big piece of her life had been violently yanked away from her forever—like pulling a rotten tooth—it left an infected hole, along with a horrible throbbing pain that would take time, and the healing grace of God, to bring things into order once more.

Carla and Darlene went to the hospital to visit with Isabelle. "Good news, Girls. I'm gittin' outta here."

"When?" They echoed in unison.

"Tomorrow—can you two come and pick me up?"

"We'll be here."

Isabelle got serious. "Sandy came by a little while ago on his way to the police station from the morgue."

"Did he tell you about Josie?" Darlene asked.

"Yes, he did. Darlene, I want to thank you for being there with her. You surely have the gifts of an encourager, and a supporter, and God is using you. How's she doing right now?"

"It's tough, and she's grieving, but she'll make it!" Carla answered.

Isabelle continued. "You know, Josie quit growing when she was fifteen years old. In many ways she's still emotionally just fifteen. Whatever her reasons for hooking up with Roger, she had a big hole in her heart and life that he filled—some needs that he met. The Lord is giving me the sense that there's something in her past before she was fifteen that she's dealing with silently and alone. Whatever that was, it changed the direction of her whole life."

"I agree, Isabelle," Carla responded. "I think sometime back there in her childhood, she may have been sexually abused, and she's buried it in some deep dark closet of her mind."

"I think you're probably right, Carla. We'll need to help her search for that missing piece of the puzzle in her life. She needs to find out who God intended for her to be, and then we must help her to grow and develop her life piece by piece into the image of Christ. Only by God's healing grace will it all come together. She'll have complete victory when she finds some meaning in her awful tragedies."

Carla opened her Bible to Ephesians 2:10. "Listen to this, Girls, 'We are God's handiwork, created in Christ Jesus to do good works, which God prepared in advance for us to do'. Let's claim that for Josie!"

"Gather 'round, Girls," Isabelle commanded. "Let's git this prayer meetin' goin'!!"

The three women began to sing enthusiastically,

Praise the Lord, Hallelujah;
Praise the Lord, Hallelujah;
Praise the Lord, Hallelujah;
Praise His Name, Praise His Name!

His Name is Jesus, Hallelujah;
His Name is Jesus, Hallelujah;
His Name is Jesus, Hallelujah;
Praise His Name, Praise His Name!

Glorify the Name of Jesus;
Glorify the Name of Jesus;
Glorify the Name of Jesus;
Praise His Name, Praise His Name!

As they were singing, one of the nurses walked by, stuck her head in the room, and waved. She went on down the hallway singing.

They all prayed earnestly—they prayed for each other, and they prayed for Josie. They thanked God for Isabelle's healing, and for the wonderful medical staff that had cared for her.

"We'll see you tomorrow, Isabelle," Carla said, as she and Darlene turned to leave.

Isabelle waived her good arm and out loud praised God, "Praise the Lord; let the Son shine in this room, and may He ever be with you both as you minister in His Name." She laughed a loud and hearty laugh so typical of the always effervescent Isabelle.

Darlene knocked on Josie's door. "Come on in!" Josie yelled from inside.

Stevie was quick to open the door. "Hi, Miss Darlene," Stevie said.

"Hi, Stevie, where's your mom?"

"She's gettin' cleaned up. I know we're goin' to chapel, an' I think she wants to wash her face and dress up some for Jesus! I think she's been cryin' about my dad."

Darlene smiled. "Can I sit down, Stevie?"

"Sure, sit anywhere you like!"

"I know she's been crying about your dad. Did you tell her you love her?"

"I tell 'er that, an' I tell 'er she don't need my dad no more, 'cause she's got me."

Darlene pulled Stevie to her and gave him a big hug. "You're exactly right, Stevie; she's got you, and right now that's what she needs more than anything else..."

Stevie piped in "...except for Jesus!!"

Darlene couldn't help but laugh. She tickled Stevie on the ribs, and he started laughing too.

Josie emerged from the bathroom and looked at the scene. "What are you two doing?"

They just kept on laughing and tickling, so she started laughing too. They all laughed until they had tears in their eyes.

"Oh my, my," Josie said. "That was fun! I needed that. By the way, what were we laughing about?"

Darlene and Stevie gave each other blank looks. They started laughing all over again while they headed downstairs to the chapel where the service was already in progress. Josie was surprised to see Carla at the podium preaching. After the short service, Josie asked Darlene about Carla.

"Is she a preacher like Isabelle?"

"Yes, she is," Darlene answered. "Hasn't she told you?"

"Told me what?"

Darlene smiled. "Carla's an ordained minister and is in charge of the women's division here at the mission!"

"A **minister**?" Josie was clearly surprised.

Darlene laughed. "Yes, a minister! At Isabelle's request, her denomination permits her to live here as part of the ministry staff."

"How **great** is our God!" Josie mumbled to herself.

Everybody was happy to see Isabelle back at the mission. Her smiling face and encouraging words had been missed. She took time to visit with everybody in person. She particularly wanted to visit with Josie. "Let's take a walk, Josie."

As they walked around the block outside the mission, Josie noticed the rundown buildings and old warehouses in the area. There were a few residential blocks, but even they were showing lack of care. "This's a pretty bad area isn't it? Do you feel safe walking around here like this?"

Isabelle looked at her. "Josie, **you** probably would not be safe if you were by yourself, but everybody in this area knows me. I've been in most of the homes here and have ministered to them in one way or another over the years. Many of them come to the mission for church on Sundays. As long as you are with me, you are safe."

"I guess you know what went on at the morgue a few days ago?"

"Yes, Josie I know. Sandy came by the hospital and told me about it. I know it hasn't brought any closure for you, but when the funeral home has the ashes ready for you, perhaps we can talk and make plans for a small service wherever it is you want to put the ashes. Maybe that will bring some closure for you."

They walked in silence for a while. Josie was taking in the stale odors from the surrounding buildings. Open garbage cans littered the street, and piles of paper were lying in bundles waiting to be picked up. Even worn out furniture was deposited against the curbs. They rounded a corner, and the mission was ahead. Twilight was beginning, and the colored lights from the roof of the mission building illuminated the sky, and seemed to cast a welcoming glow onto the street below. From a distance, it surely did look like a lighthouse guiding the ships to safe harbor.

"Have you decided how you want to dispose of Roger's ashes, Josie?"

Josie looked at Isabelle and stopped walking. "I think I have—yes, I think I have. You know the river that runs along the highway on the other side of town? There's a place along the highway that's high up on a bluff overlooking the water. That's where we stopped when we were running from Lancaster. It's where Roger ditched the car that brought us here, the same car that I was driving when he killed the convenience store clerk in Lancaster. That's where our lives and our tragedies in Rock City began. That's where I want to scatter the ashes in the water, so the river will carry them down and away from us all forever."

"That sounds good to me, Josie. We'll plan something. There is one thing you will need to do, or Roger will never go away in spite of his ashes floating down the river."

"What's that?"

"You must forgive him. As God has forgiven you, so you must forgive him, and release him from any bondage in your mind and your heart."

"Bondage?"

"Yes, bondage is a chain that can't be broken. It binds people together. Love can be a chain of bondage, especially if you love the wrong person, or even the right person for the wrong reasons, and I know you loved Roger, and you had your own reasons. Hate can also be a chain of bondage, and I know from your reactions at the morgue that you hated him—for your own reasons. Even an unwillingness to forgive can make a chain of bondage, because it keeps the two of you bound together in unforgiveness. When you forgive him, you set him free, and you set yourself free. And then God is free to pour out His healing grace into your life."

When they arrived back at the mission, they went straight to the chapel for a short service of praise. Besides the music, only Reverend Isabelle spoke a few words of encouragement.

After supper, Josie went looking for Carla.

CHAPTER ELEVEN

Next morning, Carla found Josie in the laundry room. "Hey, Josie, Detective Sandoval is here and needs to talk to you. Is it okay if he comes in here?"

"Yeah, Carla; show him into my fancy office!"

Within moments, Sandy was in the doorway. "Hi, Josie, I have some serious business to talk about."

Josie walked to him and put out her hand. When he took her hand, she pulled him into a gentle hug. He showed his embarrassment with a red face and a slight movement to step back away from her.

"Why Detective Sandoval, I do believe you are embarrassed," she teased.

"Well, it's just that I...well, I...I'm not used to that sort of thing—uh at least when I'm on duty."

"Don't be," Josie said. "You come highly recommended as a father figure, so expect it some more."

Josie laughed, but Sandy looked bewildered. Finally, he smiled. "Thank you, Josie, I take that as a great compliment—and by the way, you come highly recommended as a fine daughter figure." They both laughed.

"Now we need to be serious!" Sandy said. "A police officer named Dave Brand from Churchill called me."

Startled, Josie looked up from folding clothes, surprise written all over her face. "I think I remember him, but I didn't know him personally. So what'd he call about?" She began to feel butterflies in her stomach.

"Well, do you remember Will's and my telling you we needed to track down Roger's family?"

"Yeah, why?"

"Officer Brand told me that there had been an altercation at your mom and dad's house, between John and Doris Brown and your mom and dad. The Brown's were blaming you for Roger's death, and taking it out on your parents. A neighbor called the police, and that's when Officer Brand became a part of things. The Browns picked a fight with the police, and had to be tear- gassed by Brand's partner. Evidently there was a lot of violence on Brown's part, because even after he was restrained, he kicked out the window of Brand's police cruiser. To make a long story short, the Browns were taken into custody and hauled away to be charged with disorderly conduct, resisting arrest, and assaulting a police officer. Your dad must be a fine person because even though Brown tried to assault him, he refused to press charges. According to Brand, your dad's a big man and can take care of himself."

Josie was wide-eyed and anxious as Sandy related the story. "How did the Browns find out about Roger?" She asked, with worry hanging on every word.

"Josie, the shooting at the court house has been all over TV and the newspapers. Will found their contact information and called them. He tried to interview them about Roger's health history, but they were not cooperative. Of course, Will had to identify himself and let them know some of the details."

"So, what now?"

"Josie, according to Officer Brand, the Brown's made threats against you. They, of course, know that you are in Rock City where Roger was killed. Will refused to give them any information about you or your whereabouts, but they can easily find it in the newspapers. In Churchill, the Browns were indicted and given a hearing. They naturally pleaded not guilty. After that, they were turned loose on a bond pending trial. Brand told me they had jumped their bond, and he believes they're headed in this direction. He gave us the description and license number of the car he believes they're driving. I'm sure they're going to try to find you, and eventually they'll track you down at the mission. Of course, we'll try to find them first. We've already received a warrant from Churchill for their arrest."

"So, what can I do, Sandy?"

"I'm going to talk to Isabelle and let her know. We're also going to increase our presence in this neighborhood by having uniformed police patrols around here more often, especially during the night hours. You should not leave the mission campus to go anywhere by yourself. Make sure somebody is always with you. I'm going to suggest to Isabelle that Darlene go with you, and that Martin Green accompany the two of you anytime you need to leave the mission. Green's loyal to Isabelle because of his friendship with her dad in prison. He knows the street, and he knows what to look for."

Sandy put his hand under Josie's chin and forced her to look at his face. "Please, Josie, please...please follow my instructions and call me the instant anything looks amiss."

Josie took a deep breath. "I will, Sandy, I promise, I will."

As he was about to leave, Sandy reached into his pocket and pulled out an envelope. "By the way; Will told me to give you this. It was sent to his office with your name on it."

For several moments Josie just stared at the envelope. Very slowly she reached for it and looked at it. Tears formed in her eyes as she held it to her heart. "It's from my mom and dad," she choked. "Thanks, Sandy—thanks for being my daddy today." She pushed the envelope into the back pocket of her jeans and returned to the laundry.

For days, Josie carried the envelope in her back pocket without opening it. Every so often she would reach back and touch it, as if to make sure she wasn't dreaming and it was still there. She was heading for the chapel for her morning quiet time when she heard Carla's voice down the hallway.

"Josie, Sandy's on the phone and needs to talk to you."

Josie picked up the phone, "Hi, Sandy, what's up?"

"I've got good news and bad news," Sandy said. "Which do you want first?"

"I'll take the good!"

"Will Brent called a few minutes ago and it looks like the DA is not going to try to prosecute you as an accomplice in Lancaster. Will's been in contact with some other jurisdictions, and they're closing their investigations on Roger and his crime spree. You'll be getting an official letter from his office in a day or two that will release you from everything bearing on the prosecution of the killing in Lancaster, and the car thefts here."

Josie breathed a big sigh of relief. "That's wonderful, Sandy. Now, what's the bad news?"

"Doctor Trumbel called a little while ago, and said that John and Doris Brown had been to her office trying to claim Roger's remains. She told them they had no rights to the remains, and advised them they could not make any kind of claim. She refused to tell them that Roger was being cremated at Valley Funeral Home or where they could reach you. Sooo, they **are** in town, and we will be looking for them. Just remember, they are also looking for you. Remember what I told you and call me the instant anything comes up, you hear? These people may be dangerous, and I wouldn't put anything past them! Oh, and Josie, we may have to move you for awhile; think about it."

Josie's Gift

"I hear you Sandy and don't worry—I will call."

"Sandy, this is Will Brent. I just got word that John and Doris Brown were at the Valley Funeral Home, inquiring about the remains of Roger Brown. Because of privacy issues, they couldn't give out any information. Apparently the Browns are going to all the funeral homes in town and asking. Just thought I'd alert you. If I hear any more, I'll let you know."

"Thanks for the call, Will. I'll get right over to the funeral home and make sure they don't give out any information, and that they call me if the Browns show up again."

Sandy walked into the Valley Funeral Home and paused in the middle of the main hallway to look around. He didn't see anyone that matched the description of the Browns, or that looked suspicious. He noticed mourners in a small chapel off the main hall to his left where a body was lying in state. Another chapel to his right looked to be empty. He walked to a receptionist who had been eying him. He showed her his badge and asked for the owner or manager. The receptionist punched a button on the phone and spoke to someone in another room.

"A Detective Sandoval is here to see you, Sir."

"Thank you, Julie, show him in."

The office was neatly arranged. All around the room were samples of various things pertaining to funeral arrangements. It was a fairly large room, so it didn't look cluttered. As was his custom, Sandy glanced around and made some mental notes, extended his hand to his host, and introduced himself.

"And I am Joseph Solensky, owner of the funeral home. How may I be of help to you?"

"Mister Solensky, I understand that a Mister and Missus Brown made contact with you recently?"

Josie's Gift

"Yes, they were right here in my office just yesterday. They were asking about the remains of Roger Brown. Of course, I told them that even though he was their son I could not give them any information, and I could not say even if Mister Brown's remains were here."

"That was wise of you," Sandy said. "Since the information about a funeral or a memorial have not been arranged, the information should remain confidential, at the discretion of Missus Josie Brown, wife of the deceased."

"I shall see that it is, Detective."

"Thank you—and one more thing. We have a warrant from Churchill for the arrest of John and Doris Brown, so if they happen to come back, figure out some way to keep them here and call me. Here's my card. By the way, is there a back door to this building that's accessible to the public?"

"Yes, would you like for me to show it to you?"

"Yes, please."

The two men walked out of the office. Sandy was alert to everybody standing around.

"Julie, I'm going to show Detective Sandoval around, and I'll be back in a few minutes."

Sandy looked carefully at the layout of the building. When they got to the back door, he noted the hallways leading there, and opened the door. He walked outside and looked around. There was a parking lot surrounded on three sides by hedge and a few small trees, but no vehicles were parked there. Sandy turned to Solensky, "Mister Solensky, when is Roger Brown scheduled for the crematory?"

"First thing in the morning!" Solensky replied.

"And at what time can the ashes be picked up?"

"They will be ready around five o'clock tomorrow afternoon."

"Thank you Mister Solensky. We'll have an unmarked car around here overnight, just in case. I'll find my way out. Thank you for your help."

Sandy walked out through the back door, through the parking lot, around the building and back to his car in front parking lot. When he got to his car, he remained standing beside it and dialed the mission on his cell phone.

"Hi, Carla. This is Sandy; can you get Josie on the phone?"

Within moments, Josie was on the phone. "What's up, Sandy?"

"I'm at the Valley Funeral Home. I talked to Mister Solensky, the owner. Roger goes to the crematory first thing in the morning, and his ashes can be picked up at about five o'clock. I'll pick you up and bring you over here tomorrow afternoon. You can sign some papers and take Roger's ashes with you. I don't advise keeping them in your room. Ask Isabelle if she can keep them in her safe for you, until you make plans for whatever arrangements you have in mind. Another thing, I think it would be wise for you and Stevie to come and stay with Joann and me for a few days, to throw the Browns off. From the newspapers and TV, they know you're at the mission, and that's where they'll look for you."

"Thanks Sandy, I'll be ready. I already have a plan for the ashes, and I'll tell you about it tomorrow. I'll see what Isabelle thinks about Stevie and me staying with you."

At the Fiesta Inn Motel, John and Doris Brown were discussing their failure to locate and claim Roger's body. John was thinking and looking at a city map. He had all the funeral homes and their locations marked. He and Doris had been to all of them asking questions. They all gave him the same answer as Solensky at Valley Funeral Home. John also had the city morgue location marked. He was studying it intently. Doris was watching television.

"Doris, I'm certain that Roger's body has to be at the Valley Funeral Home. It's closest to the morgue, and from the owner's reactions when we were there, I figure it must be the place."

"So, what's your plan, John?"

"They won't likely keep him at the funeral home any longer than necessary, and my guess is they'll cremate him as soon as Josie gives her permission, and she's probably already done that."

"Why do you think they'll cremate him?"

"Because, I don't think Josie has any money for any kind of proper burial, and the county'll have to pay for it. They'll go the cheapest way and that would be to cremate."

"Now what?"

"Well, they usually schedule cremations in advance, and they'll take the body to the crematory in the morning and pick up the ashes the same day. We'll go to the Valley Funeral Home tomorrow morning and watch for the hearse to leave with a body."

"Are you planning for us to kidnap the body or what?"

"No, my Dear, we'll just watch—I don't care anything about the body or the ashes. As far as I'm concerned they can scatter them in the nearest garbage dump because that's what Roger had become—**garbage**. The ashes have to lead us to Josie sooner or later."

"And what will we do with Josie?"

"Nothing!" A sinister smile crossed John's face, and he laughed. I don't care about that Mexican Jew either. She can rot in Hell."

"Then why are we going to all this trouble? You know they're looking for us because we left Churchill without permission."

"Think for once Doris—think!" John said condescendingly. "Josie has a child, a little boy who should be six years old."

Doris looked intently at John for several moments. "I uh...I think I see, John, but what you're considering is against the law, and we'll be in deeper trouble than we are already."

"Doris, by the time the authorities find out anything about what we're going to do, we'll be far away, and we'll have a child named Roger!" He smiled, "Get it."

"I get it, but I don't like it."

"You don't have to like it, Doris, just do as I say, when I say it!"

Next morning just as Sandy was checking in at the police station, he got a call. "Sandy this is Smitty."

"Yeah, Smitty, what's up?"

"I've been watching everything coming and going here at the funeral home. There's a car with two people parked just about fifty yards down the street. The side doors where the bodies are taken in and out, is visible from that location."

"Can you see if it's a man and woman in the car?"

"Yeah, it looks like a man and woman, but I can't be sure. The light is bad, and the windows are tinted pretty dark."

"Okay, Smitty, stay put! I'll be right there."

Smitty pulled to the curb a ways behind John and Doris and parked. John looked up in his rear view mirror. "Damn!"

"What is it?"

"There's a cop behind us, watching. I should've known!" He started the car and pulled away from the curb and headed down the street, looking every few seconds in the rearview mirror.

"How'd you know it was a cop, John?"

"Just a feeling I have. It just didn't make sense. There're no businesses around here that anyone would be parking to go shopping. I'm sure by now they know we're in town."

"Sandy, this is Smitty. The car just pulled out and drove down the street. You want me to follow 'em?

"Yeah, but don't get too far from the funeral home, it could be a false alarm."

"Okay Sandy! I'm on it. Stay on the line for a few minutes."

Smitty drove in the direction that John and Doris had taken, but they turned the corner by the time he had pulled out to follow. "Sandy, I've lost 'em."

"Okay, get back to the funeral home but make a note of the make and model of the car. Did you get the license plate number?

"Yeah, it's a late model—looks to be this year, blue Ford Taurus, license number OMB, that's Oscar, Mike, Baker, two-five-seven. Repeat, Oscar, Mike, Baker, two-five-seven."

"Okay Smitty, I got it. I'll run it through the state data base and get back to you."

A few minutes later, Sandy called back. "Stay on your post, Smitty. I'm sending a relief for you who'll be there the rest of the day. The vehicle is registered to Tri-State Car Rental, and was rented to guess who?"

"Yeah, John Brown!"

"Okay, Smitty, good work. Now we know what they're driving, but we've got to assume they may turn the car in and go to another rental agency. Carl will be relieving you so give him the info and a description, but next time we see them, they may be driving a different vehicle. I've instructed Carl to be close to the crematory and to follow the hearse back with the ashes before five o'clock. I'll be there with Josie at the same time. Can you tell if the hearse has left with Roger's body yet?"

"Yeah, they're just now pulling out."

"Okay, the crematory's across town so follow it, stay close and keep your eyes open. Keep in contact with Carl so he'll know where to intercept you and take over. Let me know if that Ford Taurus shows up anywhere enroute."

"Sandy, this is Carl. I just got to the crematory, and they're unloading two bodies. I don't see anything suspicious around here."

"Okay, Carl, drive around the block a few times just to make sure everything's okay, then go back to the funeral Home and stay there. Check in with Solensky and have him tell you before they leave to go pick up the ashes. Tell him they might want to do that in something other than the hearse so it won't be so obvious. Oh, and tell him I have a plan, and I'll be over in a few minutes to make the arrangements."

"Okay, Sandy, I'll keep in touch. In the meantime, I'll check out all the motels to see if they've registered. So far they've not been very careful about their identity, but then, they are amateurs."

"Hi Carla, This is Sandy. Tell Josie and Isabelle I'll be over there about one o'clock. Also tell them there's going to be a change of plan regarding the disposition of Roger's ashes. I'll explain when I get there."

"Okay, Sandy, I'll get it done right away."

"What'll we do now, John?" Doris asked.

"Right now we're going back to the motel and check out. I'm sure they know we're here, and will be checking all the motels, and probably the car rental agencies."

"I'm afraid, John. This is going to get us into a lot of trouble."

John looked at her, his eyes narrowed in anger. "We're into it too far to back out now. We go on with the plan, you hear?" He demanded.

At the motel, John instructed Doris. "Okay, Doris, here's the key. Go into the room and pack as fast as you can. I'll go to the office and check out."

"Checking out so soon, Mister Brown? You've only been here four days."

"I uh...had a call from my business, and I need to be home tonight for an important meeting tomorrow."

"I see, well we appreciate your business, and please remember us when you're back in Rock City. It's been a pleasure serving you. Here's your receipt, and your credit card."

"Thank you! Your staff has been very kind, and we appreciate your good service."

John walked back to the room. "Got everything, Doris?"

"Everything's packed."

"Okay, I'll get started getting things into the car."

Doris closed the door to the room and got into the car. "Now what?"

"We have to check into another hotel. It'll have to be a cheap place that isn't likely to ask questions or ask for an ID because we're going to change our names. Let's see—from now on you are uh...Melinda, and I will be Bill. Yeah, that's good...Melinda and Bill. Our last name has to be something common—how about Smith? Bill and Melinda Smith, that sounds good."

"Okay, John!"

"Bill, dammit!" he yelled.

"Okay, Bill, I forgot."

"Don't forget again...Melinda!"

"Where now, Bill?"

"We turn this car in and get something else, Melinda. Most likely they've got this license number and have checked it out. Get on your cell phone and find the number of a taxi; call 'em and have 'em pick us up at Tri-State Car Rental."

Doris did as she was told. The taxi arrived at the car rental about ten minutes after they got there, just enough time for John to look through the Yellow Pages and to write down the address of a cheap motel on the east side of town.

The driver helped load their baggage into the taxi, and then drove them to the motel. The driver was a little surprised they would be staying at this particular place. "You two runnin' from somethin'?" he asked.

"Thanks for the ride but why we're here is none of your business!"

Josie's Gift

John went inside and registered as Bill and Melinda Smith. The taxi driver parked in front of the room and helped Doris unload. John stuck out his hand and gave him his fare and a nice tip.

The driver looked at the money in his hand, "Thanks Mister...uh...!

"Smith...Bill and Melinda Smith." John quickly answered.

Inside, the room smelled like stale food and stale smoke. All the furnishings looked as if they were worn out. Paint and finish was chipping away from the corners, and the dresser drawers were sloppy and loose.

"Couldn't we have gotten something better?" Doris complained.

"Yeah, I know this looks bad but it'll have to do. Now we've got to find a car. I'll go talk to the motel clerk."

The clerk was sitting with his feet propped up on a low shelf under the counter, and was chewing on an unlit cigar. When he saw John come in, he jumped up. "Yes sir, Mister Smith. What can I do fer ya?"

"Well, I need a car for two or three days."

"There ain't no rental agencies around here, Mister Smith," he said shifting the cigar to the other side of his mouth.

"Yeah, I can see that. Listen, have you got something here like an extra vehicle that I could rent?" John pulled two one hundred dollar bills out of his wallet where the clerk could see. "I'll pay you well if you've got something I can drive."

The clerk's eyes brightened, and he bit down on the cigar and swallowed. "Hold on just a minute—lemme go to the back and talk to the missus."

He soon returned. "Okay Mister Smith, she says it's okay. The two hundert'll git you two days. Every day after that'll be another hundert, and you fill it with gas before you bring it back."

John laid the two hundred on the counter, and the clerk handed him the keys. He drove it around the building and parked in front of the room.

"Now what?" Doris asked.

"We're going back to the funeral home and wait for the ashes!"

Back at the funeral home, they drove around the area, and picked out a spot where they could watch the side door. This time they stayed far enough away that they wouldn't likely be noticed. It was four o'clock.

When Sandy got to the mission, Isabelle, Carla, Darlene, Josie and Stevie were waiting. "Okay folks, here's what we're going to do. Instead of driving to the funeral home to pick up the ashes, we're going straight to the crematory. I've arranged it with Mr. Solinsky for the funeral home driver to have papers with him for Josie to sign. Josie will sign the papers, and we'll take possession of Roger's ashes. Since two bodies were brought there this morning, the driver will still have an urn of ashes to take back to the funeral home. If the Browns are waiting at the funeral home, they'll see the driver take an urn into the building. I'm hoping they make a move at that time. If they do, my man Carl will be there waiting. Now what's the plan for disposing of Roger's ashes?"

Isabelle and Josie explained the plan. Isabelle looked at Josie. "Are you ready, Honey?"

"Ready as I'll ever be, Isabelle."

"Okay everybody, let's get on the road!" Sandy barked.

Everything went off without a hitch at the crematory. Josie signed the papers and took possession of Roger's ashes. She was crying when she reached for the plain metal box. She tried to imagine Roger inside, but no matter how hard she tried, she realized it was nothing but ashes and that Roger wasn't there. Wherever he was, she honestly hoped he was at rest. It had become clear to her lately that Roger was a tormented soul, and he could never be at peace. Why? She didn't know. Maybe she and Carla could discuss that question.

They arrived at the river bank at the site Josie selected. Will Brent was waiting for them. It was a beautiful day with a clear blue sky and the air was very still. Puffy little clouds drifted aimlessly through the sky with seemingly no place to go. Josie closed her eyes, and her mind drifted back to the courthouse and the shooting. She had to put her hand over her mouth to keep from screaming.

Sandy told them to wait in the car for a few minutes just to be sure they weren't followed. Will walked to the driver side window and spoke to Sandy. "I haven't seen anything suspicious."

As they all got out of the car, Josie held the box very gently. Stevie was at her side crying quietly. She looked at Isabelle and handed her the box. Isabelle opened it slowly and took out the plastic bag that was inside. The bag was sealed at both ends. Sandy got out his pocket knife and carefully cut off one end. Isabelle handed the bag to Josie, who was by this time sobbing uncontrollably. Sandy took her hand and walked her to the edge of the embankment. They could still see tracks in the mud below where the stolen car had plunged over the side and into the water.

Josie handed Stevie one red rose they had bought. She looked up at the heavens and said a silent prayer for the soul of Roger. Isabelle read a passage of scripture and pronounced a blessing on the ashes and upon the little group gathered there. Isabelle nodded at Josie who leaned over the embankment and began to slowly shake the plastic bag. The ashes floated down to the water, and patiently made their way downstream with the current of the river. She choked at the words she knew she had to say.

"Roger," she sobbed. "I forgive you for all the pain, for everything you did to hurt me. Please forgive me for any offense I committed against you. And God, please forgive me for the decisions I made that resulted in this awful life of tragedy. God, forgive me for what this has done to my family and to Roger's family. I am so...so sorry!"

She shook the bag hard, and the rest of the ashes floated down to the water. She suddenly quit crying, as if a burden had been lifted. She bent down, picked up a rock, put it in the bag and threw the bag and the rock as hard as she could. The bag and rock went under the water. Within a few seconds, the bag surfaced without the rock, floated downstream with the ashes, to be lost forever in riverbank soil far, far away. Josie felt a sense of relief flood her soul like the water of that river had washed away all the pain and bad memories.

She turned to Stevie and helped him to throw the rose into the water. "Daddy," he sobbed. "I forgive you too... please don't forget us...wherever you are."

Stevie began sobbing, "I'm so sorry, Daddy...so sorry!" For the first time, Stevie grieved over Roger's death.

Isabelle still held the steel box that had contained the ashes. She handed it to Josie. "What do I do with this," Josie asked.

"Whatever you want to do with it," Isabelle answered.

Josie looked again at the river. The box was heavy. She turned, and in one motion cast the steel box as far as she could into the water below. Then she turned to her friends, "It's over," she said. "Let's go home."

On the way back to the mission, Carl called Sandy. "Hi, Sandy, nothing's going on here. There's been absolutely no suspicious activity!"

"Okay, Carl, let's call it off. We'll catch up with the Browns at some point. They're bound to make some mistakes, and we'll get them. In the meantime, I want you to check with Tri-State Car Rental Agency and see about that blue Taurus. Then start checking with all the motels. As soon as you have anything, call me, okay?"

"I'm on it, Sandy."

The Browns did not see the funeral home driver, in a plain car, stop in the back parking lot and enter the funeral home with a single steel box. They assumed they were there at the wrong time or at the wrong funeral home.

"Let's go back to the motel, Doris and get something to eat along the way." John sounded defeated and tired. "We have to make another plan."

CHAPTER TWELVE

Back at the motel, the Browns settled in for the evening. The next morning, John believed he had a plan that would work. When Doris emerged from the bathroom, he had a smile on his face. "Doris, instead of concentrating on Josie, we'll concentrate our efforts on finding an opportunity to get our hands on Stevie."

"How'll we do that?"

"What was the name of that place they mentioned in the paper, the Lighthouse or something like that? Think! Doris!"

"Wasn't it Lighted Way Ministries? Is that where you think Josie is? Do you think she could have found a job?"

"No, I don't think so—I don't think she's had time and besides she doesn't have any skills. The paper said there's a mission here. That must be where she's living." John handed Doris the phone book, "Look in the Yellow Pages and find the address and phone number of that place. While you do that I'm going down the street and get us some breakfast. When I get back, we'll eat and then drive over there and look around."

Sandy's phone rang. "Hi, Carl, any luck yet?"

"Not a thing, Sandy. They're smarter'n I thought. They turned in that blue Taurus yesterday afternoon. Will got me a search warrant and met me at the agency. Smitty and I went through the Taurus with a fine tooth comb to see if they left anything behind. I'm running finger prints lifted from the vehicle right now. The clerk at the agency positively identified the Browns from the poster photos I showed him from Churchill. We also got copies of the papers they filled out and the receipts with their credit card data. Will contacted the bank that issued the credit card and there's no activity as of yesterday."

"How about the motels?"

"I checked with every motel in town, Sandy, and got a hit on the Fiesta Inn Motel. Browns checked out just before they turned in the car. The clerk there also positively identified them. Brown gave some story about having to go back to Churchill for urgent business. We have copies of the motel bill and credit card receipt—same credit card he used at the car rental. Where do we go from here?"

"Okay, check with the bus lines and the airlines and see if there were incoming passengers at anytime in the past week or so. My theory is that they drove one of their own cars here and then stashed it somewhere. But check the bus and airlines just to make sure. Get the info Brand sent us on the car he thinks the Browns left Churchill in. I think they plan to use that car to get out of Rock City, but by the time they leave it'll probably have stolen plates on it. There're several self-storage places in town. After you get the info on Browns' car, check them all and find out if they stored a car. Put out word to all patrol units to check the park-and-ride lots, the parking lot at the bus station and the lots at the airport. Check with all the other motels and the car rental agencies. They must have checked in somewhere, and they're driving somebody's car. Find out if they have a cell phone and get the call records. Oh, and by the way, when you call Brand, find out if the Browns have any relatives in this part of the state. You got all that, Carl?"

"I'm on it, Sandy. I'll get back to you when I know something."

Thirty minutes later, "Sandy, Carl here. I just talked to Brand in Churchill. One of the Browns' cars is not at home. I've got the make and license number; it's a light blue Chrysler 300, license XTZ, that's X-ray, Thomas, Zulu, four-five-seven. Brand's already checked with Browns' other two sons, and except for Roger's death, they don't know anything about any of this. Both said they hadn't had contact with their parents in more than two years. Neither of them knows of any relatives here in Rock City. I asked them to call you or Will Brent if they have any contact with either of their parents. They both seemed cooperative. Phone records indicate several calls since they've been in Rock City. I'm pinpointing cell towers on a map to see if there're any connections with their activities. Brand also told me that news media are camped out at the Brown's home hoping for a story."

"Hmmm, good job Carl! Looks like they've stashed the Chrysler here somewhere. That car shouldn't be hard to spot unless they get rid of it for something else. What about the bus and airlines, any passengers named Brown?"

"No, not in the past week. As to the car, there's nothing meeting the description of the Chrysler in any of the self-storage lots, and nothing suspicious in any of the other parking lots."

"Yeah, Carl, and without the car, we're at a dead end. Get your pictures transmitted to all patrols and have the uniformed guys check all the cheap motels to see if anyone recognizes them. Maybe they'll see the uniformed cops and panic and make a mistake."

There was a knock on the Brown's motel door. John jumped up and looked puzzled. He pulled the curtain back slightly and looked out just as the man was knocking again.

It was the motel clerk chewing on his cigar. John opened the door and looked around.

Without invitation, the clerk stepped inside the door and closed it behind him. "I hate ta bother ya Mister uh...Smith, but uh...ya see they wuz a cop here a while ago and showed me some pitchures."

Doris gasped, put her hand over her mouth and excused herself to the bathroom where she got sick at her stomach and vomited. John looked at his wife then back to the clerk. "So what does all that have to do with us?" he asked.

"Waal it's...uh...time for another two hunnert fer the car! An also I'm gonna have ta raise thu room rate on ye!"

"You can't do that," John shouted. "I'll pay for the car, but we agreed on twenty-five dollars a night for the room."

The clerk chewed a little on the cigar in his mouth, turned his head, opened the door and spit. "Ya see Mister...uh... Smith, you an yer wife wuz on that pitchure thu cop showed me, an so it's gitten jest a mite outta thu ordinary, shall we say, fer thu two of you ta be here."

John got into the clerk's face and growled. "You son of a..."

The clerk was calm. "Now, now, Mister...uh...Smith; or maybe it's Mister Brown. Ya see, I didn't tell thu cop nuthin'—not a danged thing! But I sure coulda told him you wuz here. So ya see, I jes gotta raise thu rent on this here room, or ya might jes find me runnin my mouth off."

John looked down at the floor. He decided not to do to the clerk what was on his mind. "Okay, this time you win, how much?"

"Waal, I think a hunnert a night should be about right seein' as how you folks has been right nice guests so far. An' I'll jest take enough fer five days in advance and five hunnert extra in advance fer thu car."

"That's not fair," John thundered.

"I'll tell ya what I c'n do fer ya. If'n ya check out an' return thu car ahead of thu five days, why I'll jest refund some of yer money."

"Get outta here you cheap..."

"Now, Mister Brown, lets keep this affair in a civil tone!"

John got out a roll of money and handed the clerk a thousand dollars. "Go buy yourself a new cigar!"

The clerk left and John turned his attention to his wife. He found her sitting on the toilet stool fully clothed and white as a sheet. "John," she screamed. "We're in trouble, aren't we? We're going to jail, aren't we?"

"It's nothing I can't handle, Doris. Now get off that stool and wash your mouth out and come and lay down for awhile."

Doris got up off the stool and started to turn, but she vomited again, this time in the sink. John turned on the water and got her a glass. "Get hold of yourself, Doris. We'll make it through this together."

"John, I'm scared. I've never been so scared in all my life. We should just give ourselves up and take our punishment before it gets worse."

"No," John yelled. "We will not give up—we're going to succeed, and we're going to get Stevie for our own."

After Doris settled down, John found the pictures they had copied from the newspapers in Churchill. They clearly showed Josie, Stevie, the mission and Isabelle. They had done a very nice write up on the mission and its ministry. The article also had a picture of Roger from the high school yearbook. "Doris, you lie around here and rest. I'm going to drive to the mall and get some of these newspaper pictures blown up." He smiled, "Don't you think it's nice they're in color?"

While he was out, John went to the public library and researched the Rock City Papers for articles about Roger's killing. Some of the pictures of Stevie and Josie were better than the Churchill ones so he copied them. He also copied a picture of Detective Sandoval. In one of the pictures, the media were interviewing him in his front yard, but he couldn't see house numbers or street signs. He signed in to use one of the computers. He got online and did a search of the Sandoval name in Rock City. He breathed a sigh of satisfaction. He had the address and even a phone number and the name of his wife. He got everything together and headed back to the motel.

At the motel, he spread the pictures out on the table. "Look at these, Doris and study them. Here's a picture of Josie, and here's Stevie. We have to be able to recognize them quickly if we see them on the street. I'm sure the cops here know we're in town, and so far we've outsmarted them. Now, if you were the cops what would you do to protect them?"

"Well, probably put cops all over the mission area," Doris answered.

"I don't think so, Doris!" He smiled, "You know why?"

"No, why?"

"I think they'll separate Josie and Stevie for safety reasons." John smiled again, thinking about how smart he was, and it gave him more self-confidence.

"So, now what?" Doris asked.

John thought for a few minutes turning over ideas in his head. "First thing is: we've got to keep an eye on the mission to see if anybody picks up either Josie or Stevie. Let's head for the mission and find a way to watch without being discovered."

When they got to the mission neighborhood, they felt like the car they rented from the motel clerk fit right into the surroundings as it was an older model and somewhat beat up. In the yard behind the mission building, there were children playing. They watched for awhile and decided there were too many adults around to attempt anything there.

"Look, John, there's Stevie." Doris pointed at the boy holding a ball.

John looked carefully. "You're right, Doris, that's him all right. Let's put a little distance between us and the mission and park where we can watch."

Sandy's phone rang. "Hi, Sandy, this's Josie. I've been thinking about relocating like you suggested. I talked it over with Isabelle and also with Will, and they have a suggestion. Maybe it would be better if Stevie and me were in two separate places. How about you take Stevie with you and I stay here. I have duties here and I really need to stay with it."

Sandy sighed. "I'm concerned about the plan, but it might work best after all. That way the Browns wouldn't be able to get at both of you at the same time. Okay, Joann will pick up Stevie this afternoon so please have him ready."

"Thanks Sandy—thanks for everything."

At lunch Josie told Stevie of the plan, but she didn't tell him about the Browns looking for them. Josie had Stevie's things packed, and they were waiting at the entrance when Joann drove up. Stevie hugged his mom and got into the car.

"John, look! There's someone in that car picking up a boy. I'm sure it's Stevie."

John was half asleep but suddenly came to life when he heard Doris. He started the car and looked. "You're right, Doris—it's him. Let's go."

When Joann pulled away from the mission, John waited a few seconds, looked to see if anybody was watching and then pulled around the corner from where he was parked and followed Joann and Stevie. He stayed as far as he could away from them but yet managed to keep sight of Joann's car. He looked at the city map he had. "Doris! I believe they're heading for the Sandoval's home. That must be the detective's wife in the car. We'll follow them for a little while longer just to be sure then we'll head back to the motel.

Tomorrow, we'll go by the detective's house and watch for awhile."

The next morning after breakfast, John got out a pair of his oldest jeans and shirt. He then went around the motel and rubbed them in the dirt. Back in the room, he put on the dirty clothes and baseball cap. "Doris, I think it would be best if I go alone this morning. They're going to be looking for a man and a woman. If I go alone wearing these dirty clothes and in the rundown car we're driving, I can easily pass for a handy man. When I get back, we'll make a plan."

John drove by the Sandoval home carefully noting the open garage door and Joann's car in one space and the other space empty. He figured that Sandy had already gone to work. He also noticed there was very little activity around any of the homes, indicating this was probably a working class neighborhood and nearly everybody was gone to work. He parked and boldly walked up the sidewalk to the front door and rang the doorbell. When Joann opened the door he took off his cap and nervously introduced himself as Bill Smith.

"Ma'am, uh...I'm out of work. Do you or any of your neighbors, that you know, have any lawn work they need done?"

"No, Mister Smith. I'm sorry you're out of work, but all the yards here are taken care of by a service."

Just then two boys came bursting into the room and to the door. John smiled as he recognized one of them as Stevie.

"Well, sorry to have bothered you, Ma'am, I'll be goin' now."

He tipped his hat. "Nice lookin' boys you got there!"

John got into his car and drove back to the motel. "He's there Doris. I saw him up close an' he's the nicest lookin' boy you'd ever want to see. Let me change these clothes and while we eat lunch, I'll tell you what we're going to do."

They drove to a restaurant across town and near to the Sandoval home. John looked at everybody. After they were seated, he described the plan to Doris while he continually looked up at everybody passing by the table.

The next morning they got in the car, and Doris drove them to the mall. Doris parked behind a car in a full row and acted like she was waiting for someone to leave a parking space. John got out with a screwdriver and pliers and quickly removed a rear license plate. They left the mall parking lot and drove straight to a storage facility where they had parked the Chrysler. Doris waited while John unlocked the door, put the new license plate on the rear of the Chrysler and backed it out. They drove back to the motel and parked both cars in front of the room.

The cigar-chewing clerk saw what was going on and came to the room. "Looks like ye got ya a new car?"

"Well, it's not new, but we needed something. Here's your keys back, and we're checkin out."

The clerk rolled the cigar around in his mouth a few times. "Waal, hope ye have a nice trip, wherever yer goin'."

"We will," John replied. "And don't worry about the refund. In fact, here's an extra couple a hundred for your trouble. Never can tell when somebody might just come around asking questions."

"Yer sure right about that!" The clerk took the money and the keys John handed to him and walked back to the office rolling the cigar around in his mouth as he walked.

John turned to Doris. "Okay, let's get everything out of this room and get out of here."

Sandy's phone rang. "Sandy, this is Will."

"Yeah, Will, what's up?"

"I just got a call from Brand in Churchill. He says the Browns emptied their bank accounts before they left. Looks like they mean to stay away for a long time."

"That's a new twist. Call the DA's office in Churchill and ask them to issue a warrant to Brand for a search of the Brown's home. Then call Brand and ask him to look for any important papers or anything they may have left behind that could tell us where they're headed when they leave here. Right now my theory is they won't leave without Josie and Stevie. They'll go for Josie and when they find out Stevie isn't with her, they may work her over to get her to tell them where he's at."

"Okay, Sandy, I'm on it."

Thanks Will. I'll call Isabelle and tell her to be on the lookout."

"Sandy, this's Will."

"Yeah Will."

"I just got a call from Brand in Churchill. They searched the Brown's home. If they had any important papers at the house, they took 'em with them. He also found out that they had a safe deposit box at the bank, but they had emptied it and cancelled it out."

"Anything else, Will?"

"Yeah, something that may or may not be significant. Brand found several brochures from a couple of retirement resort areas in Florida. He and I both think they may head in that direction when they have what they want."

"Good work, Will—sounds like a winner. I'll get with the Department of Public Safety guys and have them look at all the possible ways of getting from Rock City to Florida. Maybe we'll have a head start on them."

"I really hope we can get 'em here before they can do any harm to Josie or Stevie—or anybody else for that matter. I don't trust 'em, and I believe they would be capable of hurting anybody that gets in their way—and that could mean any of our friends at the mission."

"Okay, Will. Keep me posted on anything else you or Brand uncover."

John and Doris drove from the motel straight to the Sandoval home. As they drove by, they noticed Stevie and another boy were playing in the back yard, and Joann was sitting on the back patio watching. They parked two blocks away so as not to draw any suspicion.

"Okay, Doris this is it. You come over here and get in the driver seat so you can drive. When we go toward the Sandoval's again, stop about a half a block away and park, but keep the engine running. If Joann Sandoval is still out there watching the boys, you call her on the phone. Keep her busy for as long as you can—use some excuse like a church affair and ask her to participate by baking some pies or something. As soon as she goes inside to answer the phone, drive up beside the yard. I'll get out and grab Stevie and bring him to the car. Then you take off and don't spare the gas. Got that?"

"I'm really scared, John!"

"Just do what I say, and everything will work out."

Doris drove very slowly. She could see Joann sitting on the patio so she made the call. Joann ran into the house to answer it, and Doris drove beside the back yard. John jumped out and ran to Stevie and picked him up and ran back to the car. Stevie was screaming all the way. Just as John was getting into the back seat with Stevie, Doris pushed the accelerator to the floor and sped off.

They had a preplanned route to take them away and Doris stayed with it. John had to hold Stevie down in the back seat. He was kicking and screaming. John tried to reason with him, telling him that they were his grandparents and just wanted to take him for a ride to get some ice cream. He calmed down a little but was crying quietly.

Doris kept on driving, and John kept talking to Stevie. "Stevie, now we're going to get your mama so she can go with us. She told us where to find you."

Stevie looked puzzled. Anticipating seeing his mama, he finally quit crying.

"Sandy, They've got Stevie," Joann was yelling on the phone, "They've got Stevie!" She was crying uncontrollably.

"Okay, Joann settle down and try to be calm. There's a uniformed officer patrolling that area—I'll get him over there immediately. Now try to tell me what happened. I'm heading that way."

Sobbing, she tried to explain, "...it was a blue car and two people. The boys were in the backyard...the phone rang and I ran into the house...I heard both boys screaming and by the time I hung up the phone and ran outside...I saw a blue car pulling away and I heard Stevie screaming..."

"Did you get the license number, Joann?"

No, it all happened too fast..." Sob.

Sandy hung up and called Carl. "Carl, I just got a call from Joann. The Browns snatched Stevie from my backyard just a few minutes ago. They're on their way to wherever, probably Florida. Check Brown's cell phone and find out if they made a call within the last fifteen minutes, and if it was to my house. Notify the state DPS guys, and get them on the highways with an APB. Issue an Amber Alert for relative abduction of child. Also, better notify the FBI. Get an alert to all our patrol units in Rock City."

"Okay, Sandy, I'm on it."

"Carla, this is Sandy. It's urgent—the Browns have abducted Stevie from my backyard. Get Josie and Isabelle and bring them both to my house. I need them there with Joann—she's going crazy with guilt. Oh, and Carla, start praying."

"Okay, Sandy, we'll be there as soon as we can."

Sandy reached to the floor of his car, picked up a red flashing light and put it on his dash. He turned on the red light and his siren and headed home. When he got there, the uniformed officer was trying to talk to Joann and Davie. Sandy ran up the walk and into the house and grabbed Joann and held her in a tight embrace. He sat her down on the couch and walked to the kitchen. He picked up his phone and called Carl again.

"Carl, Sandy. You've got the license number for that blue Chrysler right?"

"Yeah, I got it out to all units and agencies."

"Good, now check and see if any license plates have been reported stolen today or yesterday. Then get back to me."

"I already thought of that one and just got word that a plate was stolen from a car while it was parked at the Forrest Mall. Here's the number: Baker, Juliet, Alpha, three, niner, two. I've already broadcast it. You were right about using their own car and stolen plates."

Sandy turned his attention back to Joann and Josie. Both were crying uncontrollably. Josie felt like she wanted to die—as if somebody had ripped her heart out of her chest and was gleefully crushing it. She collapsed into Sandy's arms.

"What will they do to him, Sandy?" Josie sobbed.

"Well, the good thing about this situation, if there can be a good thing, is that it's highly unlikely they will harm him in any way. We're just going to have to wait this one out, and at some time or other, we'll catch up with them. I know that doesn't make you feel any better, but at this moment, that's the best we can do. We've got every resource we can muster on this case."

Josie sat down on the couch with Joann, who was still crying, and the two women held hands. "Josie, I'm so, so very sorry. I should have been more watchful. It's all my fault and I feel just awful about it."

"Joann, it's not your fault—it's not anybody's fault." Josie's growing anger at the Browns was beginning to come out. "It's the Brown's fault, and I hope their souls rot in hell for what they're doing to my son."

Isabelle joined the two women. "Look it's all in God's hands now; let's join together in a time of prayer." Everybody bowed as Isabelle knelt on the floor and lifted her hands to heaven: "Lord Jesus, look down here on this humble home, shine your light of perfect love into every window and door and into every heart. Dispel the darkness of despair and worry that has enveloped us all and replace it with sunshine and light and hope and faith. We pray, Almighty God for the safety of Stevie. As the Browns are speeding down that highway, put an angel in their way to protect them from all harm. And Lord, in spite of their evil intentions and actions, bless the Browns and bring someone their way to show them the love of Jesus. We pray in His almighty and blessed name. AMEN."

Isabelle quickly took charge and asked Joann where she kept her coffee maker. Joann started to rise from her seat when Isabelle gently pushed her back. "No, Honey—you just sit there with your husband and Josie, and the two of you get some comfort from Sandy's strength. Carla and I'll take care of things."

With that, Isabelle and Carla went to the kitchen where they found what they needed and got the coffee started. Isabelle looked through the cupboards until she found cups and saucers. Carla found the sugar and creamer and some cookies. They brought the cups and saucers into the living room along with the cookies. Then Isabelle brought the coffeepot and started filling everybody's cup. "Looks like this's going to be a long night, sisters and brothers, so let's settle in and praise the Lord."

Isabelle lifted her hands to heaven and began to sing. Soon others joined in. After fifteen minutes of praising God with songs, the mood began to lift.

Sandy's phone was buzzing and he got up and walked to the kitchen to answer it. "Yeah, Carl, what've you got?"

"That call to Joann came from Brown's cell phone. It was a decoy to get Joann out of the backyard."

"Anything else, Carl?"

"Not yet, but we're monitoring everything that's coming in."

"Thanks, Carl, stay with it. Let me know whenever anything comes in."

Before they all broke up, Joann convinced Josie to stay at her home until there was some word about the Browns. Josie was too weary to argue.

Doris was still driving when they passed the city limit sign. They were staying on the county roads so as to not attract attention. "Uh...Grampa, I need to pee real bad," Stevie said.

Doris pulled over to the side of the road, and John got out with Stevie. Stevie took care of himself and then got back into the car. John began to relax a little since Stevie hadn't tried to run away.

"Doris you come and ride back here with your grandson, and I'll drive."

Doris got into the back seat. "Hi, Stevie, I'm your grandma Doris. I love you very much." She got hold of his arm and pulled him to her and hugged him. "It'll be okay, Honey...I promise you it'll be okay. Now, why don't you try to get some sleep."

Stevie began to whimper. "I thought we wuz goin to pick up my mama."

"Uh...she decided she couldn't go with us just now," Doris lied. "She told me that after she got everything taken care of, she would take the bus to wherever we were going."

"Can I call her and talk to her?"

"Well, I uh...tried to call her a few minutes ago, and she didn't answer so she must be out or busy or something. Don't worry, it'll be all right."

"Where are we going?" Stevie asked.

"Umm, we're uh...uh going to Florida. Do you know where that is?"

"No—is it a long ways away?"

"I'm afraid so Stevie, It's going to take us several days to get there."

Stevie looked up at Doris. "Are you really my grama?"

She laughed, "Yes, Stevie I am really your grandma. I'm your daddy's mom, and John is his daddy."

Stevie laid his head against the side of the door and closed his eyes. Doris gently pulled him to her and laid his head in her lap. She quietly sang a little song she remembered singing to her own sons many years ago. Soon Stevie was sound asleep. For a long time, Doris just looked at Stevie, felt his breathing and his warmth against her lap. It felt very good—a feeling she hadn't had in many years. As she watched his rhythmic breathing, she realized that he was her flesh and blood and that she loved him. She also realized that she had never had this feeling with Roger. It seemed Roger was cold and indifferent from the beginning of his life.

CHAPTER THIRTEEN

It was late into the night, and to avoid police patrols, they were staying on the paved farm-to-market roads. Half asleep, Doris felt somebody tap her on the shoulder. Suddenly, she was wide awake; raised her head and looked forward through the windshield. She saw alternating flashing red lights a short distance ahead, and John wasn't slowing down. She screamed as loud as she could at John.

John suddenly regained a groggy consciousness and saw the lights. He instinctively grasped the steering wheel braced himself with his hands, and simultaneously hit the brake with his foot, pushing on it as hard as he could. By that time, the train was already on the crossing. Doris was still screaming and holding onto Stevie, who was crying. The car stopped just a few feet from the train and slid sideways parallel to the tracks. John's head bounced forward, his body was lifted up and forward by the sudden stop, and his head was sent crashing into the windshield. His chest was violently slammed against the steering wheel, and when the car stopped, his head was hanging over the top of the steering wheel.

Doris and Stevie were both buckled in with their seat belts, or they would have been on the floor against the front seat. Other than being sore where the seat and shoulder belts were fastened around their bodies, they were uninjured. When John's chest hit the steering wheel, and his head hit the windshield, he was knocked out cold. The car was still in gear and started to creep forward, when unexpectedly, the engine went dead and it stopped once again. Doris was sure she saw a figure in white reach into the car and turn off the ignition. She unbuckled her seat belt, got out of the car and walked around. There was a fragrant smell in the fresh spring country air, but there was no one anywhere to be seen.

Doris reached into the car and pulled Stevie out and held him in a strong embrace for several long minutes. "It's all right now, Stevie," she whispered to him.

"What happened Grama?"

"We almost hit a train, Honey," She looked at the noisy train speeding by, its iron wheels slapping the joints in the rails. She thought about the whole incident. She looked down at Stevie and spoke. There was fear in her voice. "I know this sounds crazy, but I think the good Lord sent an angel to help us. It wasn't for me or Grandpa, the angel came—it was for you."

She got down in front of Stevie at his eye level and with tears in her eyes, very quietly, she said, "...I love you, Stevie, very, very much." Then she put him into the back seat and turned to her husband who was still unconscious.

Doris shook John several times and slapped his face to try to awaken him but he didn't respond. Now she was worried. She could see where his head hit the windshield and saw the massive bloody bruise on his forehead. She felt his chest, and his breathing was very shallow. She felt for a pulse, but it was so weak she couldn't feel it. She looked back at Stevie whose worried look gave her the courage to do what she had to do. For a moment she considered driving on and dropping John's body somewhere, but looking at Stevie, she knew she had to do what was right.

"Come up here, Stevie and help me get Grandpa into the back seat." It was then she noticed John was not wearing his seat belt. With Stevie helping, she managed to pull John out and get her shoulder under his arm and push him into the back seat. Then she got her cell phone out of her purse and pushed 9-1-1.

"Hello," the pleasant voice said. "What is your emergency?"

Doris was beginning to feel the adrenaline draining out of her system, and her voice was shaky. "We've had an accident, and my husband is injured and unconscious. We are driving a blue Chrysler. I and my grandson are okay."

"What is your location, Ma'am?"

"I uh...I'm not sure. I was asleep and wasn't watching the road signs. My husband was driving. I know we are at a railroad crossing on a blacktop farm-to-market road."

"Ma'am can you see an identifying sign on the farm-to-market road?"

"No, I don't see anything."

"Do you see any markers near the tracks in either direction?"

"No, I don't see anything there either."

"Okay, now listen carefully, I have no idea where you are, however I'm alerting the EMS and Sheriff. Are you okay and is the car okay to drive?"

"Let me see." Doris turned the key and the car started. "Yes, I'm okay, and I can drive it."

"Is your grandson okay too?"

"Yes, I think he's okay."

"All right, when the train is clear of the crossing, drive on across the tracks and keep going until you see the first sign of any kind along the road."

"Okay, first sign of any kind." The train had cleared, and Doris drove across the tracks.

"Ma'am, don't hang up—I'll stay with you 'til you find a sign."

It seemed like an eternity, but five minutes later there was a sign. Doris stopped and picked up the phone. "Hello!"

"Yes, Ma'am, do you see a sign?"

"Yes, it says 'Littleville 5 miles.'"

"Good job, Ma'am, we can pinpoint your location. An ambulance is on the way. Now, just keep on driving as fast as it's safe to do so, and when you see the red lights of the ambulance ahead of you and coming toward you, pull over and stop. Turn off your headlights and turn on your emergency flashers and wait. I'll stay with you 'til you see the flashing lights. It shouldn't be long."

The emergency operator alerted the sheriff and also gave him the description of the car. He recognized it from the Amber Alerts that had gone out yesterday. He was right behind the ambulance when they came in view of car lights ahead.

Doris pulled off the road as she had been instructed; turned off her headlights and turned on her emergency flashers. Within a minute, both the ambulance and the sheriff were on the scene. She spoke to the emergency operator and informed her of the situation.

"You've done a good job, ma'am. The sheriff will take care of things from here. God bless you."

Stevie got out of the car when she did and stood with her. "Grandma, I'm scared."

"Everything's going to be okay, Stevie, help is here."

"Is Grandpa dead?"

"I don't know, Honey. The EMS will let us know, and they'll tell us what to do."

Doris opened the back door of the Chrysler, and the EMS technicians immediately got to work on John. The sheriff walked over to Doris and began asking questions. She got her wallet out of her purse and showed the officer her driver's license.

"I'm Doris Brown and that's..." pointing to where the EMS was working, "...that's my husband, John. I believe that we are fugitives!"

The sheriff looked surprised and laughed. "Yes Ma'am, I believe you are." He smiled. "I'll need to ask you some questions, but let's get your husband taken care of first, Okay?"

"Whatever you say, Sheriff."

One of the EMS technicians walked over. "Sheriff, the man's still alive, but barely. We're prepping him for the ambulance ride, and we'll take him straight to town. The hospital there may not be able to do anything and so they'll have Air Life alerted." The technician walked back to the ambulance, closed the doors and sped off.

"Ma'am," the sheriff said. "Can you drive the car? I can get a deputy here in a few minutes to pick it up, and you and the boy can ride on in with me if you'd rather."

"At this moment I'd rather go with you, Sheriff."

Doris and Stevie got into the car with the sheriff, and they sped off behind the ambulance. Doris's mind was beginning to grasp the severity of the whole situation, and she began to cry. Stevie leaned over from the back seat and got hold of her hand. "It's gonna be all right, Grama! I believe Jesus is taking care of us."

Doris's heart swelled with love. "I believe he is too, Honey." She said. She leaned her head over on Stevie's hand. "I'm so proud of you, Stevie. I'll bet your mama's missing you."

"Yeah, I know she is, but I know Reverend Isabelle's there with her, and Jesus's there too."

When they arrived at the hospital, they immediately wheeled John into emergency. An admissions nurse came to Doris to get identity information. "Can you get his wallet from his pocket," Doris asked.

"Sure," the nurse responded. "I'll bring it to you, and you can get what we need."

The nurse brought the wallet, and Doris got all the information needed. The nurse took his driver's license and insurance cards and copied them and brought them back. "Can I go to the emergency room where my husband is now," Doris asked.

The nurse glanced at Stevie. The sheriff spoke up, "Ma'am I'll stay here and watch the boy, you go on in with the nurse. You and I can talk when you come back."

Doris followed the nurse and Stevie followed the sheriff. "Are you hungry Stevie?" The sheriff asked.

"Yeah, a little."

How about you and I sitting in those chairs over there. I'll call my deputy to bring us a peanut butter and jelly sandwich. Do you like peanut butter and jelly?"

Stevie smiled big. "I sure do!"

"Hi, Jerry, Mort here. Did you bring that blue Chrysler in? Good! Go through it and see if there's anything significant besides clothes. Lock it up in our impound lot. Oh, and call the authorities in Rock City and also the FBI and let 'em know we have their people here. The man's in the hospital in bad shape, and the woman and the boy seem okay, although I'm going to have them looked over before we leave here just to be sure. We need something to eat over here so bring us two ham and cheese sandwiches, one peanut butter and jelly sandwich, and a glass of milk. We c'n get coffee here."

"I'll be there in thirty minutes Sheriff."

Sheriff Mortenson turned his attention back to Stevie. "Is it okay if I ask you some questions Stevie?"

Stevie looked up at the sheriff. "Detective Sandoval asked me some questions too—after my dad beat up my mom, and she was in the hospital real sick—bleedin' and everything."

Sheriff smiled. "So your dad beat up your mom real bad, huh?"

"Yeah, it wuz real bad—she wuz sick for a long time. Then we moved over to the motel, and then after my dad's trial we went to the Lighted Way Mission."

"You sure have a good memory, Stevie. Is Doris Brown your real Grandma?"

"Yeah, she's my dad's mama."

"And John Brown is your real Grandpa?"

"Yep. Say, do you know Detective Sandoval in Rock City? He's my friend you know!"

"No, I'm sorry to say I don't know him—but I'll bet he's a real nice fellow!"

"Yeah, and a real good cop. He shot my daddy you know—at the court house. My dad shot a bunch of people at the court house and Detective Sandoval saved a lot of people when he shot my dad."

"Did that bother you a lot—for Detective Sandoval to shoot your dad?"

"Naah! My dad was a really mean person an' he beat up my mama all the time. She was always real sad and unhappy. Now that he's gone, she's got friends at the mission, and she's got Jesus. She's doin' real good. But I think she's probably missin' me though."

Sheriff smiled. "Well Stevie, within the next few hours, your mama will know you are safe, and she won't worry anymore."

Stevie didn't say anything more and seemed to be deep in thought. For Sheriff Mortinson, the picture was beginning to come together. He remembered the awful tragedy at the Rock City Court House. It was on the national news. Miraculously, everybody survived. He hoped he would never be faced with the choice that Sandoval faced.

Jerry walked in with a sack and handed it to Mortinson. "Here's your goodies, Sheriff! Say who'se your little buddy here?"

"Jerry, this is Stevie Brown. That name ring a bell somewhere?"

"Whooeee!" Jerry exclaimed. "I remember—Rock City Court House. He took his hat off and extended his hand to Stevie. "My name's Jerry, Stevie, and I'm mighty pleased to meet you."

"Thanks for the sandwiches, Mister Jerry!" Stevie opened the sack, found the peanut butter and jelly and the milk and got to work eating.

"Jerry, what did Rock City say about the Browns?"

"They'll be bringing some paperwork as soon as they can get it together and they'll pick up Missus Brown and Stevie. They'll probably be a couple of days gittin' here though, even if they fly."

"Okay Jerry, get back to the office. I'll be there as soon as I can question Doris Brown and get things squared away here."

"Oh, by the way, Sheriff, there was a whole bunch of money stashed in that Chrysler."

The sheriff looked surprised. "Hmmm, looks like they were planning to be gone a long time! Lock it up in the safe, and we'll count it later and make sure we can account for everything."

Sandy's phone rang. He sleepily looked up at the clock; it was two a.m. "Hello, This's Sandy."

Smitty's voice on the other end was exuberant. "Good news, Sandy. We just got a call from Sheriff Paul Mortenson in Littleville, Louisiana. They have John and Doris Brown and Stevie. There was an accident, and John was pretty seriously injured, but Doris and Stevie were unhurt. They'll take care of them over there until we can get there."

"That's great news, Smitty. Get hold of Will and tell him we need some paperwork to bring the Browns back first thing in the morning."

"But, Sandy, you know what time it is?"

"Yes, I know, but get Will out of bed." He laughed. "Oh, and, Smitty, charter us a plane to be on standby, preferably a jet that'll handle seven or eight people and also call our friends at the Air National Guard Headquarters and see if they have a pilot that needs some hours."

Joann was sitting up and awake. "Was that about the Browns, Sandy?"

"Yep, they're safe and sound in custody over in Louisiana. Go wake up Josie and let her know. I'll get some coffee going. I don't think any of us will sleep the rest of the night."

Joann knocked on Josie's door. Josie opened the door—it was obvious from her expression she was worried sick, and she looked as if she hadn't been sleeping. "You okay, Josie?"

"Yeah," Josie said wearily.

Joann's face brightened, "We just got some good news, Honey—Stevie is fine, and the Brown's are in custody over in Louisiana."

Josie took a deep breath and sighed, "No joke?"

"No Joke, Honey. C'mon downstairs, Sandy's got the coffee maker going and I've got some sweet rolls in the cabinet."

Josie and Joann rushed downstairs. Sandy was holding a cup of coffee and smiling. "God has answered our prayers, Josie."

At that moment Sandy saw Josie rushing toward him and set the coffee cup down just in time. She fell into his arms, "Oh, Sandy, I am so thankful for you and Joann and everybody else who've been so good to me."

He pushed her away, a little embarrassed. "Be thankful to God, Josie. It was He who arranged all this, and it is He who deserves the glory."

Josie's Gift

Josie turned around and took Joann's hands in hers and they hugged in a long embrace. "What a relief," Joann said.

"Amen," Josie echoed. "I'm going to call Carla."

"Hello," Carla whispered into the phone. "Carla, I'm sorry to bother you at this time, but right now I'm so happy I can hardly stand it."

"That's okay, Girl. I was praying in the chapel. We have a twenty-four-hour prayer vigil going for Stevie and the Browns. So...what's the news?"

"They're in custody, Carla—and Stevie's safe."

"Where?" Carla asked.

"Somewhere over in Louisiana. Sandy's getting paperwork from Will, and they'll be going to Louisiana to pick them up and bring them back here. Isn't that wonderful? As soon as you see Isabelle, let her know. Bye for now, I love you, Carla."

Sandy, Joann and Josie sat drinking coffee until it was time for breakfast. Sandy described to Josie how things had happened to the Browns and Stevie.

The Emergency room nurse walked out to the waiting room with Doris Brown. "Well, here's the news, Sheriff. Mister Brown has a serious concussion, and he's going to need brain surgery. He has broken ribs from the impact with the steering wheel, some internal bruising and some internal bleeding. There's a good possibility of neck injuries from hangin' himself over the top of that steering wheel. The doctor feels that it's most important to treat the head and neck injuries immediately so we're arranging for a transfer to a better equipped hospital with neurosurgical capabilities. He'll go by Air Life. Our major worry is the possibility of an aneurysm or blood clot in the area of the injury so we need to move quickly."

"Okay, I'll call Jerry and have him bring the paperwork that'll put him into the other jurisdiction for the time being." He looked at Doris. "Missus Brown, we have a ham and cheese sandwich for you, and there's coffee right over there." He pointed in the direction of the coffee maker.

Doris took the sandwich and began to eat. Each bite felt like it would stick in her throat. Finally, her eyes filled with tears, and she began to cry softly. Stevie sat down beside her and put his arm around her. "It's gonna be okay, Grama...I know it is...so don't worry. I'm here to take care of you." Doris looked down at the little boy who seemed so calm in the middle of this great tragedy and confusion. She returned his hug. "Thank you, Stevie—I know you're going to take care of me."

Doris turned to Sheriff Mortenson. "What's next, Sheriff?"

He looked at her and then at Stevie. *"How could somebody like this allow herself to get into such a mess?"* He silently asked himself. He looked at the floor for a moment then back at her. "Missus Brown, I'm afraid I have to take you into custody on a possible child abduction charge. And I learned there are charges against you and your husband in Churchill. It's going to get very complicated because you crossed state lines with an abducted child. As soon as arrangements can be made, you'll be taken back to Rock City to face charges there. Ultimately, you'll be returned to Churchill to face charges there."

"Does that mean I won't be able to go with my husband?"

"I'm afraid that is exactly what it means."

She began to cry again. Looking at Stevie, "And, what about him?"

"Ma'am, right now I'm not sure. This is pretty unusual—considering the loving relationship between you and your grandson. It just doesn't seem like abduction. We'll figure out something. Let's just take it one step at a time."

Doris held out her hands, assuming he would place handcuffs on her. The sheriff, noticing her gesture laughed and was a little embarrassed.

"Uh...no need for that, Ma'am—at least not right now. I don't think you're going to be uncooperative. But, I do have to figure out something to do with you for a few nights."

Doris looked at Stevie, who seemed to be dozing off in the chair. "May I stay here until my husband is transferred?"

Sheriff thought for a few minutes. He scratched his head then looked at her. "Ma'am, my gut tells me I can trust you. It's gonna be daylight pretty soon, and Air Life will be gone with Mister Brown. I'll leave you here and go to my office to get some paperwork done on this case; then I'll send Jerry over to bring you to my office as soon as Air Life takes off. Will that be okay for now?"

"Yes, Sheriff—I promise I'll be here when Jerry gets here for me and Stevie."

Sheriff Mortenson tipped his hat and left the hospital.

All kinds of things went through Doris' mind; "*I have the credit cards so I could do pretty much whatever I want to do! I could buy a car and be gone from here pretty quick.*" She quickly realized the seriousness of her situation and knew that doing anything except 'facing the music' would be foolhardy and would complicate things more than they already were.

She dozed off beside Stevie, who was sleeping soundly. She was awakened by the nurse who told her Air Life had arrived and that they were preparing to transport her husband, and she could go and see him before they took him out. She awoke Stevie and told him they would go see Grandpa.

It was still dark outside when they got up and followed the nurse, who was in a hurry. "Stevie, they're going to take Grandpa to another hospital, and we're going to see him before he leaves."

"Okay, Grama!" He held her hand tightly.

They met the gurney just as it was being brought out of the ER. Doris took her husband's hand and spoke to him. "I love you, John. They're going to take good care of you, and you'll get well. Stevie is here and wants to say something."

She lifted him up, he patted John's hand. "It's going to be okay, Grampa. I'm going to ask Jesus to look after you. I love you; please remember that. Oh, and, I forgive you for kidnapping me!"

Doris began to cry softly as he was pushed through the doors. The helicopter was waiting outside with its navigation lights blinking. A bright light illuminated the side of the machine where a large door was open and waiting for the patient to be loaded into the cavernous interior. They walked out to watch while John was being transferred to the helicopter. When the patient was inside and everything latched down, the pilot throttled forward to increase the speed of the engine and carefully went over his checklist. He pulled back slightly on the stick changing the pitch of the rotors. As the engine reached full power, he changed the pitch some more, and the machine began to gently lift into the air. Within seconds, it was high above the building, rotated in the direction of its destination, and sped away.

When Doris turned around, Jerry was waiting behind them. He tipped his hat, "Good morning, Missus Brown and Stevie. If you're ready, we need to go to the office and talk to Sheriff Mortenson. They followed Jerry to the car and were soon headed in the direction of the office.

Doris looked around. Everything looked so different this morning. The sun was beginning to cast a warm glow on the sleepy city as it started its rise above the horizon, dispelling the darkness of the night. She smiled through her tears. *"It's all over with now! I'm uncertain, but I'm not afraid anymore."* She relaxed, squeezed Stevie's hand and felt relieved at the prospect of talking to Sheriff Mortenson.

The Sheriff's office in Littleville was located in a wing built off the west end of the county jail. Besides the sheriff, there were offices for a chief deputy and four or five others. A receptionist was located inside the front door, and the Sheriff's office was behind the receptionist. Down the hallway, there was a holding cell and two interrogation rooms. In a large open area, there were work stations with desks and computers. There was a rear door at the very end of the hallway that had steel bars and led directly to the jail. The top half of the door was heavy glass, and Doris could see people in orange jumpsuits in the hallway on the other side. They appeared to be cleaning the floors and doing housekeeping chores. She imagined herself being in there with them, assuming of course there was a separate wing of the jail for women.

Jerry ushered Doris and Stevie into the sheriff's office and closed the door. Mortenson stood when they entered and invited them to sit.

"Well," he said. "It's been a very long night for all of us. We'll try to get the paperwork taken care of and get things arranged so you two can get a nap before lunch. Mortenson got a stack of papers and pushed them toward Doris for her to look over.

"I need you to read these very carefully and make sure I have everything accurate. When you are satisfied they are accurate, I'll ask you to sign them. I have to tell you that once you sign these papers your statements can be used in a court of law. I also have to remind you that you are officially in custody and you have the right to have an attorney present before you sign these statements."

Doris looked at the papers lying on the desk and then at Sheriff Mortenson. "You know," she said. "I've always had to depend on John for this sort of thing. Now…" tears welled in her eyes; "…now it's up to me isn't it?"

She looked at Stevie, who squeezed her hand. "And now," she sobbed. "Now...I have someone who cares." Looking up at the sheriff, she said, "Sheriff, I am going to be completely honest and open, and my intuition tells me you are a good man, and you can be trusted."

"I'm flattered, Ma'am, but you must realize my job is first and foremost to uphold and enforce the law."

"I understand completely, Sheriff. To be honest with you, it's a big relief to have this over with. I was not looking forward to a lifetime of running. I knew at some point, we would be caught."

She gathered up the papers and read each sheet. She smiled, "Show me where to sign."

After she signed the papers, the sheriff brought up the matter of the money they found in the Chrysler. "Ma'am, there is one more thing. We found a considerable amount of money in the car—something in the neighborhood of a half million dollars."

Doris gasped. "I didn't realize..."

"Here's a receipt that I've signed. You keep a copy in a safe place in your purse. The money will stay in our safe until you are transferred to Rock City. You need to sign this receipt acknowledging that from what's in the safe, I've given you five hundred dollars for spending money while you are here in Littleville."

Doris looked at Mortenson with a question written on her face.

"Missus Brown, the situation we have here with you and your grandson is rather unusual, and normally, we would turn the child over to the State Department of Family Services. However, in this case, I consulted the judge. With his permission, I've made other arrangements so that the two of you can stay together. I've arranged for the two of you to stay at the La Plaza Motel near here. The money I gave you should take care of the room and your meals for several days. Here are the rules..." He showed her another paper. "I need for you to read this carefully and sign it."

Doris took the paper and read it. It said that the motel desk clerk would have a sheet of paper for her to sign in and sign out every time she left the motel for any reason. She also had to write down why she was leaving and where she'd be. She had to be in her room and locked in by nine o'clock in the evening. She had to keep a written log of every phone call she made and received. Other than that, she was free to enjoy the town. She signed the paper, kept a copy and handed it back to the sheriff.

"One of my deputies will be in touch with you periodically so keep your cell phone on and charged. Jerry is out front waiting for you. He has your luggage from the Chrysler and will take you to the motel so you can check in. They're expecting you."

"Thank you, Sheriff, you've been very understanding."

They shook hands, and the sheriff stood and showed them out.

Stevie turned around and looked at the sheriff, "Mister Mortenson, I think you're my friend like Mister Sandy."

Mortenson smiled and patted Stevie on the head. "Yes, I'm proud to be your friend."

CHAPTER FOURTEEN

After breakfast, Joann and Josie returned to bed exhausted but happy. Sandy was on his way to his office, grateful for the way things had turned out. As he was driving, he was silently planning his next moves. *"First thing will be to get hold of Will. He'll take care of whatever they'll need in the way of paperwork to bring Doris Brown and Stevie back to Rock City, and he will contact Churchill and work things out with them. Second thing will be to call Sheriff Mortenson in Littleville and find out what the disposition of the case is on his end. After that, I'll make plans for whatever develops."*

Sandy punched Will's number into his cell phone. "'Morning, Will. What's our situation in terms of getting the Browns back here for arraignment and trial?"

"'Morning, Sandy. You understand the FBI's involved because they crossed state lines?"

"Yeah, I understand, but I'm not liking it."

"Special Agent Lillian Landers, in the local field office, has been assigned to the case. She's being cooperative, but it still has to have everything cleared by them. They will be officially in charge of the case, unless they determine otherwise. So far, our case against the Browns is theft of the license plates and abduction, and of course over in Churchill they have some charges to deal with. On the other hand we do have state statutes that deal with child abductions like this one, and there's a very good chance we can retain jurisdiction if the circumstances are right. We'll have to visit with the federal prosecutor and figure out where we go with it. I'll also have to work things out with Churchill because they have charges pending, and the Browns were out on bail from there. Its kinda complicated."

"Okay, Will, I know Agent Landers. She's a good friend and has been helpful in the past. I'll let you deal with the prosecutor and with Churchill. So, where do we go from here?"

"Looks like it'll take a couple of days—maybe more, to get all the paperwork and signatures we need. At this point, everything appears to be just normal formalities—it just takes time. How about lunch today?"

"Sounds good, Will—Where?"

"How about Smokey's Steak House?" Will suggested.

"Sounds good. I'll meet you there."

Sandy walked into the police station and was greeted with…"Chief wants to see you Sandy."

"Thanks, Margaret."

"What's up, Chief?" Sandy asked, as he walked into the office.

"The news media has already picked up the story of the abduction of the Brown kid, and they're chomping at the bit for some news. I read the faxed stuff from Mortenson and looks like there's some good news. I've prepared a short news release for you and scheduled a news conference for you and Will on the steps outside the court house at eleven this morning. You can look at what I wrote and change it if you need to, then make copies to pass out to the media. You and Will can answer whatever questions they have. Just keep it short and don't forget the investigation has not been closed yet."

Sandy quickly glanced over what the chief had written. "Thanks, Chief, I'm okay with this." Sandy left the office and called Will about the news conference. "Okay, I'll be there, Sandy."

"Good morning, sheriff's office. May I help you?"

"And a good morning to you. This is Detective Randall Sandoval of Rock City, Texas, and I'm calling in regard to the Brown case. May I talk to Sheriff Mortenson please?"

"Hold on, Detective. I'll transfer your call. He's been expecting you."

A clear baritone voice came on the line. "Good morning, Detective Sandoval. I've been expecting you to call. Your little friend, Stevie calls you Mister Sandy, may I address you the same?"

Sandy laughed. "You may do that, Sheriff; I'd be pleased."

"Okay, Sandy, and you just call me Mort—that's what everybody here calls me! I'm sure you want me to fill you in on the Brown case?"

Sandy assented, and Mort filled him in on the whole situation. "I have your secure fax number from the network directory and I'll have my office fax you copies of the paperwork including the incident report and Missus Brown's statements. You can get copies to the FBI agent there at your field office. I'll also send you an inventory of everything we found in the car and copies of the paperwork on the transfer of Mister Brown for neurological surgery."

"Thanks, Mort, I really appreciate that. Just as soon as we have all the paperwork from the district judge and the Feds, I'll let you know. We have a charter jet on standby so when everything's a 'go' we'll be over there. How are you dealing with Missus Brown and Stevie?"

"Sandy, this is without a doubt the strangest case I've ever dealt with in all my years in law enforcement. That Stevie is some kid, and Missus Brown has been one hundred percent cooperative. I know this sounds a little bizarre, but the woman has apparently undergone some kind of mystical experience with angels that saved her life, and it's pretty obvious that Stevie had a lot to do with it—she is completely in love with him. I'll include her location and some phone numbers with the stuff I'm faxing."

"That doesn't surprise me, Mort. We were all praying that Stevie and the Browns would be protected by angels, and that they would find God in all this mess."

"Well, Sandy—looks like your prayers worked."

"Do you have her there in the jail or what?" Sandy asked.

"We had to decide what to do with Stevie, so with the Judge's approval, we have her close by in a motel where they can be together. Stevie promised he'd take care of her."

Sandy laughed. "That sounds like Stevie. By the way, Mort, have you had any news media bugging you there about the case?"

"Not yet we haven't, but I'm sure it's going to hit the wires soon."

"I have a news conference this morning at eleven. I would appreciate it if you would hold off until after that time."

"No problem, Sandy. I don't like reporters, and the less I have to deal with them the better."

"Okay, Mort, I'll let you go. I'm looking forward to meeting you. God bless!"

"You too, Sandy, talk to ya later."

At eleven, Sandy and Will were at the court house steps where microphones and cameras had been set up.

"Ladies and gentlemen, my name is Detective Randall Sandoval, and I'm the lead investigator in the Brown case. Standing here beside me is Will Brent, who is the chief investigator with the district attorney's office. I will read a statement prepared by the Police Department, and then either Will or I will field questions. However, we will not answer

Josie's Gift

any questions that may jeopardize our ongoing investigation. We will give you copies of this statement as soon as we are finished."

Sandy began to read from his statement. "As you know, yesterday we reported that Stevie Brown, the son of Roger Brown, who was convicted of murder and who subsequently died in a shootout at the court house, was abducted. We can now confirm that the abductors were John and Doris Brown, who are the parents of Roger Brown and grandparents of Stevie Brown. As a result of an accident over near Littleville, Louisiana, John Brown is in critical condition and confined at a hospital. Doris Brown is now in the custody of Sheriff Paul Mortenson in Littleville. Due to some very unusual circumstances, which I will not go into, Stevie is staying there with his grandmother. As soon as we have paperwork complete, we will be flying to Littleville to bring Doris Brown and Stevie back to Rock City. We'll take questions at this time."

"Detective Sandoval, you haven't told us about the condition of Doris Brown and Stevie."

"Miraculously, neither of them was injured in the accident, and both are fine." Sandy pointed to another reporter.

"Detective, is Doris Brown in jail, and if so, where is Stevie being held?"

"I'm sorry but for security reasons, we will not release that information. Another question?"

"Detective Sandoval, what is the condition and the location of John Brown?"

"At this moment we do not know his condition except that last night it was critical. For security reasons, we cannot release the location where he is being treated."

"Mister Brent, will this become a federal kidnapping case, and will the FBI and U.S. Marshalls be involved?"

Sandy moved away from the microphone so Will could answer the question. "All I can say at this point is that the FBI has been involved in the case all along, but at this moment it has not been decided whether or not it will be a federal or a state case."

Sandy stepped back and was handed a note by Smitty. He went back to the microphone, "Ladies and gentlemen, I just received something new on the case that we must investigate. There will be no more questions at this time. Thank you!"

Questions were vigorously flying around as Sandy and Will, led by Smitty, stepped away from the microphones and hurried inside the court house behind them.

Looking at the paper Sandy had in his hand, Will asked, "What's that all about?"

Sandy handed him the paper. Will looked at it, turned it over and started laughing. "This sure does look important, Sandy. We'll need to get right on it." Will handed the paper to Smitty who was laughing at a blank piece of paper.

"Thanks, Smitty," Sandy said. "I was ready to get rid of that crowd and a blank piece of paper did the trick."

From the news conference, they went directly to Smokey's Steak House. At Smokey's, Will and Sandy sat talking and drinking coffee. Both men stood when a woman walked to their table and smiled. Sandy pulled out a chair for her to sit down. "You gentlemen look mighty comfortable," Agent Landers said in a friendly tone. "Have you ordered?"

Will smiled, "You're two minutes late, and we've already ordered and eaten," he teased.

"Forgive my crazy friend here, Lil. Whenever a beautiful and intelligent woman is around, Will gets a little beside himself—no, we haven't ordered yet." They all laughed.

"I'll have water without ice and some coffee," Lillian addressed the waitress. Turning to Will, she asked "Have both of you read the paperwork from Littleville?"

"Yeah, we've both read all of it. Sandy has a copy for you in his briefcase. From here it looks to be a pretty straight forward case of a relative abducting a child with some really interesting sidebars."

Lillian turned to Sandy. "Before this was an abduction, how'd it all go down?"

"You remember the case of Roger Brown and the shooting at the court house."

"How could I forget that, Sandy? You were the hero of the day."

"Lillian, please don't use the word 'hero' relating to my actions. I was just doing my job—it's what the people of this city pay me to do. I made a decision—a decision to kill someone. I hope I never have to make that decision again the rest of my life..."

"...but if you do, you'll do what you have to do," she interjected. She put her hand on Sandy's arm, which made him slightly uncomfortable. "Sandy, that's what makes you a good cop." She could tell he was uncomfortable and smiled at him. "Okay, let's get back to the Brown's case."

At that moment the lunches arrived, and they all paused for a short prayer by Sandy and then began to eat. They agreed among themselves that it would be best to talk after eating.

When all three had finished eating, they ordered coffee and settled in for a serious discussion. They knew they would have to decide on how to manage the Brown's case. Sandy described to Lillian the details of the Browns arriving in Rock City and the events that led up to the abduction of their Grandson, Stevie. He handed her the stack of papers Mort had faxed and waited while she looked at them.

Lil looked up from the papers at Will. "According to this, the child was six years old when abducted. He was released in Littleville at approximately two AM the morning after the abduction."

"That's what we know from Sheriff Mortenson." Will responded.

Looking back at Mortenson's report, she continued. "Mortenson says that the child was offered the opportunity to be flown back to Rock City, but he wanted to stay with his grandmother and 'take care of her'. Is that one of the interesting sidebars you mentioned?"

"Yes, it is," Will responded!

"Do you think it might be a case of Stockholm Syndrome?"

"Not a chance, Lil. They've been together less than twenty-four hours and had never met before."

"Lil continued looking at Mortenson's report. "Mortenson also says that there was absolutely no indication of any violence involved, or any indication of intent to use or threaten to use deadly force."

"Another interesting sidebar, huh?" Will asked.

Lil turned to Sandy, "What was the time of Stevie's abduction from your back yard?"

"Approximately nine-thirty AM," Sandy answered.

"So, he was released within a twenty-four-hour period of time, huh?"

"That's what it looks like," said Will.

"Very interesting case!" Lil said.

"Here's another one, Lil. For the time being, Doris Brown and Stevie are staying together in a motel in Littleville, arranged by, none other than, Sheriff Mortenson himself."

Lil smiled at the two men. "Okay, you guys! I'll take this to the federal prosecutor and see what he says, but if it were up to me, I think you would have a state case, and we wouldn't need to be involved. We've got too many other things on our plate right now and we don't need a case like this one to add to it." She put her hand up, "But...don't make any hasty assumptions until you get confirmation."

"And how long will that take?" Will asked.

"Oh...I'd say not more than a year." She laughed as the two men gasped. "Naw," she said. "I know you guys want to get that kid back here as soon as possible. We'll get something to your boss just as soon as we can, Will—maybe tomorrow morning."

As Lil got up to leave, the two men stood and shook her hand.

"Thanks for lunch," she said in a very musical voice.

Sandy decided to call home. "Hi, Joann, is Josie still there with you?"

"She's taking a nap, Sandy. This whole experience has taken a big toll on her—probably even more than the shooting at the court house."

"Okay, got something to write with? Okay, here's some information on where Doris and Stevie are staying for the time being. Write this down: Plaza Motel in Littleville. Phone number there is two-two-five, three-six-one, four-nine-six-two. Room number is one-one-six. Got that?"

"I got it Sandy, I'll give it to Josie as soon as she's up."

Josie jumped out of bed when she heard the phone ring and rushed to the bathroom to wash her face then ran downstairs. "I heard the phone, Joann. Any news?"

Joann looked at Josie. She saw worry and anxiety in her eyes. "Josie, it's probably going to be a couple of days or more before everything can be arranged to bring Missus Brown and Stevie back here."

"But I thought Stevie would be coming back right away!" She blurted, with tears forming in her eyes.

"According to Sandy, the sheriff in Littleville has them in a motel until he gets the necessary paperwork from here." Joann took her hand. "Stevie wanted to stay with his grandmother and felt like he needed to take care of her."

"But what about me? I'm his mother! Doesn't he understand the Browns are bad people?"

"Maybe they aren't such bad people after all, Josie."

"Then why did they take my child away from me?" She screamed.

Joann tried to take Josie's hands, but Josie turned away screaming.

She was angry and vigorously animated every word. "He's my child—do you hear? He's mine, and I want him back. Why would he want to stay with someone who hates him?"

Joann was seeing a side of Josie she hadn't seen—but Josie was after all, a mother. She felt like she was losing an argument with Josie. "Josie, Sandy called and gave me the information on where Stevie and Missus Brown are staying. I have the phone number, but under the present circumstances and your state of mind, I'm not going to share it with you until you can think this thing through and be a little more rational and forgiving."

Josie glared at her, "Give it to me!" She screamed.

"No, Josie not yet."

"Then take me back to the mission, at least there I have friends."

Joann felt like a knife had been thrust into her heart. "Sure, Josie, it's probably time for you to go back anyway. Get your things, and I'll take you back."

In the car, a dark cloud seemed to hang over them. Josie was silent and sullen, and she didn't say one word the whole trip. She didn't even say thank you when they arrived. She got out of the car and rushed straight to her room. Joann went looking for Isabelle.

"Hi, Joann, How's Josie holding up?"

"Not very well, I'm afraid."

Isabelle got up and hugged her. She could see hurt and disappointment in Joann's eyes. "Okay, let's talk."

By the time she had finished her story, Joann had tears in her eyes. "I feel like I've failed her, Isabelle."

"No, Joann. You haven't failed. Imagine how you'd feel under the same circumstances if it was your child. Right now Josie's angry, and she's taking it out on anyone close by—and you just happened to be there when she needed an outlet. Changing the subject a little—what I find interesting is Stevie's choice to stay and take care of his grandmother. Just think what a wonderful and sensitive child he is."

Joann searched Isabelle's eyes. She smiled, "I never thought of it that way, and I'm sure Josie can't see it that way right now. Just think, Isabelle. In less than twenty-four hours, grandmother and grandson saw each other in an entirely new light."

"Yes," Isabelle said. "The light of the Lord Jesus shone into those two hearts and gave them the most precious gift of all—love! And God has a wonderful plan for that relationship."

For several long moments, Joann and Isabelle were silent—just taking time to think about what kind of child they were dealing with.

Joann took a paper out of her purse. "Here's information telling how to call Stevie and Doris Brown. When Josie had her melt-down, I decided not to give it to her. Had she called at that time, there would have been some hearts broken with harsh words."

"That was a wise thing to do."

The two women hugged. "I'll leave you now. I need to get home before Sandy gets there. Thanks, Isabelle."

Joann turned and left. Isabelle decided Josie needed some space. She walked down the hall until she found Carla and told her of the situation. "Carla, I think you can handle this best. Here's the information I got from Joann. Give it to Josie when you think she's ready."

"Okay, I'll just remind her she has some duties to take care of and we'll go from there. She'll come around."

Josie's Gift

Josie nursed her anger and brooded over Stevie for the rest of the day. She was restless and did not sleep well that night. At breakfast the next morning Carla sat down beside her. "Hi, Girl, feeling better today?"

Josie just looked at Carla, her eyes flashing anger. "Why don't you just leave me alone, Carla? Just leave me alone!"

"Josie, you have some duties to perform here at the mission, and we've allowed you a little slack the last few days, but it's time to pick up the hoe again."

Josie just glared. She got up from the table and walked at a fast pace to the stairs and up to her room. Carla waited five minutes and then followed. When she arrived at Josie's room, she was packing her and Stevie's things in a couple of old suitcases and some bags.

Carla remained perfectly calm, "Where're you going, Josie?"

Josie was so absorbed with what she was doing that she hadn't noticed Carla come to the door. "Out," Josie screamed. "Out of here ...away from this place...and away from everybody!"

Carla kept her cool and spoke kindly. "Josie, where will you go?"

In the few moments it took her to think about Carla's question, pictures of the Sundown Motel flashed in her mind, and she smiled. "I'll get by, Carla...somehow I'll get by!"

"Josie," Carla said in a direct and confronting tone. "Go over to that window and look out there."

Josie glared at her for a few seconds, then in a defiant gesture swung her head and walked to the window.

"What do you see out there, Josie?" Carla asked.

Josie looked for a few moments then turned back to Carla without answering the question. "Leave me alone, Carla!" She screamed.

"That's the street out there, Josie. When you leave here, that's where you'll be...and you'll be alone. When you get to wherever you're going, please let us know where it is so we know what to tell Stevie."

"Stevie doesn't care about me anymore. He's got his grandma, don't you know?" She screamed.

"I know he will want to know about you, so please leave us a message and let us know where you go. I'm going to the chapel now for my morning prayers. Good-bye, Josie—may God go with you." Carla turned and went to the chapel.

CHAPTER FIFTEEN

After Carla left the room, Josie walked back to the window. Through her own translucent reflection in the glass, what she saw was a bright, clear day—the sun was warm and inviting. Her soul, in its dark despair, wanted to reach out and grasp that warmth. The sky was a clear azure blue that seemed to express warmth of its own—like a giant, warm, blue hand was gently caressing the earth. She looked down at the grounds around the mission and saw color in the flowers and trees that had been planted and carefully nurtured by loving hands. Across the streets in all directions, there were rundown buildings, some abandoned, with weeds growing and trees falling down; with garbage cans on the curbs, and used and decaying furniture lying in the yards. There was no color. There was nothing to make them warm, no hands to care for them and nurture them back to life. It was almost as if they were a projection, through the window of her own cold, and embittered soul.

Her clothes, and the few earthly possessions she had, were lying quiet and waiting when she turned back to the bed. She just stood and stared at them—for long minutes she stared—with watering eyes, she stared. She thought about the mission and how broken, castaway people come through the doors and are nurtured and cared for and brought back to life by people like Isabelle and Carla, Darlene, Martin and Father Jeremy. Like those rundown buildings out there, people come here with no color and no life. And like the mission grounds, loving hands tenderly care for them and raise them up to new life.

Josie closed her eyes and screamed, "Oh God, why can't I understand this? Why is my son being taken from me by a bad woman? Where do I fit into this mess?"

She opened her eyes and was just about to walk out the door to find Carla when she spotted the envelope on top of her dresser. It was the letter from her mother that she had not yet opened and read. She picked it up and sat down on the edge of the bed. With trembling fingers, she carefully tore open the envelope and slowly pulled the letter out of its place of safety.

My dearest and my darling Daughter Josie,

Often I have thought of your soft touch and your beautiful smile—often have I longed to look into the warmth of your eyes. Dad and I have missed you so much, and we have prayed every day to Adonai Elohim for your safety and your well being. We have worried for seven long years, and now we know that our Yeshua has spared your life and preserved your soul.

We have seen you on the television and read of you in the newspaper. We are so sorry for the tragedy that has befallen Roger. We know you loved him, and we mourn for him and for you. What a beautiful son you have. Stevie looks so much like you when you were that age.

Even though you chose another way of life than the life you had with us here, we have never stopped loving you, nor have we for even one moment forgotten you. We have forgiven you for the hurt your leaving left in our hearts, for we know that hurting us was not your intention.

Josie's Gift

> *We pray every day for you and for Stevie, and we wish you well in your new-found life there in Rock City. Please, when you can find it in your heart, come home. Love and blessings upon you and Stevie, Shalom*
> *Mom and Dad*

Josie sat down and leaned back against one of the bags of clothes she had packed, her legs dangled over the side of the bed. She closed her eyes and entered a private world only she knew was there. For a few moments, she let her mind wander back in time. A little six-year old little girl was playing in the yard, chasing a golden retriever who was having the time of his life. They wrestled and played until she was exhausted, and lay in the soft grass, gazing at the clouds drifting by in the sky above. A cold nose brushed her cheek, and a warm tongue caressed her ear. A voice was calling, *"Josie! Come quickly, Mi'jita, I need you to help me with Grandpa."*

Josie struggled up to her feet and ran to the house. Grandmother enveloped her in her strong arms, and together they walked into the bedroom where Grandfather was confined to a wheelchair. *"Push him over here next to the bed, Mi'jita so we can get him up and into the bed. It is time for his nap."*

Josie pushed the wheelchair to the bed and locked the big wheels as she had been instructed, and together they managed to help Grandfather to the bed. He reached his bony hand to hold onto hers, pulled her over to him and kissed her on the cheek. Before he released her hand, he looked up into her eyes. In his characteristic guttural and gravelly voice, he said, *"Remember Mi'jita, you are a Jew—always, you are a Jew. Never forget it. Someday, Adonai will reveal a gift he has for you. It is a very special gift."*

"But, Grampa, if it is a gift then why can't I have it now?"

"You have it now, my dear Josie—but you do not yet understand it. Yes, understanding will come to you in time.

But be very careful that you do not waste it or misuse it." The old man put his hand upon her head and said, *"Adonai Elohim is your sanctuary, and He will bless you, and you will share your gift with many."* With that, he closed his eyes and rested.

At home, Ruth and Josie talked about Grandma and Grandpa. *"They have been faithful to Adonai and to Yeshua HaMashiach. Among our Jewish Believers, Grandpa has always been regarded as a leader, and often as a prophet. Our people put great faith in what he says because it is said that he has the gift of wisdom, and he talks intimately to Adonai just as Moses did of old."*

Josie just looked at her mother in amazement and could not seem to fathom any of what was said. But she had learned from the time when she could first remember, that Grandfather was a very holy man, and she held him in very high esteem as she was taught to do. He was a highly regarded Elder in the little community of Sephardim, who gathered in homes on Shabbat to celebrate their own ancestral traditions. In addition, as baptized Believers, they attended Assembly of God services on Sunday. Her father, Moisés was the old man's son and inherited the gifts and esteem of his father in the circle of local Sephardim. They all dreamed of one day having a synagogue for Messianic Jews and Gentiles alike so they could again worship like their fathers of old.

It had been a long time since Josie had even thought about those happy days of her childhood and of the family traditions that had preserved their identity for many centuries. She remembered asking her father about their ancestors. His answer: *"Our ancestors were Sephardim. That means they were Jews from Spain. Because of the Inquisitions brought upon our people by the Catholics in Spain and Mexico, they were forced to be baptized and to deny and abandon their Jewish faith for the Christian faith. The Church and the government took away their homes and lands, and the*

Sephardim were scattered throughout the whole earth. The Blandón ancestors found their way to Mexico and then to the United States. For generations we kept the deep dark secret hidden, pretending to be practicing Christians in order to avoid suspicion and persecution. We have carried our Jewish teachings and traditions in our hearts, and passed them along to our children. At some point in time, our ancestors began to understand the messianic message and the truth about Yeshua, who was a Jew and at the same time the Messiah. In the fullness of our appointed time, Adonai, opened our eyes and revealed to us His glorious truth, and our Jewish faith became whole and complete. Now, there are no Inquisitions, now there are no burnings and forced conversions, and to its credit, the Church has condemned such things. And so now, we can carry on our faith as Jews but in a Messianic tradition."

As the memories faded, Josie walked back to the window. She had always felt confused about being a Jew and at the same time being a Believer in Jesus. When she looked down at the yard below, she saw what she thought was a dream. Children had gathered in a large circle with a smaller circle in the center of the larger one. Carla was in the larger circle leading the children in songs, and they were dancing, first one way and then the other, around and around in the circles, moving in opposite directions. She opened the window so she could hear the children's voices.

*Hine ma tov
uma nayim
shevet achim gam yachad.
Hine ma tov
uma nayim
shevet achim gam yachad.*

*Lai, lai lai lai, lai lai lai lai lai
lai lai lai, lai lai lai lai.*

*Lai, lai lai, lai, lai lai lai lai lai
lai lai lai, lai lai lai lai.*

*Hine ma tov
uma nayim
shevet achim gam yachad.
Hine ma tov
uma nayim
shevet achim gam yachad.*

The English translation is: *"How good and pleasant it is for brethren to dwell together in unity" (From Psalm 133)*

    Josie couldn't contain the smile that was growing on her face. With tears in her eyes, she turned and rushed down the stairs. Even before she joined the circles, her hands were clapping above her head, and her feet were playing out the steps to the dance she remembered from long ago. She placed herself in the outer circle opposite Carla and sang and danced as never before. She was a child again, it was Shabbat, and the children and women were dancing and laughing and singing praises to Adonai. Around and around they went until she thought her heart would burst with pure joy.

    When it stopped, Josie collapsed in the grass. She was looking straight up at the beautiful azure sky with passing clouds that seemed to take the shapes of every living thing—it was as if out there somewhere, Noah's Ark was waiting to take them on board. Tears of rejoicing were clouding her eyes, and she felt whole and complete. She didn't understand it all now, but her faith was renewed in the knowledge that soon she would know and understand. Carla lay down beside her and turned her head.

"Josie, I didn't know you knew those dances!"

"They're from my childhood. Every Shabbat, all the women and girls danced like that as we and the men sang praises to Adonai." Josie raised her head up and rolled over on one elbow and looked at Carla. "I am a Believer by baptism, Carla, but..." she added proudly, "...I am a Jew by birth."

Carla sat up, "Josie, that's wonderful. You're a Messianic Jew. What a privilege to be descended from the people God chose to be his own, to give birth to the great prophets, and to give birth to our Savior Jesus Christ." She paused thoughtfully. "An elderly Jewish woman came here long ago and taught us those songs and dances. When we have more time, I want you to tell me all about your family and your heritage."

Both women stood up, turned to each other and came together in a warm and lengthy embrace. Josie felt like she had found and accepted a major part of her identity that had been lost for too many years. She went straight back to her room, unpacked and put away all her and Stevie's clothes.

For the remainder of the day, Josie's feet danced from place to place, and her heart sang those songs from long ago. As she went about her duties, she thanked God for yesterday with its pain, and for this day and the love that had brought this joy to her heart. Now she must call Joann and apologize for her behavior yesterday.

"Hi, Joann, this is Josie."

Joann couldn't believe what she was hearing. The voice was the polar opposite of yesterday. She sensed something had changed in Josie. "Yes, Josie. It's good to hear from you. How are you doing?"

"Oh, Joann, you just can't believe what has happened in my life just since yesterday. I feel like a new person."

"It sounds like you had an encounter with the Lord, Josie."

"It's more than that Joann. I've found a piece of me that I had cast aside and left behind seven years ago, a part of me that I never quite understood. I'll tell you about it later—but right now, I want to apologize for my behavior yesterday, and I ask you to forgive me. I know I must have hurt you with my words and actions."

With tears in her eyes Joann silently thanked God for Josie's experience, whatever it was. "Yes, Josie, yes, yes—I forgive you, and God forgives you."

"Thank you, Joann, for being a friend. I love you and Sandy more than I can ever express. I'll let you go now—I need to get back to my laundry."

After evening chapel and prayers, Josie lay in her bed thinking about Stevie. He must learn about his heritage. He hasn't had the benefit of a grandfather and father like she'd had, who would teach the beautiful Jewish traditions to the children.

Some inner thought drew her to the letter from her mother. She got out of bed and picked it up from her dresser and read it again. A few of the words stood out at her like a huge flashing neon sign.

"Yes, that's it!" She said to herself. There they were, and she could hear her mother's voice, *"...we know that hurting us was not your intention."*

She pondered those words and continued her conversation with herself. *"Hurting me was not Stevie's intention! His intentions were pure, unlike mine when I left home—mine were selfish, and I was thinking only of myself. Stevie, in his innocence, was thinking of his grandmother, not himself."* A thought passed through her mind, but she quickly dismissed it, *"I've been thinking like an immature teenager."*

Carla was still awake and reading when she heard the knock at her door. She unlocked the door and opened it to see who was there. "Oh, Josie! Come on in. What brings you here at this time of the night?"

Josie handed Carla the letter from her mother. "This is a letter I got from my mom a few days ago."

"You want me to read it?"

"Yes, especially that last part."

Carla scanned the letter and focused on the next to the last paragraph. "You mean this part about forgiveness?"

"The next part!"

"Where she tells you that she knows you didn't intend to hurt them when you left?"

"Yes, that part! God showed me tonight; Stevie didn't mean to hurt me when he wanted to stay with his grandmother. He was only thinking of her, not himself. And when I left home, I was only thinking of myself."

Carla smiled. Josie, I'm proud of you for that—but there's another thing here about forgiveness. You see how God's grace in forgiveness is passed on from one to another?"

Josie looked puzzled.

"Josie, your mother knew and experienced the fullness of the forgiveness of God. She forgave you, and now you must forgive Stevie. **And**, Josie you must forgive John and Doris Brown. Can you see God at work here? There was a string of evil deeds that God didn't intend for any of you, yet He has turned them all into good for all of you. That's how God works. Listen to what He says!"

She turned her bible to Jeremiah 29:11, "...'Yes, I know what plans I have in mind for you, Adonai declares, plans for peace, not for disaster, to give you a future and a hope.' Isn't our God Wonderful? And Paul says in Romans 8:28, 'We are well aware that God works with those who love him, those who have been called according to his purpose, and turns everything to their good'."

"I'm beginning to see that, Carla. Will you pray with me?"

Both women got on their knees, and Carla prayed. "Abba Adonai! It is you who is our refuge and our strength in times of trouble and in times of joy and happiness. It is you who is our light and our guide. Your Name is to be praised for the revelations you have graciously given Josie on this day, and for turning her tears of sadness and despair into tears of joy and praise. We ask in the name of Yeshua HaMashiach. AMEN."

They stood up and hugged. "Now, Josie," Carla said. "It will be very soon that you will be reunited with your son, and you will meet your mother-in-law, Doris Brown. I want you to think carefully about what you will say, and then when you open your mouth, let your words be words of healing and grace, forgiveness Josie—forgiveness."

Josie turned to leave. Before she closed the door behind her, she turned and looked at Carla, "Yes, Carla! I have learned, and I am determined to do as you say, for what you say is the truth. You are a good teacher—like my mother, who was a good teacher. Thank you, Carla, and good night!"

As Josie lay in her bed, she thought over all the events of the past two days. Then suddenly, she sat straight up in bed. *"Carla's prayer!"* She said aloud. *"Carla addressed her prayer, Abba Adonai, and closed in the name of Yeshua HaMashiach. Carla's a Messianic Jew!"* She almost bounded out of bed and headed back to Carla's room, but she controlled her impulse. *"We'll talk about that tomorrow!"* She said, and lay back and fell into a peaceful, and restful sleep.

The next morning, as soon as breakfast was over, Josie headed for the chapel and her morning prayers. She sat quietly beside Carla. When they had finished their meditation and prayer, Josie asked Carla the question that was on her mind. "Carla, are you a Messianic Jew?"

Josie's Gift

"Yes, Josie I am. My family name is Schmid, and my ancestors originally came from Austria. They fled to America in the early eighteen hundreds when wars and revolutions were breaking out everywhere in Eastern Europe." Carla smiled; "It was my mother who came here some years ago and taught the children those songs and dances."

"Darlene told me you are an ordained minister. If you are a minister, how can you also be a Jew?"

"Like your ancestors, Josie, some of mine were forced to convert, others chose to convert and live as Believers. As time went on, we began to see the wonderful truth of Yeshua and accepted him as the promised Meshiach who would save and redeem our people, and we realized that he was the savior, not only of the Jews, but of the whole world."

"How did you manage to become a minister?"

Carla laughed. "I didn't manage it—God did that part. A generation ago, my family joined the Assemblies of God Church. At that time there were no Messianic Synagogues. When I felt called to the ministry, I was up front about my ancestry. I was accepted as a Jewish Believer. I believe I am fulfilling what God intended for His people the Jews; to bring His salvation to the world." She smiled a big smile, "And the part of that world God sent me into is right here in this mission in Rock City. We work together with our Gentile brothers and sisters, Catholic, Protestant and Jewish, to bring the message that the savior has come. He died, and rose from the dead, and sits at the right hand of God the Father in Heaven. Each year, here in the mission, we celebrate the holy days of the Church and we also celebrate the holy Jewish days such as Haggadah, a Messianic Passover; and Hannukah, the Festival of Lights, and of course, Yom Kippur. Come up to my room for a few minutes. I want to show you something."

Josie's Gift

Carla opened a drawer in her nightstand beside her bed and took out a small four sided top. Holding it up to Josie she asked. "Do you remember what this is, Josie?"

Josie took the object in her hands and reverently held it up. She swallowed hard. "It's a dreidel, Carla. We had one in our family and the children played with it every Hannukah."

"Do you remember what the inscriptions on each side stand for?"

Josie thought back to her grandfather's teaching. "I know it has four letters of the Hebrew alphabet that stand for words which remind us of the miracle of the oil for the lamp stand in the temple of God."

"And, do you remember a song about the dreidel?"

Josie began to hum a tune. Then she smiled and began to sing;

"I have a little dreidel
I made it out of clay
And when it's dry and ready
Then dreidel I shall play.

Dreidel, dreidel, dreidel
I made it out of clay,
Dreidel, dreidel, dreidel,
Then dreidel I shall play."

"Did your mother make sufganiyah, latkes, and buñuelos."
"Oh, yes, Carla. Do you know to make them?"
"I'm afraid I've forgotten those things," Carla responded.
"Perhaps my mother can make some and send them."
Carla smiled. "We can dream, Josie."

Josie was awestruck. In her wildest dreams, she never could imagine that there were people—Jews like her—who were Believers, and who ministered the love of God wherever they were called. She turned back to Carla. "I wonder if God has called me?"

"Yes, Josie. He calls us all to serve Him, and He gives us gifts that are specifically designated for each one of us, and places us where those gifts can best be used for His glory. Do you think, Josie, that you're being here is an accident of fate?"

"I suppose not. I hadn't ever thought about that, but sometimes it seems like there's no meaningfulness in the things that happen—they just happen, and for no reason."

Think about it, Josie, and pray for God to show you your gifts, and help you to understand them, and show you your calling and where you are to be."

Josie was about to leave, but she whirled around again with surprise on her face. "When I was just six years old, my grandfather told me God had given me a gift, and He would bring me to an understanding of it. How odd, that you would mention it now, nineteen years later!"

"Your grandfather was a wise old Jew, Josie."

"Yes, he was," she said, as she turned to leave for her duties.

CHAPTER SIXTEEN

Doris and Stevie were spending the evening in their motel room watching a movie. There was a knock at the door.

"Wonder who that is," Doris asked, looking at her watch.

"You want me to answer the door, Grama," Stevie asked.

"Yes, Dear, I would like that very much."

Stevie rolled over out of the big stuffed chair he was sitting in and hit the floor on his feet. He ran to the door and opened it. To his amazement, there stood a man in a black suit and clerical collar carrying a basket of fruit and goodies. He turned his head, "Grama, there's a...a priest here!"

"Oh my," Doris said. "Ask him to come in!"

At Stevie's invitation, the man entered and walked to Doris. He held out his hand and spoke, "Missus Brown, I'm Reverend William Bertrund, chaplain at the county jail. Everybody just calls me Reverend Bill. Sheriff Mortenson notified me that you were here, and that you might have some needs." He placed the basket on the table and smiled at Stevie's immediate interest.

"Thank you for coming by, uh...Reverend Bill. I guess you probably know my story by now."

"Well, not all of it—only the part that brought you to Littleville. The basket is for you and Stevie to enjoy while you're here. We try to make our guests feel welcome even though they may come to us under uh...very unique circumstances."

"Stevie and I appreciate your generosity. It's a little difficult for us to get out very often because we don't have a car—that is we have a car, but we don't have access to it."

"I understand. Uh...may I sit down?"

"Oh, certainly. I apologize for not being a better hostess."

Reverend Bill turned to Stevie. "Stevie, do you go to school yet?"

"Sometimes I go to kindergarten."

"And so you are about six years old! Am I right?"

"Yep!" Stevie answered. "Reverend Bill, do you know Mister Mortenson?"

"Yes, I'm proud to say that I do, Stevie."

"He's my friend, you know! And, Detective Sandy, he's my friend too. Do you know him?"

"Well, no I'm sorry to say I don't know Detective Sandy. But, I'm sure he's a good friend and a fine detective."

"Yep," Stevie said as he bounced over to the fruit basket. He picked out an apple and turned to his Grandma, "Can I have this apple, Grama?"

"Yes, you may, Dear," Doris answered.

"Missus Brown, have you heard anything regarding your husband yet?" Reverend Bill asked.

"I called the hospital this morning and they said he was still in critical condition. He's had several surgeries to fix the bleeding problems but seems to be stable. I still can't speak to him though."

"Is there anything you need? Anything we can do for you while you're here?"

Doris thought for a moment. "Not that I can think of, just pray for my husband. We're not uh...,"

"I'm Lutheran, Missus Brown.

Josie's Gift

"Well we still appreciate your prayers. Oh...there is one thing. Would you ask Sheriff Mortenson to call my two sons and tell them where I am and why I'm here?"

"I'd be happy to Missus Brown—on second thought, I'll call them myself."

Doris went to her purse and got out a small book. She wrote down the information Reverend Bill needed to make the calls.

He laughed. "Missus Brown, I will make these calls, and I promise I will pray for your husband. As to you're not being Lutheran, my job is not to bring you Lutheranism, but to bring you Jesus and his love and healing power. I have several brother ministers, including a Catholic Priest, who work with me in the jail ministry, and I'll let them know your need for our prayers. Don't be surprised if one of them shows up to visit. We work very closely together. In the meantime, I'll make the calls as soon as I get back to the rectory."

He got up from his chair and started walking to the door. He turned and blessed Doris and Stevie and prayed for John.

"Thank you so much for coming, Reverend. Your prayers and blessings mean a lot right now. And thank you for bringing the basket."

Reverend Bill shook hands with Doris and then turned to Stevie. Stevie held out his hand, and Reverend Bill took it in his. He bent over to Stevie's eye level and said, "Thank you for taking such good care of your grandmother, Stevie."

As he walked out the door, Stevie asked, "Are you my friend now, Reverend Bill?"

Reverend Bill smiled, "Yes, Stevie I do believe we are friends now."

Doris's eyes were watering a little as she watched her grandson. She realized that she must cherish every moment because it wasn't going to last. When they get back to Rock City she probably will have limited access to him.

It was ten P.M. when Doris' cell phone buzzed. Stevie was asleep on the bed next to her. She quietly got up and went to the door leading to the bathroom and answered the call. "Mom, this's Joe Richard. I just got a call from a man named Reverend Bill. He told me about your situation. Are you ok?"

Doris burst into tears. "Oh...Joe Richard, I'm so glad you called. It's been so long since we talked."

"I know, Mom! And I'm really sorry. Right now, I'm very worried about you." Joe Richard's apology was sincere but then he began to show some of the anger he inherited from his father. "Mom, what on earth possessed you and Dad to do such a thing as abducting your own grandson?"

"Son, right now your father is in very critical condition in Big Pine, a city near here where they have a major medical facility. I haven't been able to see him or talk to him. I know we did wrong, and we will pay the price, but right now I need your help and understanding not your anger and criticism."

Joe Richard said nothing for a few seconds. "Okay Mom, I'll do my best, but please don't expect me to be happy with the situation, okay? I'll call David Lee—if we can get started within the next couple of hours, we can be there after lunch tomorrow. I understand you have Roger's little boy, Stevie there with you."

"Yes, he's here, and he's the most wonderful thing that's happened in the middle of all this tragedy. You're going to love him."

"Okay, Mom, I...I...uh...love you. Please keep your chin up, and we'll take it one day at a time. Bye for now."

Doris hung up the phone and went into the bathroom, shut the door behind her, and sat on the stool and cried. She hadn't seen either of her sons for two years and, except for Christmas cards and Birthday greetings, had no communication with them.

She got up, washed her face and went back to her bed. She was pleased that she would see her sons tomorrow. She worried about John. *"What will I do if he passes away?"* She asked herself.

Joe Richard and David Lee arrived in Littleville at three-thirty the next afternoon. They went straight to the La Plaza Motel and got a room. Doris and Stevie were waiting in the lobby when they arrived. Joe Richard walked straight to his mother and embraced her then squatted down to look at Stevie. Stevie looked up at his Grandmother.

"Stevie, Dear, this is your uncle Joe Richard—and that one over at the counter is your other uncle David Lee."

Stevie looked puzzled. "How come they have two names Grandma?" He asked.

They all laughed. By this time David Lee walked to his mother and embraced her. He put out his hand to shake Stevie's hand and squatted down to embrace him. He stood up and addressed Stevie's question about the names.

"Stevie, we each have two names because that's the way Mother named us. We had the same question you have, but long ago quit trying to get an answer."

"Why?" Stevie asked.

"Well, I guess because whenever we asked her why she and Dad named us that way, she always said, 'ask your father.' And then whenever we asked, Dad he said, 'ask your mother.' Finally, Mother just said; 'that's the way it is, so get used to it and live with it.' So, we did!"

Joe Richard turned to his mother, "Mom, we need to get our stuff into the room, and then we can talk a while."

Doris and Stevie waited in the lobby until Joe Richard and David Lee returned. They sat and talked for a long time. Doris was more interested in catching up on her sons and their families than anything else. After catching up on their lives, she finally told them the whole story of the plot to kidnap Stevie and their trip to Littleville. Not once was Roger's name brought up.

David Lee asked the question that both he and Joe Richard had on their minds, but his tone of voice expressed disapproval at the actions of their parents.

"Why, Mom—why on earth would you do such a thing? What were you thinking?"

Doris looked from one to the other and was silent. Finally she laughed. "You'll have to ask your father that question." She laughed.

Joe Richard didn't see the humor. He scowled a little and sounded angry. "Mom, what possessed you and Dad?"

Doris looked at him for several seconds before speaking— when she did, her words were carefully measured. Tears formed in her eyes as she spoke. "In some twisted way, I guess we thought we could get some peace out of Roger's tragedy by hurting Josie. You see, your father was convinced it was all Josie's fault that he was killed. Now?...now, I know we were very wrong—not just that what we did was illegal—but it wasn't going to solve our, or Roger's problems, and it could never bring Roger back. If it could bring Roger back, do you think he would be different?"

She paused for several long moments and dried her eyes with her sleeve. Joe Richard handed her his handkerchief. She continued, pointing at Stevie who was watching TV. "Look at that little boy over there. He's Roger's flesh and blood—but he's so different from Roger. There's something about him that attracts everybody—they all want to be his friend."

It seemed as if there was so much more to talk about, yet there was thoughtful silence among mother and her two sons. Finally she walked to where Stevie was sitting, pulled him up and held him in a tight embrace. "No matter what happens, Stevie, I love you more than I can say." Then she released him, took his hand, and she motioned to her sons. Cheerfully, she said, "It's time for supper, boys, let's go eat!"

Everybody was smiling when they headed out of the motel lobby and walked down the street to the restaurant.

As they sat waiting for their meals, Joe Richard asked about Roger. "Mom, uh...where is Roger buried?"

"I honestly don't know, Son. We...that is, your father and I... guessed that he was cremated because the county had to pay the bills, but we don't know where he's buried or even if he's buried."

"I know where he's buried, Grandma," Stevie piped up. "That is...he's not actually buried. They put his ashes in a box, and we threw them into the river at Rock City...an' we all cried and said goodbye...an' we told him we forgive him."

"Forgive him for what?" David Lee asked, looking directly at Stevie.

Stevie put on a worried face, looked at his grandma and then at both Joe Richard and David Lee. Doris nodded to him indicating it was okay for him to talk about it. When he spoke he had tears running down his little cheeks.

"We forgave him...uh...uh...because he was so mean all the time." He looked at his uncles again and was hesitant to go on, but Doris took over the story and told them what Stevie had told her about it, adding her own interpretation of the events.

"You see, Roger had problems—really big problems. You two were gone and not seeing what Roger had become. He dropped out of school, he used drugs and pretty much lived a life of petty crime." She took a deep breath before continuing. "He uh...also beat up Josie a lot and killed a store clerk during a robbery. Josie was hurt pretty bad by the last beating and had to have emergency surgery. She also miscarried the child she was pregnant with."

Both her sons looked down as the story unfolded. Finally Joe Richard sighed and said, "Yeah, we heard about some of that on the news but didn't realize it was that bad. Mom, we both feel guilty that we weren't there for you and Dad when you were having all your problems with Roger. I don't know if it would have made a difference for Roger, but at least we would have been there to support you." He looked at Stevie. "I'm very sorry, Stevie. I guess your life was pretty rough. So... how's your mama now?"

Stevie brightened up and smiled. "She's doin' good now. She's at the mission, you know — an' Jesus is takin' care of things for her while I'm gone."

His uncles laughed out loud. "Jesus, huh? Whatever makes you happy, I guess!"

"Yeah," Stevie said with a big grin. "Jesus'll make you happy too if you ask him."

Doris smiled and reached over and touched Stevie's hand. The conversation ended as the food arrived at the table. Doris thanked the waitress and then turned to Stevie. "Would you say grace for us, Stevie?"

Stevie bowed his head. "God is good, God is great, and we thank him for this food! AMEN"

With that, they all ate without saying much, then retired to Doris and Stevie's room to watch television.

After the news was over, Doris looked at Stevie, who was fast asleep. "I think it's time to go to bed, boys. We'll see you in the morning. After breakfast, we'll need to go to Sheriff Mortenson's office and introduce you two so he can tell you what's on the stove for Dad and me."

Next morning they all walked into the sheriff's office, and Doris spoke to the secretary. "I'm Doris Brown, and we'd like to talk to Sheriff Mortenson if that's possible."

"Good morning, Missus Brown. I remember you — is everything okay for you?"

"Yes, we're doing fine. Pointing to her sons, "These are my two sons, Joe Richard and David Lee."

The secretary reached out to shake hands. "I'm sorry, but the sheriff is out on a call at this moment but I expect him back within about thirty minutes. If you'd like to wait, you can sit here, and I'll get you something to drink."

"Thank you, Dear," Doris said. "I'll have some coffee, and I know Stevie will want juice."

Joe Richard and David Lee both asked for coffee. When the secretary delivered the drinks, she pointed to a table off to the side of the next room. "There're donuts there if you'd like some. Help yourself!"

Stevie's eyes brightened and he looked at his grandmother for permission. She nodded her approval and held up one finger, meaning just one was all he could have. He bounced into the room and returned with the prize.

The phone rang and the secretary picked up the receiver and spoke. "Good morning, Sheriff's office, may I help you?"

"This is Gordon Medical Center in Pine City, is Sheriff Mortenson in?"

"No, I'm sorry he's not, but I expect him shortly. Can I take a message?"

"Please ask him to call this number—it's about John Brown, his condition has taken a turn for the worse."

"Okay, I'll call him on the radio right now and give him your number." As she hung up the phone she looked at the Browns but decided it would be best for Sheriff Mortenson to tell them. She punched in a number on her phone and contacted the dispatcher who relayed the message.

Within a few minutes, Sheriff Mortenson walked in through a back door directly to his office and the secretary went in. As he sat down at his desk, he sighed.

"Is it bad news, Mort?" The secretary asked.

"I'm afraid so, Joyce. Show the Browns in."

When the Browns walked in, Mort stood and welcomed them. He extended his hand to shake the hands of Joe Richard and David Lee who introduced themselves. Pointing to the chairs, "Ya'll sit down." Looking directly at Doris, "Missus Brown I'm afraid we have bad news about your husband."

Doris burst into tears and Stevie took her hand. "It'll be okay Grama, Jesus'll take care of us and take care of Grampa."

Both Joe Richard and David Lee put their arms around her but said nothing. Each had his own thoughts to process. Finally Joe Richard spoke. "How bad is it Sheriff?"

"They don't expect him to live very long—maybe only a few hours but perhaps as long as another day. But, nobody knows for sure. Ya'll need to be there with him in his last hours."

"How many hours is it to drive from here to there?" David Lee asked.

"Probably about two or maybe three hours, depending on traffic."

"Can Mom go?"

"That's a horse of another color, David Lee! I'll have to take this to the Judge and get his permission for her to leave the county and I'll need to call Rock City and get at least verbal permission from them."

"So, how long will all that take?" Joe Richard asked.

Mort sighed, "Too long, I'm afraid—but it has to be done. Every 'i' has to be dotted and every 't' crossed for it to be legal. If ya'll go back to the motel and make your plans, I'll get right on this and maybe have some word in a few hours. Oh, and I'd really appreciate it if you'd not call me for information. Trust me to call you as soon as I know anything."

Doris and Stevie were both crying when they left the office and headed back to the motel. By the time they arrived,

Doris had regained control. When Stevie saw his grandmother calm down, he too calmed down and quit crying.

They sat in the lobby and talked. Finally, Joe Richard had a plan. "I think I should rent a car and go right away to Big Pine. As soon as you get word from Sheriff Mortenson, the rest of you can come in David Lee's car."

All agreed that would be best. Joe Richard called a rental agency, got his things packed and left. They all walked to the car and Joe Richard got in and opened the window. "I'll call David Lee as soon as I get there, okay Mom?"

"Be careful, Son," Doris admonished.

Stevie piped in, "I'll ask Jesus to take care of you Uncle Joe Richard."

Joe Richard reached out the window and ruffled Stevie's hair. "I'll just bet He'll do that, Stevie!" There was a hint of skepticism in his voice.

Doris and David Lee walked back to the motel with Stevie between them holding their hands. When they sat down, Doris quipped, "I wish there was a way to call Josie. I really think she should know about this."

Both Doris and David Lee looked surprised as Stevie spoke up. "I know a way Grama!"

"You do?"

Stevie smiled real big. "Yeah, I know the number at the mission!"

David Lee looked admiringly at his newfound nephew. "Good boy Stevie! Let's have it!"

Stevie thought for a few seconds then rattled it off perfectly as his uncle wrote it down.

Doris looked worried. "I'm not supposed to contact her!"

"That's okay Mom. Nobody says that Stevie or I can't contact her."

Doris smiled and looked at Stevie. She handed David Lee her cell phone. He punched in the numbers and then handed the phone to Stevie.

Josie was in the laundry when Isabelle came in with the phone. She was smiling, "A little voice is on the phone wanting to talk to you."

Josie grabbed the phone. Tears were welling up in her eyes, she could hardly speak. She took a deep breath, "Stevie, is that you?"

When she heard his voice her heart leaped in her chest. "Hi Mama. Please don't be worried now, I'm okay." Then with a smile in his voice he said, "Guess what—Uncle David Lee is here with me and Grama."

"Oh, Stevie—that's wonderful. I'm so glad you're getting to meet him. Is Joe Richard there too?"

"No, not now. He went to see about Grampa in another place! Uncle David Lee wants to talk to you, okay?"

"Okay, give him the phone!"

"Hi Josie, it's been a long time."

"Yeah, it's been a long time. How's your family?"

"They're doin just fine. Look Josie, I need to talk to you about Dad. He's taken a turn for the worse and they don't expect him to live."

"Oh, I'm so sorry to hear that. How's your mom holding up?"

"Well, with Stevie's help, she's doing okay. She wants me to tell you that she wants you to be here and be with us when we go to see Dad."

"I don't have money or a car, so that's not possible."

"Josie, this is important to Mom. I'll call the airport right now and buy you a ticket on the next plane out of Rock City. All you have to do is go to the airport there, show them your ID and get on the plane. We'll meet you at the airport here, okay?"

Josie was silent. In a flashing moment she heard her grandfather's prophetic voice. "You have a gift, Josie. Don't waste it."

"Josie, are you okay?"

"Yes, David Lee—I'm okay. I believe God wants me to be there. I'll get my things together and be there as soon as I can. God bless you, and give my love to Doris."

When she hung up the phone she turned; Isabelle was still standing behind her. "Go get your things Girl, I'll call Will and Sandy and let them know what's happening. I'll be waiting for you in the chapel where I'll be praying, then, I'll drive you to the airport."

By the time Josie was ready Will was at the mission waiting. "I'm going to drive you to the airport Josie." He laughed, "I bumped Isabelle off this job."

On the way to the airport they talked. "Mind if I tell you something real personal, Josie?"

"No, Will. Why would I mind?"

"Well, it's just that I don't want to be inappropriate but... well, I just want you to know..."

Josie broke in, "Know what Will?" She smiled coyly.

"You've been through a lot since you and Roger came to Rock City. I don't think I've ever met someone who has held up under such...uh...heartache and disappointment... uh...and outright devilish oppression." He glanced at her. "You've really changed—you've blossomed into a beautiful flower."

She searched his eyes and hung her head. "It's been bad Will—but without people like Sandy and Joanne, and Isabelle and Carla, and...you...I would have never made it. God certainly put me in the right place at the right time." She put her hand on Will's on the steering wheel, "With all my heart—I thank you, Will."

For a moment they looked into each other's eyes—both smiled. Will turned into the airport parking lot and found a spot. He got Josie's bag out of the back seat and they walked in silence into the terminal.

She reported to the ticket counter and got the information about her flight which was scheduled to take off in just fifteen minutes. At the passenger screening point, Will handed her the bag. "This is as far as I can go Josie."

She turned to him and pulled him into an affectionate embrace. "Thank you, Will. Thank you for being here and for being a...friend."

She turned into the screening booth and waved at Will from the other side.

Miraculously, Josie made the plane with only minutes to spare. It was on time, and when she stepped from the airplane into the terminal at Littleville, the first thing she saw was her son. They ran to each other and embraced for several minutes. She bathed his face in her tears and kissed him over and over again. Suddenly he broke from her embrace and turned.

"C'mon Mama. Look, it's Uncle David Lee and Grama!"

In the seconds it took to reach Doris she remembered what Carla had said about forgiveness. The two embraced and through tears Doris asked Josie to forgive her for all the trouble she and John had caused. "Josie, I am so thankful I had Stevie here with me. I don't think I could have made it without him."

Josie held her at arm's length and looked into her mother-in-law's eyes. Together they looked at Stevie. "Yes, Doris. Stevie is a true gift from God. He has been my constant inspiration." Turning her gaze back to Doris, she continued. "I forgive you Doris. I have experienced the wonderful grace of God's forgiveness for all the sin in my own life, and I give it to you in return. With all my heart I forgive you." For several moments she still held Doris' hands in hers. "To be very honest, there were times when I was very angry and I hated you and John for what you did—will you forgive me for that?"

Doris looked into Josie's eyes. "Yes Josie—oh yes, I forgive you and I hope with all my heart that you will not abandon me. You are a bright spot in this old and messed up life of mine!"

She smiled and pulled Josie into another long embrace. Both women were in tears while David Lee and Stevie looked on in awe. Stevie looked up at his uncle with a question in his eyes.

"It's a woman thing, Stevie...a woman thing. In its own way it's wonderful, but it's not something men understand very well." He smiled and picked up Josie's bag. "We best be getting back to the motel Mom.

Stevie walked between his mother and his grandmother as David Lee led the way to the car. Back at the motel they relaxed while Josie and Doris tried to catch up on all that had happened in both their lives in the past seven years.

The call came late that afternoon. "David Lee, this is Sheriff Mortenson. You're all set to go to Big Pine. I've got some paperwork here for you and your mother to sign. As soon as you want to leave, just come by here and if I'm not here, Joyce will have them for you."

"Thanks Sheriff, we'll be there within thirty minutes." David Lee turned to Doris and Josie. "Get your stuff rounded up, we're out of here for Big Pine."

CHAPTER SEVENTEEN

John Brown was strangely aware of the accident, and of being taken to the hospital. It was not actually a conscious awareness—more of a strange state of being—he had no feelings or any sense of the existence of his body. He was aware of voices, yet wasn't hearing. He was aware of lights, but couldn't see them. His existence wasn't dark, and yet it wasn't light either. He was aware of a woman's voice telling him she loved him, but he didn't know who she was. He was aware of a small child telling him he loved him and forgave him, but he didn't know who that was either. He knew he was seriously injured, but he felt no pain.

He had that same awareness of things when he was transferred to another hospital. This time the voices were different. He was aware of someone performing surgery, but he didn't know what it was for or on what part of his body they were operating. It was a very comfortable existence, yet he couldn't identify either happiness or sadness. There were no other people there, wherever he was—he was all alone—completely alone—like in a personal cell in another world. He was aware that he had a body, yet he wasn't in it, and yet every time they moved his body he went with it.

This strange altered awareness went on for some period of time—he didn't know how long, for there was no time where he was. When that time of awareness was over, he seemed to awake from the altered state and could see and hear things in the world in which he once lived. But it was like he was floating above everything. He could see his own body lying on a hospital bed and knew for sure it was his body and not someone else's. He could see the nurses coming and going and tending to the needs of his body—sticking it with needles, changing bed clothes, changing the bottles hanging from a pole, measuring liquid in a bottle hanging beside the bed, injecting medication into one or another of the intravenous tubes to which he was attached. He could hear their voices and could understand what it was they were saying.

An alarm suddenly sounded from one of the machines and nurses came running into the room. A doctor quickly arrived, looked at the machines and then shined a light into his eyes. The doctor called for 100mg of epinephrine which was injected directly into John's heart by means of a long needle. The doctor looked at the monitors and called for the defibrillator.

A technician came in rolling another machine. The technician twisted some dials and handed the doctor two paddles. He put them, one on each side of the chest of the body and yelled "clear". Suddenly the body jumped and twisted a little. The doctor listened to the chest. Green lines on a monitor were flat and a constant sound still emanated from it. The doctor called for another 100 mg of epinephrine in an IV. Still there was no activity. The paddles were again placed on each side of the chest and again the body jumped and twisted a little. Within seconds there was a faint response from the monitor and the flat lines began to course up and down, weakly but rhythmically. All of this, John could see from where he was.

The first time the alarm sounded, John felt like he was descending into a dark hole where he panicked, like he was drowning—he couldn't catch his breath. In what seemed like an eternity, he felt like he was trapped and couldn't get out. Unexpectedly, a light appeared and a shining figure came walking toward him.

"Who are you," John shouted at the figure. As the figure drew closer, he saw something in the face that was kind and yet frightening, and he realized he was looking into the face of death.

"You're Death!" John shouted with fear in his voice.

"Yes, I'm the Angel of Death," the figure responded in a soft yet imposing voice. "Angels are messengers of God, and the Father has sent me with a message for you."

"Am I dead?" John asked.

"No, not yet," Death answered.

"Then what is the message?"

"You'll see in due time, John!"

"It's awfully dark in here! Is there no light?" John asked.

"No, there is no light," Death said.

"Why no light," John questioned, growing more and more anxious and fearful thinking the angel might not be telling the truth about his not being dead.

"There is no light here because God the Father is not here. You see, God is Light, and God is Love, and where God is there can be no darkness—so this darkness is the complete absence of God," Death explained.

"Then who lives here?" John asked.

"Satan who is called the Devil lives here in this darkness, he is the ruler of it," Death said.

"But I thought Satan lived in Hell and there was fire there," John pleaded.

Death laughed. "Yes, there is fire there in Hell but not here. You see this is the portal that leads to the fire. There is a myriad of souls who are, even at this moment, passing through this dark portal on their way to Hell."

John looked around him—he saw nothing but the total darkness.

Death laughed. "You can't see them John, because of the darkness surrounding you, and because Satan doesn't want you to see them, otherwise it may turn you around."

"What about the world out there where I came from. Is the darkness there too?"

"Yes," Death answered in a very serious tone. "There is darkness there—that's where it all starts and it's like a river flowing into this place and then to Hell and the fire."

"B...B...But," John stammered. I don't remember any darkness like this!"

"You don't remember it, but it was there!"

"Why don't I remember it?"

"Because you didn't see it, your mind was closed and your eyes didn't see! Many years ago you turned away from the light, and you chose darkness as your way. Here, take my hand—let me show you something!" John reached his hand out toward Death but was afraid to take the extended hand for fear he would die.

"Will I die if I take your hand?"

"No, John—your time has not yet come. Here take my hand and you will be safe!"

John's hand was shaking as he took hold of Death's hand, but he immediately felt peace and safety once he did.

Suddenly the dark hole disappeared and it was a beautiful, bright, sunshiny day. Clouds drifted through the sky. John looked around—it all looked familiar, the flowers, the little country church, the people. Death pointed to a family sitting in the fourth row of the church—a man, a woman, two little girls and two older boys. John looked carefully but suddenly the sky overhead grew very dark and there were loud claps of thunder and lightning flashing from the sky. John cringed then turning to Death, he pointed to one of the boys.

"Yes, John—that's you. Do you remember that day?"

John was silent then his eyes filled with tears. "That was the day...sob...that was the day I was going to be baptized and give my life to Christ."

Death's eyes grew narrow and his voice changed to a challenge. "Why didn't you give your heart to Jesus and offer yourself for baptism with the others, John?"

"I don't know!" John sobbed. "I was stubborn and..."

Death interrupted "...and proud, John? And arrogant? And angry at God?"

"Yes! Yes!" John sobbed. "And I never went back. Oh God, why didn't I ever go back?"

John turned again to Death, "That's when the darkness really started in my life, wasn't it?"

"Yes," Death responded. "That's when it began to take over. Come, let's look some more." Death again held out his hand.

John stared at the hand and shook his head. "I'm not sure I want to see any more. Do we have to go?"

"John, these are things you must see! If your life is to change, we must go on!"

"You mean there's hope for me?"

"Yes, John there is hope but you must see and recognize the darkness in your life before you can grasp the Light."

Death led the way to a new place. It was beautiful beyond all description. There were many children playing and laughing. They were singing and dancing and never seemed to tire.

"Look over there, John," Death said pointing to one particular child.

John looked at the child and then with a confused look turned back to Death. "Is that... is that...someone I should know?" John asked hesitantly.

"Isn't she a beautiful child John?" Death asked, ignoring John's question.

John turned back to the child. He smiled, almost lovingly. "Yes...yes she is! She is very beautiful. Who is she?"

For what seemed like an eternity, Death just looked at John and then at the child. "John, do you remember Sophie?"

John looked very happy as the memories of Sophie came back to his mind. He had buried those memories so deep in his subconscious mind—he thought they would never come up. They were happy memories until...until the night of the prom. His thoughts began to come out in audible words, "She was so beautiful and I was so arrogant about my manhood. I just had to have her—it would do so much for my image with the other boys..."

He hung his head and turned to Death who finished his thoughts. "...you made love—actually there was no love in it—you had sex that night and a few months later when she found out she was pregnant, Sophie was forced by her parents to have an abortion."

John head came up and his eyes widened. He pointed to the child, "You're going to tell me that child back there is my child, aren't you?"

"Yes John, she is your little girl!"

"But if she was an abortion, she has known neither dad nor mom to look after her. Why is she so happy with the rest of the children?"

"You see John, many babies die a natural death and they too, never know their dads and moms—never know the loving arms of other humans. The Father has set aside this very special place for them and for all the children wantonly killed by their parents through abortions. Here they enjoy the love of the Father, and the welcoming arms of the Lord Jesus, and the fresh air of the Holy Spirit."

John didn't want to ask, but couldn't resist the temptation. "Are...are...are there others here that I should know?"

"I'm afraid so John. For years you prided yourself on how many girls and women you could get into your bed.

There are others here but you didn't know about them. The women had the abortions alone because they were afraid to tell you about it."

"So...so, how many?"

"There are three others here John. Come, I'll show them to you."

John broke out in tears as Death led him through the crowd and pointed three others out for him to see. He couldn't help but gaze for long moments at each one, studying their features. The children went about their play and were not aware of the two strangers in their midst.

"Can I touch them and hold them in my arms?" He asked.

"No," Death replied, they live in another dimension than you, and it is impossible. But now that you have seen them you will never forget them."

"Will we all be together in Heaven?"

"I cannot say, John. That is something only the Father knows." Death paused then continued. "Now I will show you three more children. These are for you and for someone else."

They walked through the myriad of children and stopped in front of three little boys. Death pointed to them. "Look carefully John and study them. These three boys are your grandchildren from Roger and Josie. She had two abortions and then one miscarriage when Roger beat her up."

John looked at the children and then back at Death. He reached out to them, but it was as if they weren't there. He could see their forms but couldn't grasp them.

"John! I told you that you could not touch them. What you have seen here are children you will never hold in your lap, or tell bedtime stories to, or kiss them good night. You will never play baseball with them or go to their graduations or weddings because they will never know those things."

John fell on his knees with his head in his hands. He was sobbing uncontrollably. His throat was choked up and his chest heaved with each sob. "What have I done? What have I wasted? It's all here, but I can't get any of it back. I can't even say how sorry I am." He looked up at Death. "Where is Roger, Death? Where is my son? Has he seen any of this?"

"No, John he hasn't seen any of this. I'm very sorry to say that he was cursing God until the moment he died."

John looked surprised. "How do you know that?"

"I was sent there to be with him. After Josie and Isabelle talked with him the Father sent me—not for Roger's sake necessarily, but because Josie and her friends were praying for him. It was for their sake I was sent. Unfortunately, he refused to see me or listen to the message I took to him through Josie and Isabelle."

"What was the message?"

"The same message that angels, and humans, take to people like Roger—God loves them, and sent His Son, the Lord Jesus, to die for them and to save them from the curse of the darkness!"

"Is there any possible way I can talk to him now?"

"No, that is not possible. I do not mean to be critical, John but—you never talked to him while he was alive so, now it is too late. You see Roger chose the darkness, just like you did, and he went deeper into the darkness with every choice he made. He grew to love the darkness and hate the light because his words, thoughts and actions became increasingly evil. He tried his best to pull Josie into that darkness with him."

"And did he? I mean pull her into the darkness too?"

"Not all the way. You see Josie's mom and dad were praying for her. Every day they pleaded with the Father to protect her and keep her safe from harm and to save her life. Many were the times when she could have been killed but the Father's love kept her safe. In the last moments of his life Roger himself even tried to kill her. You see, he had gone so deep into the darkness that that his mind was ruled by it."

"Are you saying that Roger was possessed by Satan?"

"Well, that's one way to put it—but you must remember that Satan rules the darkness just as God rules the light. Satan is darkness just as God is light. Roger, like many others who are passing through that dark portal and into the flames, chose to live in the darkness and reject the light. There is a point of turning when they make a terminal decision, and from that point they either love the darkness or love the light and they never turn back."

"What is that point of turning, Death?"

"In Roger's case it was his use of alcohol and drugs—mostly alcohol. He began drinking and using drugs at a very early age and you never noticed." Death looked John in the eyes, "...but then, you didn't ever look for it either! You were absorbed in your own life at that point, and you were blind to Roger's problems."

"So, he kept on drinking until...until he couldn't turn away from it, right? He went over that edge and it became a terminal decision?"

"I suppose so," Death answered. "You see, alcohol and drugs have many good purposes but they are things that exist on a razor's edge balanced between darkness and light!"

John turned to Death with a confused look. "I don't understand."

"Well, let me give you an example—wine for instance. I know you drink wine John. And I also know you have been drunk with wine and other alcoholic substances numerous times. To your credit though, you never allowed it to get hold of you and drag you completely into the darkness." Death held up his hand, "But—that doesn't mean that you were sinless during those episodes either."

John was embarrassed. "I'm really sorry you had to see that. I know there were times when I made a fool out of myself and Doris was furious with me for it."

"Yes, she had every right to be furious with you. Well, back to the example. You have personally experienced the negative things about alcohol and seen how easy it is to fall off that razor's edge. But think for a moment about how wine can be a holy thing and bring blessing to people who are Christians and Jews."

"You mentioned Jews!"

"Yes, John. They are God's chosen people and He still loves them and has plans for them."

"What plans?"

"The Father knows, John—trust Him. Back to the wine! You see wine is a very sacred part of the Jewish celebration of the Passover—you've heard of that haven't you?"

"Something about the Angel of Death helping them leave Egypt! Hey! Was that you?"

Death smiled. "Yes, John I was there, but there were very special angels God sent to carry out the punishment on Egypt. I just directed the traffic."

"I'm beginning to understand."

"You see, John, in God's church which is the mystical Body of Christ, the Passover is carried on in what is called the Eucharist or Communion celebration of the New Covenant. When Communion is celebrated, bread and wine are offered on the altar to represent for you the body and blood of the Lamb. It is a very sacred and solemn sacrament in which both the bread and wine are blessed and offered to become the body and blood of Christ for you as you partake of it in faith. Just as the Jews killed the Passover lamb and offered the unleavened bread and sacred wine as a symbol of their faith in obedience to the Father, so you partake in the same continuing and never ending covenant between God and His people through the bread and wine of Christian Communion."

"But I know people who go to church and even take Communion and also go out and get drunk and do all sorts of bad things!"

"Yes, I know that, and so does the Father. But—the point of turning, the terminal decision will come for each of them and they will choose either the darkness or the light. They cannot go on having it both ways. They cannot live on the edge of the razor."

"Death," John queried. "Will I remember all of this wherever it is that I'm going next?

"You are asking a very important question, John. When people live in the darkness and eventually are pulled into the fire, they will, for all of eternity, remember the evil and darkness they chose for themselves. They will be immersed into an everlasting sorrow. If that is where you end up, yes, you will remember what you have seen, just like you do now. You will plead for repentance and you will grind your teeth and curse the day of your birth, but there will be no point of turning—no chance to change."

"Must I see more?"

"Yes, John—there is more! Come!"

Death took John's hand and they came to a very nice upscale restaurant inside a very fine hotel. "Do you remember this place John?"

"It looks familiar, but I...I'm not sure."

"Here's a clue. You see that table over there in the corner?

"Yes, what about it?"

"Look carefully, John! You should recognize someone."

John looked again then quickly turned his head away. "Nobody was supposed to see us there. How did you know about it?"

"John, John—the Father's eyes are everywhere."

"Does Doris know about this?"

"It's best for you and her that she didn't!"

"Wow, that's a relief!"

"Not so fast John."

John hung his head. "You know about the others too, don't you Death."

"Yes, and so does the Father. You see how close you lived to the edge of the portal of Hell and darkness? Every time you placed your foot into that dark portal, it got easier and easier didn't it? Each step took you one step closer to the terminal decision."

"Oh Death, what must I do? What must I do....?" John was sobbing. His tears were real but seemed to disappear as they ran down his face.

"The Father wants you to know that He loves you and His will is for you to clean up your life and worship Him and Him only. You must repent, turn around and abandon all the sin from your past, and even abandon some of your friends, who are no more than enablers, and who want you to occupy the darkness with them. You must confess your sin and ask the Father's forgiveness, then accept the Lord Jesus into your heart and life."

"I know there's more. But must we go on?"

"No, John. I believe that you've seen what you need to see and it's time to return. After you return you will examine your life and you'll have the opportunity to repent and make amends to those you have wronged. Don't let it scare you, for it will be a process of cleansing for you."

"To where am I returning?"

"To the body you left a few minutes ago!"

"You mean we've only been away a few minutes and—please Death, can't I stay and be with those children. They are so happy and contented."

"John, the Father has a plan for your life and He has instructed me to take you back. There have been people praying for your life to be restored and He has heard those prayers. Remember John, it is for them you are going back—not for yourself. You really don't matter anymore. It is all for them. You have a wife, two sons, three beautiful daughters-in-law, and eight grandchildren. And never forget your children and grandchildren who are back there in heaven—tell others never to forget the women who are considering abortion and the men who made them pregnant. Your daughter-in-law, Josie, has a very special gift from God. As you transition back to your dimension, it will be her hands you will feel, and it will be her voice you will hear. Treasure her for the rest of your life and listen to her. She has been given the gift of wisdom of her grandfather and of her father."

"But she's a Jew!"

"Yes, she's a Jew—one of the chosen of God. And she is also a Believer—she has accepted Jesus as the Messiah. To her and her people, Jesus is called 'Yeshua Mashiach'. She loves you, John. When you get back, tell others that you have been to the door of death and you have seen the dark river leading to the fire. Tell them about the special place in the Father's love set aside just for the children. Warn them that they must turn from their sin and forsake the darkness. Come now."

David Lee, Doris, Josie and Stevie rushed from the parking lot into the hospital. Joe Richard was waiting for them. They sat down and Joe Richard brought them up on what was happening. "When I got here yesterday, Dad was having trouble breathing and his heart was irregular. They put him on a ventilator and have been monitoring his heart and his brain activity. Just a little while ago his heart stopped. They made me leave and I've just been waiting here for you. They're working on him now."

A nurse came and invited them to follow her. They all went into a room where a doctor met them. "We managed to start his heart again but it's very weak and irregular. His breathing is completely dependent upon the ventilator. Because of his heart being so weak, his oxygen saturation is very low. If he were to survive, we should expect possible brain damage. All we can do now is to wait and watch the monitors. I suspect it will only be a matter of one or two hours." Looking back at John, he sighed and continued. "I'm glad you all got here before he passes."

"May we go see him, Doctor," Doris asked, tears welling up in her eyes.

"Yes," the doctor answered. "Two of you can go to his bedside and the rest wait inside the door then you can change around."

The nurse led them to John's room. Doris walked immediately to his bedside with Josie holding her hand. Tears were streaming down their cheeks. Doris looked at the still form—it was so gray and seemingly lifeless. With her voice choking, she spoke to him. "We're here, John. We're all here—me and Joe Richard and David Lee and Josie and Stevie, we're all here and we've been praying for you." She leaned over and kissed his forehead and held his hand." She looked at Josie, "He looks so peaceful, Josie—more like he's just taking a nice nap."

Josie leaned over to speak in his ear. "John, it's me, Josie. I want you to know that I forgive you for taking Stevie and hurting me and I...I love you."

Josie looked at the frail form. Again she heard her grandfather's voice. *"You have a gift Josie, don't waste it."*

She looked up at the ceiling and asked God what she should do. The voice was nearly audible, "Pray for him Josie—pray for his healing—pray for his spirit to return. The Father has a plan for him."

Josie laid both her hands on John's head and stroked his hair. Then she made the sign of the cross on his forehead as she'd seen Carla do, and as she remembered seeing her father and grandfather do. She looked up and closed her eyes and the words came as she began to speak out loud. "John, the Father wants you to know He loves you very much, and

He has a plan for your life. He's healing you right now. He's healing you, John. He's healing your lungs, He's healing your heart, and He's healing your brain, and even more, He's healing your soul. Come back to your body John, it's waiting for you—we're waiting for you. In the Name of the Father and the Son and the Holy Spirit AMEN."

As Josie was praying the room brightened as if someone had turned on some extra bright lights. For a moment it was almost blinding. Then, it disappeared as if something had just passed through the room. Josie's eyes were still closed and she kept praying silently. She was startled when she felt a hand reach up and grasp hers—it scared her. She opened her eyes to see John's hand on hers. The monitor beside the bed began to beep in a rhythmic way signaling the heart was alive and he was opening his eyes to consciousness.

Josie seemed to glow with love and John pulled her gently down to his face. He was weeping as he whispered into her ear. "I knew you were coming Josie and I knew when you came into the room." He looked into her eyes, "I was visited by an angel today and the angel told me you were coming."

She turned her head and kissed him on the cheek. "Yes John, that same angel told me to pray."

Josie straightened up and pushed the call button. A nurse rushed in supposing John had passed away. She was startled when she saw him with his eyes open and holding the hands of Josie and Doris. She rushed out of the room to call the doctor who was soon at the bedside and listening to John's heart. He turned to the nurse and gave an order to see if John could breathe with a Continuous Positive Airway Pressure (CPAP) mask without the ventilator. When it appeared that his breathing was normal, he instructed the nurse to remove the tube and make him comfortable but to keep the CPAP mask in place. He instructed the nurse to monitor the oxygen saturation closely.

The doctor turned to Doris, Josie, and John's two sons, who by this time were in the room. Stevie was holding onto Josie. "Well," the doctor said looking back at John. "I can't explain this—at least medically or scientifically. So, we'll just have to call it a miracle! I'll be back in the morning to check on him. In the meantime we'll leave him hooked up to the monitors, the IV's and the CPAP until we know he's stable." With that he turned and left.

John's throat was a little sore from the breathing tube and his voice was hoarse. He motioned for them all to gather around his bed. In a voice that was almost a whisper he said through the mask, "I want all of you to know how much I love you—and I'm asking your forgiveness for not being a better husband and father. Josie I know you've already forgiven me and I treasure that. I have a long ways to go and there are many things I don't quite understand, but I know it will all come together in time. There are things about my experiences here in this bed I want to tell you but that must wait until I have my voice back. Now, I want you all to sit here with me and I want Josie to read to me from the bible and I want all of you to listen."

Josie turned around to reach for her purse. She got her bible out, opened it, and put Stevie on her lap. "I'm going to read from the book of Psalms. It's what my father used to read to us when I was a child a long time ago." As those memories came, Josie had tears pooling in her eyes. They were tears of a grateful heart. Then she remembered something else. She reached back into her purse and pulled out a white scarf which she first kissed and then put over her head.

She turned to the first Chapter and the first verse of the Psalms and began to read in a loud clear voice.

"Blessed are those who do not walk in step with the wicked
or stand in the way that sinners take

*or sit in the company of mockers,
but who delight in the law of the LORD
and meditate on his law day and night.*

*They are like a tree planted by streams of water,
which yields its fruit in season
and whose leaf does not wither—
whatever they do prospers.*

*Not so the wicked!
They are like chaff that the wind blows away.
Therefore the wicked will not stand in the judgment,
nor sinners in the assembly of the righteous.*

*For the LORD watches over the way of the righteous,
but the way of the wicked will be destroyed."*

When Josie finished she looked at John whose eyes were closed. How different he looked from the time when she first arrived in the room. His color had returned and he was no longer at the door of death.

John opened his eyes and looked up. He saw the face of Death who was smiling at him from the far corner of the room. He looked pleased at how things had turned out. Without thinking of the others in the room, John raised his arm and waved goodbye to the Angel who had become his friend. "I will remember," he said aloud. "And someday when it's my time I'll look forward to our meeting again."

Joe Richard leaned over the bed and spoke what was on everybody's mind. "What was that all about, Dad?"

John looked at his son. "When it's time to do so, I'll tell you all about it. For now, just know that I was saying goodbye to a good friend whom I know I will meet once again someday."

Joe Richard looked at the others and smiled. "I don't understand all of this, but I'm glad Dad is still with us."

Stevie took Joe Richard's hand and looked up into his face. "I know what it's about, Uncle Joe Richard. Grandpa has an angel for a friend!"

"How do you know, Dear?" Doris asked.

"Cause I saw him when he came in the room with the bright light. That was him!" He jubilantly explained. Everyone smiled but no one said a word to contradict Stevie's statement.

CHAPTER EIGHTEEN

David Lee suggested they go find a motel close by and check in. It looked like they would be here for at least a few days. They met again in the lobby after getting everything unloaded and into the rooms. David Lee and Joe Richard shared a room and Doris; Josie and Stevie all shared another. Joe Richard suggested they find a restaurant and have something to eat. "Our day has been very long and it's getting late. A snack will do us all some good," he said.

Nobody said much at the table. Fatigue and stress of the last several days had taken a toll on everybody in the family. Both boys called their wives and talked to their families. Josie became very concerned about her own family as things were unfolding with the Brown's. She decided to wait until morning to call when she was rested and fresh. By the time they got back to the motel, Stevie was fast asleep.

The next morning they again met in the lobby and went out for breakfast. Everybody had slept late and it was mid-morning by the time they sat down to order. David Lee had the papers from Sheriff Mortenson and suggested they all go to the local Sheriff's Office and check in as per Mort's instructions. After that, they could return to the hospital.

After breakfast and after getting directions, David Lee drove them to the sheriff's Office. A pleasant but matter of

Josie's Gift

fact voice greeted them when they walked in. Joe Richard asked to speak to the sheriff. "Sit down over there," the receptionist commanded pointing to a waiting area. "I'll see if I can locate him."

Doris couldn't help but notice the differences between this office and Sheriff Mortenson's office, especially the seemingly unfriendly reception. Except for the receptionist, nobody spoke to them and no offer of coffee was made. Before long a tall, mustached man in a suit and big hat walked in and looked at them. He had a blank expression on his face. The receptionist said something and he looked again. He took off his hat, hung it on a peg in his office and sat down at a big desk. At that point the receptionist motioned to them they could see the sheriff now.

The Sheriff stood as they all walked in. He extended his hand introducing himself. In turn they all shook hands and were invited to sit. In a flat, expressionless voice, the sheriff said, "What c'n I do fer ya?"

David Lee walked to the desk as the others sat down. "Uh...Sheriff, my mother, Doris Brown, is here in Big Pine because my Dad is in the hospital and until yesterday was in critical condition and not expected to live. Today he's fine, having made quite a miraculous recovery..."

"...and his name is?" the sheriff interrupted.

"John Brown. I believe he's wanted for child abduction in Rock City and some other things over in Churchill."

The sheriff scratched his chin, "Yeah, I remember now. I got some paperwork on him from Sheriff Mortenson over in Littleville. Hold on!"

He opened his desk and pulled out a file. "Okay, here it is. He's to be held here in my jurisdiction until he's recovered enough to return to Littleville."

"That sounds like it, Sheriff. And my mother Doris is here with permission of Sheriff Mortenson. We're reporting here this morning as per Mortenson's instructions." He handed the papers he had to the sheriff.

Just then Stevie piped up. "Mister Sheriff, do you know Sheriff Mort? He's my friend you know."

Sheriff just looked at him with a quizzical look. He nonchalantly answered, "Yeah I know him!"

The tone of voice and the expression on the sheriff's face told Stevie he didn't much like to talk to little kids.

The sheriff looked at the papers and handed them back to David Lee. "Yeah I got a fax yesterday about that." Looking up at David Lee, he continued. "I expected to hear from you as soon as you got here. When did ya arrive?"

"It was pretty late last night. Dad wasn't expected to live so we went directly to the hospital. We were so absorbed in Dad's condition that we weren't thinking about anything else. I apologize for that oversight."

Sheriff scratched his chin and looked at David Lee and the rest of the family. "Seems like Sheriff Mortenson's kinda loose with his pris'ners, if ya ask me." He paused. "Well, that's his business. The doctor's have instructions from me not to release yer dad 'til I give the word so don't git no ideas about skeedaddlin outta the county." He paused again, "Sure is a strange case though. Okay, ya'll c'n go on about yer business, BUT!" The sheriff raised his voice, "Don't none of ya leave here for any reason without notifyin me, is that clear!"

"Yes, Sheriff, it is clear. However I need to remind you that my mother, Doris and my dad John are the only ones you have any jurisdiction over. The rest of us are free to come and go as we please. I say that only because there is a chance one of us may need to go back to Littleville."

The sheriff looked up with fire in his eyes. "You lookee here young man. If I need to, I can find something that will put you under my jurisdiction and it could be a long time before you leave here." It was obvious that the sheriff did not like to be challenged and David Lee knew full well the kinds of things someone like this sheriff could cook up just to hold them.

"I apologize for any misunderstanding Sheriff. The rules for Mother's conduct while she's here are clearly stated in these papers Sheriff Mortenson gave us. You can be assured that we will see to it they are followed to the letter. Furthermore, we will voluntarily let you know where we are at all times if you want us to go that far."

The sheriff scratched his chin and thought for a few moments. He could see the possibility of these people becoming a nuisance calling him many times every day they were here. He relaxed a little, "Okay, what's the name of the motel where yer stayin?"

"We're at the Medical Center Motel near the hospital."

Sheriff wrote that down. "One of my deputies'll be over at the hospital sometime today to talk to the doctors about yer dad." He paused. "Say, you some kinda lawyer or somethin.?"

"No, I'm not a lawyer." David Lee answered.

The sheriff looked him in the eyes, "Well, you seem to know a lot about the law."

David Lee smiled, put both his hands on the desk and leaned over the desk slightly. In a very quiet voice he said, "I'm an investigator for the District Attorney's Office in the county where I live."

A slow smile grew on the sheriff's face. "Oh, well," he said. "That does make a difference." Then as if to get in the last word, "Just remember, young man, you don't have any authority in this state or in this county. Now, ya'll git yer butts outta here and go about yer business. Call and check back in here tomorra morning. Just leave word with the receptionist out there."

David Lee extended his hand, "Thanks sheriff. It has been a pleasure working with you."

Stevie piped up again. "Mister Sheriff, I don't think you are my friend, are you?"

Somewhat embarrassed by Stevie's remark, they all, in turn shook the sheriff's hand and turned to leave.

The sheriff just looked at Stevie, turned around, grabbed his hat and walked out a back door.

As they left the building, Stevie looked up at David Lee. "Boy, that sheriff sure is a grumpy person, isn't he?"

"Yeah, he sure is," David Lee answered.

At the hospital, they found John sitting up in the bed and smiling. The CPAP had been removed and replaced by small tubes in each nostril that supplied additional oxygen. Each in turn went to his bedside and kissed him. Doris sat down beside the bed and took his hand in hers.

Joe Richard and David Lee carried a couple of vases of fresh flowers they bought on the way and placed one on the night stand beside the bed and the other on the bed tray.

"I'm so glad all of you are here," John said, his voice still hoarse. "The doctor says I'm doing great. No residual brain damage and no heart or artery problems that they can determine. I'm very weak which is to be expected, but with some therapy, I plan to be as good as new in a few days. They made me get up this morning and walk around the room with that walker over there," he said, pointing to the corner.

"How long do they think it'll be, Dad?" Joe Richard asked.

"They said it would be a few days before they could make any prediction on that. By the way Doris, you need to go down to the admissions office and give them my insurance and ID cards so they can process me properly," he laughed.

Doris got up to leave, and David Lee accompanied her. They got the paperwork taken care of and returned. Josie got up from the bedside and turned to Doris. "May I borrow your cell phone, Doris? I've got to make some phone calls."

"Certainly, Dear."

Josie took the phone, "I'll be out in the lobby for a little while."

Josie's heart was beating a little faster than normal as she punched Will's number into the keypad. She pushed the 'call' button and waited with anticipation. The phone rang—she was anxious to hear his voice but it rang and rang with no answer. Finally the voice mail picked it up and Josie left a message. "Hi Will, this is Josie. I'd...uh, like to talk to you, so give me a call as soon as you can. Everything's fine here." There was disappointment in her voice. "God bless you, bye."

She sat down in a comfortable chair just to collect her thoughts. She decided to call Joann. Punching in another number she pushed the button and the phone began to ring. It was a welcome relief when she heard the voice on the other end.

"Good morning, this is Joann!"

"Hi Joann, this is Josie."

"Oh Josie, I'm so glad to hear from you. Where are you and how're you doing?"

"I guess Isabelle called you about John Brown! Well, he's had a miraculous recovery. It was quite dramatic. Doris and their two sons are all here and everybody's doing great."

"Any idea when you'll be home?"

"Not yet! John's getting therapy. It may be a few days before they'll predict how long he'll need to stay. How's Sandy doing?"

"He's doing just fine. He has a case in court today with Will so they're both at the court house."

"That explains why I couldn't get hold of Will. Okay, I'll let you go. I just wanted you to know that all is okay here. Tell Sandy hi for me. I love you both more than I can ever say. Please keep praying for the Browns."

"Okay Josie We'll be praying for all of you. God bless, bye."

Josie ended the call and cried. She didn't know why she needed to cry at this moment but she welcomed it. A smile crept onto her face and she realized how thankful she was to have friends like Sandy and Joann...and Will.

She felt a twinge of guilt because she kept putting off calling her mother. "What will I say?" she thought to herself. *"How can I tell her that I'm embarrassed to call? I'm ashamed for having left home the way I did!"*

Josie's fingers trembled as she punched her parents phone number into the keypad. "Hello and Shalom," the voice said.

Josie's tears cascaded down her cheeks and dropped onto her lap. She was so choked up she couldn't speak. The voice again said, "Hello!"

Between sobs Josie managed to speak, "Mama?"

"Josie, is that you?"

"Yes Mama, yes it's me!"

"Ahhh, Mi'jita it is so good to hear your voice." Ruth broke into tears. "Praise to Adonai, thanks to our Yeshua and praise to His great and holy Name. He has preserved your life and answered our prayers for you."

"Yes, Mama—thanks to Him I am safe and He has preserved my life and saved my soul. It is so wonderful to hear your voice. Before I say another word, Mama please forgive me for my disobedience seven years ago and for my pride and arrogance in not listening to your wisdom."

"Yes, Mi'jita it is all forgiven and our love for you is no less than it was when you left. We have cried before Adonai day and night for your safe return, never doubting that He would one day bring you back."

"Mama, I have so much to tell you—so much that has happened. Adonai is even now working miracles in my life, and in Stevie's life. We are so grateful for your prayers and for your faithfulness to our savior Yeshua." Josie paused to organize her thoughts then she continued. "I'm sure you saw the news broadcasts about Roger's violent death."

"Yes Mi'jita, we saw all that. We knew from what we saw that you were safe."

"And do you know about John and Doris Brown abducting Stevie?"

"Yes, we know about that. Officer Brand came by to tell us and to let us know that the resources of the local law enforcement there in Rock City as well as the State and Federal agencies were tracking them. He came back again yesterday to tell us that the Browns were in custody and that Stevie was safe and sound."

Josie continued the story. "When the Browns got Stevie they headed out of State to Louisiana. When they were just across the State line near Littleville, there was an accident involving a train. Doris and Stevie were miraculously unhurt but John was critically injured. They transported him to Littleville and then by Air Life to Big Pine where they performed surgery on his brain and treated him for the other injuries. He was in a coma and not expected to live. The family was called and Joe Richard and David Lee drove to Littleville. They paid for me to fly from Rock City because Doris wanted me to be there with them when John passed away. I went with them from Littleville and we were all there before John was to pass away. In his hospital room a bright light came in and Stevie said he saw an angel. I laid my hands on John and prayed just like I remembered Papa and Grandfather doing when they prayed for the sick." Josie choked up with her tears and couldn't continue.

"Mi'jita, take your time. I am so happy you were there. Adonai had His own purpose in your being there."

Josie regained her composure. "Mama," she said jubilantly. "Adonai made a miracle happen and John revived and is healed. They are doing therapy and he will be released sometime soon! Of course he and Doris both know they face charges in Rock City and also in Churchill but they are both at peace with it. They know that Adonai will see them through it."

"I will call the rest of the family and your friends and let them know you are fine. Ever since you were on TV from Rock City, they have all been asking about you. Papa is right here and wants to say hello!"

Josie was surprised because her father never liked to talk on the phone. "Hi Papa. I just want to say I love you and thank you for your prayers."

Moisés didn't speak for a few seconds. He had tears in his eyes. "My dearest Josie, it is so good to hear your voice. You sound just like you did the day you left. Mama will tell me all that you have said. Just remember that I love you." He choked a little as he handed the phone back to his wife.

"Mama, I'm living with some wonderful people at the Lighted Way Ministries in Rock City. I'm going to give you the address, okay?"

"Yes Mi'jita. Let me get something to write with. Okay, I'm ready."

"It's Two-Three-Three, West Third Street, in Rock City. Got that? I want you to know I got your letter. It went to the District Attorney's office and they got it to me. The letter meant a lot to me and it brought calm to my soul at a time when it was sorely needed." She paused. "I've got to go now Mama. I'll call you as soon as I know when we'll be back in Rock City. I'd like for you and Papa to come see me when I get back. Please think about it. I love you! Bye."

After talking to her mom and her dad, Josie felt a great sense of relief. She still didn't feel completely at peace though, and knew that peace would not come until she was with them and they could talk face to face.

Josie walked slowly back to John's room trying to collect her thoughts as she went. When she got to the room,

John's voice was almost completely clear and they were all talking back and forth. David Lee stood up and motioned for her to follow him into the hallway.

"What is it David Lee?"

"Josie, do you believe in miracles...um...like Angels and healing and all that stuff?"

Josie looked him in the eye. "Why do you ask?"

"Well, all morning Stevie's been talking about Jesus and Angels. I figure he must get it from you." He paused and looked down. "Uh...do you think it's a good idea to fill his mind with all that? I mean, he's pretty young and isn't mature enough to judge the merits of those kinds of things."

Josie smiled and almost laughed at his thinking. "David Lee, children come by those things very naturally. Nobody has to, as you say, 'fill their minds'. Very often God allows little children to see things we don't see because they have no doubts and we adults are full of doubt—like you are right now. A good example is the bright light in your Dad's room yesterday. We all saw a bright light but Stevie saw an Angel in that bright light."

David Lee took his gaze away from Josie. He was beginning to feel argumentative. "Look Josie, I believe in God and all that, but I don't believe God performs miracles in this day and age. Back in the early days of the church, they didn't have doctors and they needed miracles. But now we have doctors and miracles aren't necessary."

Josie was still smiling. "Yesterday, I heard an audible voice telling me to pray for your Dad. Furthermore that voice told me what to pray. You didn't hear it because the message wasn't meant for you—it was meant for me. You can believe whatever you want, and I and Stevie will still love you—but why don't you ask your Dad about miracles and God and angels?"

Josie's Gift

David Lee didn't want to give up. "Since he was dying, don't you think those things could have been hallucinations? I've heard that people who are dying do that all the time!"

"And I've heard about just as many or even more people who have seen bright lights and Angels when they have near death experiences. David Lee, yesterday, if your dad was dying as you say he was, then, today he'd be dead and we'd be making different plans. Even the doctor couldn't explain the miraculous recovery. You really need to talk to your dad about his experiences."

David Lee smiled. "Thank you Josie." He paused and looked intently into her eyes. Still feeling his doubt, "I really want to believe you. It would make things so much simpler."

As they walked through the door to John's room, Josie pulled her Bible out of her purse. Going to John's side she asked him if he'd like her to read before lunch. She sat down beside the bed and turned to Psalm Chapter 2 and read the entire chapter. Soon after she finished, an aide brought John's lunch tray. They all gathered at the bed and Doris asked Josie to bless the food.

"Bless us oh Lord in the gift of this food which you have so graciously provided and which good hands have prepared for our nourishment. May Adonai be blessed forever in His bounteous love and mercy! AMEN."

When she opened her eyes she saw David Lee look her direction. There was a certain admiration in his expression. She smiled and turned to John. As Joe Richard raised the head of the bed Josie pushed the tray where he could comfortably reach it.

John looked at them all. Then he took Stevie's hand. "This little fella's hungry! Why don't you all go to the cafeteria and get lunch so you don't have to watch me eat!" He laughed a hearty laugh.

As they sat at the table to eat, David Lee spoke. "Do all of you see what I see in Dad?" He looked around the table.

"He's changed—I can't ever remember seeing him in this state of mind ever in my life."

"You're right, Dear." Doris said.

"I see it too," Joe Richard agreed.

They all looked at David Lee. "I think Dad's undergone some kind of powerful transformation—he's changed—and it's all for the better. We'll see how real it is when we get back to Rock City and the charges he faces."

In the midst of this serious conversation, Stevie raised his hand as if he were in school. They all looked at him. His eyes went from one to the other then he said, "I think Grampa met Jesus!"

Both Doris and Josie had tears pooling in their eyes. Joe Richard and David Lee just looked at Stevie in wonderment. Finally everybody laughed.

"Praise Adonai from whom all blessings flow, both great and small!" Josie said in a sing-song voice.

Joe Richard, always the one to drag everybody back to reality said, "So, what about the future?"

They all looked at Josie. "Our God is big enough to handle every matter," she said. "What we have to face is small in His eyes. We need to make a plan to get back to Littleville, take care of things there, and then get us all back to Rock City where the music has to be faced. I have good friends in Rock City and I believe things will go smoothly. I also believe that Sheriff Mortenson is a good Christian and will help us as far as he can go with it. So, let us rejoice in our savior, Yeshua, and go with the confidence that He knows the way and we need only follow it."

When they returned to John's room they were met with the doctor talking to the deputy the sheriff had sent. The deputy tipped his hat and introduced himself when they came into the room. He explained his visit and then suggested they

Josie's Gift

go back into the hallway where there was a waiting room not far away. Stevie stayed with his grandpa.

The doctor spoke first. "I see no reason why Mister Brown could not be released day after tomorrow morning, that'll be Wednesday. Unless there are complications we don't see at this moment, I'll order that he be discharged and Missus Brown or one of the sons can sign the paperwork. We'll get it accomplished in plenty of time that you all can get back to Littleville before nightfall."

The deputy spoke. "I'll let the sheriff know and I'll git the paperwork ready fer ya ta take back to Sheriff Mortenson. I'll bring it over first thing Wednesday mornin." The deputy smiled and tipped his hat again. "It's been real nice meetin you folks. I'll check in with ya in the mornin so there'll be no need fer callin the sheriff."

They all shook hands with the doctor and the deputy and went back to John's room.

"Well, Dad!" David Lee said. "Looks like you're all set to go. Wednesday we go to Littleville and then as soon as things are taken care of there, we go on to Rock City to face the music."

"I know! The doctor and the deputy told me before you came back. I'm looking forward to getting out of here and getting all this mess straightened out." He smiled and looked around at his family. "I'm confident that it will all turn out for the best and I'm not in the least worried about it."

Doris got out her cell phone and handed it to Josie. "Here Dear, you call the authorities in Rock City and let them know of the developments here. Joe Richard, you call Sheriff Mortenson and let him know we'll be looking forward to seeing him Wednesday evening. We'll probably need to stay the night in Littleville and then get on the road to Rock City the next morning. Joe Richard, how long do you think it will take us to drive from Littleville to Rock City?"

Well, we have Dad to think about, so we should give it at least two days. We'll play it by ear and if he gets too tired we can stop and extend the drive time."

Wednesday morning they all showed up at the hospital by nine o'clock. The deputy was there with the papers they needed. Doris felt some relief they wouldn't have to go by the sheriff's office and deal with anything there.

"We'll folks, I think everything's set fer ya ta git on yer way this mornin. Sheriff decided it would be best to put one of the boys in charge so to speak, so Mister David Lee, if you'll jest sign right here," he pointed to the space.

David Lee read the page very carefully and when he was satisfied, he signed two copies. He addressed his family, "This paper says that I am solely responsible for the welfare of Dad and Mother and to see that they get to Littleville. Furthermore, the minute we get to Littleville, we are to go directly to Sheriff Mortenson and check in with him. He will give us instructions for the rest of the trip. It's only about a two to three hour drive. We can stop about half way and eat lunch."

They all checked out of the motel later in the morning as planned and drove to the hospital to pick up John. David Lee issued instructions. "Mother, you give Josie your cell phone and I'll give you mine. The two of you can communicate if it's necessary to let us know if you need us to stop before we have lunch."

John and Doris got into the rental car with David Lee; Josie and Stevie got in Joe Richard's car and they immediately got on their way.

When they arrived in Littleville they went immediately to Sheriff Mortenson. He seemed genuinely glad to see them. He extended his hand first to John and introduced himself. Then he shook the hands of the others. He turned back to John. "Mister Brown, I'm glad everything has turned out well for you. Frankly, I'm surprised to see you in such good shape."

John looked around at his family. "Sheriff, I do believe God had a lot to do with this and it is to the credit of the prayers of my family and of good men like you—and I sincerely thank you for your prayers, and for the way you treated my wife and grandson while they were here."

Stevie walked rapidly around the big desk and tugged at Mort's arm. "Mister Mort, Grampa saw an angel and he also met Jesus while he was in the hospital."

Mort smiled and said, "You're right Stevie, I can see that he did." Then he addressed the others. Missus Brown I'm waiting on some instructions from Rock City authorities on getting you two back there. I told them I thought you and your sons could be trusted and there would be no need for any law enforcement personnel to come here and accompany you. However, that decision is theirs to make so we'll wait and see. In the meantime your Chrysler is in our impound lot and is serviceable if you can get a new windshield put in. I've called around and have the name and address of a company here who can do it in a matter of a couple of hours. If you'll call them, I'll have Jerry drive it up here to the front of the building. Oh, there is the matter of the stolen license plate." He looked at John and Doris.

"You should have found the authentic plates in the Chrysler under the back seat." John said.

"That's correct," Mort replied. We put the originals back on the Chrysler and sent the stolen one back to Rock City. So, as soon as you get the new windshield, the Chrysler's legal."

He handed Doris a slip of paper and she called the number. "They have the windshield in stock and can get it installed as soon as we can get there and have it ready to go by six-thirty," she said

Jerry brought the car up and Mort suggested that Doris, Josie and Stevie take the Chrysler to be fixed and John, David Lee, and Joe Richard stay behind so they could talk.

After Josie and Doris were gone Mort turned to David Lee. "When we went through the car we found a considerable amount of money stashed under the back seat. I have it here in my safe." Handing David Lee a piece of paper he said, "Here's an audit of how much it was and the amount we gave your mother for her expenses while she was here."

David Lee whistled and handed it to Joe Richard. Joe Richard handed it to John. "We emptied our bank accounts and savings before we left Churchill. We intended to set up a new life in Florida." John laughed, "Funny how things turn out isn't it?"

"Yes, it is," Mort replied. Looking at Joe Richard and David Lee, he continued. "Because of your dad's legal problems, you two boys will be the custodians of that money in trust for your parents. There's no indication it was any part of a crime and it won't be needed for evidence. I would suggest that you take the money over to our bank here and buy a bank draft so you're not carrying so much cash around. With your parents' permission, of course, you can take out what you feel you will need for expenses. I'll need to call the bank President and let him know you're coming with this amount of cash. That way they won't have to question it. You'll need to explain it for the record because they have to report to the feds cash deposits over ten thousand dollars—just to make sure it's not drug money. I'll have Jerry go with you to the bank for your own safety."

Joe Richard spoke, "That sounds good Sheriff—and we are all very grateful for your kindness and understanding. While we're out, I'll turn in the rental car and David Lee can get us a pair of hotel rooms back at La Plaza."

"You boys call me just as soon as you have your mom and dad settled and everything taken care of at the bank.

Now, as soon as you sign this paper, I'll get the money from my safe. Jerry's waiting for you outside."

The money was stacked carefully in a suitcase with a strap around the outside. When they walked into the bank, carrying the suitcase, customers looked curiously at the suitcase and then at the deputy who was following them. A bank officer immediately met them and ushered them into a private office. Once their business was done, David Lee and Joe Richard shook Jerry's hand, thanked him for his help and left for the motel. On the way, David Lee called Mort to let him know they had been well taken care of at the bank. At the motel, they got rooms big enough for the three men to stay together and the two women with Stevie to stay together.

By six-thirty, Doris, Josie and Stevie got to the motel with the Chrysler sporting a brand new windshield. They walked to the familiar restaurant down the street to eat supper. The hostess seated them at a large corner booth that was semi-circular in shape.

When they were finished eating, they ordered desert and coffee. As they settled in for relaxed conversation, John startled everyone. "Now, I think it's time for me to tell you about my experience of dying—or almost dying—I'm not sure which, while I was in the hospital." He looked around at each member of his family. "Some of this is difficult for me. I ask your patience and your forgiveness for the things I'm going to say."

"Dad, maybe...some of those things are stuff you shouldn't tell us," David Lee said.

"And maybe the restaurant is not the place for it," Joe Richard interjected.

Stevie looked sleepily at his mom, laid his head on her lap and went to sleep.

"Do you think the motel lobby would be any better?" John asked.

David Lee looked around. "Probably not," he said.

Josie's Gift

John gave David Lee a look of sympathy and he took Doris' hand in his. "My sons, I know you will be disappointed in me for the things I've done—all of you will. This is not easy, but I trust that our love can endure the telling and will support us as a family after it's over. I'm not the man you knew before the accident. I know God in a way that none of you can know Him, at least right now. I want what has happened, and what I will confess to you tonight, to make us a stronger family."

By the time he finished telling about his experience with the angel; John had tears in his eyes. "I hope all of you can understand how important this is to me—and for that matter to all of you as well."

Doris was crying, but for a different reason than John. She was looking down at the floor; she took her hand from his and looked up into his expectant face. "John, I never dreamed—it's almost like I've been married to two different men all these years—one of them I didn't know at all."

"Doris," John said. "I can't tell you how sorry I am for the kind of man I've been. You have every right to be angry and disappointed. I humbly ask for your forgiveness, and as soon as I can talk to a minister, I will ask God for forgiveness. Please, Doris—please forgive me."

Doris just looked at her husband. Slowly she reached her hand back across the table and took John's which was trembling. "John, I should be angry, I should be telling you I want a divorce. I should be yelling and screaming at you." Just then she felt Josie's hand on her other hand. She continued, "John, I forgive you but my trust is in God. It will take time for me to trust you again."

Josie spoke to them both. "For those who are in Christ, all things are new. Now your lives are new, and the old things have passed away into that dark hole John was in when he was in the hospital."

Josie's Gift

David Lee and Joe Richard were somewhat embarrassed by their father's openness and frank confession about his life. John turned to them. "Boys, I ask you both to forgive me for the hurt I brought to your mother and for what I neglected so many times with both of you and with Roger. Had I been a better father, Roger might have turned out differently."

The boys just sat and stared at their father. David Lee looked at Joe Richard, then at his mother. "Dad, I can't speak for my brother but I forgive you. It's all gone now. You'll remember the faces of those children for the rest of your life."

"I too forgive you Dad," Joe Richard said, "And I agree with David Lee."

Josie was stunned at the revelation about her abortions. Nobody said anything while she collected her thoughts. Finally she spoke, "John, I've been feeling a lot of guilt over those abortions. I want to blame it all on Roger and say that he forced me into it, but in the end, that terminal decision was mine to make." She spoke as she looked intently at John, "There's no excuse for what you did, and there's no excuse for what I did. I have asked God for forgiveness and now I'm asking my angel to relay a message to my three babies in Heaven that I love them and please, oh please, forgive me for what I did. John, I envy you because you were given the privilege to see them and watch them play, and I won't see that until I get to Heaven. Thank you, John, for telling us about that experience you had. I will treasure it and bless you for it the rest of my life." She hung her head, "I will grieve for Roger for a long time knowing he will never see those babies."

Joe Richard, ever the doubter, asked the question that had been on his mind since David Lee had talked to Josie in the hospital. "Dad, don't you think you might have been dreaming all of that? You know things like that don't happen nowadays!"

John smiled. "Joe Richard, were you there with me when the angel visited me and showed me the things of my past?"

"Well, I guess not."

Stevie raised his head and rubbed his eyes. He looked at his grandpa.

"Actually," John said. "It isn't a guess. You know you weren't there. Now, listen to me, all of you." John said in a stern, almost reprimanding tone of voice. "I've been through a very special experience, and I'll never forget it, nor will I ever deny it. It was as real as I am sitting here with all of you. I know that I had an experience that has changed my life forever. I was at the very door of death, and I saw the awful darkness that had become a part of my life. God has given me a second chance, and I intend to use it to glorify Him for whatever time I have left on this earth."

Everybody except Joe Richard was smiling. Stevie piped up, "Don't worry Grampa, I saw him too—the angel I mean."

The waitress came back to see if they needed anything more. Seeing all the tears, she asked, "Is everything okay folks? Is there something wrong?"

"No, Dear," Doris answered. "We've just heard a wonderful story of angels and healing and Heaven."

The waitress choked up a little. She put the ticket on the table and hurriedly left. Josie, prompted by an inner voice, got up from the table and followed her. She tapped her on the shoulder. Looking at the name tag, she asked, "Are you okay Becky?"

"I need an angel in my life right now!" Becky blurted out.

Josie looked around, "My Name's Josie Brown, and we're staying down the street at the La Plaza Motel. When you get off work, come by. I'll be waiting for you in the lobby. I can help you with the angel problem." Josie looked around, took a glass of water from Becky's hand, "Thank you for the water Becky!"

When she got back to the table, Joe Richard asked, "What was that all about?"

Josie smiled, "Becky needs an angel in her life, and I'm going to see that she gets one."

CHAPTER NINETEEN

As soon as she got off work at nine PM, Becky walked to the La Plaza Motel where Josie was waiting for her in the lobby. Josie smiled and waived; Becky walked over to where she was sitting. Josie greeted her and invited her to sit down. "I'm only going to be in town for a day or two," Josie said. "But I'd like to help you. When we met in the restaurant, you looked like you needed a friend—someone to talk to."

Becky was tall for a woman, but shapely. She had stringy brown hair and with a little make-up in the right places, would be very attractive. Right now, she looked haggard and depressed. She looked at Josie for a long time, searching her eyes, before she spoke. "I don't know why I'm here; I shouldn't be here—but yeah, I need someone to talk to. It seems like I was drawn to you...as if someone sent you to the restaurant just for me. But, all the way over here I kept telling myself, this is crazy, and you wouldn't want to hear about my problems. Even if you knew my problems, there's nothing you can do." Becky got up and started to leave.

Josie stood up and took her hand, determined to stop her from leaving. "Becky, I believe it was God who arranged our meeting—He has some purpose for it. I want to help you, if I can. You look to be about the same age as I am, and you look like you're in trouble. I may not be able to change your circumstances, but I can help you deal with them—and besides, I know someone who loves you and who can change your circumstances."

Becky was hesitant and looked at Josie for several moments. Finally, she sat back down. "Who do you know that loves me and can change my circumstances?"

That person is Jesus, Becky. He brought people into my life, and my life and circumstances changed, and He can do the same for you."

Becky looked puzzled. She hung her head. "I...I'm not sure if I should tell you everything or not. If Ronnie ever found out I was talking to someone, he'd be furious and..."

"...and beat you up?" Josie interrupted. "And Ronnie is...?"

"...my boyfriend. Sometimes we live together. Yeah, he'd beat me up! How'd you know?"

"Let's just say, I've had some firsthand experience with someone like that. Have you heard about a guy named Roger Brown? He shot up the courthouse over in Rock City, Texas, a couple of months ago—it was on all the national news channels."

Becky's eyes widened. "Are you...?"

"...yeah, I was married to him for seven years."

"When Roger was arrested, the judge put me and my son in the custody of a woman named Reverend Isabelle Jefferson, at a place called the Lighted Way Ministries. At the time, the authorities were investigating me as a possible accomplice to Roger's past crimes. At the mission, I found people who loved me and helped me through the tragedy. Best of all, they introduced me to Jesus Christ. I have come to know Him in a personal way, and He's changed my life. I have no money, no car, but I'm still at the mission. I work there in exchange for board and room for me and my son.

Josie's Gift

I'm here in Littleville because of the generosity of my ex-husband's family."

Becky nervously looked around. She gasped when she saw a car drive very slowly around the parking area outside. It drove under the canopy and stopped. The driver waited for a few minutes and then started driving around again. "Oh my God! It's him; it's Ronnie, and he's looking for me. I got paid tonight, and he wants my money."

Josie had Doris' cell phone, and promptly called the sheriff's office. "Good evening, this is Josie Brown. Is Sheriff Mortenson in tonight?"

"No, I'm sorry he's not in. Can I get someone else for you?"

"Is Jerry working tonight?"

"Let me see—yes, he is but he's on patrol."

"Could you call him and give him my name. We have some trouble at the La Plaza Motel, and we need some help quickly."

"Okay, Missus Brown, I'll call him."

Just as Josie hung up the phone, Ronnie parked his car and barged in through the doors. He looked around and walked straight to where Josie and Becky were sitting. He had tattoos on both arms and other exposed places on his body. It was obvious from the way he moved and the way he looked, that he was high on something. He was enraged when he saw Becky there with Josie. By the time he got to where they were sitting, he was yelling at Becky at the top of his lungs. "What are you doin' here you damn bitch? You were s'posed to meet me in the parking lot at the restaurant." He shifted his gaze to Josie. "An' who's this bitch with you?"

Josie was beginning to fear for her and Becky's safety. Her heart was beating fast, and her palms were sweaty. She wanted to call David Lee but was afraid to take out the cell phone again.

Josie's Gift

When the desk clerk saw what was going on, he hurried over and confronted Ronnie. "What's going on here?"

Ronnie put his face squarely in front of the clerk and shouted. "None of yer business, Dumass! Now git outta my face and leave me and my girlfriend alone. We'll settle things without you buttin' in."

"I'm sorry sir, but you'll have to leave, or I'll call the police."

Becky moved between the clerk and Ronnie. She took hold of his arm. "Ronnie, I'm sorry, I know I shouldn't be here. C'mon let's go."

Ronnie spun around and knocked Becky onto the floor. Josie got down and helped her up enough that they could crawl away from Ronnie and the clerk. Ronnie took a swing at the clerk who ducked just in time. As he was trying to get out of Ronnie's reach, the front doors burst open and Deputy Jerry Walker came in, his right hand on the grip of his pistol. "Police, hold it Ronnie! Don't make a move. Put your hands behind your back and get down on the floor!" He yelled.

Ronnie was surprised and partially obeyed. He put his hands behind his back but didn't get down on the floor. He was seething with rage. Just as Jerry walked up to him, Ronnie swung, knocking Jerry to the floor. Both the women screamed in horror. In a flash Jerry's Taser was out of the holster and pointed at Ronnie's body above him. Ronnie screamed in pain and went down, totally immobilized and lying in a fetal position. Jerry got on top of him, rolled him over and handcuffed his hands behind his back. He was breathless when he got up. He looked around and spoke, "Everybody okay?"

The clerk was shaken, but in control. Becky was crying, and Josie was holding her. Jerry keyed his handheld radio and called for police backup. Officers took Ronnie away, and a tow truck took his car to the police impound lot. Jerry sat down with Josie, Becky and the motel clerk to get their statements.

"Jerry, you seemed to know Ronnie?" Josie asked.

"Yep, sure do. We've had trouble with him for years. Every time we think we've got him on something, an attorney hired by his old man, gets him off. I think this time we've got something that'll stick—two charges of assault and battery, one charge of assaulting a police officer and interfering with an officer in his lawful line of duty—and we have witnesses. After we go through the car, there may be some drug-related charges."

"What now? Josie asked.

"I need to take statements from all three of you and take a few photos of the scene."

"If Ronnie finds out I talked to you, he'll kill me!" Becky whimpered.

"He's going to be out of the way for a while, Becky. We'll keep an eye on things." Jerry replied.

"But, he's got friends, and I know they'll be looking for me when they find out Ronnie's in jail. Two of them were in the car when he drove up. They're probably hanging around the motel right now."

"Becky, I can't tell you not to worry because you're right about Ronnie's friends. What I can tell you is that we'll do everything we can to protect you."

Josie was thinking. She interrupted the conversation, "Jerry, is there a Christian mission or a women's shelter here in Littleville where Becky can stay?"

"No, I'm sorry to say there's nothing like that here and nothing I know of that would be safe."

Josie smiled. "Can she leave the county and the state?"

Jerry scratched his head and thought for a few seconds. "I suppose she can...um...she'll for sure be needed to testify. For that matter, Josie you'll be needed too. So, both of you will have to come back here for that."

"Then it's settled," Josie said with a big grin on her face. "Becky will go back to Rock City with me and live at the mission where I live." Josie was confident but she didn't consider that God might have other plans for them.

Becky was stunned. "You mean leave here and relocate to Rock City—and I can live with you?"

"Yep!! Where do you live Becky?"

Becky hung her head, "I live down the street a couple of blocks in a ratty apartment building. It's called the Crown Royale Apartments, if you can believe that!"

"Jerry, can you take her down there to pick up the things she needs and bring her back here?"

Jerry was startled and looked at both women. "Well, I...um...this sure is unusual, but I guess for her safety, I'll need to go with her. Now, can we get on with takin' yer statements?"

By the time Jerry had written everything down from his three witnesses, it was nearly midnight. "Okay," he said, getting up from his seat. "I'll have all this typed up and ready for ya'll to sign sometime tomorrow. I'll have Mort call Josie, and she can spread the word."

Josie took Becky's hand. "It's gonna be okay, Becky, just trust in God our Father and the angels he surrounds us with."

Becky looked at Josie, she was puzzled at what she said. "You mean God is somehow interested in us—right here—right now?"

"Yes, he is!" Josie replied. "He loves you, and He wants the best for you. His promise in the bible is that He has a future and a hope for all of us (Jeremiah 29:11). You go with Deputy Walker and get your things from the apartment and come back here."

Becky followed Jerry to his patrol car. When they got to the apartment building, Becky gave Jerry instructions to drive to the back. Her apartment was on the second floor, and the entrance was at the top of the stairs. Jerry parked, and Becky opened the door and looked around. "You see anybody familiar, Becky?" Jerry asked.

"No, I don't see anything!"

"Okay, go on up and get some things packed and leave your door open. I'll wait here for you and keep an eye open." Silently, he said to himself, *"Mort's gonna kill me for this!"*

Unexpectedly, Jerry heard a scream—then another louder than the first. He opened his door and looked up at the open apartment door—another scream. He put his hand on his Glock forty and headed for the stairs. Halfway up, he heard another scream and knew for sure it was Becky. He unholstered the Glock and pushed a small switch on the grip, which turned on a laser sight. He bounded two steps at a time the rest of the way up, all the while keeping a wary eye on the door and the windows on either side.

When he reached the top, he turned and placed his back against the wall just inches from the door. He listened and tried to determine where Becky and whoever assaulted her were, relative to the door. He could hear commotion and scuffling as if someone was fighting. Thinking he could surprise them, he took a deep breath and swung the Glock in his right hand around his body and into the door opening. At the same time he yelled, "Police! Don't anybody move."

He moved his head and his Glock in an arc covering the living room but nobody was there. He heard more scuffling and someone falling on the floor. It was coming from the next room, which he figured to be the bedroom. When he swung around and through the doorway with the Glock always pointing where his eyes were focusing, he saw a man holding Becky from behind, his right arm around her neck. He had a large knife in his left hand, with the point of the blade poised against the skin on the side of her neck.

"Back off, Deputy," the man commanded.

Jerry moved his eyes around the room to see if anyone else was there. With the Glock still pointed in the direction of Becky's assailant, he slowly backed up in the direction of the wall behind him. From that vantage point, he could see the window and the door to the living room as well as the closet door.

"You'll never get outta here alive," Jerry shouted.

The man just grinned and a let out a nervous laugh. "You got no choice, Mister Deputy! It's gonna be either me or her. I git a slug, and her throat gits my knife. You drop that gun on the floor, and she goes with me." He laughed an evil laugh. "An' maybe, jest maybe, there's a chance she'll live..." he tightened his right arm on her neck, and pushed the blade a little into the skin. "...that is, as long as she...uh cooperates!"

Back at the Motel, Josie was getting concerned. Becky and Jerry should be back by now. She got out the cell phone and called the sheriff's office and asked them to get hold of Mort. She felt a premonition that both Becky and Jerry were in trouble. After she hung up, she walked outside and looked down the street in the direction of the apartments. She looked up and prayed. An inner voice seemed to be saying, "*Go!*"

She ran as fast as her legs would move in the direction of the apartments. As she got close, she couldn't see Jerry's car so she ran around to the back. Several people, hearing the commotion, were gathered at the base of the stairs. She saw Jerry's car close to the stairway, and up on the second floor she saw the open door, which she guessed was Becky's apartment. She bounded up the stairs, and throwing caution to the wind, ran inside. She screamed at Becky.

From the bedroom, Becky screamed back. "Don't come in here Josie. Go back to the motel, please!"

Josie paused. Something inside her again said, "*Go!*"

She walked into the bedroom and saw Becky and her assailant. When the assailant saw Josie, he turned his gaze in her direction. "Don't come any closer," he yelled. He tightened his hold on Becky, and Josie could see the knife point depressing the skin on Becky's neck. A small trickle of blood began to ooze from a small wound. Josie turned to her left and saw Jerry against the far wall with his pistol still pointed at the assailant.

Josie prayed. She let her hands fall down to her sides with the palms open to the front. She fixed her eyes on the assailant, "Look, I have nothing to hurt you with." She took a slow step forward.

"Stop," he shouted.

Josie stood still and just looked into the man's eyes. She could see in her mind the courtroom and Roger shooting wildly. She could feel Isabelle at her side, hearing a shot, and saw her falling, nearly trading her own life for hers. Josie spoke calmly, "Mister, I don't know your name but just listen to me please. Let me take Becky's place—you can have my life for hers—please."

The man listened—he looked her up and down. A sinister smile crossed his lips, and he was quiet as he thought about his situation. "Okay walk real slow over here."

Josie obeyed. When she was close enough to touch him, he quickly threw Becky off to the side and grabbed Josie around her neck. He pulled her in front of him and held the knife to her neck. "Now Miss Josie—whoever you are—me an' you are goin' fer a ride. Back off Deputy, or she dies."

Jerry lowered his pistol and watched helplessly as the man and Josie walked slowly to the door and onto the landing outside. Only then, did he go to Becky to check on her. He and Becky then ran to the front door where they saw the man backing down the stairs still holding the knife to Josie's throat. Two accomplices who had been waiting in a car down the street came racing in the direction of the man and Josie. The small crowd of neighbors scattered. The car stopped briefly, the back door opened, and the assailant pushed Josie inside, got in beside her and they sped away.

Josie's Gift

As they passed the stairway and the open door, one of them fired a shot that went wild. Jerry fell on the landing and pulled Becky with him. He carefully looked at the license plate as best he could as the car zoomed past under the security light. He repeated the numbers to Becky. They repeated the numbers together so they could remember them.

As the car with Josie sped away and turned into the night, a police car drove up and came to a screeching halt. Jerry got Becky on her feet, and they hurried down the steps.

"Oh, Mort, am I glad to see you!"

Mort very quietly spoke into Jerry's ear, "Jerry, I'm gonna kill you for this!" He laughed. "Now give me a minute while I call for uniformed officers to secure this place and get the crime lab people in there to scour it."

After he got off the radio, Mort told Becky and Jerry to go back upstairs and wait. By this time Becky was crying uncontrollably. Jerry wasn't sure what he should do. He wanted to comfort her, but at the same time recognized that his position might not allow it. Finally he couldn't hold back. He took one of her hands and pulled her to him and tried to comfort her. When she calmed down, he had her sit on the old worn out couch in the living room. When he looked up, he saw Mort with an impish grin on his mouth but a scowl in his eyes.

Mort sat down. "Okay," he said. "Let's start at the beginning. Tell me the whole story!"

"First, how'd you find us here, Mort?" Jerry asked.

"Josie called me before she left the motel lobby. I went to the motel and the clerk told me he heard you and her talking about going to Becky's apartment to get her things. He told me Becky told you two that her apartment was just down the street a couple of blocks, so here I am! And it looks like just a mite late."

"I'm really sorry, Mort, things were movin' really fast, and I had to make some judgments."

"We'll deal with that later. You get a description of that car and the license number?"

As the uniformed city officers and the crime lab people arrived, Jerry was giving Mort the description and the license number. Mort tore off a page from his notebook and gave it to the first officer on the scene. "Get out an APB out on this car, pronto!" he commanded. "There's three suspects and a woman hostage. We want 'em alive, you hear?"

"Yes sir, Sheriff."

"Jerry, you go in there with the crime lab people and tell 'em what happened in that bedroom. I'll get another deputy over here to help us with the Browns back there at the motel."

Mort got on his portable radio and requested a deputy. He then turned his attention to Becky who was still crying and looking terribly distressed. "I'm sorry, Ma'am, but I've got to know what's happened here tonight and how Josie Brown got into this. Instead of me asking questions, why don't you just start from the beginning and tell me how it all came about."

"Okay, Sheriff... I'll...do my best." Becky began with meeting Josie in the restaurant. She detailed everything. "I hope we can get Josie back!" she said as she again broke into tears.

"We'll get her back Becky—I promise you, we'll get her back. Now, can you give me the names of those three who abducted her?"

"They're all friends of Ronnie's. The one who was holding me is named Sam Jobst. The two in the car, I can't say for sure, but are probably Jorge Sánchez and 'Big' Larry Canfield. They all hang around with Ronnie."

"Jerry," Mort yelled.

"Yeah, Sheriff?"

Mort tore a page out of his notebook and handed it to Jerry. "Go to the computer in your patrol car and look up these names. See what we have on any of them." Jerry bounded down the steps to his car.

Just then the second deputy arrived. "What can I do, Sheriff?"

"Jimmy, I want you to go back to the La Plaza Motel and get the Brown family. The motel clerk will phone their rooms. Git 'em over here as quick as you can! No, wait! On second thought, tell 'em to wait in the lobby. I'll be right there."

"I'm on it, Sheriff," Jimmy said, as he turned to leave.

Just then, one of the crime lab personnel poked his head around the bedroom door. "Hey, Mort, I think you need to come in here and take a look."

"Be right there." Mort turned to Becky, "What am I going to find in there, Becky?"

Becky was hesitant, "There's...a...a big stash of drugs in the closet."

"How long has it been there?" Mort asked.

"Just a couple of days! They were getting ready to break it up and peddle it."

"You talkin' 'bout Ronnie, Sam, Jorge, and 'Big' Larry?"

Becky put her head down in her hands on her lap. "Yes... and...um others," she said.

"Who are the 'others', Becky?" Mort asked.

"I...I don't know!"

Mort had the feeling she was lying. "Were you in on their drug business, Becky?"

"NO!" Becky shouted.

"Then why were the drugs being kept in your apartment?"

Becky looked up at Mort and sighed. "When you been beat up a few times, and when four or five guys take turns with ya whenever they want it, you kinda learn to do what yer told, Sheriff."

Mort just looked at her. Her eyes reflected a deep and habitual sadness, and she looked resigned to whatever fate came her way. "Well," he said. "There's a good side to this, if you can call it that. I've got a hunch you're innocent in all this—especially from what I know about Ronnie and his friends. However, finding the drugs here in your apartment gives us an excuse to take you in and hold you on suspicion. That'll mean you'll be in protective custody, and you won't have to worry about Ronnie or his friends..." Mort looked into her eyes, "...or the 'others'."

Mort got up from his seat and headed for the bedroom. "You wait right there, Becky, I'll have Jerry take you in and get you settled.

Becky looked up at Mort. She shook her head in agreement, and lowered her eyes in resignation.

At that moment, Jerry came back, carrying some papers. "Okay, Mort, the Browns will be waiting for you in the lobby at the motel, and here's the dope on the suspects. They've all got records of drug dealing and felony assaults, plus a bunch of other stuff. You name it, and they've done it. There's pictures there, too."

"Thanks, Jerry," Mort said. Looking back at Becky, he continued. "There's a pretty sizeable stash of drugs here in the apartment. I'm confident they don't belong to Becky, but we need to take her in and book her on suspicion. That'll keep her away from Ronnie and his bunch for awhile. Be sure to inventory everything and photograph it before any of it is removed. Oh, and get the sheets off that bed and have the lab look at 'em for DNA."

"Okay, Mort, I'll take care of it." Jerry reached out his hand to Becky and helped her up. He turned to Mort with a sheepish look. "I don't need to cuff her do I, Mort?"

"Naa, Jerry. She'll be okay. Have her show you the drug stash and ask her if there's anything else in the apartment we should know about. And when you git to the office, have them transmit these pictures to all units in the area." Mort smiled as he turned to go outside and down the stairs to his car.

When he got to the bottom of the steps, news media people were ducking under the crime scene tape and heading for him. He decided it would be best to talk to them before they got more information than they should have. The questions started coming.

"Sheriff, was this a drug raid or what?"

"No, this was not a drug raid. It's a hostage situation involving three male suspects and a female hostage."

"Who's the hostage?"

"At this moment, we're not releasing any names until relatives have been notified."

"Do you know who the suspects are?"

"We're not sure on that. We expect to have more information on their identity tomorrow."

"Do you have a description of the car involved?"

"Not for sure—nothing we can verify at this time. That'll be all, ladies and gentlemen. Please leave the immediate scene and stay behind the crime scene tape. All the officers on the scene have been instructed not to give any interviews or information regarding the crime. I will schedule a news conference for sometime tomorrow, and your respective media will receive notices. Thank you very much."

When Mort got to the Motel, a very worried Brown family was waiting for him. The clerk offered to get them all some coffee.

Mort sat down and sighed. He looked at each one and especially at Stevie who was sitting on Doris' lap. He asked them to tell him what happened at the restaurant that would bring Josie and Becky together.

John spoke for them all. "I was telling about my experiences at the hospital in Big Pine, and we were all in tears."

Stevie broke in. "Mister Mort, Grampa saw an angel!"

Mort smiled, "Thank you, Stevie, I'm glad you told me. That's an important bit of information. Go on Mister Brown."

"As I said, we were all in tears, and the waitress...um Becky Hall...came to our table and asked if everything was all right. We said it was, and she began to get a little teary eyed herself, and walked away. That's when Josie got up and followed her. Josie told her if she needed to talk with someone, to come here to the motel lobby after work, which she did. We all went to our rooms and went to bed."

Mort turned to the clerk. "What happened here after Becky got here?"

The clerk described the scene when Ronnie walked in and how he verbally assaulted the women and then physically assaulted him. He described how the situation escalated when Deputy Walker got there, and how Becky ended up going to the apartment with Jerry, and how Josie followed.

Mort just stared at the front doors for awhile. He could picture in his mind all that happened as the clerk described it. Everything the clerk and John said was consistent with what Becky told him. "Okay folks, here's what we know. Josie traded places with Becky into the hands of the abductor, a known bad guy named Sam Jobst. She's in a car with Jobst and two others. They're dangerous, and at least one of them has a gun. They may have more guns in the car or in their hideout, wherever that is. My hunch is they'll hole up, and they likely won't treat Josie very well. It's entirely possible they could kill her when they figure they no longer need a hostage. Jerry got a good description and the license number of the car, and we've got every unit in the state looking for them."

Stevie was in tears. He looked around and said, "I know Jesus will take care of my mama!"

Mort went to Doris and took Stevie up into his arms and held him. "Yes, Stevie, Jesus will take care of your mama."

For several minutes, Mort walked around and held Stevie then gave him back to Doris.

"Missus Brown, why don't you and Stevie go back to your room and see if you can rest. I'm going to talk to your husband and sons for awhile."

Doris tried her best to keep from crying. She thought of Josie's parents and how worried they would be. She was thinking she should call them when it hit her— *"Josie has my cell phone."* She ran back to Mort and the men, with Stevie following.

"Sheriff," she almost shouted. "Josie has my cell phone."

Their mouths dropped open and they stared at Doris.

"If the phone's on, can't they ping it and find out where it is?" Joe Richard asked.

"Boys, that's the best news I've had all night. They can't tell us exactly where that phone is, but they can get mighty close. What's the number?"

Doris gave him the number and he immediately called his office and relayed the information. "Okay, folks, we should have something soon—that is if she left the phone turned on. Let's pray she did."

Mort asked the clerk for another cup of coffee. The other men passed on the offer of more coffee. Their spirits were lifted by Doris' news.

"Well, we need to talk about tomorrow," Mort said. "I should be hearing from Rock City with instructions on what they want to do about extraditing Mister and Missus Brown. They'll have to return there as soon as word arrives. That means you all may not be here for the conclusion of this situation with Josie. What I would suggest is that, since David Lee has custodial responsibility, he drive his mom and dad, along with Stevie, back to Rock City. Joe Richard can stay here so he can look after Josie when we find her." He looked around at them all.

"Can't you stall them at Rock City, Sheriff?" John asked.

"I don't know! That might be a possibility. I'll see what I can do when they contact me. Regardless, I think one of you should call Reverend Jefferson at the mission and explain things to her. They'll want to know, and they can all pray. We're going to need lots of prayer."

Joe Richard looked at his brother and then spoke. "Okay, Sheriff, your suggestion is a good one, and that'll be our plan 'A'. If you can get Rock City to put off extradition, then we'll all stay. First thing in the morning I'll call the mission." He looked around, "Does anybody have that number?"

Doris spoke up, "She used my phone to call when we were all at the hospital, but Josie has it." Then she remembered, "Stevie knows it!"

Stevie beamed as he spoke the numbers from memory. Joe Richard wrote it down. "Thanks, Stevie. Now, let's all get a little rest. Sheriff, here's my cell number—if you get any word call me."

"Okay," Mort said. "I'll do that. You folks all get some rest if you can. It's gonna be daylight in a few hours. I'll call if anything develops. I best be getting' on back to the scene and see what Jerry's come up with. Good night—what's left of it. And by the way, the news media may be around wanting to interview you all. Please keep all this under your hat for Josie's sake. I talked to them over at the apartment and told them we couldn't release the name of the hostage so that's the first thing they'll want to know. Please don't say a word."

After talking to the motel staff and asking them not to make any statements to the news media, Mort tipped his hat, turned toward to the front doors, and left. The Brown family decided to get together in one of their rooms to pray and to nap if they could.

CHAPTER TWENTY

When Jobst pushed Josie into the car, he hit her on the back of the head so she fell over on the seat unconscious. When she began to rouse and tried to sit up, he pushed her down again. He leaned over on top of her and forcibly kept her on the seat beside him. In the process, he tried to fondle her breasts, and in response, she pushed one of her hands under his and pushed it up. At the same time, she bent her head down far enough to get hold of his hand with her teeth. She bit into his flesh as hard as she could. He screamed and temporarily rolled back off her and leaned on the opposite door with blood gushing from the wound. Josie reached for the door handle and tried to open the door. It was locked, and the child lock feature was engaged. She was trapped, and she knew it.

When Jobst recovered his wits, he doubled his fist and hit her on the side of her head as hard as he could. She lost consciousness and again collapsed onto the seat. In the front seat 'Big' Larry Canfield yelled back at Jobst. "Leave her alone, you hear? LEAVE HER ALONE!"

"Okay…okay," Jobst yelled back. "The bitch bit my hand!" He took out his handkerchief and tied it around his hand, which by this time was throbbing.

They drove around for what seemed like hours. Josie regained consciousness with a swelling lump on the side of her head and with a miserable headache. She decided to pretend she was still unconscious. She didn't know how long they had been gone from the apartment and had no idea of where they were headed. She thought of Stevie and what he might be doing right now. That thought gave her the resolve she needed to stay alive. She thought of the Brown family and knew they were praying for her. She knew that people back in Rock City were praying as well. Suddenly she felt a sense of calmness sweep over her and knew that somehow God would see her through this. Her mind went to Will, and she smiled inwardly at the thought of him.

"Where you figurin' to take this bitch?" Jorge asked no one in particular.

"We're headin' for Ronnie's dad's ranch," 'Big' Larry responded. "We can lock her up there and git us something to eat. We'll make a plan for disposing of her as soon's we know we don't need her for a hostage no more."

Josie heard what was said, and by the sound of the car, could tell when they pulled off the main road and started down a gravel or dirt road. After about ten or fifteen minutes, she felt the car stop.

'Big' Larry got out and opened the back door where Josie was still pretending unconsciousness. Turning to Jobst, "What'd you do to the bitch, you knucklehead."

"Dammit, she bit me."

'Big' Larry looked at his two partners. His eyes narrowed, and his face puffed in anger. "Now, you two Creeps listen up good! We need this bitch alive, YOU HEAR? There ain't no harm of any kind to come to her. There's always a chance we'll need her to bargain with!"

Sam looked at Larry and growled. "Ain't no harm in us havin' a little fun with her, if ya know what I mean."

Larry got right into Sam's face. "You harm that woman in any way, an' that includes havin' yer fun with her, an' I'll smear yer ugly face all over that cabin! YOU HEAR?"

Sam looked down, "Yeah, I hear."

Larry yelled, "I DIDN'T HEAR YA, SAM!"

Sam looked up and yelled, "YEAH, I HEAR YA!"

Larry continued. "Now, you two git that bitch outta the car and into the cabin. Lay her on the old sofa and tie her up."

Sam and Jorge did as they were told. Josie still pretended to be unconscious. They put her on the couch, and tied her up. She heard Jorge say, "Don't you think one of us should stay behind?"

Larry just looked at him. "How stupid are you Jorge, an' how stupid do you think I am? Do you think I'd trust either one of you to stay behind? Now git into the car and let's go."

They all got back into the car and Josie heard them drive away. She maintained her pretense of unconsciousness just in case one of them was left behind.

"Where we goin'?" Sam asked.

"There's an old shack about a mile from here. Ronnie's old man keeps an old pickup there. We're goin' back to town, and we'll need somethin' else to drive."

First thing next morning, Sheriff Mortenson called Rock City and talked to Sandy. "Mornin' Sandy, Mort here. I need ta know what you want in terms of extradition of the Browns back to Rock City. But first, we have a complication involving Josie."

"Go on."

"Well, Josie befriended a young woman named Becky Hall at a restaurant down the street from their motel. One thing led to another, and Josie was taken hostage by three bad guys. They got away real early this morning. They took a shot at my deputy as they departed. I'll tell ya the whole story later. If ya turn on yer TV you'll probably see a little

Josie's Gift

bit of it on the morning news. I have a news conference at eleven o'clock, and I'll give a few more details. I can't give away too much, or it might jeopardize Josie's safety. We've got a statewide APB out on the car. Fortunately Josie had Doris Brown's cell phone with her. We're hoping her abductors didn't discover it and that she has it turned on. Anyway, what's your plan Sandy?"

"Will Brent at the DA's office has the extradition papers. I'll call him right now. My guess is that we'll be on the next plane out. Can you have one of your deputies pick us up?"

"I'll do that honor myself."

"Thanks, Mort. We should be there early this afternoon."

When Mort hung up the phone, Jerry walked in with a map. "Jerry, I thought you was going off duty and would be home sleeping."

"Not on your life Mort. Looks like Josie left the cell phone on. We've got some areas marked on this map where she could be. We can't pin it down yet because the cell towers out there are not very close together."

Mort laid the map on his desk and studied it. "What time was the last ping?"

"About six this morning, and it came from the same location as the previous one."

"That means they've stopped somewhere in that area. How often do they ping that phone?"

"About every fifteen minutes. Problem is there've been no returns from the phone since that last one at six. That means either the bad guys found the phone or the battery has run down."

"Good work, Jerry. Get word out to concentrate efforts in that area and get a chopper out there."

"Okay, Mort, I'm on it." Jerry turned and left the office. He was dead tired, but adrenaline and sheer will power kept him going. He wasn't about to give up.

Josie's Gift

Mort decided to have a talk with Becky and called the women's jail to have her brought over. When she arrived, Mort put a county road map out in front of her and asked her to look at it. "Becky, we've been having the cell company ping the phone Josie's carrying, and we've had some luck. It seems when they left your apartment, which is right...here." He pointed. "They then drove out in this direction...and then over here to this area...then over to this area where we think they stopped somewhere. The cell phone ping was coming from the same area twice in thirty minutes." Mort pointed out the area with his pencil. "Are you familiar with anything out there at all? Did they ever take you out there for anything? Or do you remember them talking about anything out there?"

Becky studied the map. She asked a few questions about some of the symbols then looked some more. Finally she looked up, "I don't recognize anything, Sheriff. I'm sorry." She broke into tears, "I can't stop thinking of Josie."

"Think of her a lot Becky, and as you do pray for her." Mort scratched his head as he was thinking. "Becky, do you think if Jerry drove you out to that area you might recognize something?"

Becky shook her head. "I doubt it, Sheriff. I don't think I've ever been out there. They did everything with me at my apartment. I'm truly sorry."

"That's okay, Becky," Mort said. "You just keep on praying, and if you think of anything that might help us, have the supervisor in your cell block call me, okay?"

Mort walked with Becky back to the holding area and turned her over to one of the female guards.

Mort went back to his office and got a cup of coffee on the way in. He sat for a long time studying the map. "There's got to be something," he said to himself. Finally he got up and walked out to his secretary. "I'm supposed to have a news conference this morning. Call all the media and let them know I'm postponing it. Patch me through to the other law enforcement agencies for a conference call and find out what time the next plane will come here from Rock City. Oh, and tell Jerry to keep the SWAT team at the ready for a five-minute lead time, and that I need to see him."

As soon as he got back into his office, the phone rang. "Sheriff, you're good to talk to the other agencies now."

"Thanks." Mort punched some buttons on his phone. "This is Mort, any of you folks got any news."

One by one they all reported they had nothing. Roads were all blocked, and nothing fitting the description of the car had come in or out of the area. The chopper pilot reported nothing from the air. He had seen one pickup, older model, on one of the ranch roads, but nothing suspicious.

"Okay, thanks all of you. Let's keep the pressure on. They're going to make a mistake sooner or later. I just hope its sooner."

Jerry walked into the office just as Mort's phone rang. "Mort, this is Sandy. We're on our way in a National Guard jet. Pilot says we'll touch down at Littleville in one hour."

"Okay, Sandy. I'll be there waiting for you. I assume you'll be taxiing to the military buildings on the east side of the field."

"Yeah, you got it right. See you in an hour."

"Sit down Jerry," Mort commanded. "You look tired."

"You do too, Mort"

"Anything new?" Mort asked

"Nothing," Jerry answered.

"Okay, let's brainstorm a little bit. There's got to be a break somewhere in this case. The danger to Josie gets worse as time goes on. We've got to keep the pressure on those creeps so they'll think they have to keep Josie alive for bargaining power." Mort thought for a few minutes. "I'm going to put out a news release and identify all three of 'em and hope they're listening to the radio. You think it'll work?"

Jerry thought for a minute. "What're the other options? Like you said if we wait too long it gets more risky for Josie. I say you go ahead with it. Another thing I thought of — I can check the courthouse records and find out who the property owners are in that area..."

Mort interrupted, "...that's brilliant, Jerry! But all we need to do is go to the nine-one-one office down the hall. They have computerized maps and records of all that. Go get on it! I'm going to make up a news release and get it emailed out immediately." He looked at his watch. "Then I've got to get to the airport and pick up Lieutenant Sandoval and his pal from Rock City."

As Mort typed up a simple news release he began to feel as if they were making some progress.

> *To: All news media*
> *From: Sheriff Mortenson*
> *Subject: Abduction*
> *New information has been uncovered relative to the abduction of a woman from the Crown Royale Apartments yesterday. The identity of the woman abducted is Missus Josie Brown, who lives in Rock City. Her abductors have been identified by a witness on the scene as Sam Jobst, Jorge Sánchez and 'Big' Larry Canfield. All three are known felons and are extremely dangerous. We have some indication where they're hiding out. More information as it becomes available.*

As Mort walked out of the office, he grabbed his hat. Speaking to Joyce, he said on the way out, "There's a news release on my computer. Please get it to all the media ASAP. I'm on my way to the airport. If Jerry comes back, keep him here until I get back. Oh, tell him to put someone on surveillance at Becky's apartment in case those creeps come back looking for her."

"Yessir!" Was the reply.

At the airport, Mort parked and headed into the military terminal to wait. He asked about a National Guard arrival from Rock City and was told it was in the pattern and would land in five minutes.

As the jet taxied to the terminal, Mort recognized the distinctive markings. As soon as it stopped and shut down, a side door opened and a ramp was let down to the tarmac. Two men dressed in suits and each carrying a briefcase and a small travel bag walked down the ramp. Mort went out to meet them.

Sandy extended his hand and introduced himself and introduced Will. Out of curiosity, Mort asked how they rated a trip on the National Guard aircraft.

Sandy explained, "We have one of the main state squadrons stationed at Rock City. Those guys always need training flights to keep up their skills—they're real good about letting us tag along whenever they need to fly."

"Glad to have you guys here," Mort said. "We've had quite a time since the Brown's accident."

"What's this about Josie?" Will asked.

"I'll tell you the story in the car on the way to my office. First, we'll get you two checked into the motel where the Brown's are staying. Then we can relax and talk official stuff over some coffee and donuts at my office. Oh, have you two had lunch?"

"Yeah," Sandy replied. "Joann, my wife packed us a nice lunch for the flight. These National Guard planes don't have flight attendants or food."

"Unless of course you happen to be a high-ranking state official or one of the generals," Will interjected.

At the motel, Sandy and Will checked in. The Browns and Stevie happened to be walking into the lobby. Stevie ran to Sandy and Will and hugged them both. Then he hugged

Mort. Turning back to Sandy and Will, he said, "Mister Sandy, Mister Mort is my friend."

Sandy and Will smiled. Will said, "I'm sure he is, Stevie. You have the best friends in the world."

Stevie introduced them to the Browns who were curious about how long it would be before they would go back to Rock City.

"Within the next couple of days," Sandy said.

As they drove from the motel to the office, Mort described the events leading to Josie's being taken hostage. By the time they reached the office, Sandy and Will had all the details.

"How dangerous are these guys, Mort?" Will asked.

"Well, all three have long rap sheets—some violent stuff, but so far no murders—at least that we know of. But we consider them dangerous and apt to do most anything if pushed into a corner," Mort replied.

When they got to Mort's office, he introduced them to Joyce, his secretary.

Sandy smiled. "Well, I've been looking forward to meeting the sweet voice I talked to on the phone!"

She smiled at Sandy and went about her business.

Jerry was waiting for them in the office. Mort introduced Sandy and Will to Jerry.

"Mort, I think we have a bingo."

"Okay, talk!" Mort commanded.

"Look here," Jerry said, pointing to an area on the map. "Ronnie's old man has property there, and the boundaries are roughly along this creek, then a fence line about here, and back to the road. It's a pretty good size piece of property, several thousand acres and has several dirt ranch roads going in and out of the place. Now, look right here," pointing, "and here," pointing. These are small buildings of some kind. One or both may be cabins with living quarters, but nobody knows."

Josie's Gift

"Good job, Jerry. My hunch is they're hid out in one of those buildings, and they've got Josie there." Mort scratched his head and looked at Sandy. Here's the plan! Jerry, you get a plainclothes officer to go with you to Ronnie's old man's office. I want you to squeeze him and see if he'll talk. Either way, bring him in and hold him on suspicion of being an accessory to kidnapping. I'll get the SWAT team on the way out there with instructions to hide out near both buildings and to watch what comes and goes. They'll have the authority to move with whatever force is required when needed. I'll get that chopper back in the air and have him high enough that he can see as much of the area as possible without attracting attention with his noise. What do you think, Lieutenant?"

"Sounds like a good plan, Mort. You've got all your bases covered. If Josie's in neither of those buildings, then what?"

"Then...then we're back to plan 'B'. Somehow we'll round up those three thugs and make sure they talk. Okay, let's get going!"

Just then the radio crackled. It was Deputy Bill Green on the stakeout at Becky's apartment. The whispered voice said, "Mort, I've got a visual with someone going up the steps at the apartment. Looks like he's got a key and is trying it in the door. Okay, door's open, and he's going in."

"Anyone else around?" Mort asked.

"No, it looks like he parked his car around the corner out of sight. No one else around."

"Okay, move on that apartment right now and hold whoever it is. I'm on my way!"

Mort turned to Sandy and Will, "let's go!"

Josie's hands and feet were beginning to get numb from the ropes binding them. Her captors had been gone long enough she figured they would not be back anytime soon, so she tried her best to twist the rope and loosen the knots. Unsuccessful, she swung her body into an upright position

Josie's Gift

with her feet on the floor. She looked around. The closest thing she could see was a water glass on the table. It took her several tries, but she managed to stand up. She hopped over to the table and hit it hard enough with her hips that the glass fell on the floor and broke. The bottom of the glass was intact with the top part broken, leaving several jagged and pointed pieces still attached.

When she bumped the table, she lost her balance and started to fall. To stop herself from hitting the floor and being cut by the glass, she leaned over the top of the table until she felt stable. Her head was bruised with a big lump on the side, and it was throbbing with pain. The activity with the table made her a little dizzy. When she felt better, she looked at the glass and looked at the couch. Still leaning on the table, she used her feet to kick the glass toward the couch. It stopped within inches of where she needed it to be.

She moved around the table little by little until she was leaning over it, facing the couch. With her feet, she was able to move herself and the table inch by inch toward the couch. Now, all she had to do was get down on the floor in a sitting position, with her back to the couch and the glass between her hands. She moved very slowly so as not to slip. At the same time, she moved the glass to a position against the couch. Using her hands behind her back and her knees, she was able to slide to the floor in a sitting position with the glass right beside her. She turned just enough to get hold of the glass with her hands and then turned again so her back was against the couch. She was now in a position that she could use the jagged edge of the glass to cut the rope around her wrists.

By the time she was in position, Josie was tired and her hands were numb. She was afraid she would not know if she cut her wrists. She laid her head back against the couch, closed her eyes and prayed earnestly for her angel to guide her movements. She took a deep breath and very carefully began the slow up and down movements of the rope against the glass. Suddenly, she felt a sharp prick on the skin of her wrist. She immediately stopped, readjusted the glass, and pushed her buttocks back against the glass so as to keep it from moving. Again, she got into a slow rhythmic movement of the rope up and down on the jagged edge of the glass.

After what seemed like an eternity and several stops to rest, the rope finally broke free. She sat and rubbed her hands until she again had feeling, then she untied her feet. Slowly she got up and tried to walk. Her legs were weak, and her feet were still numb. Holding onto the table for support, she kept moving until the blood circulation was restored. She knew she had to get away from the cabin as soon as possible. She went to the cupboards to try to find something to eat to take with her. There were several boxes of cereal in the cupboards and some bottles of water in the fridge. She grabbed one box of cereal and two bottles of water and headed for the back door.

Attorney Albert Russell moved slowly and carefully up the steps. With each step he looked around. At the door, he inserted a key. Taking one last look around, he went into the apartment and shut the door behind him. Deputy Bill Green moved quickly, but quietly, up the stairs and burst into the apartment with his gun drawn and out in front. At the same time, a well dressed man stepped out from the bedroom with a very surprised look on his face. Green engaged his laser sight and commanded the man to get on the floor.

The man's voice displayed his arrogance. "Deputy, you're going to hear from your boss for this. My name is Albert Russell; I'm an attorney here, and a very influential one at that. Now why don't we just forget this whole thing and pretend it didn't happen. I've got plenty of money, and I can make it worth your while."

"Mister Russell, I've already heard a lot about you, and none of it was good. Now you git yer butt down on that floor and roll over on your stomach and put yer hands behind you."

"What are the charges?"

"Well, let's see now. How about breaking and entering and tampering with a crime scene fer starters. And we'll just add accomplice to kidnapping?"

"Your boss is going to hear about this!"

"He already has, Mister. Now git yer hands behind yer back."

Green put his handcuffs on Russell and helped him to his feet. Then he patted him down.

"What do you think you're doing?" Russell commanded.

"I'm jest doin' what the law says I'm supposed to do, Mister Russell." When he got to Russell's waist, he exclaimed, "Well, well—lookee here." He pulled a small caliber pistol from a hidden holster.

"I have a license to carry that handgun, Deputy. Just look in my wallet."

Green just smiled. "I'm not touchin' yer wallet, Mister Russell. Now, you have the right to remain silent, and you have the right to an attorney. Anything you say can and will be used against you."

Just then Mort, Sandy and Will came up the stairs and stepped cautiously into the apartment.

"Lookee here, Mort. See the big fish I jest caught—in the very act you might say!"

Mort smiled when he saw Russell in handcuffs. "Well, I'm not surprised." He immediately got on the radio and called the deputies assigned to go to Russell's office and told them to come over to the apartment.

Russell instantly, and angrily, addressed Mort. "Sheriff, I'll have your job for this. You've got no cause for this arrest. I'll see to it that you're thrown out of office. You know when we get downtown I'll post bond and be out in a matter of a couple of hours."

Mort looked at him and calmly said, "Maybe...and maybe not, Mister Russell. We'll just have to wait and see won't we? We might just take our time getting downtown." Mort turned to his deputy. "Bill, take Mister Russell back to the office and make sure he's still there when I get back. I'm going to have a look around here. Oh, and take the scenic route."

"I'll see to it, Mort," Green answered.

Will sat on the worn out couch while Mort and Sandy scoured the rest of the apartment. "Ya know, Sandy, there's got to be something here that old man Russell came back for."

Sandy was looking through some things in the closet. "Hey, Mort look at this."

Mort went to the closet, where Sandy showed him two pairs of pants and two shirts. These sure aren't Becky's," Mort remarked. Looking more carefully he could see they were expensive clothes, and the shirts looked tailor made. Mort turned up one of the shirt tails. "Well, I'll be. Here's the initials 'A' – 'R'. Looks like Mister Russell was a pretty regular visitor to this apartment. Let's look in the drawers of that dresser over there."

Sandy pulled open the drawers one by one. "Looks like women's stuff here. Wait a minute," he said as he pulled out the very bottom drawer. He took out several pairs of men's underwear and T-shirts. A couple of expensive looking neckties were neatly folded and tucked in along the side of the drawer. "Any shoes or socks? He asked Mort.

"None that I can see. My gut tells me this stuff belongs to Attorney Albert Russell. We'll collect it and send it to the lab for them to check out and verify. There may be some prints on those belt buckles."

Suddenly, Will called from the living room. He had the old couch torn apart and found some hidden compartments inside. That's interesting," Mort said. "I'm going to get the crime scene guys back in here. They missed some stuff when they supposedly scoured this place yesterday."

The other two deputies arrived, and Mort gave them instructions. "I want this place secured and nothing disturbed till this is over. Make sure those crime scene guys go over every nook and cranny. Dust everything for prints—I want every set of prints identified."

Mort motioned to Sandy and Will, "Let's go and see what's developing elsewhere in this case.

As they were on their way back to the sheriff's office, the radio crackled. "Mort this is Chopper Two, we have visual on a person running out the back door of the cabin. We're going to take a closer look."

"I'll wait," Mort said.

Chopper Two came back. "Mort, looks like a female, and she's running northeast away from the road."

"Okay, Chopper Two. Keep a visual on her, and if you can, find a place to land and pick her up, set that ship down and get her."

"Will do, Chopper Two out."

Suddenly the radio crackled and an anxious voice came, "Mort, we've spotted a pickup pulling into the drive at the cabin. Three men getting out and looking around."

"Chopper Two, are you armed?"

"That's affirmative, one SWAT with AR-15 automatic weapon and telescopic sight."

"Chopper Two, stay on location and try to keep an eye on both the female and three subjects. SWAT One is on the way."

"Will do! Oh, I think I see the SWAT on the way in a black Hummer. I'll get on the secure frequency and let them know what they've got here."

"Okay, Chopper Two. I'm on my way. Keep your radio open so I can monitor."

"Affirmative, Mort. Chopper Two out."

Mort turned to Sandy and Will. "You guys want in on this?"

"Let's go Mort. Lead the way." Sandy replied. "Wouldn't miss it for the world."

When they got into the car, Mort immediately turned the radio to the secure frequency so he could hear the conversations between Chopper Two and SWAT One.

"SWAT One, this is Chopper Two—I'm hovering above you, high altitude. Female ran from cabin a few minutes ago heading north away from the road. You have three male subjects just arrived in light colored pickup at cabin. When you get close I'm going to low altitude and see if I can scare them out."

"Roger, Chopper Two, SWAT One nearing cabin. Pickup truck visual. Let us know if anyone emerges from cabin."

"Will do, SWAT One. Going down now!" Chopper Two banked into a sharp turn and began a rapid descent. When he was at tree-top level, the suspects began running from the cabin. "SWAT One, you in position? They're coming out. I need to get back up high and try to locate female."

"Roger, Chopper Two, we're in position. We have three subjects visual."

A bull horn bellowed. "Police! Stop where you are and lay on the ground. If you are armed, throw your guns away from you!"

Canfield looked in the direction of the noise. He pulled a gun and fired. Three shots rang out, and Canfield went down. He was wounded in his hip—he rolled over and began firing again. As he fired, Sánchez and Jobst ran around the cabin

Josie's Gift

and tried to run into the woods. Two more shots rang out, and Canfield's body jerked and lay still. He was dead.

A loud voice interrupted the escape of Sánchez and Jobst. "Police! Stop where you are and throw your guns away and lay down on the ground face down. Canfield's dead and you're next!" Both subjects froze in their tracks. They looked around confused at what was happening. Jobst threw a gun away and lay down on the ground. Sánchez screamed, "I'm not armed," then lay down on the ground.

The SWAT Team members approached both men with their rifles at ready and pointed at the two subjects. Neither Jobst or Sánchez made any move to resist. Both were handcuffed and hauled away to the Hummer.

On the other side of the building, members of SWAT One looked down at Canfield and shook their heads. The leader got on the radio. "Chopper One we have three subjects under control—one dead. We'll need an ambulance."

Mort broke in, "SWAT One, good job—ambulance on the way. Chopper Two anything on the female?"

"Nothing yet, Mort!"

"Okay, her name's Josie Brown. Captors are in custody, one dead. Use your bull horn and see if you can coax her out into the open, she couldn't have got far. We're just about to the cabin. Let us know if you locate her and if you can, find a place to land to pick her up!"

"Will do, Chopper Two!"

After several circling passes of the area, Chopper Two finally saw a figure cautiously crawl out from some brush. She looked up and waved. The bull horn blared, "Josie Brown, we're police, you're safe now—your captors are all in custody. Stay where you are and stand in the open where we can see you. We're going to look for a place to land to pick you up."

A few minutes later, the SWAT in the chopper spoke on the intercom and pointed to a spot. "Okay, that looks good," the pilot replied.

Chopper Two circled around and back to where Josie was standing. Again the Bull Horn blared. "Josie follow us."

Josie looked up and waved. She followed the chopper and noted the place beyond the trees where she saw it disappear toward the ground. She ran as fast as she could until she saw the chopper waiting, engine running. She collapsed before she could reach the machine. The SWAT member jumped out and ran to carry her back. He got her into the back seat and helped her fasten her safety harness then got back into the front seat. He pointed his thumbs up—the pilot throttled up, and the chopper slowly lifted into the sky.

"Mort, this is Chopper Two. We have the female secured and are heading back to the landing pad on your roof."

"Job well done, Chopper Two. I'll see you there."

Mort turned to his guests and sighed. "Well somewhat of a happy ending here, but Canfield's mother is going to have a very sad day. I feel sorry for her, but I'll personally visit her and let her know what happened. You guys ready to go?"

"Good Job, Mort—great police work." Sandy said.

Mort turned to the SWAT Team. "One of you guys stay here with the body; the ambulance'll be along momentarily. The rest of you go to the shack and see what's in there then come back and pick up your guy. My guess is, there's a car in that shack we will be mighty interested in. I'll get Jerry out here to haul your cargo in."

Mort got on the radio. Jerry, this' Mort."

"Yeah, Mort."

"We need you at the cabin out here, Jerry. We've got human cargo that needs to go to jail."

"I've been listening into your conversations out there, Mort. I'm already at the gate. We'll pass on the way."

"Jerry, alert CSI and have them bring the hauler for a car. I want the cabin, the shack, and the car scoured. Oh, and tell 'em they better do a better job with this than they did on that apartment, or they'll all face some discipline."

"Got it, Mort. I'll see to it, out."

When Mort, Sandy and Will arrived back at the office, Josie was already there. A nurse was treating the cut on her wrist from the glass and the scratches and bruises from her run in the berry bushes and the brush in the woods. The nurse looked at the lump on the side of her head and recommended it be looked at by someone at the hospital.

When Josie saw Will and Sandy, she immediately ran to them. She literally fell into Will's arms and burst into tears. Sandy just smiled. Will held her for several minutes until she regained her composure. He looked sheepishly at Sandy.

Josie looked at Sandy and then hugged him. Sandy walked her back to the nurse to complete the first aid.

Mort spoke. "Well, I hope it will be my turn when that nurse is done with you."

Josie just smiled. "I love all of you. I surely thought I would die out there, but by God's grace I'm safe, thanks to angels named Mort and Jerry." She looked at Sandy and Will, "You two are my very best friends, and I can't thank you enough for being here at this time. I know all of you've been praying, and I appreciate that. Our God is so good!"

When the nurse was finished, Josie rose from the chair and walked directly to Mort. She threw her arms around him and hugged him.

When she released him, Mort spoke, "Josie, being sheriff's a job for me, but its times like this that I wouldn't give it up for all the money in the world. Now, we need to get you to the hospital to have that head looked at. How about you go with Will? Sandy and I will stay here and talk about what's going on with the Browns?" He looked at Will. "You okay with that, Will?"

"Be glad to do it, Mort," Will said. "Just point me in the right direction and give me something to drive."

"Good, just tell the attendant at the hospital that Josie is a material witness and is in the care and custody of the county. Have them call me to verify. Oh, and have Josie call the Browns at the motel. They're probably frantic. And by the way...nobody, and I mean nobody...is to know Josie was there at the hospital. Be sure she checks the right space on the confidentiality form."

CHAPTER TWENTY-ONE

After Will and Josie were on the way to the hospital, Sandy turned to Mort. "I know enough about your case here to know that Josie's going to have to stay here in Littleville for the time being isn't she, Mort?"

"I'm not sure, Sandy. With Russell involved, it looks to me like this is going to get a lot bigger and much more complicated. There's a lot more to this than just Russell and his young buddies. Whatta you think?"

Sandy thought for a few moments before he spoke. "If it were my case, Mort, I think I'd be looking into the possibility of a connection with the syndicate or with one of the big-time Mexican drug lords orchestrating things."

"My thoughts exactly, Sandy. You think we could squeeze old man Russell for information?"

"Or use him for bait," Sandy said, with a smile on his face.

Mort looked at his watch. "You make a lot of sense. Let's go get a bite to eat. Whatta ya say?"

"I'm ready, lead the way."

Mort had an idea. "I think I know just the place!"

On purpose, Mort drove by the motel and pointed it out to Sandy. "Now, there's a restaurant just down the street from the motel that has very good food."

They pulled into the parking lot and parked. Mort radioed his dispatcher so she'd know where he was. Before they got out of the car, Mort spoke. "This is where Becky was working when she met Josie. I think I'd like to talk to the manager. Let's see if we can flush him out!"

A very pretty young hostess showed them to a table. "Will this be okay, gentlemen?" She asked with a thick Spanish accent.

"This'll be just fine."

"Someone will be here in a few moments to take your drink order."

"Thank you, Miss..."

"...Juanita," she replied.

Mort smiled and casually looked at the menu. Out of habit, Sandy looked around and unobtrusively glanced at everyone who was visible. A young man wearing a white shirt and black pants came to the table. "My name is Enrique, and I'll be your waiter today. May I take your drink orders Sirs?"

"Enrique...?" Mort asked.

"Enrique Martínez Talamantes," He said proudly.

Sandy looked up, "Okay Enrique Martínez Talamantes, water for me please."

Mort was watching the young man closely. "I'll have water also. Oh, and...uh, is Becky working today?"

Enrique's eyes widened in surprise. "No, uh...no, she's not working today." He had a worried look on his face, but said, "I'll be right back with your water and to take your order."

Sandy watched the young man hurry to the back. He saw the young man's head above a divider—he was soon joined by another older man. "Mort look to your left, just behind that divider."

Mort turned his head, his eyes quickly took in what Sandy was seeing and then turned back to the menu. Still looking down at the menu, "What do you make of it Sandy?"

"Let's just watch and see what happens. Just keep your eyes on the menu!"

Within a few minutes the second man looked over at Mort and Sandy and then quickly turned and left. "I'm going to the bathroom Sandy. Watch our waiter."

Mort stood up and casually looked around for the bathroom. As he did, he saw the second man disappear into an office to the side of the kitchen and in the rear, near the far end of the building. He spotted the bathrooms and headed in that direction. He only spent a few minutes washing his hands and then headed back to the table. Enrique came to take their order, but instead he told them to follow him; the manager wanted to talk to them.

When they walked into the office, Enrique closed the door and left. Mort's eyes followed him out and took note of the door to see if it was locked—it wasn't. The office was rather elaborate for a restaurant manager, and the furnishings were more expensive than one would expect in a common office. He noted the man who had been with the waiter standing to his left against the wall and facing the desk, his hands clasped in front of his body. He wore expensive boots, slacks and an embroidered, short-sleeved shirt.

Mort moved to a place directly in front of the desk, and Sandy moved to a place against the wall directly opposite the man who seemed to be a bodyguard. Sandy eyed the bodyguard carefully. He noted tattoos on both arms and a bulge inside his shirt on his right side, which Sandy concluded was likely a gun.

The man behind the desk was dressed impeccably and expensively. He immediately stood and reached across the desk and introduced himself. "Ah, Sheriff Mortenson, I have heard many good things about you. I am Juan Velasco Salazar, and I am very happy to welcome you to my restaurant."

Mort extended his hand, and the two shook hands. He glanced down momentarily and noticed small bits of tattoos barely showing beyond Salazar's jacket sleeve. Turning to Sandy, he said, "And this is Detective Sandoval from Rock City, Texas." Salazar turned and extended his hand to Sandy and the two shook hands.

"Yes," Salazar said in a melodious tone. "Rock City, I wonder if that might be an appropriate place to open another of my fine restaurants?"

"I'm sure Rock City would welcome you Señor Salazar." Sandy's Spanish pronunciation of the name was flawless, and Salazar smiled approvingly.

Salazar smiled and sat down. He invited Mort and Sandy to sit. "Can I get either of you a drink?"

"No, thank you," Mort answered, as he sat down.

"Thank you for your hospitality, but I don't drink," Sandy said in a friendly tone.

"So, my friends—you were asking about Becky Hall?"

"Yes," Mort replied.

"Just what is it you would like to know?"

"Well," Mort said. "For starters, how long did she work here?"

Salazar thought for a few moments then motioned to the man standing against the wall. He spoke something in Spanish, and the man left the room. Mort looked at Sandy. Sandy said nothing. He didn't want Salazar to know that he spoke and understood Spanish.

"We will have your answer very quickly, Sheriff."

Within minutes, the man returned with a file, handed it to Salazar and again stood against the wall with his hands clasped in front of him.

Salazar opened the file and thumbed through several papers. He smiled, "Yes," he said in the same melodious tone of voice. "Here it is. She began to work here two years ago." He looked up at Mort. "And, what is your interest in her, if I may ask?"

"We're looking for her. We think she might have information on some drug business here in the county."

Salazar stiffened, his eyes narrowed. "But, I saw her on television the other night when the police raided her apartment."

"And she hasn't been seen since." Mort lied, not letting on he noticed Salazar's change in demeanor. "Some thugs were trying to get away from police, and they took her hostage. Her friend stepped in and the thugs got away with her friend as a hostage instead. In the melee, Becky slipped out and completely disappeared. We think she's been stashed away by her contact, whoever that is."

"Has the friend been found and rescued?" Salazar asked.

"No," Mort lied again. "We've captured the creeps who abducted her—one was killed in the action, but the other two are now in custody."

"Well," Salazar replied. "I am very sorry about the trouble Becky is in. Of course, we had no idea she was involved in anything illegal. You already know her address so what more do you need?" He asked trying to sound helpful.

"Just one more question, then we'll be on our way. "Do you know if she was close to any of the other staff here at the restaurant?"

"No, my friend. I am not that close to my employees. However, you may feel free to talk to anyone who is working right now, casually of course so as not to arouse my customers. I hope you find her; her record here is a good one. She was one of our best waitresses, and of course we would welcome her back."

Mort stood and turned to leave. He nodded to Sandy, and both men shook hands with Salazar and thanked him.

"Señores, you will of course stay for dinner? You will be my guests!"

Mort looked at Sandy and nodded. "Thank you, Mister Salazar we'll do just that. You've been very kind and helpful."

The bodyguard led them back to their table and snapped his fingers. Enrique returned with a big smile and took their order.

"Let's not talk shop in here, Sandy. Just talk about the food and..." He stopped talking when he saw the bodyguard leave the restaurant. "You see that, Sandy?"

"Yeah, I saw it."

"Well, Sandy," Mort said. "Tell me about your family."

"Wife's name is Joann, and she's absolutely wonderful. We have two kids, and one grandson, with another on the way. We get to keep Davie a lot when he gets home from kindergarten. He's a really bright kid. Stevie stayed with us while Josie was in the hospital, and it was a real joy to have the two of them around."

"You mean Stevie..."

"Yeah, that Stevie. How about you, Mort? Got any family?"

Wife's name is Susan. She's great too." He paused. "Ya know its darn hard to be a cop's wife."

"Amen to that, Mort. Ya have to appreciate what they must go through every day, worrying about us. Any kids?"

"Yeah, we have three...adopted. The youngest is still in high school. The oldest is attending the FBI Academy, and the middle one, a girl, is married and has given us two grandkids."

They finished their meal in silence, but observed everything going on. When they got up to leave, they left a tip and waved to Enrique, who smiled and waived back. "Nice kid," Sandy commented. "Wonder if he's connected?"

Outside and in the car, Mort spoke what was on both their minds. "I wonder how many of the employees are connected in some way, and what role Salazar plays in this?"

"Did you notice the inconsistency in Salazar's comment about not knowing his employees, but at the same time seemed to know what a good waitress Becky is," Sandy asked.

"Yeah, I noticed. I also noticed how much his demeanor changed the moment I mentioned she may have information on the drug business in the county." Mort thought for a few minutes as he drove. "You know, Sandy I think Becky knows a lot more about all this than she's told us. And I also think she's really scared because she may know something the big guys don't want her to talk about."

"Josie's picture has been all over the media after the kidnapping so we have her to worry about, Mort. What's your plan for her?"

"You're right, but right now I don't have a plan. We don't have a legitimate charge to be able to hold her, plus there's her son to think about. When we get back to the office, we'll get together with Jerry, Will and Josie and figure something out. For sure, she has to be protected."

"One more thing, Mort; did you notice the tattoos on the arms of Salazar's bodyguard? I'm pretty sure one of them is a likeness of what the Mexican drug gangs call *La Santa Muerte*. It signifies their allegiance to a peculiar saint they call 'the holy death'. The little bits of tattoos we saw on Salazar's arms may be the same figure. That so called saint is thought to be the guardian of the worst of sinners. There are numerous small shrines in Mexico that have been set up to honor her, and many go to those shrines to pay their homage and ask for protection while they are carrying on their murderous businesses. It is said that as long as one keeps his vows to her, she will protect him from harm, no matter what the crime."

Mort looked at Sandy with questions written all over his face. "Tell me more."

"It seems to be a mixture of superstition and Catholicism. Nobody knows the origin, whether it came from Europe or South America, or where. But it seems to be closely related to the Mexican drug cartels and the trafficking of drugs into the United States. Devotion to her has also generated a folk saint named Jesús Malverde, who is said to have been hanged over a hundred years ago in the Mexican State of Sinaloa. He's the saint of 'honorable thievery', kind of like Robin Hood. We're seeing some of this stuff in the border areas on the United States side. Even though the Catholic Church has condemned these practices, the cult of *La Santa Muerte* and Jesús Malverde thrives. Check out Señor Salazar; I have a feeling he may be originally from Sinaloa. He's must be pretty confident, showing off those tattoos."

"Thanks, Sandy. I'll check that out and do a little research. This situation we have with Salazar is beginning to look much more serious than I thought."

The x-rays of Josie's injuries did not show anything to be overly concerned about. She was strongly cautioned to call the emergency room doctor if she had any unusual headaches, blurred vision or mental confusion. While she was waiting for the test results, she called David Lee and told him everything that had happened and to not worry about her; she was all right. She asked him to please bring Stevie down to the sheriff's office for her. After she hung up she called the mission in Rock City.

A familiar, pleasant and melodious voice answered the phone. "This is Isabelle Jefferson. How can I be of service to you?"

"Hi, Isabelle, it's Josie."

Josie's Gift

"Oh, Josie, I'm so glad you called. We've been worried sick about you and of course have been praying day and night."

"Thanks, Isabelle. I love all of you for that. How are things there at the mission—Carla and Darlene?"

"They're fine, Josie. Are you still in Littleville?"

"Yes, and I may be here for some time. I'll have to tell you all about it later, or you may be seeing some of it on the news. Will and Sandy got here yesterday so we've been visiting a lot."

"How's Stevie doing," Isabelle asked.

"Well, I haven't seen him for almost two days. Right now I'm at the hospital with Will, and we're about to go back to the sheriff's office."

"The hospital?" Isabelle yelled. "Why are you and Will at the hospital?"

"I got hit on the head, but I'm okay. At the jail, the nurse said I should have my head examined at the hospital." She laughed.

"Isabelle couldn't help but laugh. "Hit on the head—jail—hospital—you sure you're okay, Girl?"

"I'm okay, Isabelle, just keep praying for me—I mean us! I gotta go. God bless you, bye."

"Wait, Josie, don't hang up!"

Josie almost hung up, but waited. "What is it, Isabelle?"

"Josie! Your mom and dad are here."

Josie didn't know what to say. She broke out in tears. "Isabelle, please keep them there. Don't let them come here to Littleville under any circumstances. I hope to be back to the mission in a few days. Maybe get Carla to look after them—she can relate."

"I understand and agree, Josie. Is it okay if they call you?"

"Yeah, give them the number I'm calling from. It's a cell phone that belongs to Doris. Thanks Isabelle, I love you more than you will ever know. Give my love to Mom and Dad. God bless, bye."

Will saw the tears. "Is everything okay, Josie?"

She smiled and took his hand. "Much better now, Will. My mom and dad are at the mission in Rock City. They went there expecting to see me, but...let's go."

Back at Sheriff Mortenson's office, Josie and Will joined Sandy, Mort and Jerry in Mort's private office. "Any of you need anything before we get started?"

Each in turn said nothing was needed so Mort began. "This whole thing has turned into a very complicated investigation that I believe has some pretty serious and far reaching implications. Everything I'm telling you must be kept in the strictest of confidence, is that clear?" He looked at each one as each nodded ascent.

Mort continued. "Sandy and I had dinner at the *Las Palmas Especiale Restaurant* today. We went there with the idea of trying to find out what we could about Becky. We were introduced to Mister Juan Velasco Salazar, who's the owner. I don't want to go into details just yet, but we believe Becky knows more about a major drug operation than she's letting on. Sandy and I both think there are probably ties to either the syndicate or one of the Mexican drug cartels. We also think that Russell and his young buddies are involved. I have no idea yet how it all fits together, but we will launch a full-scale investigation and bring in the State and Federal resources, if they are interested."

Josie was wide-eyed, and her eyes were beginning to tear up. "But how could someone like Becky get involved?"

"When we went through Becky's apartment, we found a lot of things that connected her to Russell and the drug business. We think Russell is up to his neck in it, but as of yet, we can't prove anything. Becky got in through her relationship with Albert Russell and his son Ronnie. She just made a bad choice of friends, and once in she couldn't get out—except in a casket."

Turning to Jerry, and handing him a piece of paper, Mort continued. "Jerry, I want you to run the names on this list through every data base you can get into. I want to know everything about them. I want to know if Salazar owns any other businesses around here or anywhere else. Look into immigration records and find out where Salazar is from. I want to know all about Attorney Albert R. Russell. Get into the court records and identify whom he's represented. Find out if anytime in the past he's ever represented Becky or Salazar."

Jerry got up to leave. "I'm on it, Mort!"

"One more thing, Jerry. Russell won't be in custody more than a few hours. When he leaves here I want him tailed. I want to know everyplace he goes, and whom he visits with."

Mort turned to Sandy and Will. "Now, we've got to decide what to do with Josie. Because of her association with Becky and her abduction by Ronnie's friends, her life is in danger. She's going to be needed here for grand jury testimony and for any follow-up trials. Unfortunately, we don't have a safe house here in this county so she may need to be taken elsewhere. I know the state people and the Feds have such places. Whether they'd be willing to take the responsibility for her, I don't know...and of course there's Stevie to think of."

"What about taking her back to Rock City?" Sandy asked.

"That's a good possibility, but it's also out of state. I'd probably have to get a court order." You work with the district attorney in Rock City, Will. Whatta you think?" Mort asked.

"I think it can be done, Mort. Witnesses can be hidden just about anywhere as long as they're available when needed. The problem as I see it would be getting her back here from

Rock City. When she is here, it would be for several days or possibly weeks at a time, and you would still have to put her in a safe place."

Mort scratched his head. "What about a compromise. She goes back with you until the investigation is ready to go to the grand jury. Then she comes back here, and we keep her as long as needed. That'll give me some time to get something in place here."

"The other possibility," Will recommended, "would be to take sworn depositions before she goes back to Rock City. Sandy's and my problem right now is that we have to get back to Rock City with the Browns."

"Yeah," Mort replied. "We need to get the Browns out of that motel as soon as possible. I have a hunch Mister Salazar or Attorney Russell may have some business connection with that motel." Mort scratched his head and thought for a few moments. "Why don't you two guys call back to your National Guard friends and find out if you can get a jet to take you and the Browns home?"

Josie was listening wide eyed and worried. "What about Stevie?"

"I think it would be best if he goes back with the Browns," Mort answered.

Mort punched a button on his phone. "Joyce, do we still have Russell Senior in custody?"

Joyce's voice had a little laugh in it. "Yeah, we do, Mort, and he's mad as a wet hen!"

"Okay, I need to keep him at least overnight. Call the district clerk and see if we can get a hearing tomorrow afternoon so we can keep him at least that long."

"Mort, he's already had a visit from an attorney. I'm sure they are getting ready to file papers to get him out on bail."

"Okay, Joyce, speak to the district clerk, and use that sweet voice of yours to get everything stalled for at least twenty-four hours."

"Okay, Mort, I'm on it now. I'll do my best."
"Thanks, Joyce." Mort backed away from the intercom. While Mort was on the intercom, Will called the National Guard headquarters in Rock City. He turned to Mort. "We'll have a National Guard jet in here by noon tomorrow."
"Good," Mort said. "Now all we need to worry about is Josie." He turned to Josie. "Do you feel comfortable staying at the motel tonight, Josie?"
"I guess so," she said with worry in her voice and her eyes."
"Sandy and I are both checked in there, Josie. We'll be close by," Will said.
"Besides," Mort added. "My hunch is that as long as Russell Senior is in custody, she'll be safe." He handed Will a card. "The woman who owns this beauty shop is named Betty. I'm going to call her. She can be trusted, and we'll have her work on Josie and change her appearance as much as she can. I'll have Joyce take her over first thing in the morning. Neither Salazar nor Russell has ever seen Josie in person so hopefully they won't pick up on anything from news media. Now, all of you need to get back to the motel. It's been a long day, and we all need some rest. Oh, I think it would be a good idea to stay out of the lobby as much as possible and find a new place to have breakfast. Here's a card for a place over by the airport. It's a ways from the motel, but I'm going to let you use my personal car. Check out of the motel before you go for breakfast."
Turning to Will and Sandy, Mort asked, "Do you guys have your personal weapons with you?"
"In the briefcases, Mort, in the trunk of your car." Sandy replied.
Mort punched the button on his intercom. "Joyce, we need temporary weapons permits for Detective Sandoval and for Will Brent."
"Okay, Mort."

"Okay, as you two leave, Joyce will have ID cards for you and will take your pictures. Carry those cards and carry your weapons. In the morning, I'll send Jerry over to help you get out with the Browns and your luggage. See you in the morning."

Meanwhile back at *Las Palmas Especiale,* Juan Velasco Salazar had Enrique Martinez Talamantes brought into his office.

Salazar smiled at the young man. "Ahh, Enrique. You have been a very dependable and valued employee here, and I am sure I can trust you." Salazar's eyes narrowed.

Enrique stood straight with his chin up, "Sí, Señor Salazar, you can always trust me. I and my family are in your debt."

Salazar looked Enrique straight in the eyes, then stood up and walked around to the front of the desk where the young man stood. He put both hands on Enrique's shoulders. "My young friend, your father was a valuable asset to my business interests in Mexico City until his...uh...untimely death at the hands of ruthless men."

"Sí, Señor, I was very young, but I remember very well. You brought us here and have taken good care of us. If it were not for me and my sister working here, we would be milking goats in Culiacán, Sinaloa."

Salazar laughed at Enrique's sense of humor, then his eyes narrowed, and he looked serious. "I have a very important assignment for you tonight."

"Whatever it is, Señor, I will do it." He smiled and felt privileged to be called upon to do something important.

"Here is what I want you to do. Do you remember the two gentlemen who were here asking about Becky?"

"Sí, Señor!"

"The one is our local sheriff—the other is a detective from Rock city, Texas. I have been informed that the detective and his friend are staying at the motel. I do not know their business here. You are to go to the motel and hang around observing anyone who comes and goes in the company of the detective. Sometime during the night, take a nap and then be alert in the morning to see who is with him again. Here is a cell phone that connects directly with my private number."

Enrique took the cell phone and carefully put it in his pocket. "When should I call you Señor?"

"As soon as you make your first observation, you are to call. Just press the number One button, and it will automatically call me. I will give you instructions after that. Do you understand, Enrique?"

"Perfectly, Señor!"

"And, Enrique..."

"Sí, Señor?"

"...keep yourself out of sight! That detective knows your face."

Enrique was excited about his assignment. He went into the bathroom, changed his clothes, neatly folded his black pants and white shirt, and went to his car. On his way out, he spoke to his sister, the hostess. "*Hermana*, I will not be back tonight. Tell Mamá I have a very important job to do for Señor Salazar."

Juanita gave her brother a very worried look. She looked around and then spoke softly, "*Mi Hermano Amor,* you must be very careful. This does not look good."

Just then she saw Salazar's bodyguard come toward the front of the restaurant. "Go, *Hermano*," she commanded.

As Enrique hurried away, she turned to the bodyguard. He put his hand under her chin and pulled her face up. "You are very beautiful, Juanita. Perhaps someday you and I... what did Enrique tell you?"

She laughed and fluttered her eyes, pretending to enjoy the attention. "He said to tell Mamá that he will not be home tonight." With a disgusted tone of voice she went on,

"Probably some girl he met." Turning to the bodyguard, she said coyly, "Is there something I should know about?"

"No, Juanita, do not worry your pretty head." He smiled at her and turned away.

Sandy, Will, and Josie joined the Browns back at the motel. They were all tired and needed rest, especially Josie. When they drove in and parked, they didn't notice the small compact car that was parked a row behind them, nor did they notice the young man sitting in the car. The parking lot was well lit, and when Sandy exited Mort's car, as was his habit, he looked carefully around the lot. That's when he noticed the young man in the compact car. The face was familiar. Sandy locked the car and nonchalantly followed Will and Josie inside.

Sandy spoke to them all. "Folks, Mort's instructed us to not spend any time in the lobby. I'll explain later. Let's all go upstairs to our rooms, and Doris, Josie and Stevie get some rest. Will and I need to talk to Joe Richard, David Lee and John for a little while, which we will do in their room. We're going to make a change in our room, and then we'll meet you. Goodnight."

Sandy spoke to Will, "Go get our room changed so we have a room on this side of the building looking directly over the parking lot, if possible. I'll explain later."

Sandy headed to the room he and Will shared and waited. As soon as Will arrived, they picked up their few things and went to the new room. "That clerk was inquisitive about why we wanted to move!"

"What'd you tell him?" Sandy asked.

"I told him we were expecting someone during the night and just needed to be able to see when they drove in. He seemed satisfied when it had nothing to do with us being unhappy with the accommodations. Now, you want to tell me what this is all about."

"Okay, turn off all the lights and come over to the window with me. You see that compact car parked two rows behind our car?"

"Yeah, why?"

"There's a young man in that car, and I believe it is Enrique Martínez Talamantes, our waiter at the restaurant today. I'd like to know why he's there and if he was sent to watch us."

"Do you think he recognized you?" Will asked.

"I'm sure he did. We're going to keep an eye on him tonight and see if he leaves the car. I'll take first watch, and we'll alternate throughout the night. You go over to the Brown's room and explain what's going to happen tomorrow."

Three hours later, Sandy was barely able to keep his eyes open. He awoke Will to take his turn at watch. "See anything, Sandy?" Will asked.

"Yeah, right after you went to bed, I saw him make a cell phone call. Otherwise he's still there, and it looks like he's asleep."

"Okay," Will said. "I'll take it from here."

After changing watches twice more during the night and not observing the young man exiting the car, both Sandy and Will got a little careless and allowed themselves to sleep. Sandy woke suddenly, sprang out of bed, and walked to the window. It was just getting daylight and the young man was nowhere to be seen, but the car was still there. Sandy woke Will, and he also took a look. "Whatta you make of it, Sandy?"

"I think he's still around but just not in the car. You stay here and watch the car. I'm going to get dressed and go downstairs. I'll look around and see if I can spot anything. I'll pretend I'm going for exercise."

Sandy walked around the lobby but found nobody. Finally he walked outside and completely around the motel.

When he got back to the parking lot, the car was gone from its parking space. He walked around all the rows of cars and didn't find the car. He also glanced into every car parked there to see if anyone might have relieved Enrique on his mission. He found nothing suspicious so went back to the room and reported to Will. "He must have figured his mission was over or else his boss called him back to the restaurant."

"I think you're right. Just before you returned, I saw him come back to the car, make a phone call and leave."

"I have a plan," Sandy said. "Let's get everybody checked out of here, and we'll split up. The Browns and Josie will go to the restaurant Mort suggested. You and I will go to *Las Palmas* and act like nothing happened. Let's just see if Enrique is there and what he might have to say."

"Sounds like a good plan, Sandy. I'll go tell the Browns, while you take your shower and get dressed. After breakfast, they can go directly to Mort's office and we'll meet 'em there. I think I should call Mort and let him know about this, don't you?"

"Yeah, that'd be a good idea. Sometimes I forget this isn't our jurisdiction."

CHAPTER TWENTY-TWO

Sandy and Will drove to the *Las Palmas Especiale* as planned. After looking carefully around the parking lot, they walked in through the front door. Juanita's friendly voice greeted them. Sandy called her by name. Her smile told him she was pleased that he would remember her. In perfect Spanish, he told her they were very pleased to be back to enjoy such a fine restaurant. Juanita looked surprised and smiled. She picked up two menus and showed them to a table. She looked at Sandy, and in Spanish told him that a waiter would be along soon.

Will smiled at Sandy. "What'd she say?"

Sandy kept his gaze on the menu. "She said that a waiter would be here for our order. Do you see Enrique anywhere in here?"

"No, but I'll get up and go to the restroom. That'll give me a chance to look the place over." Will spent enough time in the restroom that nobody would be suspicious then walked back to the table. "I don't see hide or hair of Enrique: and don't see anything of Salazar or his bodyguard either. Must be too early for them, or else they were up all night, ha!"

A waiter showed up dressed just like Enrique. In a thick Spanish accent he said, "Good morning, Señores, may I get you some of our special coffee?"

Josie's Gift

Sandy looked at his name tag then spoke to him in Spanish. "Yes, José, we'll both have coffee and a small orange juice for me." Looking at Will, he asked if he wanted juice. Again he spoke to the waiter in Spanish, "My friend will also have coffee and orange juice."

In English the waiter said, "I will be right back, Señores."

Will spoke. "I didn't know you spoke Spanish so well."

"My family lived in Mexico for ten years while my dad was an engineer for Pemex. Knowing Spanish sometimes comes in handy. Right now I want to impress Juanita—I want her to trust us. Her language skills tell me she is from the Mexican interior and has been to school. José is probably from the same area as Enrique and Juanita. My hunch is that Salazar has connections in wherever it is Juanita and Enrique grew up. I'm glad neither Salazar nor his bodyguard are here yet. That might give us a chance to talk a little with Juanita."

José returned, and they ordered their food. After they had eaten and downed another cup of coffee, Sandy motioned José to bring them the bill. "You leave the tip; I'll go to the front and pay Juanita."

"Was everything okay, Señores?" She asked in Spanish.

In Spanish, Sandy complimented the food and the service, and gave her a large bill with his business card under it. Her eyes looked from side to side, and she quickly put the card in her pocket. When she pulled her hand from her pocket, she had a green piece of paper which she carefully put with the bills she gave to Sandy in change. She thanked him, again in Spanish, and wished them both a fine day. Sandy carefully folded the bills and put them in his front pocket.

Outside in the car, Sandy asked Will if he had seen Juanita put the piece of paper in with the change. "Yeah, what do you think it means?"

Sandy started to back out when he saw Salazar's bodyguard get out of a blue Lincoln parked at the side of the building. Sandy rolled down his window and shouted to Salazar as he exited the Lincoln. In Spanish he said, "Thank you for feeding us so well, Señor Salazar. We are leaving today to go back to Rock City. I hope to enjoy your hospitality when we return to Littleville."

Salazar walked over to the car followed by his bodyguard. He bowed slightly and spoke to Sandy in Spanish "It has been our pleasure, Señores. I hope we may again meet, perhaps in Rock City when I open another restaurant."

The two men shook hands. Sandy continued to back out and turned into the street. They drove straight to Mort's office. The Browns had not yet arrived.

Mort looked surprised. "Where's the rest of your crew, Sandy?"

"We've had an interesting night and morning, Mort." He proceeded to tell Mort about Enrique watching them in the parking lot and his disappearance in the morning. Then he related their experience at the restaurant. "I know you advised that we not go back to *Las Palmas* for breakfast, but we wanted to see if Enrique was around. He wasn't, but his sister Juanita was there as usual. On the way out, she gave me a note folded with the bills in my change. We met Salazar as we were leaving the parking lot. Here's the note." Sandy pulled the folded bills out of his pocket and handed the green slip of paper to Mort.

Mort looked at it. "Have you read this, Sandy?"

"Not yet, Mort."

Mort handed the note back to Sandy. "Take a look! It's in Spanish."

"Sandy read the note and translated it. She's really scared Mort...for herself and her brother. She says Enrique was sent on some kind of secret assignment by Salazar last night, and he didn't come back home. He wasn't home when she left for work. She believes there are bad people there at the restaurant, and bad things going on. She doesn't want Enrique to get involved. At the end, she's pleading for help."

"Well," Mort responded. "That confirms what we suspected about Salazar doesn't it?"

Just then, the Browns walked into the office. "Good morning everybody," John said. Looking at Sandy, "We're ready when you are, Sandy."

Sandy turned to David Lee and Joe Richard. "Well, Boys, I guess you two will be driving back to your homes."

Joe Richard responded. "Yeah, we've both got jobs to get back to. Sometime in the next few weeks we'll be in Rock City. If there are any court proceedings involving Mother and Dad, it's for certain that we'll be there. You let us know and keep in touch if Mom and Dad need anything."

The men all shook hands. Josie hugged them all. She hugged Stevie and Doris. Stevie whimpered and held on to her. They had decided that Stevie will go with David Lee, and that Joe Richard will drive the Chrysler. They will drop Stevie and the Chrysler off at the mission in Rock City where Josie's Mom and Dad are staying. John and Doris will fly back to Rock City in the custody of Sandy and Will.

David Lee picked Stevie up in his arms, and with Joe Richard, headed for the cars. Josie walked with them and waived as they drove away. It was a teary goodbye for everybody.

Back in the office, Sandy spoke, "Mort, what've you decided to do with Josie?"

"Joyce is going to take her to the beauty shop for an appearance change right now. During the day, we're going to hire her to do some work around here. Her nights will be spent in a special cell we have between here and the jail. It's a kind of 'safe-keeping' cell we use when someone needs protection. It's isolated and there'll be no contact with any other prisoners or outsiders. However, it's outfitted much more comfortably than the normal jail cells—almost like a motel room. One of our secretaries here is just about the same size and shape as Josie, so we're going to dress her to look like Josie and take her with us to the airport. I put out the word last night that Josie would go back to Rock City with you."

Sandy looked at his watch. "It's time we get on to the airport. You're a good cop, Mort. Wish we could work together more often."

They all said their goodbyes, hugged Josie, and put her into the hands of God. Will was the last to hug her. He looked at Josie and then bashfully down at his feet. He pulled a small box out of his jacket pocket and handed it to her. "Here, Josie. This' something I got for you that I know you can use. God bless," he said as he looked up to meet her gaze.

She smiled. "Thank you so much, Will. You're a great friend and I thank God for bringing you into my life. Whatever this is, I'll treasure it." When she hugged Will, she clung to him a little longer than the others.

"C'mon, Will, time to go," Sandy said with a big grin on his face.

Will looked one more time at Josie and then turned and followed Sandy toward the door.

Mort got his hat and told Joyce where he was going to be. Josie's double met them at the car. On the drive to the airport, Mort floated an idea with Sandy. "Sandy, there's a Tri-State Task Force getting organized to deal with the Mexican gangs and the drug syndicates in the area. How about me pullin' some strings and getting you on it? Your Spanish skills would be a valuable asset to the Task Force."

Sandy thought for a few minutes and looked at Will. "Yeah, I think I'd enjoy that, Mort. I think I'm ready for a change. Go for it!"

"It all has to go through the governor's office, Sandy, so when you hear something, it'll be from your governor's office. This stuff is all top secret, and nobody is to know anything, not even your wife."

"I think Joann can handle that Mort."

"We'll have top-secret, encrypted communications equipment so it's going to mean a very different life for you."

Sandy's cell phone rang. "Hey, Sandy, Smitty here. Change in plans. You're not coming back on a National Guard jet; it'll be a private charter. You're to go to the private terminal with the big Cessna sign. When you get there, don't identify yourself, but drive in and park outside the fence near the fuel pumps. The tail number on your plane is, November three-three-two Lima Tango, and it's a Citation Seven. We've used it before. You're to wait in the car 'til it lands. When it gets to the fuel pumps, go straight to the aircraft and get on board."

"Okay, Smitty, thanks. Any reason for all the secrecy?"

"You'll hear about it when you get here."

"Thanks, Smitty, see you this afternoon."

At the airport, Mort parked close to the fuel pumps, and they followed Smitty's instructions. About thirty minutes later, a Citation Seven landed and taxied to the pumps. "Okay folks, tail number matches our instructions...let's go. Both Mort and Josie's double followed them up the ramp and boarded the plane. Mort left the plane first. Fifteen minutes later, Josie's double, now dressed as a man, exited and got into the car with Mort. They backed out and drove off immediately."

After Sandy, Will and the Browns got settled in the plane, the pilot asked if everybody was buckled up. Flight was expected to be two hours and fifteen minutes. The pilot contacted ground control and they were cleared to taxi to, but hold short of the runway. Another Citation Seven with National Guard markings was finishing his checklist and moved onto the active runway. The engines whined, and the aircraft began to move. Suddenly it stopped and the pilot shut the engines down. Three crew members could be seen evacuating the aircraft as emergency vehicles were careening around the taxiway and toward the grounded jet.

Sandy's pilot then contacted ground control and asked for instructions. He was instructed to taxi back to his original position on the ramp and wait for instructions. The airport was shut down and no flights were to leave. All incoming flights were routed to other destinations. On the intercom, the pilot notified his passengers. "Folks, we're going to be delayed for an indefinite period of time. Stay in your seats for the time being. There's an emergency of some kind involving that National Guard jet." Special equipment was brought in and the National Guard jet was towed to a remote area on the airport followed by the emergency vehicles.

The radio crackled. "November three-three-two Lima Tango prepare to taxi in ten minutes."

"November three-three-two Lima Tango, Roger."

After a few minutes ground control was back. "November three-three-two Lima Tango, taxi to runway one-eight and hold short."

"Roger, three-three-two Lima Tango."

The pilot again turned on the intercom. "Okay folks, buckle up; we're ready to roll."

"November three-three-two Lima Tango, you're number three in the takeoff sequence. Hold short."

They watched as two other aircraft taxied onto the runway and took off. The pilot was cleared for takeoff and contacted Departure. He began his takeoff roll.

As soon as they lifted into the air, Departure called. A voice with a tone of urgency said, "November three-three-two Lima Tango, when you reach fifteen hundred feet make a sharp right turn heading zero-niner-zero degrees, continue climbing."

"November three-three-two Lima Tango, copy and turning to heading zero-niner-zero degrees; that's off our flight plan."

"November three-three-two Lima Tango, you're being routed around the emergency area. Look to your left, and you'll see the emergency vehicles. Continue to one-zero thousand and hold; we'll clear you to two-five thousand and your flight plan heading in three minutes. Then contact Houston Center."

The pilot spoke on the intercom. "Folks look out the left of the aircraft. You'll see the emergency vehicles with that National Guard jet. We'll be back on our flight plan in a couple of minutes."

The remainder of the flight was uneventful, but all were worried about the National Guard aircraft back at Littleville. As soon as they landed and put down the ramp, Smitty was there to meet them. "Sandy, Mortenson wants you to call him as soon as you get to the office."

"Okay Smitty, let's go. Oh," turning to Doris and John, "Smitty, This is John Brown and his wife Doris. We've all had quite an interesting time in Littleville."

Turning to Will, he issued more instructions. "Will, try to get an arraignment hearing for the Browns ASAP so they can be released on bond. I'll call Isabelle and see if she can take 'em at the mission. I'll also call Sheila Langdon and see if she can represent them. In the meantime, we'll have to put 'em in our holding cell."

"Okay, Sandy, I'll do my best." Will answered.

Smitty, Sandy, John, and Doris got into Smitty's car and headed for the police station. Will headed for his car in the airport parking lot.

When Will got to his car and was about to back out of the parking space, his phone rang. Opening the phone he recognized the number. "Hi, Josie, I was hoping you'd call."

"Will, thank you so much for the phone. I really needed it. I noticed you put some numbers into my address file for me. Your number is the first one I called."

"I'm glad you called me first. That means a lot. By the way, that phone takes pictures and you can send them to me. You can also receive pictures. I'll tell Isabelle to send you pictures of Stevie. I'll also give Joe Richard and David Lee your number when they get here. How'd the makeover go? Did it change you a lot?"

"It did change things a lot. I also have some new clothes—the kind of stuff I don't ordinarily wear when I have a choice."

"Take a picture of yourself and send it to me, okay?"

"Okay, Will. I gotta go. Bye for now. Shalom aleikhem."

On the way home from the airport, Sandy called Sheila. "Hi, Sheila, I need a favor."

"Sandy, for you favors are no problem. Who've you got for me?"

"John and Doris Brown," Sandy answered. "Can you come to my office ASAP?"

"I'll be there, Sandy. I'm with a client right now, but I should be finished in about thirty minutes."

"Thanks, Sheila, I owe ya one!"

Next, Sandy called Isabelle. "Sandy! It's so good to hear your voice."

"We just landed and are headed for my office. We've got John and Doris Brown in custody, and they're going to need a place to stay for a little while. Can you manage at the mission?"

"We'll manage, Sandy. I'll get over to your office as soon as I can get away. I'm anxious to meet them. I'm sure they can use a little pastoral attention about now."

"Thanks, Isabelle. I'll tell you the whole story when you get to my office."

By the time Sandy was finished talking on the phone, they were turning into the parking lot. "Smitty, you take the Browns and book 'em in. Put them in the holding cell together and put something comfortable in there so they can relax. Get 'em whatever they need! They're probably hungry."

"I'll take care of it, Sandy," Smitty replied.

Sandy breathed a sigh of relief when he sank into his office chair. He picked up his office phone and dialed his home number. "Hi, Darling! We just landed, and I'm beat. I need to be here at the office for quite a while yet, but I need to see your smiling face. How about you picking up something for us to eat and something sweet and come to my office?"

"Oh, Sandy, I'm so glad you're safe. I'm glad to have you back. I'll be there as soon as I can. I love you!"

"I love you too, Joann!"

Smitty walked into the office. "Okay, Sandy. The Brown's are booked in and settled."

"Good! Sheila should be here soon. Now you want to tell me about the change in travel plans this afternoon?"

"We had a mysterious phone call this morning, Sandy. A girl named Juanita said there was a bomb planted on your National Guard jet. She said you'd know her. I went ahead and contacted Mortenson and told him."

"Fortunately, they got that plane stopped before there was a catastrophe. Did Juanita say anything else?"

"No, that was all. No last name or where she was calling from. The chief was skeptical but decided it would be best to make the change in plans."

"Were you able to trace the call?"

"Yeah, we've got the number and the location of the call."

"Good work, Smitty. Just before we took off from Littleville, there was an emergency with a National Guard Jet that was just beginning his takeoff roll when he unexpectedly stopped and shut down. Was that one of our National Guard aircraft?"

"No!"

"I think I know who Juanita is, and we owe her our lives. Sit down, I'm going to call Mortenson."

"Hi, Mort, what's up on your end?"

"Did you guys see the emergency with that National Guard Jet when you took off?"

"Yeah, we saw it, very dramatic."

"Three crew members on board managed to get off. I went directly to the scene as soon as I could. By the time I got there, the military had taken control, had it roped off, and were still trying figure out where the bomb was located and how to take it out safely. I talked to the officer in charge of the investigation. He told me, he thought for sure that it was a bomb and it was probably set to go off by an altitude sensing device or a cell phone from the ground. It seems to be a pretty sophisticated job."

"Any idea who would target that aircraft and why Mort?"

"I think I know what's on your mind, Sandy. You're wondering if you and the Browns might have been the target. It's exactly like the aircraft you flew up on, and it landed a couple of hours before your charter landed. There was ample time for someone to hide a device somewhere on the plane. The officer at the scene says the crew was on a training mission. I have a hunch someone thought Josie was on that flight. Right now all this is just speculation, but I'll get with the investigating officer and tell him what I think. I hope they'll let me in on the investigation."

"So, when the news gets out that Josie was not on that plane, whoever was responsible will think she's here in Rock City. Am I right?"

"I think you're right, Sandy. It's going to be a few days before anything is released to the news media about what happened. What we need to do in the meantime is to figure out a plan for Josie here and for Stevie there in Rock City. There might be a way we could plant some information and flush the vermin from their holes."

"Mort, I've got some news from here. The change in our travel plans was no coincidence. Smitty, my partner tells me he got a call this morning from someone named Juanita, who said a bomb was planted on our plane. I think you and I both know who that Juanita is! Of course that National Guard jet was exactly like the one we went to Littleville in so naturally the bomber thought that was our plane."

"Holy...! I think Salazar's in this up to his eyeballs, Sandy. But how did Juanita know who to call?"

"I slipped her my card when I paid for breakfast. When she called my office number, Smitty answered and immediately called you."

"I think I'll go back to the restaurant for a meal and try to find out where Juanita lives. We'll need to find a way to watch her for a while. If Salazar has any idea she made that call, he'll put a green light on her."

"Mort, I just happened to think of something. I noticed this morning when we had breakfast at the restaurant that Salazar drives a light blue Lincoln. You might be able to watch for that Lincoln and get into the restaurant when he's out doing something else."

"Okay, Sandy. Thanks for the info. I'll get on it right away. I'll try to get the cooperation of the military and keep all this under wraps for as long as we can."

"Okay, Mort, we'll keep in touch. Let me know immediately if anything develops. I think Josie's safe for the time being in your cell, but she's going to get tired of that."

"I agree, Sandy. I plan to have a talk with her and see what we can do. We may be able to get Becky to spit out some more information by allowing her to visit with Josie. Of course, those visits will be in one of our interrogation rooms so none of the other inmates will be wise to what we're doing."

"Okay, Mort. I trust your judgment to do what's best. Just call if you need anything from here."

Sandy turned to Smitty, "Do we have a recording of Juanita's phone call, Smitty?"

"I'm pretty sure we do, Sandy."

"Let's make a copy of that on a CD and send it to Mortenson. Also get the info on the origin of that phone call and send it to him."

"I'll take care of it." As he turned to leave, Joann walked into the office. "Oh, hi, Joann, good to see you."

"You too, Smitty."

She watched Smitty leave, walked around Sandy's desk and wrapped him in her arms. "I'm so glad you're back and safe. Is there any of it you can talk about?"

"Not yet, Joann!" He looked into her eyes, and their lips spontaneously entwined in a kiss that passionately said they had missed one another.

When Sandy looked up, Will was standing in the doorway. "See what you're missing, Will!"

"Yeah, I've thought about that. We can't get an arraignment for the Browns 'til tomorrow or the next day. However, Judge Jacobson says they can be released on a bond if we can get the paperwork taken care of before his clerk closes up for the day. Sheila's with them right now so she'll take care of it. Isabelle just got here too so God is looking over them."

"Thanks, Will."

Sandy and Joann enjoyed their meal together. Sandy told her about their trip and shared what he could about the situation with Josie. "Joann, I can't overstate the amount of danger Josie's in. If the bad guys find out where she's staying, they'll find a way to get to her." He paused. "Changing the subject, let's go downstairs. You can meet the Browns and have a talk with Isabelle."

"What do you want me to tell her?"

"Just tell her to pray. Josie's in the protective custody of Sheriff Mortenson for the time being, but that doesn't means she's in no danger."

"When will she be able to come back?"

"Will thinks they can take some sworn depositions from her, and then maybe she can come home. When the trial starts for those guys who kidnapped her, she may have to go back and testify, unless the judge will accept the depositions in lieu of personal testimony." He sighed, "Sooo, this may go on for quite a while." Sandy sighed and looked up as if to breathe a prayer.

Joann reached for his hand. "I love you, Detective Sandoval. You're a fine cop. I worry a lot about you, but I always know you'll do the right thing and that God will take care of you."

Still holding her hand, he stood up. "Let's go see what's going on with the Browns."

Downstairs at the holding cell, Sandy introduced Joann to John and Doris. It was a rather awkward meeting for Joann, who knew nothing of John's near death experience and his powerful conversion. All she could think about was the morning she answered the phone, and John abducted Stevie from her backyard. John smiled and immediately stepped to Joann and took her hand, "Missus Sandoval, I want to apologize for our actions in abducting Stevie. I'm sure you were terrified, and I apologize for having hurt you so. Will you please forgive us?"

Joann could see the pleading in John's eyes. She looked at Doris who was teary-eyed. "Yes, of course, Mister Brown — all is forgiven."

"Please, dispense with the mister and missus; we're John and Doris. Your husband has been so very gracious, to us, and we want to count you as our friends."

Joann's voice grew soft and kind. She looked directly into John's eyes. "Of course, Mis...uh John. Sandy has told me you have quite a story to tell, and I'm anxious to hear it."

She stepped over to Doris and put her hands on Doris' shoulders and drew her into an embrace. Doris, I can see God's gracious hand in all of this—we've all been brought together under unusual circumstances for the purpose of some plan the Father has for all of us. None of this is coincidence. I'm also anxious to hear all about Josie. It seems she has turned into somewhat of a heroine."

Sheila stepped away to take a phone call. She returned within a few minutes. "Well, folks it looks like it will be first thing in the morning before the clerk can process our bond application." Her face brightened into a smile. "But," she continued, "Judge Jacobson has approved a release to Reverend Isabelle on personal recognizance. Will's going to bring some papers over in a few minutes so for the time being, we make ourselves comfortable."

Doris turned to Isabelle. "Reverend Isabelle, tell us about the mission and what our lives will be like there."

Isabelle described the ministry of the mission and what their routines were like. When she finished, she looked at John then Doris. "There is one thing you need to know."

"What's that, Dear?" Doris asked.

Josie's parents, the Blandóns are also staying with us. They came here expecting to see Josie. Looks like the Father has some purpose in that too, doesn't it?"

Doris and John looked at each other and smiled. "That's wonderful, Dear!" Doris responded.

"We're anxious to see them. We owe them an apology," John added. He turned to Isabelle, "You know something, Reverend, after my experience with the angel in the hospital, I told my family about my sinful life, and they forgave me. I told them that as soon as I could get with a minister, I was going to confess those sins again and ask for prayer and forgiveness."

"John," Isabelle said. "If that's what you want, I'll be very happy to do that for you and to pray with you so that you may complete your relationship with Christ." She turned to Sandy. "Sandy, may I use one of your private rooms to meet with John?"

Sandy smiled and led the way to a vacant office that was close by. John told his story to Isabelle and confessed everything as best he could remember. He was sincere and tearful. When he finished, Isabelle laid her hands on his head and spoke. "John, I can say with complete assurance that God has forgiven all your sins as He promised in the scriptures. *"If we confess our sins, he is faithful and just and will forgive us our sins and purify us from all unrighteousness (1 John 1:9).* Now I'm going to pray for you, and I would like for Doris to come in. Is that okay?"

"Absolutely," John answered.

Isabelle stepped out and asked Doris to come in. She put their hands together and then enclosed them with her own. "Doris, you are to be commended and admired for your willingness to forgive your husband. God is very pleased with that and will bless you for it. John, you are to be commended and admired for your willingness to take full responsibility for your actions of the past and also for all the trouble resulting from the abduction of Stevie. God will bless you for it. Now, I'm going to pray for the two of you. 'Heavenly Father, in the Name of Jesus Christ I give my blessing to this couple whom You have joined in marriage, and I ask for You to confirm Your love and blessing upon them throughout this legal process and for the rest of their lives together. I also ask blessings upon their sons and grandchildren—that you will guide them and direct their paths. May John's experiences be a testimony to them of your gracious love and forgiveness. May the angels continue to watch over them, In Jesus Name; AMEN.'"

When they returned to the holding cell, Will had arrived with the papers for the release of the Browns. John raised his hand and spoke. "I want all of you to know how much Doris and I appreciate all you have done for us. We consider all of you to be our friends. With your support and God's grace we can 'face the music' so to speak and find our place in ministering to God's people."

John and Doris signed the papers followed by Isabelle.

"Folks, it's been a long day. Let's all go and get some rest!" Isabelle suggested.

Everybody went their own way except for Sandy and Will. "What's on your mind, Will?" Sandy asked.

Will sighed. "Nothing, and everything if that makes any sense. I can't forget the sight of that National Guard jet at Littleville this morning and how close it came to being us. And—I can't get Josie out of my mind. I strongly believe she's in a lot of danger, and Salazar's bunch will go to any length to get at her. I sure hope Mort can connect Salazar with Russell and shut the whole business down."

"I agree, Will. The sad thing is when Mort shuts that bunch down there'll be another bunch that will slide right in and take over—then it starts all over again."

"Unfortunately, you're right. Goodnight, Sandy—goodnight Joann. We'll get together sometime tomorrow in court."

"Goodnight Will!"

Josie's phone rang. When she opened it, she saw Will's name on the screen. "Hi, Will, glad you called."

Hi, Josie, it's good to hear your voice. How're things going?"

"Okay so far. Did they tell you I have a job now? The county is actually paying me for working for Sheriff Mortenson. And," she added, "I get board and room free." Her voice dropped, "I wish you were here, Will. I feel really alone."

"I wish I was there too, Josie. I wish I could...uh, well I'm praying for you. God is there with you."

"Oh, Will! How long will this process go on? I'm tired of it already."

"How long it goes on will depend on the judge. I will say this—when they're finished with you, I'm personally going to go over there and bring you back to Rock City. Maybe I can bring Stevie with me. Would you like that?"

"Yes, Will! Oh, yes I would like that very much."

"Count on it, Josie." Will was feeling a little awkward. "I...uh have to let you go now. I just wanted to hear your voice and tell you goodnight."

"Thanks, Will, good night. Give Stevie a hug for me when you see him."

At the mission, John and Doris were welcomed by Moisés and Ruth Blandón. John immediately asked their forgiveness for his actions at their home. Moisés smiled and the two men shook hands while the women hugged each other. "Let's have a snack." Isabelle suggested. "A bite to eat and a cup of coffee would be welcome right now."

In the dining room they all sat around a table and chatted, John and Doris telling more of their experiences in Littleville. Moisés and Ruth were most interested in Josie's wellbeing. John told them what he could and reassured them that Josie was safe. Of course, John knew nothing of the events involving Albert Russell and Juan Velasco Salazar or of the real danger facing Josie. He knew only of the kidnapping of Josie, her escape, and the capture of her abductors.

"Brothers and Sisters, it's time we get the Browns settled and let them know a little of the routine around here. I'll get Carla and have her help out. Stevie should be arriving sometime tomorrow evening if everything goes as planned. Then we can have a wonderful family reunion."

CHAPTER TWENTY-THREE

David Lee and Stevie were on the road heading for Rock City, with Joe Richard following. David Lee pulled into a truck stop restaurant. Joe Richard pulled in beside him. Neither of them noticed the van that pulled in a couple of spaces away. They all went inside and ordered coffee and meals. David Lee looked at Joe Richard, "What's on your mind, Brother?"

"I think I'll drive on through tonight. That'll get me to Rock City sometime in the morning. You and Stevie go on however long your butts can hold out and get a motel for the night. I'm really anxious about Mom and Dad. Whatta you think?"

"Sounds okay to me."

After their meal, Joe Richard hugged his brother and Stevie, and then he got on the road. David Lee and Stevie continued for another couple of hours and pulled into a motel. After they registered, they got out of the car what they would need for the night and closed the door and locked it.

An hour after they arrived, they were getting ready for bed and watching TV. There was a knock on the door. Joe Richard got up to see who it was. Without thinking he unbolted the door and started to open it when two men barged in and shut the door behind them. One of them had a gun.

"Well, Well, this must be Stevie," the man with the gun said as he walked toward Stevie.

Stevie jumped out of the bed and ran for the closet. Just before he could close the door, the man grabbed him and pulled him back. Stevie was crying—he knew something was wrong. The man slapped him and threw him onto the bed. David Lee started to rush to Stevie, but the other man hit him on the head with a small club. David Lee was dragged up from the floor where he fell and was thrown into a chair. The man with the gun laughed, all the while keeping his gun pointed at Stevie.

When David Lee regained his senses, he asked, "What's this all about and who are you? How did you know us?" His head was throbbing, and he shook it from side to side.

The man with the gun motioned to the other man who produced a pair of handcuffs. He pulled David Lee's arms behind his back and placed the handcuffs on his wrists. The man waived the gun in Stevie's direction and spoke. "Now, Mister Brown, as long as you do as you're told and cooperate, nothing bad is going to happen."

"What do you want?" David Lee asked, his head beginning to clear.

"Right now, just some information—it's that simple. You give us the information, and you go free."

"What about Stevie?" David Lee asked.

"Let's just say he's our little insurance policy just to be sure you do as you're told and to ensure your information's correct."

"And if I don't cooperate?"

The man laughed. "I wouldn't advise that course of action, Mister Brown. You won't like the consequences."

Stevie sat on the bed crying. He was looking from one person to the other and watching what was going to happen to his Uncle David Lee. David Lee met his glance. "Stevie, everything's going to be okay. Pray to your Jesus for us."

The man with the club laughed and turned his attention back to David Lee. "Mister Brown, I'm going to ask you a simple question, and you can give us a simple answer." His smile was sinister, his teeth were dirty brown and needed lots of dental work. He had a tooth missing from his lower front.

David Lee's law enforcement training was beginning to influence his thinking. He looked carefully at the man, memorizing every feature, trying to think about what their intentions were for himself and Stevie. He knew instinctively that he couldn't trust them to keep their word, whatever he told them. He studied the man with the gun. He spoke silently to himself. *"The gun is a revolver, probably thirty-eight or three fifty-seven. Kind of strange he would be so armed. I would expect professionals to both be armed. Most professionals in the business of abductions prefer automatics. This man's face is scarred, and he looks rough at the edges — not the kind of look one would expect from someone who's a professional."* He felt confident he could describe them both and certainly could recognize them in the future. His assessment of their personal qualities told him they would be making mistakes sooner or later. He decided to play along.

"And your question?" David Lee asked.

The man smiled. "Now we're gettin' somewhere, Mister Brown." He leaned close to David Lee's face, his breath smelled like rotten eggs. "Mister Brown, we would like for you to tell us where Josie Brown is at this moment. We figure she is either in Littleville or in Rock City. Which is it and where is she being kept?"

Just then the gunman's phone rang. He opened it, "Yeah!"

"You got what I'm after?" The voice on the other end asked.

"We got 'em. Right now we're tryin' to get information."

The voice on the other end screamed. David Lee could hear the voice but couldn't make out the words. "That's not your job, dammit. You bundle them up and bring them to the place I told you—you got that? And don't attract any attention getting out of there! There's to be no harm to either of 'em! Is that understood?"

"Yes sir, Mister Russell," the gunman sheepishly replied.

"Dammit, don't use my name!" Russell screamed.

"Yeah, yeah, yeah! Whatever!"

David Lee kept looking down and pretended he didn't hear, but now he knew someone named Russell was behind this, and he wanted Josie for some reason. It was probably connected to her kidnapping by Russell's son and his buddies.

The two kidnappers tied up Stevie, gagged him and then wrapped him in a blanket. They gathered up David Lee's and Stevie's personal items and headed for the door; one of the men carried Stevie. Outside, they put both their captives in the back seat of the van and locked the doors. The two abductors jumped into the front seat, backed out, and headed for the highway.

The windows of the van were darkly tinted, and the night was moonless so it was difficult to see outside. However, David Lee took careful mental notes of which way they turned out of the motel parking lot and of business lights along the way. It seemed to him they were heading back in the direction of Littleville. When he saw the sign welcoming them to Louisiana, he knew for sure.

Several hours later, they pulled into the parking lot of a rural dance hall and beer joint. It was well lit up with neon signs and music blared from inside. The driver got out and went inside. He soon returned with two cases of cold beer; then with a beer in hand, and one in each pocket, he went back inside. His buddy yelled at him, but he continued walking.

David Lee took note that the guy remaining in the car was the one with the gun. He started drinking the beer the driver left him. Soon the driver returned to the car and grabbed another beer and stuffed his pockets. This routine went on for another hour. The last time the driver came back to the car he was stoned out of his mind, and his buddy was passed out in the front seat. He grabbed some more beers and staggered back into the beer joint.

David Lee figured he might have a chance to get out of the car. By this time, Stevie was asleep. He turned his body as far as he could so he could reach the door lock with his feet. Then he kicked off his shoes and tried to get the lock with his toes. It took several tries, but he was finally able to unlock the door and move the door handle so that he could push the door open when he needed it.

He nudged Stevie and woke him up. He leaned close to Stevie's face and told him to be very quiet. Stevie obeyed. With his teeth, he got the gag out of Stevie's mouth. He whispered to him to turn around, and he worked on the rope that was wrapped around his body. Again with his teeth, he managed to untie the knot. Stevie unwrapped himself from the rope as David Lee whispered to Stevie to push the side door of the van open. Stevie, very quietly, pushed the door open and climbed out of the van and to the pavement. David Lee followed him.

David Lee's hands were bound by the handcuffs, but he clumsily ran toward a dark area of the parking lot where there were trees and bushes. They hid themselves and watched. David Lee whispered to Stevie, "Are you okay, Stevie?"

Stevie was breathing hard. "Yeah, I'm okay."

"Okay, I'm very proud of you. Now I'm going to hide you right over there behind me in those other bushes. Then I'm coming right back here and wait so I can watch the van. You'll be able to see me from where you're hiding. No matter what you see happen, you stay hidden and don't make a sound. You pray to your Jesus to look after us, okay?"

Stevie did as he was told as David Lee watched the van and the beer joint. He lay down on the ground and struggled to pull his legs up through his handcuffed hands so that his arms would be in front. Then he turned his attention back to the beer joint and the van. Before long he saw the gunman get out of the van and stagger off a ways and relieve himself near another car. He returned to the van without noticing that his passengers were not there.

Before long, the driver returned. He too was so drunk he didn't notice his passengers were gone. He got into the van, started the engine and backed out. He headed the van toward the highway and spun out getting onto the road.

David Lee walked back to where Stevie was hiding. "Stevie, get into my back pocket and get out my cell phone." He laughed to think how dumb these guys were. They didn't even search him.

Stevie got out the phone. "Okay," David Lee said. "Dial nine-one-one and then hold the phone up to my ear."

A very nice voice answered. "Nine-one-one; what is your emergency?"

David Lee spoke in a loud whisper into the phone. I and my six-year-old nephew were abducted from a motel in Texas and driven back to Louisiana. We are in the parking lot of a beer joint called the **Bad Alibi Lounge.** We've managed to escape but my hands are still handcuffed."

"A sheriff's unit is on the way. Do you need medical services?"

"No, I don't think so. We'll watch for the sheriff's car."

"Keep calm, it should be no more than a few minutes."

No more had David Lee hung up the phone than he spotted the van with their drunk abductors come careening back into the parking lot with its side door swinging wildly. It came to a screeching halt close to where they were originally parked, and the two men climbed out. The gunman was holding his revolver and pointing it in every direction. The driver ran around the parking lot looking for their passengers. Both men were staggering and fell multiple times.

At one point, David Lee thought the gunman was coming in their direction, but instead he turned and ran to another point on the periphery of the parking lot. At the same time, a sheriff's car came careening into the parking lot and drove around. He spotted the two men, and with his loudspeaker, ordered them to stop. The gunman swung around and pointed his pistol at the deputy, who immediately fired at him. He went down onto the pavement screaming. The other man gave up without resisting. The deputy walked slowly to the gunman and kicked the pistol away out of his reach. Then he turned to the other man and ordered him to spread his legs and put his arms on top of the car. He got everything out of the man's pockets, including a key ring, and handcuffed him." He then got on his radio and called for another deputy and the ambulance.

David Lee got Stevie, and the two of them ran into the parking lot where the deputy had just finished handcuffing the driver of the van. David Lee held his hands out in front of him, showing the handcuffs he was wearing.

"Are you the guy who called?" The deputy asked.

"Yes, I'm David Lee Brown, and this is my nephew, Stevie Brown."

The deputy introduced himself as Ron Frazier and shook hands with both. As he shook Stevie's hand, he looked up at Deputy Frazier, "Mister Frazier, do you know Sheriff Mortenson?"

"Yes, as a matter of fact I do!" Frazier replied.

Stevie smiled, "he's my friend you know."

Frazier smiled and patted Stevie on the head. "Okay, let me lock this guy up in the cage in my car, and while the ambulance is getting here, you can tell me what happened.

When the deputy got his prisoner locked up, he turned back to David Lee. "Let me see if any of these keys will fit those cuffs." He tried the keys, "Nope, won't work. Lets fish around in the pockets of that guy on the ground and see if he's the one with the key." The deputy rolled the man over so he could get into his pockets. He was moaning in pain. Blood was coming from the right side of his chest. The deputy found another key ring, and two of the keys looked like the type he was looking for. He tried them and got David Lee free.

By that time, the ambulance arrived, followed by the second deputy. The EMS personnel quickly got the gunman loaded up and ready to go. They spoke to the deputy and left with their siren blaring. By this time, a large crowd had gathered in the parking lot to see what was going on.

David Lee pointed out the van that they had come here in and told Frazier what he could about the abduction. They called for a tow truck to take the van. "Why don't you get whatever you have in the van and bring it to my car. We'll go into town and get your sworn statements."

When they arrived in town, Deputy Frazier showed them into his office. "How 'bout some coffee and something to eat?" Looking at Stevie, he asked, "Would you like a glass of milk and a nice fat donut?"

Stevie perked up. "Yessir," he said.

The deputy made a call, and within a few minutes, a very polite attendant, dressed in a jail uniform showed up carrying coffee, milk, donuts, and sandwiches.

As Frazier took notes, David Lee went over the whole experience from the time they left Littleville. "Any idea why these two guys took such an interest in you?" Frazier asked.

"I heard the guy with the gun answer his cell phone. Whoever he talked to was mad and shouting. I heard the gunman say, 'Yes sir, Mister Russell'. I'd suggest you call Sheriff Mortenson over in Littleville because I know he's been working a case involving Russell and Stevie's mother, Josie Brown. Josie was abducted and beaten by Russell's son and three of his buddies. Right now Josie's in Mortenson's protective custody. I'm sure Mortenson would like to talk to our two friends you've got here."

"Okay," Frazier replied. "Just as soon as it's decent office hours, I'll call Mort and let him know what we've got. Now we've got the problem of the motel where you were staying and your car which is still there. Have you got your motel receipt with you, and by any chance do you have your car keys with you?"

David Lee reached for his wallet. "Here's the receipt, but I don't have the keys. We left in kind of a hurry."

"Good, I'll call the sheriff over there and see if he can get somebody to the motel and dust that room for fingerprints and secure the room and your car. Meantime, after you two get a little sleep, I'll have one of my guys drive you over there to get your car. There's a pretty nice motel down the street from the office here. I'll call them and get you a room. One of the other deputies will take you over there. Since this crime crossed state lines, the FBI will be interested, and they'll want to talk to you before you leave here. I'm sure you want to get home, and I don't want to be the bearer of bad news, but you may have to hang around for a few days while the investigation is ongoing."

David Lee pulled out his wallet and showed Frazier an ID and badge, "I understand the problem, Ron."

Frazier looked at the badge and ID. "Yes, I guess you would understand."

David Lee got his cell phone out of his pocket and punched in Joe Richard's number. "Good morning, Brother!"

"Good morning David Lee. What's up?"

"Where are you?"

"I'm about two or three hours from Rock City, why?"

"I need you here. Stevie and I are in the sheriff's office in Parchville.

"In the sheriff's office! What on earth for?"

"We stopped at a motel for the night, and two thugs abducted us. We're fine, but I need you here. Can you come back? I'll tell you the whole story later. Right now I've got to call Josie and let her know Stevie and I are okay. Would you mind calling Mom and Dad and tell them Stevie and I won't be getting there as planned. They can spread the word to Sandy and Will."

"Okay, Brother, I'm turning around and heading for Parchville."

The morning after David Lee and Stevie's abduction, Mort was on his way to his office when his phone rang. "Mornin', Jerry, what's up?"

"As predicted, Albert Russell posted a bond and was let go early last evening and, Junior went with him. The judge said there wasn't enough evidence to hold onto 'em any longer."

"What about Josie's abductors?"

"Judge insisted on keeping them."

"Good, maybe we can squeeze 'em and get some information. In the meantime, get with the DA and see if he can get a warrant to search Russell's home and office. Make sure it covers all files, furniture and computers."

"Okay, Mort, I'm on it. Oh and the sheriff over in Gordon County needs to talk to you. Something about David Lee and Stevie Brown. One more thing, crime lab reports are back, and Russell's prints were all over Becky's apartment, and his DNA was on the bed sheets. That means either he or Junior had a romp in the sack with Becky very recently."

"Thanks Jerry. I think we're just about ready to take Albert Russell to the Grand Jury."

When Mort walked into his office, Joyce was on the phone. He heard her say, "He just walked in, wait one."

"Morning, Mort, a deputy in Gordon County wants to talk to you."

Mort picked up the phone. "Sheriff Mortenson, What can I do for you?"

"Mornin' Mort. This is Deputy Ron Frazier in Parchville in Gordon County. We have a Mister David Lee Brown and his nephew Stevie Brown here. Last night, they were abducted from a motel about three hours across the state line into Texas. They were brought back across the line into Louisiana where we picked them up. Mister Brown is very observant and heard one of the abductors talk to someone named Russell on the cell phone. Brown said you would know who that is."

"Ron, this is a real break for us. I'm on my way to your office right now. It'll take me about two hours to get there." Mort grabbed his hat, and as he walked by Joyce, he gave her instructions. "I'm on my way to Parchville—I'll probably not be back 'til late tonight or maybe even tomorrow. Call my wife and let her know. Tell Jerry to call me as soon as he can."

"Okay, Mort, have a good trip."

When Mort arrived at the Gordon County Sheriff's office, he was met by Deputy Frazier. "Hi, Ron, good to see you again."

"Good to see you too, Mort. I think last time was at the meeting of the Sheriff's Association of Louisiana, if my memory serves me right."

"That's right, Ron. By the way, where's your boss?"

"He's on vacation so I'm holding things down. Sure wish he was here—this case looks like a big one."

"It is," Mort added. "We believe there's a connection with one of the Mexican drug kings."

"Well then, what we've got here are a couple of really little fish from a big pond!"

"That's about the size of it. Where can I find David Lee Brown and Stevie? I want to spend some time with them.

I also need to see if I can squeeze the two little fish. When the feds get here, the fish will be out of our hands. They'll be taken back to Texas for prosecution because that's where they committed the crime."

"Okay, Mort. Let's start with the two little fish and see what we can find out. I've got one here, and one's in the hospital with a hole in his shoulder from one of my bullets. Where do you want to start?"

"Let's start with the one you've got here. Did you do a background on him?"

"Yeah, here's what we've got so far." Ron handed Mort a folder.

Mort looked at the information in the folder. "Quite a long rap sheet, but mostly small stuff. Gimme just a minute."

Mort got his phone out and punched in Jerry's number. "Jerry, this's Mort. Look into the computer and see what we have locally on a guy named Paul Jacobs, and another guy named 'Little' Tony Blanchard. Get Becky into one of the interrogation rooms and see if she recognizes the names then call me back."

"Okay, Ron. Let's go see what this guy has to offer."

"Follow me!" As they walked, Ron punched a number into his phone. "Bring that guy we brought in last night into the interrogation room."

When they got to the interrogation room, the prisoner was seated at a table, very nervously looking around. Both Ron and Mort watched through a one way glass. "Ever see this guy before?" Ron asked.

"Can't say as I have." Mort studied him a little more. "He looks like the kind of scum Ronnie Russell has around in his gang. They all have that same look—you know? Grimy skin, stringy and unkempt hair, wrinkled and oversize clothes, and tattoos everywhere. Their eyes are sunken and dark—they look mostly sad. We have two of 'em in custody right now— two of the three that abducted Josie Brown."

"Two of the three?"

"Yeah, one of 'em was killed by a SWAT in the course of Josie' rescue. They're all just kids, probably early twenties." Mort looked at Ron. "Give me your tablet for a moment."

Mort took the tablet and wrote four names on it: Ronnie Russell, Jorge Sánchez, Sam Jobst, and 'Big' Larry Canfield. What's this character's name?"

"This one is Paul Jacobs. Of course that could be an alias, but that's what his driver's license says."

"And the one in the hospital?"

"That one is 'Little' Tony Blanchard."

Just then Ron's cell phone rang. "Frazier!"

"Deputy Frazier, this is Connie at Memorial Hospital. Mister Blanchard passed away about ten minutes ago from complications of surgery. His remains are on the way to the morgue."

"Thanks, Connie!" Turning back to Mort, "Well, looks like we won't have to worry about Blanchard—he just died."

Mort was quiet for a few moments. "You know Ron, these things happen, but it's such a waste. I feel so sorry for his mom and dad. No parent intends to raise their kid to turn out this way and have to identify him on a slab in the morgue."

"Yeah," Ron added. "As a cop you hope to God you never have to take someone's life, but it happens."

Mort looked into the younger man's eyes. "I know how you feel. People call you a hero, Ron—but you're never proud of what you had to do."

Ron shook his head. "Well, let's get back to Mister Jacobs. What's your plan?"

"Let's let him believe his buddy in the hospital is still alive and talking. I'm going to bring up those names I gave you, and you watch for signs of recognition. I'm particularly interested in the connection with Ronnie's old man, Albert Russell. If I engage you in a conversation, just play along."

"Let's get on with it." Ron opened the door, and he and Mort sat in chairs on the opposite side of the table from Jacobs. Ron introduced himself and Mort. When he mentioned that Mort was Sheriff over in Littleville, Jacobs' eyes showed attention.

Back in Littleville, Jerry met with Becky in an interrogation room. Becky looked worried. Jerry greeted her. "Hi, Becky. Are you doing okay?"

"Yeah, sort of," Becky replied. "The word from a couple of the inmates is that Albert Russell and Ronnie are out on bail, and there's been people lookin' for me and for Josie."

"Umm," Jerry responded, not wanting to give any hint of assent or denial. "Becky, here's some evidence we got from your apartment." He opened a folder and began to list some things. "First, we found some of old man Russell's clothes in your closet. His fingerprints were all over your apartment, and his DNA was on the bed sheet. We figure he had been there within a few days before Josie was abducted." He paused to see if Becky would respond.

Becky hung her head and didn't say anything.

Jerry continued. "We also found a compartment in the couch, and it had drug residue on it. Your closet was also used to store drugs. In fact almost every cabinet in the place had drug residue. It begins to look like you're up to your neck in this thing, Becky. It could mean a very lengthy prison term. You could help yourself a lot if you'd talk to us about what you know."

Becky began to cry softly but remained silent.

"There's a couple of more names I want to run by you. Tell me if you know anything about them. Do you know someone named Paul Jacobs?"

Becky looked up. Her eyes showed recognition.

Jerry continued, "Do you know someone named 'Little' Tony Blanchard?"

Again Becky's eyes showed recognition.

Jerry continued, "What do you know about the connection between Juan Salazar and Albert Russell."

Becky stood up and screamed. "I can't tell you anything—you hear, nothing! They'll kill me!"

Becky, listen to me. "If we can put those people behind bars, there's nothing they can do to you. We'll do our best to protect you."

Becky sat back down and put her arms on the table and rested her head on them. "Can I talk to Josie?"

Jerry thought for a few moments. "Yeah, I think that would be possible."

Josie walked into the interrogation room and immediately took Becky's hands and lifted her up and hugged her. "It's going to be all right, Becky. I've been praying for you, and I know for sure God has a plan for your life, and the plan doesn't include you being killed by gangsters or spending your life in jail. God wants to bless you and keep you safe."

Becky pulled away from Josie. "I wish I had your faith, Josie. They want me to tell everything I know about Albert Russell and his connection with Salazar. Those men will have me killed if I talk."

"Becky, they're going to try to have you killed whether or not you talk. They need you out of the way. Let me tell you about some things that have happened since you've been in here. You remember the Browns who were with me at the restaurant?"

Jerry interrupted. "Let me tell it Josie. I have some new details not even you know about. Becky, this is a very serious situation. They're after Josie as well as you. We had assumed that a National Guard jet was going to fly Sandy and Will and Mister and Missus Brown back to Rock City for trial. We put out the word that Josie was going with them. However plans got changed and a charter was arranged instead. Someone put an explosive device on a National Guard jet while it was on the ground here. Authorities managed to intercept it before it got off the ground so thankfully, none of the three crew members was injured or killed. Detective Sandoval, Will Brent, and the Browns were on the private charter, and Josie was here with us. The information that Josie was with them was planted by us. The bad guys just assumed that they would be on the National Guard jet because they came here on an identical plane."

Becky looked at Jerry—she was bewildered. "My God," she said. "Three innocent people could have died!"

"That's right, Becky. And what neither of you know until now is that David Lee Brown and Stevie were on their way to Rock City that same afternoon. When they stopped at a motel over the line in Texas for the night, they were abducted by two guys named Jacobs and Blanchard. The abduction was arranged by Russell. We know that from talking to them. On their way back here they stopped at a beer joint and got drunk. David Lee and Stevie managed to escape and called nine-one-one. They were taken to Parchville by a deputy. Blanchard died in a shootout with the deputy, and Jacobs is in custody. Mort left this morning to go over there to talk to them."

"Are Stevie and David Lee okay?" Josie whimpered.

"Yeah, Josie—they're fine. You'll be proud of Stevie when you hear the whole story.

Becky just looked at Josie for several long moments. She burst into tears and grabbed Josie and hugged her. "I'm so, so sorry Josie. You saved my life. Now, I must help you. Even if it means my life—I must help you." Becky looked at Jerry. "Wha...what do you need from me?"

For the next two hours, Becky answered Jerry's questions and told him everything she knew. When they were finished, Josie took Becky's hand. "I'm very proud of you, Becky. God is going to make this tragedy turn out for good."

CHAPTER TWENTY-FOUR

As soon as Albert Russell and his son Ronnie were freed from jail, Albert made some phone calls, and they headed for *Las Palmas Especiale* for dinner. Enrique greeted them, "Good evening, Señores, I am very happy to see you out of jail. What can I get for you to drink?" Both men ordered beer. "Sí, Señores, I will be right back."

When Enrique brought the beer, Albert Russell spoke to his son. "As soon as we're finished eating, I want you to call your mom and let her know we'll be at the ranch. I don't want anyone else to know where we are, is that clear? I don't want any of your seedy young gang members to know where we are. We're going to hang out there for a few days 'till things cool off a little here in town."

Ronnie muttered something into his beer glass, which made him sound like he was talking into a hole. Albert reached across the table and grabbed the glass. "Dammit, Ronnie, don't do that. Do you understand what I want you to do?"

"Yeah Dad, I understand!"

"I don't want you talkin' to anybody—not even your slimy friends. Don't screw this up, Son—our lives may depend on it! What guns you have, take them with you to the ranch along with all the ammo you have available."

Ronnie looked at his dad. His face took on a worried look, he frowned, his eyes narrowed. "But Dad, you're the king here, nobody'd dare take you on."

Albert looked up as Enrique brought their meals. After both men had eaten, Enrique brought the check. Albert looked at his son. "Okay, Ronnie, you get outta here and head for the ranch. Call Mom on your way and otherwise don't talk to anybody."

Russell watched his son leave and ordered another beer. He gave Enrique some money and told him to go pay the bill for him. When he was nearly finished with the beer, Enrique returned to the table. "Señor Russell, Señor Salazar would like for you to go to his office."

"Thank you, Enrique." He took his time finishing the beer and then left the table to go to Salazar's office.

"Ah, Señor Russell!" Motioning to a chair, Salazar continued. "Please be seated, my friend. And what brings you here so soon after being released from jail?"

As an act of defiance, Russell sat in a different chair than the one designated by Salazar. The two men looked at each other with confrontation in their eyes. Neither spoke. Russell became increasingly irritated. Finally he stood, leaned over Salazar's desk, and pointed his finger in Salazar's face. The bodyguard moved ever so slightly in Russell's direction, his muscles on alert to move when directed to do so.

Russell's eyes narrowed, "Did you tip off the police to Becky's apartment?"

Salazar looked at his bodyguard who moved into a position behind Russell. He leaned back in his chair, took a cigar from his shirt pocket, sniffed it, and put it in his mouth. He rolled it around on his tongue, then took it out and held it in front of his face and looked at it. He was still looking at the cigar when he spoke.

"I did not do such a thing, Señor."

Russell leaned a little further over the desk. "You lying son of a bitch—you are to leave Becky alone—is that clear?"

Salazar smiled. "Señor Russell, I think you are mistaken about something very important. You see, I do not take orders from you—you take orders from me." Salazar's face turned into an angry snarl. "Now, get out of my office. When I need you, I will summon you."

"Why you son..." He was interrupted by Salazar's bodyguard, who physically turned him around, and gave him a shove toward the door. The two men looked intently at one another. Russell looked at Salazar, narrowed his eyes, and walked out the door.

Salazar, still fingering his cigar, stood up and turned to the bodyguard. "He knows too much. We can't afford his arrogance and his many mistakes. Eliminate him and his son! And, plan it very carefully."

The bodyguard turned and quickly left.

A week later, Albert and Ronnie Russell were sitting on the front porch of their cabin drinking beer. "Ronnie have you been to the shack in the last few days?"

"No," was the curt answer. "Why?"

"I was wondering if the old pickup was still there. There's supposed to be some crates of AK-47s and lots of ammunition in the shack that's ready and waitin' for us ta deliver 'em. We need to check it out. First thing tomorrow morning, we'll drive over there and see if Salazar's ponies have brought that stuff in yet."

"And, if that stuff's there?"

"I've got a plan Son. I know who those guns are supposed to go to. One little trip and we make ourselves a bundle of money."

"Salazar's not going to put up with that, Dad! You know what he can do."

Albert stomped his feet as he stood up and yelled, "Salazar be damned. I've got enough on him that we can go into our own business, and he can go to hell!"

Both men staggered into the cabin and got ready for bed. The next morning they ate breakfast, got into the Jeep and headed for the shack. What they didn't see was a total surprise to both. The pickup was missing. "Where the hell's the pickup," Russell yelled at his son.

"I don't have any idea," Ronnie curtly responded. I've been in jail, remember?"

"The sheriff must have taken it in when they rescued Josie Brown from the cabin after your stupid friends abducted her." Albert looked around at the sound of another voice.

"Well, well, Señor Russell, you are of course, correct," the voice behind them said. Both men turned around to face Salazar and three of his men with AK-47s pointed at them. "Are you looking for something besides the pickup, Señor?"

Russell was stunned. "We uh...we were just checking to make sure your shipment of arms was safe," he said, his face twitching nervously.

"Yeah," Ronnie interrupted. "That's exactly what we were doin'."

Salazar was infuriated. He walked over to Ronnie and slapped him hard on the side of his face, almost knocking him down. As Ronnie cowered away, Albert started toward him. Someone grabbed him from behind, hit him on the head, and he fell.

"Tie their hands and take these stupid idiots to the cabin. You know what to do!" Salazar commanded.

The three men dragged Ronnie and his dad outside to a waiting SUV. Salazar got into his Lincoln and motioned to his bodyguard. He backed the Lincoln out of the drive, and sped away, dust collecting in the air behind them.

Ronnie's eyes showed the fear he was feeling, knowing that any moment he expected to be shot. Albert, being pushed along by one of Salazar's men, staggered to his feet and stumbled toward the waiting vehicle. All he could do was scream angry curses at them.

At the cabin, both men were forced into chairs and bound to the chairs with rope. A guard stood in front of them glaring and fingering the trigger of his weapon. It was obvious he would take pleasure in shooting them. The other two looked into the refrigerator and found the beer and began drinking. It wasn't long before all three men were bragging about being the one to kill these two stupid Gringos. One of them pulled a knife and began to pretend to cut Ronnie's throat, the sharp blade leaving a slight red line as it passed around his neck. Ronnie's eyes were bulging, and he was screaming and pleading for his life. He felt warm liquid in his pants and knew he was urinating. Salazar's men, seeing the growing stain, obviously enjoyed the emotional torture they were inflicting on their captives. Alternately one of them put the barrel of his gun against Ronnie's head and then pulled it away, all three laughing at Ronnie's reactions and at his wet pants. Then they repeated the process with Albert.

While his men were enjoying their devilish antics at the cabin, Salazar and his bodyguard were on the ranch road leading away. As they neared the gate leading out of the property, Salazar motioned for his driver to stop.

"Something is not right!" he exclaimed. He looked around carefully in all directions, but he could see nothing. He motioned for his bodyguard in the back seat to get out of the car and check out the gate. As the bodyguard prepared to open the gate, three sheriff's deputies emerged from the brush, all carrying pump action shotguns. The bodyguard froze and lifted his arms into the air. Salazar ordered his driver to floor it, break through the gate and keep on going. At the same moment as the driver put the car in gear, three deafening shotgun blasts rang out, flattening both front tires.

Steam was billowing out of the radiator. Salazar ordered his driver to back out and turn around. Three more shotgun blasts from behind flattened the rear tires. The car was immobilized.

Deputies emerged from the brush and surrounded them. The occupants were ordered out of the car with their hands in the air. The driver emerged, pistol in hand and started shooting. A hail of bullets riddled his body, and he died instantly. Salazar was ordered out, and he complied. He was met by Sheriff Mortenson.

"Ah, Señor Mortenson. We meet again. Perhaps we can discuss this matter and come to some sort of...shall we say... agreement. I'm sure you are...a very reasonable man."

Mort snarled at the suggestion. "Mister Salazar, it is a great pleasure to meet you again, especially under these circumstances. I am very sorry, but I don't discuss matters such as this with scum like you. Remember, Señor, you are not in Mexico. Your bribes will not work in my county. You will have your chances to discuss it with the judge. **Now!** Lay on the ground face down."

"But, Señor, it is very dirty down there and there may be insects."

Mort laughed at his cowardice and pushed him down. "You're under arrest. You have the right to remain silent, everything you say can and will be used against you in court. You have the right to an attorney." Mort laughed. "Oh, by the way your attorney is back yonder in that cabin and at this very moment under arrest along with your other henchmen. Any questions?"

Salazar scowled and sneered. He narrowed his eyes, and spit at Mort's feet. "Someday, Señor, I will see you with your face in the dirt."

"I doubt that will occur, Salazar!"

Mort put handcuffs on Salazar's wrists and lifted him up to a standing position. As he did, the black tinted rear window of the Lincoln was slowly lowered, and an arm appeared with an AK-47. Two shots rang out in quick succession followed by a shotgun blast. The shotgun blast tore out what remained of the window and hit the gunman in the chest. Like a domino, Salazar who was hit in the back, spun around and went down backward falling into Mort. Then everything was quiet. When Jerry ran around the car gun in hand, Mort was lying on the ground with Salazar on top of him. Jerry looked at Mort who was struggling to push Salazar's body off of his stomach so he could get up. Jerry quickly dragged Salazar to the side.

"Are you okay, Mort?"

"I don't know, Jerry, but thanks for the help." He winced as he tried to move his left arm. "I think I'm hit." He looked down at Salazar who was staring blankly up at the lazy clouds floating overhead. One of the other deputies bent down and felt for a pulse. "He's dead, Mort!"

Mort shook his head. Jerry tied his bandana around Mort's arm and helped him over to a car where they had a first aid kit. An ambulance had been prepositioned and was quickly on the scene.

Back at the cabin, and scared out of their wits, Albert and Ronnie Russell were pleading for their lives. Their tormentors were taking great pleasure in taunting them and laughing at their cowardice. They were so busy laughing and drinking, they failed to notice the sound of a SWAT vehicle as it drove to within one hundred yards of the building. Six men dressed totally in camouflage, and with their faces partially blackened, got out and carefully made their way to the cabin, each taking a position at one of the doors and windows so that all sides of the building were in sight of someone.

The team leader carefully walked up to the porch and crouched near a window. Peering inside, he saw what was going on. He turned to his right and made some hand and finger signals, then he turned to his left and did the same. Several of the SWAT team repositioned themselves. When the leader was satisfied that everyone was in position, one of the team threw a rock through the window near the other end of the room from where the Russell's and their captors were occupied.

When the gunmen responded to the broken window with gunfire, a bullhorn blared for them to give up, lay down their guns and come out with hands in the air. One of the captors swung his gun around toward Albert Russell. Two shots in quick succession put the gunman on the floor. A second gunman screamed something in Spanish and tried to shoot his way out the door but was quickly brought down in a hail of bullets. The third gunman seeing his two friends lying on the floor, and probably dead, hesitated for a few seconds but dropped his gun and raised his hands.

The SWAT leader went first to Albert, untied him from the chair, lifted him up and quickly twisted his arms around behind him and put handcuffs on his wrists. "Mister Russell, you're under arrest for conspiracy to illegally distribute drugs and weapons and conspiracy to commit murder. You have the right to remain silent, anything you say can and will be used against you in a court of law. You have the right to be represented by an attorney."

"I am an attorney, you fool," Albert screamed. "Can't you see I'm the victim here! You can't arrest me! I'll have your job for this."

"Victim or not, Mister Russell. You're under arrest."

Ronnie was handcuffed and given the same reading of his rights as was the drunk gunman, who by now was joking with the SWAT team members. Speaking to the SWAT leader, the gunman blurted in broken English, "Señores! I can tell you much! You will treat me well?"

"That'll be up to the judge, but it may help."

The gunman smiled as he was led away. Ronnie had urinated repeatedly and was very uncomfortable. Albert was screaming and cursing. The gunman was giggling at the whole spectacle.

Ambulances picked up the dead gunmen, and the prisoners were taken in by sheriff's deputies. Jerry helped Mort into his car and sped away toward the hospital.

Back at the office, the first thing Mort did was call his wife. Then he asked Joyce how Becky was doing. "She's holding on, Mort," Joyce told him. "Josie's been with her every minute since the stabbing. How's yer arm?"

"It's okay—hurts a lot but okay. No bones broken, just a hole. Josie?"

"She's an amazing woman, Mort. She has a real gift. It seems like she can talk straight to God, and God hears her."

"God hears all of us Joyce."

"But—this is something real special; something you only read about in the Bible."

"Well," Mort said. "It's about closing time here, and we've done more than a day's work. Let's go visit with Becky and Josie. I need to tell 'em about our fishing trip today. Besides we're going to have the news media all over us real soon. If we leave now, we'll be ahead of 'em."

When Mort and Joyce arrived at the hospital, the doctor was there to talk to them. "How's she doin' Doc?"

"She's doing just fine. The stab wound was deep—it left a small cut on her liver and lower portion of her lung. I think we were able to patch it all up, and she'll recover with no problems. She lost a lot of blood so she's weak, but she's awake. We figure she must have been lying near her bunk for several hours before the guards discovered her."

"Is it okay if we go in for a visit?"

"Sure, but don't stay too long."

"Thanks Doc."

Josie was sitting on a chair beside the bed holding Becky's hand. With her other hand she was very gently stroking Becky's head. Josie looked up as Mort and Joyce walked in. Mort walked immediately to Josie and gave her a little hug and then turned to Becky and leaned down and kissed her forehead. Becky smiled. Mort stood back, and Joyce hugged both women.

"Oh, Becky...it's so good to see you. I don't pray very much," Joyce confessed. "But I've been praying for you. Somehow I feel like God is going to take care of you."

Becky smiled, and looked at Mort's arm. Pointing she whispered, "What happened?"

Mort smiled, "We went fishing today, me and a bunch of my deputies, and I just happened to get in the way of a bullet."

Becky frowned, and her eyes expressed worry. "Are you okay?"

"Yeah, I'm okay." He added, "And you're okay now too. We had a little roundup out at Albert Russell's ranch this afternoon. We have both Russell's back in custody for good and two of Salazar's gunmen along with 'em. Salazar and three of his henchmen are dead. Out of twelve law officers involved, I'm the only one to get the Purple Heart—and I didn't even draw my gun." He laughed, "Now you can live your life in peace." As an afterthought, he said, "I hope you've learned something about who you can trust..."

"...And who not to get involved with," Becky added. She looked at Josie, "I am so glad that Josie was here for me. As tragic as things have been, it seems like God had it all planned and under control. Even the pain and disappointment have been worth it to live to see this moment. I have God in my life now," she beamed. "I'm a new person. And...I guess that *Las Palmas Especiale* will be under new management?"

"I can't tell you that, Becky. I'm sure the state will have a claim, and of course the Feds will take it because of drug money. It'll take a long time to investigate and trace the money Salazar used to buy it. They'll have to interview every single person who works there now or in the past. I'm sure when it's all said and done there'll be more people charged as co-conspirators. They'll be going through all the records and files. It'll undoubtedly be closed for some period of time."

"That's sad. It is a fine restaurant, and some good people are going to lose their jobs."

"That's all just a game to people like Salazar, Becky. They really don't care about who they hurt in the process."

Mort turned to Josie. "We best be goin'. Do you need a ride back to your cell, Josie?"

"I'll stay here, Mort, as long as Becky needs me. They'll let me sleep here, but I could use a change of clothes. Maybe Joyce could go to my cell and pick some things for me."

"Are you eating?"

"Yeah, they always seem to have an extra tray. I don't know where it comes from, but I think Jesus is multiplying the loaves and fishes, and they bring them on a tray for me."

As Mort and Joyce were about to leave the room, Mort's wife, Susan walked in. She rushed to her husband and hugged him. He hugged back with his good arm. When she let go, she looked at the arm and started crying. "How bad is it, Mort?" She asked.

"Not bad...not bad at all." Mort quickly turned and introduced her to Josie and Becky.

"Mort, there are reporters and microphones set up outside. I think they want to hear from you."

Mort looked at Becky and Josie, "Good night, girls. I'll probably see you tomorrow sometime."

Josie followed them out. "Becky's been talking a lot, Mort—I mean about Salazar and Russell and all."

"That's good Josie, but it won't do any good for you to tell me any of it. It would be second hand knowledge of events and not admissible in court. When Becky's strong enough, maybe tomorrow afternoon, I'll come over with Jerry and we'll make sure she's ready to testify in court. She's going to be a key witness in nailing this case down and in tying the Russell's to Salazar. Thanks for everything, Josie. You've been a Godsend."

Mort took his wife's hand, and they walked toward the hospital entrance. A hospital spokesperson met them and let them know about the news conference. "We scheduled the news conference only because they've been bugging us about the stabbing at the jail and the condition of Becky. We've not released any names. Now that you're here, we thought it would be a good idea for you to talk to the media people after the doctor says his word or two."

Mort sighed deeply and looked at his wife. "I really need to talk to them, Sweetheart. That's the only way I have to quell rumors and get control of runaway investigations by reporters."

"I'll wait for you, Mort." Susan replied.

Soon the hospital spokesperson and the doctor joined Mort at the hospital entrance, and they all walked out to the microphones together. The hospital spokesperson talked first. "Ladies and gentlemen we have here Doctor Hassim Akan, the attending physician, and Sheriff Paul Mortenson. Doctor Akan will speak first on the condition of the prisoner who was stabbed at the County Jail facility last night. Doctor Akan!"

"Good evening. When the patient was brought in, she had a serious stab wound in the lower left chest area and had lost a considerable amount of blood. Following three hours of surgery, the wounds were cleaned and sutured, and she is resting comfortably. We do not expect that she will have any lasting complications." Doctor Akan waited for questions.

"Doctor, approximately what time did the patient arrive at the hospital."

"She arrived at the emergency room at eleven-thirty last night."

"Was she conscious?"

"Yes, she was conscious but in extreme pain."

"What's her condition at the moment?"

"We are listing her in 'critical condition' for the time being, for medical reasons."

"Doctor, what's the patient's name."

The hospital spokesperson stepped in and answered the question. "Because this case involves a crime that is still being investigated, it is the policy of the hospital not to release any personal information on the patient. Now, Sheriff Mortenson."

"Good evening. As already indicated, the female patient was in our custody when she was assaulted and stabbed in her cell last night. The case is under intensive investigation, and the jail is now on lockdown pending our findings. We have information on the perpetrator and the motive for the assault, and we expect to file attempted murder charges soon. There may also be other charges in connection with this case. Questions?"

"Sheriff, does this case have any connection with the gang you and your deputies broke up this afternoon when you raided the ranch of Albert Russell?"

"I can acknowledge that we broke up a significant drugs and firearms operation this afternoon and captured or killed several persons during the course of the operation. However I cannot make any statements about connections until both cases have been fully investigated. Because of the firearms and drugs issues, there will be federal authorities who will be looking closely at the ranch and will have charges of their own. We will be coordinating our investigation with theirs."

"Sheriff, was the abduction of Josie Brown in any way connected with either of these cases?"

"I cannot comment on that as it could jeopardize our investigation still in progress."

"Sheriff, how did you know about the situation at the Russell ranch?"

"I cannot give out any details on that."

"Sheriff, do you have the names of those arrested and those killed this afternoon?"

"No names!"

"Sheriff, did you receive a tip about the Russell ranch?"

"No comment!"

"Sheriff, how was Juan Velasco Salazar involved in the drugs and firearms operation?"

"No comment."

"Sheriff, was Salazar one of those killed?"

"No comment. Ladies and gentlemen, things are developing fast in this investigation, and I will be scheduling news conferences outside my office on a daily basis over the next few days. There will be federal authorities taking over part of the case, and they will join me. You will all get notices. Thank you for your cooperation and good evening."

Mort, Doctor Akan, and the hospital spokesperson all walked away from the microphones and back into the hospital. Mort took Susan's hand, and together with Joyce, they walked to the car. "We'll drop you at the office for your car, Joyce, and I'll see you in the morning. Right now, I need to get my arm up in the air and relax and take some acetaminophen for pain. I need some of Susan's tender loving care."

"Why, Mort," Susan kidded. "What you mean is that you want to be waited on! I thought big strong cops like you didn't ever have pain."

They all laughed.

Jerry was waiting when Mort arrived at the office next morning. We've got a ton of forensic info from Russell's shack out at the ranch. Not only that, but Salazar's driver is talking."

"What about the character at the cabin?"

Jerry laughed. He was so drunk that he doesn't remember much about what happened there. But, he is willing to talk about Salazar and his connections in Mexico."

"Are either of those guys legal?"

"We traced what we could of their origins. Neither of them had any papers indicating citizenship or legal status."

"Okay, we'll hold both of 'em 'til we're through questioning 'em, and if nobody comes to claim 'em, we'll keep 'em locked up for trial. Bring in someone from the local FBI office when you are questioning. And, be sure they waive their rights to an attorney. Otherwise, we'll have to wait until the judge can appoint someone. Now, what've we got from the crime scene?"

"We found five cases of AK-47s. They all had Chinese markings and were wrapped in a preservative that the lab quickly identified as typical of Chinese imports. We also found eight, maybe ten thousand rounds of ammo, looks like stuff from North Korea. Everything was dusted for fingerprints. We have warrants for Russell's office, home and cabin. We also have warrants for Salazar's office and home. We'll begin serving those this morning."

"Any idea how those weapons were smuggled into the United States?"

"Well, Mort, you know the Chinese have contracts to manage several important ports here in the U.S. I always figured it would only be a matter of time before they got comfortable enough to begin bringing in contraband—probably weapons. Weapons are trucked to New Mexico or Arizona and ponied across the border into Mexico." Jerry's expression turned serious. "There is something else we need to look into Mort. Those weapons may have gone from China by way of a third party to a Mexican port and then across the border for use by gangs here. The Feds tell us that the cartels have established beachheads in most major cities and all along the southern border. They're stockpiling weapons for whatever actions and goals they have in mind."

"I hadn't thought of that, Jerry. That's a good theory. Back to Salazar—I assume there's a Missus Salazar?"

"We don't know, Mort. There's nobody at the house except for a housekeeper and yard staff, all illegals. We'll ask some questions."

"Find out if there's a Missus Salazar, and if there is, find out where she's holing up. I know there's a Missus Russell. She may or may not know anything about her husband's business or his connections to Salazar. Question her but be kind, and when you're goin' through the house don't leave it in a mess!"

Jerry got up and turned to leave. I'll see to it, Mort!"

"Thanks Jerry."

Josie awoke from her makeshift bed and looked at Becky who was sleeping peacefully. She looked at the clock; it was seven. She knew breakfast would be here soon. She used the bathroom, got herself dressed then awoke Becky. Within a few minutes breakfast was brought in.

"How're you feeling this morning, Becky?" Josie asked.

Becky smiled. "Much better, thanks to your prayers. I'm not ready to run the marathon, but I think I could walk around the room and down the hall."

"We'll wait for the doctor to approve that, okay?" Josie was interrupted by her cell phone ringing. She looked at the screen. "Good morning, Will, it's always good to hear your voice. What's new over there?"

"Josie, it seems all the news is from Littleville. Mort's been all over the news media. And how's Becky? I'm just guessing that she's the one who was stabbed at the jail."

"She's doing great, Will. She's right here, and we're eating breakfast. Wanna say hi?"

"Yeah!"

Josie handed her phone to Becky. "Hi, Will," she said, her voice still a little weak.

"I'm sure sorry about the stabbing, but I'm happy you're doing so well. Josie has a gift of prayer, and I know it works. You have our prayers here in Rock City. I'll let everyone know I talked to you."

"Thanks, Will. I'll give the phone back to Josie."

"Will, I guess you know about David Lee and Stevie by now. My little Stevie's quite the hero!"

"Yeah, we've heard. I'm just guessing that Mort has finally been able to put Russell away and has nailed down Salazar.

"Mort wouldn't talk about it, but I think you're right. Some of the bad guys were killed, and Mort was wounded in the arm. That's all I know. Everybody here's making him out to be a hero. As far as I'm concerned, he deserves the accolades."

"Has Becky been able to talk about Russell and Salazar yet?"

"Yeah, she's been talking to me. Mort's coming over this afternoon with Jerry to make sure she's willing to testify. She's a lot more confident now that Russell and Salazar are out of the way. I think she'll be the star witness and a national hero when this all comes up in court."

"Yes, but it also makes her a marked woman. The people above Salazar may put a green light on her. But then again, maybe not. They're probably in Mexico and may be glad to get rid of Salazar and Russell. I'm glad Becky's got you. You've got an angel that goes everywhere you go. Well, I need to go, Josie so I'll have to hang up. I just want you to know I miss you. God bless!"

Thank you, Will, I miss you too. Blessings and hugs, bye."

Josie smiled as she closed her phone. *"Will's a wonderful person,"* she thought to herself. *"I think I have feelings for him, but I need to know more about him."*

Becky saw the smile in Josie's eyes and in her face. "Will's a wonderful guy, Josie. I think he really cares for you."

Josie's feet began to feel light, like they wanted to dance. Her voice began to feel free like she wanted to sing. Her arms began to feel like she wanted to embrace the whole world. "Yes, Becky. Yes, he is a wonderful guy."

CHAPTER TWENTY-FIVE

"Mornin', Joyce," Jerry said as he headed into Mort's office.

"Mornin', Jerry." She said pleasantly as he walked by. Joyce didn't look up from the paperwork that was occupying her mind.

"Mornin', Mort," Jerry said.

"Mornin', Jerry! Grab a cup of coffee and sit down... what's on yer mind?"

Jerry poured himself some coffee. "How's the arm doin'?"

"The arm's doin' fine. Pretty sore but still in one piece. Doc says no infection. How's your investigation comin' along?"

Jerry took out the notebook he always carried. "Tho't I'd bring ya up on the goins on with the feds, an' what we've learned from the interrogations, both the fed's and ours."

"Okay, Jerry, you been workin' on it for more than two weeks, let's hear what ya've got!"

Jerry looked at his notebook. "First of all, about the weapons and ammo we found at Russell's ranch. I already told ya that those AK-47s are all Chinese made, and the ammo is North Korean. It seems they came through Venezuela then to Mexico."

"How do you know that, Jerry?"

"Markings on the crates and on some of the ammo! Plus, the preservative used on the guns and ammo is typical Chinese."

"Go on!"

One of Salazar's boys told us the weapons came across the border at a remote spot in Arizona under the protection of cartel militia operating on the Arizona side. Then they were brought here by several vehicles traveling different routes."

Mort scratched his head. "And...they were headed for...?"

Jerry smiled. "...Islamic Jihadists in Detroit!"

"Holy...You were right, Jerry. They were headed north, not south. So, what's their status as of now?"

"Hold onto yer seat, Mort! The feds are pullin' the plug on the whole investigation."

Mort's eyes widened, and his forehead furrowed. "Why?"

"Dunno, word is, orders from somewhere on high, very likely the U.S. attorney general's office in Washington. My thinkin' is, a decision was made at the top...but, that's just me thinkin'."

"Any word on why?"

"I talked to a buddy of mine in the bureau, and he told me confidentially that the word in their circles is that our president doesn't want to embarrass the president of Mexico, or the Muslims in Detroit...for his own reasons...probably political stuff. The field boys at the bureau are pretty frustrated. They feel like they've got a real smoking gun, and they don't like having the rug pulled."

"This'll get out, Jerry! The media'll pick it up, and it'll get out. Who will they throw under the bus?"

Jerry scratched his head. "That's another story, Mort. I really don't know...but somebody'll go down!"

"Maybe we can give the attorney general the benefit of the doubt and assume they want to fish for trophies."

"That's possible, Mort. But I don't believe it for a minute!"

"What about the finances for the operation? Any info on that?"

"The bureau boys believe the money is coming from the Iranian Revolutionary Guard, funneled through an embassy in Houston—probably the Venezuelan embassy. They pay guys like Salazar to pony stuff across the border and then deliver it to Detroit and other United States destinations. It's big money."

Mort scratched his head again and thought for a few moments. "That means the Mexican cartels and gangs are broadening their business contacts aren't they? No wonder there's been so many assassinations."

"Looks like it, Mort. Friends at the bureau say the gangs are also escorting Middle-Eastern folks through Mexico and into the United States through Arizona. They have armed Mexican militia who operate on both sides of the border, as far north as Phoenix. They're armed to the teeth with automatic weapons, rocket launchers and grenades…even some fifty cal BMG's (Browning Machine Guns). They smash anybody who gets in their way. The Mexican government doesn't want to know about it, and our government denies its happening. One more thing: rumor has it that *Los Zetas* (Mexico drug gang) has taken over a couple of ranches near Laredo, Texas, and are attempting to establish a corridor like in Arizona. It's all hush, hush stuff they don't want to get out, but, it's also just rumor at this point. That's not all…the Sinaloa cartel had a major meth operation in Oklahoma that was busted up not long ago. So, it's not surprising at all, one of the cartels is operating in our neighborhood."

"I feel sorry for the federal and local law officers in Arizona and Texas. They don't have the firepower or the authority to intercept." Mort sighed. "Okay Jerry, where does that leave us, and the cases we have against these guys here?"

"We've got cases we can make stick in our state courts... no doubt about that! The feds want to act like nothing happened. They took those AK-47s..." Jerry grinned, "...and we've got lots of good pictures! We did the feds a favor by taking Salazar and his buddies out of the business, but don't expect any thanks."

"Good work, Jerry! Did you ever find Missus Salazar?"

"Not a trace, Mort." Jerry flashed a big grin, "For some unknown reason, the taxes haven't been paid on their home, and the restaurant was a lease. They let the state sales taxes, unemployment compensation fees, and some debts to creditors pile up. It looks like they were planning to abandon everything and move on real soon."

"Since the feds have pulled out, any chance the county could seize the business and the home for taxes owed?"

"Can't say, but I can sure ask the county attorney to check it out. Might have to be shared with the state."

"I've been bothered about that guy in the Lincoln that shot Salazar and me." Mort rubbed his arm. "Have you managed to get any info on who he was or why he did what he did?"

"We've been able to glean some stuff from interpol sources in Mexico. His name is Hadan Al Kolhani, aka, José Santleban. At one time, he worked as a double agent for some unidentified cleric in France. The only theory I can come up with is that it was his job to keep an eye on Salazar. He was a relatively low-level employee in the Mexican federal police a few years ago and traveled numerous times between the U.S. and Mexico on so called 'official business'. He defected and joined a cartel—better pay. He's been hangin' around a bunch of bad guys from everywhere in the world. I think he was planted in Salazar's organization by someone in the Mexican government with connections to the cartel. It was

Josie's Gift

pretty obvious that someone at a very high level somewhere couldn't afford for Salazar to go to trial. There's a bunch of pieces to that puzzle we'll probably never find now that he's dead."

Mort shook his head. "You're probably right. Too bad the feds don't want to go any further with it. What about Missus Russell; did you get anything from her?"

"When I talked to her, she was pretty upset, Mort. But, when we went to her home, she was one-hundred percent cooperative. We were able to go through the house, bring out computers and file cabinets...lots of evidence! I'm pretty convinced that she had nothing to do with the old man's illicit businesses, and knew nothing about his mistresses. I feel sorry for her. She's a really nice lady...has class... doesn't deserve what she's gettin' from her old man. She does have some other children from a prior marriage so she has some family support."

"Did you find anything connecting Russell with any of the women in our jail?"

"Yeah, Mort! Angelina De Leon was one of his clients... owed him a lot of money! Becky identified Angelina as her assailant so we know there's a connection with Russell. I still need to question her and see if we can get an admission...maybe make a deal of some kind. What we got from Russell's files indicate she has a criminal record...and a long relationship with Russell, probably one of his mistresses. We also found out Russell once defended Becky on a charge of driving while intoxicated. That's probably how she got involved in his business. He was using her in more ways than one. The DA's pretty sure he can get immunity for Becky in exchange for her testimony. Angelina may get off with a lighter sentence if she cooperates and talks."

"Are any of our cases scheduled for the grand jury anytime soon?"

"Not any time soon, Mort. The DA's office is trying to organize the evidence and get their cases in order. There's a lot of overlap so they've got to organize things so they have the best chance of convictions. I'm sure you already know that the judge has ordered Albert and Ronnie Russell held without bond...pending formal arraignment. Salazar's helpers are all being held similarly, because they pose a flight risk. The Mexican Embassy has been more than a little noisy about its citizens being in our custody, but the judge has been firm. They're ours until the court decides on their fate."

"You've done a good job, Jerry! I hope, when I go full-time with the task force, you'll be appointed to this office. You'll make a good sheriff."

"Thanks Mort, I'll remember that. By the way, how's Becky doin'?"

"She's supposed to be released from the hospital tomorrow. Joyce is going to help her and Josie find an apartment they can share. Then they can move quietly away from the jail. Josie can keep on working here as long as she needs to. In fact I'm going to promote Joyce to be dispatcher supervisor, and she'll train Josie to take over her job as receptionist."

"I think that's a good move, Mort. That'll help keep Josie in Littleville." He sighed, "I think she'll eventually go back to Rock City, though. She's been a godsend here, that's for sure. Maybe we can help Becky find a job too...when she's strong enough. I wonder if she and Juanita could partner and open up *Las Palmas Especial?*"

"Good thought, Jerry, but we've got to get Juanita a legal status before anything like that is even a remote possibility."

"Yer right...I was jest thinkin', hopin'."

Mort tore off a page from a small pad and handed it to Jerry. "Here's the Talamantes' address, Jerry. I want you to go visit with Juanita, Enrique and their mother. Go in street clothes and an unmarked car. Promise them they have nothing to fear from us, but, that if they try to head back to Mexico, their lives could be in real danger from the cartels down there. Tell them to contact us immediately if they have problems with any of Salazar's associates we don't know about, or with the feds. Let 'em know we'll do everything we can to protect them. I think Juanita's smart enough to play along with Salazar's friends or the feds until she can get in touch with us. Tell Juanita and Enrique, in exchange for their testimony, we'll do our best to get them on a fast track to a legal status, like a green card and citizenship. They're good people and will make good citizens. See if the DA will go along with it. Impress on him that Juanita and Enrique are key witnesses in Salazar's businesses. I'm sure Enrique thought he was doing Salazar a favor, when he told him about overhearing Albert and Ronnie's plans about holing up at the ranch. We have Juanita to thank for telling us about it. Thanks to Juanita and Enrique, everything came together at the ranch and not somewhere here in town."

Jerry got up from his chair and turned to leave. "Mort, you have a way of making sure my plate is full, ha! See ya later."

"I know you can handle it, Jerry!"

As the weeks went by, Josie was enjoying her new job at the sheriff's office. She got to meet people, and her welcoming smile was attractive to everyone who came into the office. She learned quickly, and the three weeks of working with Joyce were very beneficial for her. They had become good friends in the process. Josie felt good about herself, in the knowledge that she could learn, and could develop her abilities into some job skills. She was also able to attend G.E.D. classes and earn her high school diploma.

Becky was working as a waitress not far from the sheriff's office, and she and Josie were able to visit a little each day. Using money from Josie's mom and dad, they bought a second-hand car that served both her and Becky.

Moisés and Ruth both had jobs at the mission. Their willingness to work hard and their skills were an asset to the ministry. Will picked them up at the mission and took them out to eat at least once a week. He was fascinated by the culture and beliefs of Messianic Jews. Moisés and Will became very good friends. The mission became Moisés and Ruth's place of worship, although privately with Carla, they practiced some of the ancient Shabbat and high Holy Days traditions as their ancestors had done for hundreds of years. They spent time with Carla, encouraging each other in their Jewish traditions. It also gave them an opportunity to practice what they knew of the Hebrew language.

Josie missed Stevie, who was still in Rock City with her parents. She had to think about getting him enrolled in school in the next month. She hadn't decided whether it would be in Rock City or Littleville. The trial of her abductors was still at least four weeks away, and she had to stay in Littleville at least that long.

David Lee Brown was able to return home after the investigation of his and Stevie's abductors was completed, but would have to go back for the trial.

Having waived trial by jury, John and Doris Brown were tried before Judge Jacobson in Rock City. The judge found them guilty by their own admission, and gave them a suspended sentence, and probation. He released them to return to Churchill. They were to serve their probation there, along with whatever sentence was imposed by the judge at Churchill. It turned out the Churchill judge gave them each two-year's probation, and made them pay restitution to the city for damage to the police cruiser. Moisés and Ruth Blandón testified on behalf of the Browns, and since they had no previous criminal record, and were deemed to pose no future threat, the judge was lenient. John and Doris joined a community church and became active members. John blessed many with his telling of the story of his conversion and near-death experience with the angel. They worked with their church to establish a non-denominational mission in Churchill patterned after the Lighted Way Ministry Mission in Rock City.

Although Josie talked to her parents and to Stevie nearly every day, she missed her family, especially Stevie. She also talked to Will every day. She missed him...he was so different than Roger. Roger's strength came from his need for prowess and power. On the other hand, Will's strength was something inner, a quality of personality and spirit that exuded comfort and peace. Will was responsible and thoughtful.

Josie was realizing that her feelings for Will were growing beyond just friendship. In his absence she dreamed. Many were the times she wished he were there. She imagined herself in his arms. Their relationship was a comfortable one, she felt no need to worry or wonder where he was, or what he was doing. She always knew that he was where he was supposed to be...and, he was in her heart. At times she had to pull herself up to reality, lest she develop a fantasy of Will that could turn out not to be true.

Josie didn't know if she was in love...or if her feelings were real. She had no idea what being in love would feel like. At times she caught herself trying to capture feelings like the ones she had for Roger...but she couldn't. The feelings she had for Roger would be foreign to Will...they didn't fit his personal qualities. Whatever her feelings for Will, she was feeling comfortable with them...she felt as if they fit the relationship. Yet, when she stood back and evaluated her feelings, she was disturbed...she didn't know what he was feeling or thinking about her. She also realized she knows very little about him. She knows he's a district attorney's

Josie's Gift

investigator, that he has a college degree in criminal justice and a law degree on top of that, though he had never practiced law. She knows he's about the same age as Roger—but, who is he, really? Her feelings were confused...like a dream and he wasn't really there...maybe he wasn't real, but just something her imagination made up. She concluded that she needed to go back to Rock City...to know Will.

Finally, a trial date was set for Josie's abductors. *"At last,"* she thought. *"This whole ordeal will be over, and I can get back to my life."* She asked herself over and over, *"Shall I stay in Littleville or go back to Rock City?"* Then, she rationalized, *"On the one hand, I've made many friends in Littleville and will miss them. On the other hand, I feel like I'm drying up spiritually...not growing in the Lord... something is still missing in my life. I really need Isabelle, and Darlene, and Carla. I miss the close spiritual bonds we shared at the mission. It's a relationship in which our common bonding is Jesus. I'm not ready to make it totally on my own. The experiences in Littleville with John and Doris...with Mort and Jerry...Joyce and Becky, have been wonderful and I've grown from them, but I don't feel ready for God's calling on my own. I need to go back to Rock City and the mission...I need to grow...up!"* The confidence she had felt during those experiences was drained. Like an athlete at the end of a grueling race, she felt her strength consumed. She needed a fresh new breath of wind...a new burst of spiritual energy.

She agonized over her parents. *"I need time with them. I have to repair that relationship, whatever it will take."*

Josie's thoughts were captured by the story of Jesus and his disciples (Luke 10). After they had been with Jesus for a time, listening to him teach and watching him perform miracles, he sent them out two by two with instructions to teach, and to heal, and to cast out demons. They tried their wings so to speak. They did as they were instructed, and they were successful. But, they returned to the Master for further and more advanced training.

"They must have felt like I do now," Josie thought to herself. *"It was wonderful experience for them, but they needed more. So they went back to Jesus, and he took them to the next level in their training and ministry. I must go back to Rock City! That's the only place I can put the pieces of my life back together. But, what about Becky? I feel some responsibility for her! I can't just walk away from her."*

The phone rang in Isabelle's office. "Hi, Isabelle, this is Josie!"

"Hi, Josie. How're things going in Littleville?"

"The trials are starting tomorrow, and after I testify, I'll be ready to go home to Rock City and the mission. I miss you so much."

"We miss you too, Josie. And...Will misses you too. Did you know he's been in contact with the DA's office over there, keeping tabs on those trials and when you'll be called to testify?"

Josie's heart skipped a beat. "No! Why on earth would he do that?"

"Well, Honey...if you can't figure that one out...!"

"I'm flattered...Oh, Isabelle! I don't know what to think any more. I miss him so very much. I have feelings that I can't understand. I have so many feelings I need to sort out... and I need you and Carla and Darlene to bring me down to earth and help me deal with those feelings. I need to grow more in the Lord. Right now, I feel like I'm wandering in a desert. I don't have the bearings I need to grow up, and to be what the Father has planned for me."

Isabelle could hear in her voice, the tears that were filling Josie's eyes, the beating of her heart searching for something. "Josie," She said, "More than anything else, right now you need to get closer to the Father. Read your bible, and as St. Paul says, 'pray without ceasing'. Correct me if I'm wrong, but my guess is you've let up on your daily bible study and prayer life."

Isabelle could hear the breathing that signaled a pause at the other end of the line. Josie took a deep breath. "Of course, you're right, Isabelle. You're always right."

Isabelle continued, her voice raised in encouragement. "Let every breath you take, be a prayer breathed to the Father who loves you. You're going to make it, Girl. We're waiting for you. Remember, the Father has given you a gift, Josie."

"What is my gift, Isabelle? Right now I'm not sure I have a gift!" Her voice still expressed her discouragement.

"Look at your hands, Josie. You've used your hands for healing others, and for comforting and blessing them. That is the gift the Father has given you. He used unexpected circumstances to place you in Littleville, because He had a purpose for you there...people He wanted you to bless. Because of your gift, lives there have been changed forever. Now, He wants you to come back here."

Josie was silent for a few seconds processing, then, stumbled over what she wanted to ask. "Isabelle, can I...uh, bring Becky back with me?"

"Josie, do you think that is what the Father wants, or is it something you want? Listen to the Father's voice, Josie. He'll tell you. Whatever is His will, we will accept it."

Josie felt encouraged. Talking to Isabelle always had that effect, *"That was surely one of her gifts,"* she thought to herself. "Thanks, Isabelle, I love you. Tell Mom and Dad and Stevie, I'll see them all very soon. Bye for now." She hung up the phone feeling comfortable the Father would say Becky should go to Rock City and the mission with her.

The trials seemed to drag on with no end in sight. The defense attorneys repeatedly asked for delays, claiming they needed more time to study the evidence presented by the

DA's office. Finally, after four weeks of haggling over admissibility of various pieces of evidence, Judge Jacobson issued an ultimatum to the defense attorneys, "Today is Thursday; you **will** be ready for trial on Monday morning at nine. There will be **no** more delays."

Josie punched a familiar number into her cell phone. She was anxious to talk to Will; she needed to talk to him about her testimony.

Will flipped open his phone and recognized the number immediately. "Hi, Josie!"

"Hi, Will! I'm getting anxious about testifying."

"Yeah, I'm sure you are. I know all about the delays. That's a common tactic of defense lawyers. I'm glad the judge put a stop to it...that was the right thing to do. I've also dealt with enough witnesses to know that as time goes on, they get increasingly nervous about the proceedings."

"Will, what do I do? The DA has been very understanding and has tried his best to help me."

"Did he go over the questions he'll ask you?"

"Yes, he did."

"Did he go over the kinds of questions the defense is likely to ask?"

"Yes, he did that too, but, I'm still nervous. I'm afraid I'll get on the witness stand and just stammer, and not remember anything. What do I say?"

"Honey...," the word slipped out without Will even thinking about it, "...all you need to think about is telling the truth. Keep it simple and tell the truth. Don't try to explain anything that you're not asked to explain. If they ask you a 'yes' or 'no' question then answer it 'yes' or 'no'. If the question is designed to trick you, the DA will straighten it out on his redirect."

Josie didn't immediately notice the 'honey' in Will's statement. It wasn't until after she hung up that it hit her. The more she thought about it, the more she felt like he had

Josie's Gift

real feelings for her. It made her feel encouraged, not only about the trials, but also about going back to Rock City. But now, another hurdle: she must talk to Becky, and to Mort, and Joyce, and Jerry. They needed to know she had decided to return to Rock City.

"I think we all knew that you'd be going back to Rock City, Josie." Becky said, after Josie broke the news to her.

Josie didn't quite know how to say what was on her mind. She stammered a little. "Becky, remember one time we talked about you going to Rock City and starting a new life? Uh...do you think you would want to go to Rock City with me when I go back?" Josie then proceeded to tell her all about the mission, and all about Isabelle, and Carla, and Darlene. There was excitement in her voice, like a used car salesman trying to close a deal.

"Josie, I think you're about the most wonderful friend I've ever had...in my whole life." She paused and looked intently at Josie. "I love you like a sister, and you've taught me so much about God and Jesus, and about life. I'll never forget you...but...no, I can't leave Littleville. God has given me a chance for a new life here."

Josie was not convinced. "But, Becky, every time you turn around you'll be reminded of things in your past...of people who wanted to kill you...of men who used you." Josie pleaded, "You can start over in Rock City...it'll be a chance for a new life, without all that past." Disappointment hung in her voice like the car salesman losing a sale.

Becky smiled, "I've prayed about it, Josie; I really have prayed. The Father has something here for me. And, yes, I'll be reminded often of the pain and hurt, and of all the disasters of my life. But, each time, it will also remind me of the Father's love, and how He sent you into my life to show His love for me. And you know what?" Her eyes brightened, and she smiled, "Sheriff Mort's wife Susan, is going to work on getting a shelter set up for women like me. I think it'll be a ministry very much like the mission in Rock City." Tears began to well up in Becky's eyes, "And you see, I'll have a ministry to help other women...just like you've been helping me." She paused thoughtfully. "And you know who God is putting on my heart?"

"No, who?"

Becky smiled again, "Angelina DeLeon!"

"But, she tried to kill you Becky!"

"That's true, but God loves her just like He loves me. I want to do for her what you've done for me."

When Becky finished, Josie was speechless. Her eyes were filling with tears. She was disappointed, even a little jealous, but very slowly, a big smile crept across her face, and she reached out and pulled Becky to her. They hugged each other like two matching pieces of Velcro. Josie was disappointed that Becky didn't need her any more, and yet realized that the Father's assignment for her was finished in Littleville. Now, Susan and Mort would take Becky to a higher level of spiritual growth and service. Josie's thoughts turned back to Rock City, *"I'm free to go back to Rock City. Isabelle was right...the Father has spoken His will about Becky."*

Monday morning came like a ghost, and except for alarm clocks, did not announce its arrival. It was a typical day in Louisiana, warm and humid. The sun was bright and a few clouds spotted the sky above...and by noon it would be uncomfortably hot. Josie thought of that day when Roger was to be sentenced...and how he tried to kill her and others in a similar courtroom. She guessed all courtrooms were very much alike, and she decided she didn't like them.

Josie walked into the courtroom and took a seat near the front. It was a couple of rows behind the rail that separated the attorneys and the accused from the audience, just like at Roger's trial. She had to close her eyes and pray just to keep her mind from seeing Roger with a gun in his hand, his red eyes like projectors, rapidly flashing the flames of hell onto everything he looked at. When she let her mind wander to pictures of Roger, it was a hellish sight. They seemed to form an out-of-control continuous loop of snapshots, playing over and over in her mind until she had to physically shake herself from that slideshow of destruction. She often wondered how many lives had been destroyed in Roger's torrid wake of hate. This was one of those times when she found it difficult to shake the images. She was tempted to leave her seat, and wait outside the room until she was called by the bailiff. She prayed and convinced herself that she could make it. She glanced over at Mort who seemed aware of her distress. She flashed a weak smile.

The courtroom filled quickly, and the attorneys took their places. Several police officers were present for testimony, as were members of the sheriff's department, including Mort and Jerry. The defendants, Jórge Sánchez and Sam Jobst, both in handcuffs and ankle shackles, were led in by a bailiff and took their seats beside their respective attorneys. The bailiff stood, and in a loud voice commanded, "All rise." When the judge walked in and seated himself behind the bench, the bailiff proclaimed in a sing-song voice, "The twenty-first District Court of the State of Louisiana is now in session, Judge Jim Wells presiding."

Members of the jury were ushered in and took their places. They were sworn in as a group. The list of charges was read: aggravated kidnapping, assault with intent to inflict bodily harm, illegal possession and carrying of weapons, resisting arrest, attempted murder of a police officer, sexual assault, and conspiracy to distribute drugs. Both the defendants pleaded 'not guilty'. As the charges were read, the courtroom was abuzz with whispered voices.

The judge pounded his gavel, and everything became quiet.

Josie's Gift

In a stern voice, the judge asked the DA and the defense attorneys if they were ready. "Yes, Your Honor," they both answered.

Jórge and Sam both turned around to look at the people in the courtroom. They spotted Josie. Their mouths curled down on one side the way she'd remembered Roger. In the half smiles, and slit eyes, she thought she could see the same face of evil she had seen in Roger when he turned and looked at her. It sent shivers up her spine. She looked down at her feet and began to pray silently, *"Our Father…!"*

Opening statements were made. They were long and drawn out with lots of gestures, and at times, some theatrics. Josie grew bored and increasingly nervous about what she was going to say in answer to the questioning. Finally, the judge called a recess for lunch. She stood up, stretched, and turned around to look at the audience. That's when she heard the familiar voice of a child.

"Mama!" Stevie shouted, running down the center aisle toward her.

It was a total surprise, and she immediately squatted down to pull him into her arms. "Oh, my Stevie, I've missed you so much." Mother and son hugged. Josie closed her eyes, which were filling with tears. She didn't notice the man who walked up to stand behind Stevie. She pushed Stevie away to arms length, "Let me look at you. I think you've grown!"

A man's voice spoke. "I think so too, Josie!"

She looked up and met the eyes of Will. He was smiling. She stood up and he reached out and drew her to him. She willingly put her arms up around his neck and molded her body to his embrace. It was a long, almost passionate embrace. Stevie looked up in admiration while Josie's tears made wet stains on Will's shirt.

Mort and Jerry saw Will and hurried over. Josie turned around and backed slightly away from Will at the sound of Mort's voice. She didn't let go of Will's hand. "Hi, Will,"

Mort greeted. "What brings you over here on a hot day like this?" Mort looked at Josie and paused, "Let me guess," he said with a big grin on his face. "It's good to see you, Will." Turning toward Jerry, he continued, "Jerry and I have to meet with the DA over lunch, so we'll see you back here this afternoon. I'll be first witness on the stand, followed by Jerry, so I expect Josie won't be up 'til tomorrow morning or later."

"Okay, Mort we'll see you later." Turning back to Josie, "Let's go get ourselves some lunch, whatta ya say?"

Josie smiled. She felt the warmth of Will's hand and for several seconds just looked at her hand in his. It seemed so right. She smiled up at him and then at Stevie, who took her other hand. The three of them walked out of the courtroom, down the stairs, and onto the street. Will directed them to a café close by.

They all ordered their meals. Josie was filled with a sense of wonder she had never experienced. She silently reflected on her circumstances, *"It's like I've found the lost coin Jesus told about in one of his parables. There's no need to question, no need for explanation...Will and Stevie are here, and that's all that matters. I've heard girls talk about the term, 'soul mates'. I have no idea what that means except that it seems to be used to describe a perfect relationship. Could Will and I be soul mates?"* She asked herself silently.

Back in the courtroom, Josie sat with Will and Stevie. It gave her a feeling of confidence and strength. They all listened to Mort first, and then Jerry, tell in exact detail, the events of that night at Becky's apartment. Josie could see it all like it was happening again, right now. She heard the defense lawyers try to cast doubt on Jerry's testimony, insinuating that he was at the apartment for reasons other than law enforcement business. Jerry stuck to the facts, often referring to the little notepad he carried.

Off to her right, she saw Becky walking in. Their eyes met, and they smiled at each other. Josie knew Becky would be grilled unmercifully by the defense attorneys. She prayed for Becky to be strong and tell it just as it had happened. Becky's testimony would be agonizing, because she knew they'd try to make her out to be a simple whore whose only interest was what she could get from Albert Russell, Ronnie Russell and the members of Ronnie's little gang. They would try as best they could to point the finger at her character and imply she was a liar.

As the afternoon wore on, both Mort and Jerry handled their selves impeccably. Josie was proud of their professionalism and how calm they were when they were questioned. She could see why police had to make accurate notes on their criminal cases because they constantly referred to their notebooks and police reports.

At four-thirty, the judge declared a recess until nine A.M. the next morning. He gave some instructions to the jury, rapped his gavel, after which the bailiff shouted, "All rise!" The judge walked out of the room, and the jury followed. There was a jumble of whispers and comments as he left.

Becky joined Will, Stevie and Josie. Jerry walked over and suggested a way down to the first floor and out to the parking lot, which would avoid the news media gathered at the steps. "Mort will make a statement to them, as will the DA and the defense attorneys," he said. "They don't need us."

They all followed Jerry, and when they got outside, wished each other a good night and left for their respective homes or jobs.

"Stevie and I will follow you ladies to your apartment," Will suggested. "That way I'll know where you live. I'll leave Stevie with Josie and drive to my motel. I'll pick all of you up at six, and we can find someplace to eat. You can bring me up on what's gone on since I left."

"How about Mort and Jerry?" Josie suggested.

"Good idea," Will responded. "I still have the sheriff's office on my cell phone directory. I'll give 'em a call."

Will arrived and knocked on the door of the apartment promptly at six. Both women had showered, fixed their hair, and dressed up. Josie had freshened Stevie up as well. Josie opened the door, "Come in, Will."

Will looked at both women and then looked again. "What did I do to deserve to take two gorgeous women out to dinner?" He laughed. Josie and Becky both giggled, and each put an arm in Will's, and they marched down the steps to the car. Stevie was laughing hysterically.

At the restaurant, Josie and Becky again each placed an arm in Will's, and they promenaded in through the front door. They were still locking their arms in Will's, as he asked for a table that would be big enough for the four of them plus Mort and Susan and Jerry and his wife. Seeing the charade, the waitress grinned and showed them to a table. She bowed and very formally asked if this would be okay. Everybody laughed as Will held the chair first for Josie, and then for Becky. Stevie watched in starry-eyed wonder. They were soon joined by Mort and Jerry, along with their wives.

As they talked among themselves, there was a conscious avoidance of the trial and the courtroom happenings of the day. Mort was sitting next to Will and brought him up to date on the issues with Salazar and Russell. "Will," Mort asked. What do you think of Jerry's theory that those arms and ammo were heading north to Jihadists in Detroit?"

"You know..." Will answered. "...that the Mexican drug cartels and their militia are operating pretty openly in southern Arizona and southern Texas, so it's little wonder, that arms and ammo are moving this direction. Local law enforcement officers, as well as federal Border Patrol officers are receiving personal threats from the Mexican Militia.

Snipers take potshots at 'em from Mexican side of the border. The cartels pay a bounty to anyone who kills an American officer. I don't know what can be done about it, but I've lost all confidence in the federal government. From the administration on down, they seem to be hiding their heads in the sand and pretending it's not a problem."

Will continued, "We haven't seen the full extent of it yet in Texas, but I expect its coming. Killings, kidnappings and terrorism are moving north along the Rio Grande. There've been killings in Nuevo Laredo and now Piedras Negras and in Ciudad Acuña. Wouldn't it be something if we saw Muslim Jihadists and Mexican drug cartel militia joining forces?"

"Will, don't you think they're already organized and operating in Texas? Except for El Paso, they just haven't started the kidnappings and killings like they have in Arizona."

"You're probably right, Mort. Yep! You're probably right. It's only a matter of time." Will changed the subject. "By the way, I've applied for a U.S. Marshall's Service position."

"Does Josie know about that?"

"Not yet, Mort. I plan to tell her soon as I hear something more concrete. On second thought," he said sheepishly, "I guess I should tell her right away."

The food arrived, and Mort asked that they join hands and pray. Mort prayed, not just for the food, but for justice and mercy for them all. And they all said, AMEN.

After dinner, Will drove Josie, Becky, and Stevie to the apartment. There were awkward moments when he got out of the car and walked with them up the stairs to the door. He turned to Becky and gave her a hug and said goodnight. Then he reached for Josie's hand and drew her into a strong embrace. She relaxed and gave herself over to the warmth of it, breathing deeply and wishing he would kiss her.

Becky quickly recognized the situation, took Stevie's hand, and led him inside the door. Josie smiled at him, then turned around and pulled Will's face down to hers. Their lips met for just an instant in what was a light expression of affection. She pulled away, cocked her head slightly, and smiled at him, "Goodnight, Will. Can you pick me up in the morning for court?"

"I'll be here, Josie." Before she could turn away, he put his hand under her chin, lifted her face and kissed her again. He smiled, "Goodnight, Josie."

When Josie got into the apartment, she felt like her feet weren't touching the floor. She was experiencing feelings she could never remember having before Will came along. Becky was helping Stevie get ready for bed; she looked at Josie. Their eyes met, and they both smiled understandingly. "You're very blessed, Josie," Becky remarked.

Josie took Stevie by the hand and led him to a pallet she had fixed for him on the floor in her bedroom. As he dragged himself into the covers, he looked at Josie, and with a smile asked, "Is Will going to be my daddy?"

His question caught Josie totally by surprise, she had to think quickly, "I...I uh...don't know, Honey. That's something we'll have to pray about and see what our Heavenly Father thinks about it. It'll be up to Him." She knelt beside him, and they said their prayers together. Stevie rolled over and was soon asleep.

Josie went back to the living room where Becky had settled into a soft Lazy Boy, reading her bible. Becky closed the bible and looked up at Josie. "We need to pray together about tomorrow," Becky suggested. The two women stood, held hands, and prayed each for the other, knowing that tomorrow would be a very anxious and stressful day for them both.

"Goodnight, Becky," Josie said as she turned to go back to her bedroom.

"Goodnight, Josie."

CHAPTER TWENTY-SIX

The apartment grew quiet as Josie readied herself for bed. Her thoughts were a jumble of worry about her testimony tomorrow, about her relationship with Will, and about Roger Brown. As she lay in her bed, sleep refused to come to her anxious mind. She tossed and turned as snapshot loops of Roger, of her abductors, and of Will, all kept coming around like a continuous slide show over and over in her brain.

Sleep came grudgingly only after long, emotionally draining battles with shadowy images floating through her mind like the dark clouds whirling around a thunderstorm. She periodically awoke after a few hours of fitful sleep, hearing her own voice whimpering and sometimes sobbing. Finally her weariness caught up, and in the wee hours, she finally slipped off into a deep sleep. But the nightmare, after a long absence, returned...that black hole...she was spinning round and round, and deeper and deeper into the hole that seemed to suck her into its depths. She lacked the strength to pull herself out...and no hand reached down to rescue her. Then she felt the smothering...the pain in her body...the wanting to scream...an inability to breathe. As the crescendo of the dream reached its peak, she awoke with a start, sitting upright in the bed, sobbing uncontrollably. She shook her head and looked around, not knowing for a moment where she was. Stevie was breathing regularly and quietly, sound asleep on the floor beside her. She felt compelled to go to the bathroom and wash herself...she didn't know why...but she had to do it. When she crawled back into bed, she felt drained of every ounce of energy, but drifted off into a sleep that was fitful and shallow.

She was just beginning to relax when her alarm went off. She raised herself, shut off the alarm and swung her feet off the side of the bed. When she tried to stand, she felt shaky, wobbly, like she'd been running for her life all night. She stumbled to the bathroom. Seeing Becky eating breakfast, she spoke, her voice weak and insecure. "Good morning, Becky," she said wearily.

"Good morning Josie, you look worn out, like you were in a fight last night."

"I feel like it," Josie said stumbling on into the bathroom.

Becky shouted through the door. "I have to get to work and then over to the courthouse. You want me to get Stevie up for you and get him started on breakfast?"

"Please, Becky." Josie shouted back.

After showering and clearing her head, Josie opened the door and looked into the kitchen. Stevie was eating his cereal and looking at the pictures on the box. She looked up, breathed a prayer, pasted a smile on her face and greeted Stevie. "Good morning, Honey. Did you sleep well?"

"G'morning, Mama. I slept good, but once I woke up and heard you crying."

Her voice dropped and she furrowed her eyebrows, "Honey, Mama's worried about some things right now... you know...the court and all. But, everything's going to be all right." Then she smiled and lifted her eyebrows, "I'm so glad you're here, Sweetheart." She gave him a hug and started for the bedroom to dress.

"Mama," Stevie shouted.

She turned, "Yes."

"Jesus'll make it all okay...I know He will!"

"Yes, my Darling. Yes, He will make it all okay." Now her smile was genuine, and she closed the bedroom door behind her.

Josie dressed, looked at herself in the mirror, dabbed a little color to her lips and face, then laid out Stevie's clothes. She walked to the kitchen where Stevie was just finishing his cereal and gave him instructions to get himself dressed. "Will's going to be here in just thirty minutes, and he'll take us back to the courthouse. We need to hurry and be ready."

"Okay, Mama." Stevie bounded off the chair and headed for the bedroom.

Josie got a bowl from the cupboard and sat down at the table. Her stomach felt like it was in knots and she didn't feel like eating. She figured she needed the nourishment, so poured the cereal into the bowl followed by milk. As she ate, she prayed. *"Unusual to be praying while I'm eating,"* she thought to herself. Then she remembered St. Paul's words, *"Pray without ceasing."* She smiled at the thought, *"Praying and eating...and at the same time."*

After eating and praying she felt better. She startled a little when she heard the doorbell. Remembering that Will was going to pick her up, she went to the door. Will stepped into the room and Josie immediately took both his hands and pulled him into an embrace. She felt more confident now that Will was here.

Becky was the first witness called to testify. In a kindly and considerate manner, the DA asked her about the sleazy relationship she had with Ronnie Russell and the gang. His strategy was to get the relevant bad stuff out in front and deal with them openly. Becky told the truth. As expected, the defense attorneys attempted to drag every other ugly spot in her life up in front of her, like the driving while intoxicated charge. They insinuated that she had sexual relationships with numbers of other men. They tried repeatedly to paint her as a common whore. Repeatedly, the DA objected to the line the defense was taking, saying that those things were not relevant to the case. The judge sustained the objections and each time, warned the defense to stay with the facts of the case. Their reply was always that they were trying to prove that Becky was not a credible witness. When she finally stepped off the witness stand, she was in tears. In the end, Becky's cool head and honest and open demeanor impressed the jury.

Josie was the last witness the DA called to the stand. It was her personal story that his questions were designed to bring out. The SWAT leader and the helicopter pilot had previously testified and laid the groundwork for Josie's testimony. She kept looking at Will for courage. He maintained a smile and often winked and mouthed his pride. The DA's questioning got deep into her feelings during the ordeal; the physical pain of being assaulted in the car, of being tied up in the cabin, of her run through the brush, and of her hopeless fear when she heard the shooting, fearing they were shooting at her.

When it was the defense's turn to call witnesses, they called only the two accused, who repeatedly claimed that it was Becky who wanted sex with them, and that she wanted to be part of the drug dealing. They claimed that Josie was a willing participant, and that she initiated sex in the back seat of the car. Upon cross-examination, the DA was able to punch holes in the defense case by noting that when Josie was taken to the hospital after her rescue, there was no evidence of sexual contact. He easily painted the defendants as liars.

After four long days of intense arguing and detailed closing statements, the case went to the jury. The deliberations took only two hours. When the jury filed back into the courtroom; the judge asked for their decision, the defendants were found guilty on all seven counts. The judge rapped his gavel and dismissed the jury. He scheduled a punishment hearing for a week away.

Will watched and listened to the entire proceedings. Each day he told both Josie and Becky how proud he was of them.

Before they left the courtroom, Will asked Josie and Becky to sit down for a few moments. "The news media is going to be waiting on the front steps. I think the two of you should make statements. Mort and the DA will be first to go to the microphones. Of course, the defense attorneys will also make their statements." He showed them a piece of paper. "Here's a statement I wrote that you can read. There's something for each of you to say. Look at it and see if I've captured your feelings about this whole ordeal."

The women read it and looked up at Will. With tears of relief and joy, Josie spoke. "Will, I can't tell you how much it's meant to have you here. Neither I nor Becky would have had the time or forethought to put together something like this. Thank you." She leaned over and kissed him on the cheek. Becky, who was on his opposite side, leaned over and kissed him on the other cheek. He blushed and grinned.

On the courthouse steps, both women walked to the microphones, and amidst clicking cameras and TV news videos, they made their statements. Becky was first.

"My name is Becky Hall. During my life here in Littleville, I gave little thought to how things might turn out for me. I feel happy and relieved that I can now disconnect from an ugly past and go on to a new life. This has been an awful ordeal, not just the trial, but everything, including my own bad decisions and actions leading up to it. Our Heavenly Father sent Josie into my life, and I was introduced to Him. Now I have a personal relationship with Jesus, and I plan to walk a totally different way. Thank you all for being here. My prayer is that God will have mercy on Jórge and Sam, and

that they will find Christ in their new life in prison. I have forgiven them for their treatment of me." She smiled and turned to Josie.

"*My name is Josefa Blandón Brown. I am known to my friends as Josie. I came here just three months ago without the slightest idea that I would ever be involved in a criminal case such as this. I believe it all happened for a purpose, and that purpose is standing here beside me.*" She turned, took Becky's hand and smiled. "*I thank God that He gave me the courage to do what I did and that He has been a wonderful part of my life. Now I can go back to Rock City and rebuild my relationships with my family, and with my dear friends. Like Becky, I hope that Sam and Jórge will find Christ in their new lives in prison. I want to thank someone who has become a dear, dear friend and who has encouraged me and supported me through this whole ordeal, Mister Will Brent.*" She turned to Will and embraced him in front of the cameras.

"You added that last part," He nervously whispered into her ear.

That evening they all celebrated over grilled steaks at the home of Mort and Susan. After dinner outdoors, Mort stood to speak. "The last three months here in Littleville have been the most exciting and at the same time the most blessed I have ever experienced. We have all seen miracles of deliverance of life and spirit by the gracious and wonderful power of our Heavenly Father. It proves beyond any shadow of doubt that He provides angels to guard our lives and preserve our freedoms. I can't help but think of how much we have been blessed by Josie coming into our lives. Even that was a miracle of grace. I am pleased that Will has been here and shared some of it." Turning to Will and taking a piece of paper from his pocket, he continued. "Will, this was faxed from your office to mine today." Handing it to Will, he shook Will's hand and said, "Congratulations on being chosen to become a U.S. Marshall, a very elite and historic body of law officers."

Josie stood and hugged him. She whispered into his ear, "You didn't tell me about that." She grinned. "Will Brent, I'm so very proud of you."

Next, Jerry stood to speak. "Josie, we're going to miss you, but I know Will is glad to have you back. I know God is going to bless you and Will." Looking at Becky he continued, "Becky, you've been literally pulled from the fires. We can all see how much your life has changed. I know I speak for Mort in saying we're glad you plan to stay in Littleville. You still have more court appearances to make, and we will all be praying for you and helping you in every way possible." Looking at Susan, "I know Susan has some plans that include you, and I know God will bless you, along with her."

Everybody stood and clapped. All had tears of joy and were sad to be seeing Josie and Will leave. Susan called for them to all hold hands, and pray. After the prayer, she and Mort went to each one, laid their hands on their heads and gave them a personal blessing as the Spirit led. When they got to Josie, Susan had a word of prophecy. "Josie, the Lord has wonderful plans for your life. You will see true love, and your testimony will bless many. God will restore your seven years of loss and will bless you a hundred-fold. You still have mountains and rivers to cross, but the Lord will bring them down before you, and make your paths straight." Then, she got a worried look on her face and looked directly into Josie's eyes. "Josie, I see an interruption to your dreams; it will bring you much sorrow, but, do not be afraid. At the end of that time, you will experience joy unspeakable and full of glory." Then she hugged Josie. It was a long and tearful hug.

Everyone said, "AMEN."

Back at the apartment, Josie began to pack what few things she possessed, leaving most everything including the car, for Becky. While Will waited, she tucked Stevie into his pallet and walked back to the living room. Will stood to say goodnight. He hugged Becky then walked to the door. Josie followed. They walked out onto the landing, and she closed the door behind them.

Taking Will's hands in hers, she looked up into his expectant eyes. "Will Brent, I am so thankful that God brought you into my life." She stood on her tiptoes and kissed him on the lips. She let go of his hands and Will drew her into an embrace. Again their lips met, this time with passion and longing."

Josie backed off just enough to look directly into his eyes. She cocked her head coyly and grinned, "Goodnight Will."

As she started to turn and step to the door, Will spoke. "Josie, there's something I want you to know."

"What's that?"

He smiled and laughed, "I'm going to be a U.S. Marshall."

"Oh, Will. I know that!"

He took her hands again and drew her close, "Josie, I... uh, Josie...what I mean is, I love you!"

She smiled back at him and laughed. "I know that too, Will."

"Well," he said.

"Oh Will, I love you too, and I hope God brings our lives together. Goodnight!"

Will turned and walked back down the steps. He turned and shouted over his shoulder, "I'll pick you up at about eight in the morning. We'll eat out for breakfast and then head for Rock City." Josie stood and watched until he was in the car and driving away.

For a long time, Josie lay in her bed, her mind a jumble of thoughts and images. She was thinking and dreaming about what life would be like with Will. She also pondered Susan's prophecy and what it might mean. She was almost asleep when she shot straight up in bed. *"I need to get to know Will,"* She said to herself. She put her head on the pillow and prayed, finally going to sleep.

In the wee hours, she stirred, half conscious and half asleep. She thought she heard sounds...footsteps...then a light. She felt an intense fear come over her, and she covered her head. Then...the black hole returned. For the rest of the night she struggled with the familiar nightmare.

When the alarm went off Josie threw her legs over the side of the bed and stumbled to the bathroom. As usual, Becky was already up. Josie immediately got into the shower. She felt that same overpowering need to wash herself. But, no matter how much she washed, she never felt clean.

Becky met her coming out of the bathroom. "I want to tell you goodbye, Josie." She took Josie's hands, and the two women hugged. "Please write, will you? And, call once in a while."

Josie looked at Becky and for several moments said nothing.

"Are you okay, Josie?"

Josie forced her mind into the present, "I'm okay, Becky. It's just that I hate to leave you. I never had a sister, and you're the closest thing to that in my life. I love you, Becky. Please pray for me...and for Will. And when you get some vacation time, come to Rock City for a visit."

"I will, Josie...I promise. I love you too, and I'll never forget you. I never had a sister either, so now we're sisters in Christ."

Josie's face brightened as Stevie walked out of the bedroom rubbing the sleep out of his eyes.

"Time to say goodbye, Stevie." Becky said as she kneeled down in front of him.

Stevie looked at her and sighed. "Are you my Aunt Becky now?" He asked.

Becky grinned, "Yes, Stevie. I guess that's right. I'll be glad to be your Aunt Becky!"

She hugged him, looked at her watch, and stood to leave. "Gotta get to work." She blew kisses as she walked out the door.

Josie smiled at Stevie. "Will's going to be here soon, and we're going out for breakfast."

Stevie bounded off to the bedroom. He soon emerged fully dressed dragging a small suitcase containing his clothes. Josie went to the bedroom, dressed and got her things together. By the time she got back to the living room, Will was at the door.

"Good morning, Josie; good morning, Stevie," He said cheerfully.

He immediately went to Josie and they hugged. He kissed her lightly on the lips, all the while out of the corner of his eye, watching for Stevie's reaction. Stevie seemed to enjoy what he was seeing. He bounded over to where his mother and Will were standing, and took Will's hand. Will bent over and gave him a hug, lifting him off the floor. "Let's be on our way; breakfast waits, and then...Rock City." They followed Will down the steps to the car. Will got everything loaded and then opened the back door for Stevie and the front door for Josie.

"All buckled up?" Will asked.

A resounding 'YES' from two voices, answered his question.

CHAPTER TWENTY-SEVEN

For the first hour in the car, Josie spent her time talking to Stevie, pointing out to him interesting things along the way. Will was occupied with driving and following the road signs. At times, Josie chanced a glance in Will's direction. She admired him. He was handsome, had a polished personality, and was a good Christian. From time to time, Will caught her sideways glances and smiled back approvingly. Their eyes communicated what they both were feeling. Stevie slipped off to sleep, his head hanging over his shoulder harness.

Josie couldn't help but make comparisons between Will and Roger. She thought back to the time when she first disobeyed her parent's demands that she not see Roger. It seemed so exhilarating then...pushing the limits to construct her own identity...to make her own decisions. She rushed past her parents' values never thinking about consequences. At first, she hadn't given any thought to how her parents would feel and what their reactions would be if they found out what she was doing. There was excitement in pursuing her independence. It made her feel older and grown-up.

Every day, Roger came for her at school. He gave her lots of attention. She had no problem seeing his faults, but she was his princess...her kisses would heal his broken life...

he promised. She had used all kinds of excuses to get out of the house in the evenings to see Roger. She thought everything was working out for them, and they could be together forever. Then, one night he pushed her beyond her ability to maintain control—she gave in to him, and they had sex in the car. After that, there was more...and more...until she couldn't stop. He became possessive and began to abuse her verbally. Then, she began to miss her periods...pregnant? Of course not! There had to be a mistake...but it was no mistake.

Josie found herself staring out the side window...almost as if she was in a daze. She heard a voice, "Mama, I gotta go to the bathroom."

She pulled her thoughts back to the present moment. "Okay, Honey."

Will heard what Stevie said. "I'll stop at the next gas station or restaurant."

Stevie began to whimper, "But, I gotta go real bad... right now!"

Will looked at Josie, who nodded her approval. He turned on his right signal and pulled off the highway. "Just open both doors, and step out near the car and do it, okay?"

Soon they were back on the highway, and Stevie lapsed into a sleepy nod. Will let out a little laugh, "...ah, the advantages of being a boy!"

Josie laughed. "Will Brent, you better hope I don't have to do that."

He looked at her, his eyes wide. "We'll...uh...uh stop at the next facility just as a precaution."

Within thirty minutes, a town was in view. Will found a convenience store and stopped. "While you two go to the bathrooms, I'll fill up with gas and get us a cup of coffee. Then we can be on our way."

In another hour it was time for lunch. They stopped at a restaurant, ate and were on their way again. The day was getting hot, and the sun was beginning to beat in through the windshield as they travelled west and southwest. Will drove for a couple of hours and decided to stop. He found a picnic area along the highway and pulled in and parked. From the looks of the landscape and heavy forest all about, he decided they were getting pretty close to the Sabine River and the state line. Josie woke up when the car stopped. She got out with Will, and they walked together just to stretch and get themselves awake.

"Would you like for me to drive for awhile, Will?"

"Thanks for offering, Josie. That would be a nice relief. All I need is just a couple of hours."

Back in the car, Will dozed off and on for the next two hours. When he felt wide awake, they stopped, and he took over the driving. The sun was beginning its descent below the hills and trees in the west, and Will began looking for a motel. He pulled into one that looked decent. There was a restaurant next door where they could eat. Josie looked at Will and smiled her approval. He went into the office and booked two rooms. He drove to their room numbers and parked. Before they got out he turned to Josie, "Do you want Stevie to sleep with you in your room or with me in my room?"

Josie thought for a moment then smiled, "I think the men should sleep together in their own room."

Stevie looked at them both and smiled at Will. He was pleased to be identified with the men.

"Okay," Will said, "Let's get our things settled in the rooms and go to the restaurant for a bite to eat.

After dinner, they gathered in Will and Stevie's room to watch television. When Stevie began to nod off, Josie got him ready for bed and tucked him in. They all gathered around the bed and prayed for a safe trip. They should be in Rock City by mid-afternoon tomorrow. Stevie was quickly asleep.

"Time to turn in, Josie. I'll see you to your door."
"That's not necessary, Will."
"I'd like to make sure you get there safely," he laughed. "Actually, I don't want to alarm you, but this is the same motel where David Lee and Stevie were abducted. I'm sure nobody is following us, but I'm always alert."

When they got to Josie's door, Will drew Josie into a hug and kissed her. "Goodnight, Josie. Be sure to lock your door with the safety lock and chain and don't open it for any reason. If anything happens, call me on my cell…just don't open the door." He waited as she stepped inside and he heard the bolt close and the chain latch on the door.

Next morning after breakfast, they were back on the road. Josie's thoughts wandered from Roger to her parents. *"The reunion this afternoon will be wonderful,"* she thought to herself. *"We have seven long years to catch up on."* She decided that unless they brought him up, she would not discuss Roger or his crime spree. She didn't want to talk about the killing or the shootout in the courtroom. That segment of her life was something she wanted to make sure stayed in the past. They would have Stevie to talk about.

Josie looked over at Will. This trip was making her feel as if they were a couple. He met her glance and smiled back. She leaned her head back and closed her eyes. *"Maybe things are happening too fast with Will. Maybe I should slow down 'till I know more about him. For all I know he may turn out just like Roger! No, that wouldn't be possible with Will…he isn't that kind of person!"* She shivered. *"I wonder if I'm letting go of my feelings too quickly, just like I did with Roger."*

She turned her head again to glance at Will. This time she frowned, and her face showed worry. Will noticed. He reached over and laid his hand on top of hers on the seat. She looked down at his hand. *"This hand is kind,"* she thought.

At about eleven-thirty, Will pulled off the highway and into a restaurant parking lot. Stevie woke up and looked around. "We gonna eat?" He asked.

"Yep!" Will shouted. "We gonna eat!"

Josie walked close to Will. She liked the idea that people would see them as a couple with a little boy.

The hostess showed them to a table and left menus. Soon a waitress came and took their orders for drinks. When she came back they were ready to order.

Josie looked around, *"Traveling with Will is so different than traveling with Roger,"* She thought. *"We never stayed in nice motels, and we never ate in nice restaurants. It was always cheap, smelly motels and convenience stores for sandwiches and chips and junk food."* She looked at Will. *"I don't need any magic kisses to change him into a handsome prince. He came that way!"* She smiled and looked at her son who was enjoying all of it. *"Stevie doesn't have to worry about Will getting drunk and yelling and hitting us both. What a blessing God has brought my way,"* She thought to herself. She looked around at people sitting at the other tables, hoping they could see what a fine couple she and Will were, and what a fine son they had. Josie was feeling complete...she had God, she had Will, and Stevie. *"Surely,"* she thought, *"God has led me beside the still waters and to the green pastures. My cup is overflowing...He has set the table before me."* (Psalm 23)

Will noticed Josie's quiet, pensive mood. He saw her watery eyes. He reached over to hold her hand, "Josie, are you okay?"

She looked at him and then at Stevie. "Yes, Will. I couldn't be better!" She smiled.

Will wondered what she was thinking, but decided not to ask. He had begun to notice there were times when she needed to be alone in her thoughts. *"She's been through a lot,"* He thought. *"Maybe things are going too fast. I wonder if there are issues that could come between us."* He dismissed his thoughts as the meals were delivered and set before them. They held hands while Will prayed.

After lunch, Will turned to Josie, "Do you mind if we walk around a little bit? I really need to stretch my back and loosen up my legs."

Josie looked at Stevie and smiled. "We don't mind, Will. We can all use a little exercise."

After they were on the road about an hour, Will suggested to Josie that she call Isabelle and let her know they would be there in a couple of hours.

When they got close to Rock City, things began to look familiar. They drove along the river and soon came near the spot where she had scattered Roger's ashes. "Will," she shouted. "Please stop, please."

By the time Will could react, they were past the spot. He turned the car around and pulled over to that familiar high place along the river. He didn't like the idea, but could understand why Josie would want to stop. Josie slowly stepped out of the car and cautiously walked to the edge of the high river bank. Stevie followed her. *"This is Josie's moment,"* Will thought to himself, *"I'll wait in the car."*

Josie and Stevie stood together looking into the brown, murky water. There was a fresh, warm breeze blowing in her face that made her cotton skirt and her long, brown hair flow in the air behind her. Stevie held her hand. She bowed her head and tried to pray. Nothing came to her mind, no words formed to give voice to her feelings. Finally, she raised her eyes to heaven and prayed silently, *"Lord, I don't know what or how to pray at this moment; you know my heart. Please, Father, see fit to give me total peace. There's no possible way I can give myself to Will, until I can find total healing for my damaged life."*

She looked down at Stevie, he was crying softly. Like a contagious disease, his crying brought tears to her eyes.

Then, out of the blue, almost as if a tide of water was washing over her, she shivered and her mind felt at peace. She looked down at the flowing water carrying sticks, leaves, and other natural debris downstream to parts unknown to anyone but God. "Goodbye, Roger," She whispered, "Goodbye forever."

She smiled at Stevie and led him back to the car. She leaned in the open window, smiled at Will, cocked her head slightly, "You got room for a couple of passengers, Mister Brent?"

Will laughed. "Yes Ma'am. Sure do." Will saw in her face that she had resolved something in that short time she and Stevie looked into that water. He was glad they stopped.

As they drew nearer to the mission, Josie became increasingly nervous about the coming reunion with her parents. A lot of water had flowed under the bridge in the last seven-plus years. She had changed and was sure they had changed. When she last saw them, Moisés was still working...now he was retired. Ruth was strong and wise...and now?

When Will pulled the car up in front of the Mission and stopped, two people walked out of the building. Isabelle, Carla and Darlene waited inside. Stevie jumped out of the back seat and ran to his grandparents. He embraced them both. They waited on the sidewalk for their daughter. Josie was sobbing before she opened the door and stepped out of the car. She ran, like a child would run; she fell into their arms...the three of them fastening themselves to each other as if they were clinging to a life raft. Tears and more tears flowed, choking off the words that were pushing for expression. For long moments, they all hugged and cried, then hugged and cried some more. Will carried Josie and Stevie's suitcases into the building. On the way, he managed to lean over and give Isabelle a passing kiss on the cheek. He did the same as he passed Carla and Darlene.

Will dropped the suitcases in the hallway and then went back outside. He greeted both Moisés and Ruth with hugs and kisses on their cheeks. He turned to Josie and hugged her and gave her a passing kiss on her lips. "I need to get over to my office and see what's waiting for me there."

Isabelle called after him. "Will, how about you having supper here with us this evening? We'll make it special."

"Thanks, Isabelle, I appreciate that. I'll be here."

Over the next week, Josie resumed her duties at the mission. She spent every spare moment with her parents, trying to catch up on the lost years they had been apart. Josie couldn't get over how much her family had changed. At times she lay awake at night wondering if her reckless disobedience had contributed to their gray hair and wrinkled faces. On the other hand, she saw how they conducted themselves at the mission and carried out their duties, and she was very thankful they both had good health, thanks to Adonai.

Will was beginning to feel left out, but understood Josie needed this time for recapturing memories and for making new ones. At the same time, she was beginning to miss him. They talked on the phone every evening, but it wasn't the same as being together. By the end of the week, Will asked Josie for a date.

"Will Brent!" she exclaimed. "Are you asking me for an honest-to-goodness date?"

Will, somewhat taken aback by her comment, responded in a way he thought afterward could have been better. "Yeah, Josie, a date...you know, like you and me going out for the evening...just the two of us!"

Josie started laughing.

"What're you laughing about? This is serious!"

"Oh, Will, I was just thinking, we've been kissing, traveling together, holding hands, but," she giggled, "we've actually never been out on a real date." In her mind though, she realized she had never in her life been out on a real date, not even with Roger.

Will started laughing with her. "You're right. So this will be our very first date. And, I need to tell you that it's my policy not to kiss until the third date."

"Will Brent, if you were here I'd hit you—with my laundry basket." The two of them laughed together, excitedly. It felt good, to tease, to joke, and to laugh.

"Everything doesn't have to be so serious, does it Will?"

"No, it doesn't. I love to hear you laugh. It means you're healing. I'll pick you up tomorrow at six. We'll have dinner and then take in a movie."

"This is exciting, Will. We're really going to court...no pun intended, if you know what I mean!"

"I know what you mean, Josie. I love you!"

"Bye, Will, I love you too!"

The next evening, Josie was waiting when Will arrived at the mission. They drove to an upscale restaurant. Soon after they were seated, a young waiter brought them water and asked if they would like anything to drink. Will looked at Josie, "Would you mind if I have a glass of wine?"

"Not at all, Will. In fact, I'll have one too. I'll let you make the selection." Josie thought to herself, *"This is a date, and we're in a fancy place, wine is surely fitting."*

The waiter left and gave them time to look over the menu. "If I may," Will said, "I would suggest the red snapper. It's absolutely delicious."

Josie smiled. "That sounds good."

When the waiter returned with their wine and some fresh baked bread, Will ordered for them both.

Josie was overwhelmed. *"Is this what the lords and ladies do on their dates?"* She asked herself. This whole experience was utterly new to her. She reveled in what she was seeing and experiencing. She felt like Cinderella at the Prince's Grande Ball. "Oh, Will, this is absolutely wonderful.

Just the two of us together—do you realize we've never had time together for just the two of us."

Will smiled, reached across the table and took her hand. "Yes, I realize that. And we need more of these kinds of times together to be able to really get acquainted."

Josie looked down at her hand in his. She couldn't resist the question that was on her mind. "Will, how is it that you're not married? I can't believe some woman hasn't captured your heart."

Will shifted his glance in embarrassment. "Josie, I uh...I was married once. I'm divorced."

Josie's face showed her surprise. She wished she hadn't brought up the subject, at least not now. "What happened?" As soon as the question was out of her mouth, she wished she had never asked it.

Will put on a weak smile. "You have every right to know all about that part of my life...and, I intend to tell you the whole story—but, another time. This is our first real date. I want it to be about you and me and not about anyone else... not Roger...not my ex-wife—just you and me. It's right that you now know I'm divorced, just like I know about your marriage to Roger."

Josie could see in his face and hear in his voice that he wasn't yet ready to tell her the rest of the story.

Will picked up his glass of wine and held it out, "Here's to you and me, Josie...and to the future."

Josie smiled, picked up her glass and touched it to his, "Here's to us, Will; to you...and me, and to the future." Their glasses clinked and each took a sip of the wine. She looked up from her glass, "I love you, Will," She whispered.

"I love you too, Josie," He whispered back. "By the way, I have no children."

Josie just smiled. "Will, I am so glad God brought you into my life."

"And I am glad that He brought you into my life."

They looked up as the waiter brought their food. Will watched, as Josie tasted the red snapper. "This is delicious, Will. You have good taste in food and wine."

"And good taste in women?"

"Yes, Will, you have good taste in women! Everybody gets one chance to strike out."

The rest of the meal was given to eating and to light conversation about the future. "When will you know about your new job with the U.S. Marshall's Service, Will?"

"I got a letter today. I'm scheduled for the next class. I have to report to Glynco, Georgia in six-weeks, and I'll be there for seventeen and a half weeks."

Josie frowned. "You have to go to school?"

"Yep, back to school. There's a lot that goes into U.S. Marshall training. They're pretty picky about who they select so it seldom happens that somebody doesn't make it."

"Do you get to come back home on weekends?"

"I'm not really sure about what the schedule will be like, but I'm pretty sure I'll get a little time off."

Josie looked at him. Her mood was a little depressed; her eyes spoke her feelings. "I'll miss you!"

"I'll miss you too, Josie." Will smiled and tried to brighten the mood. "This is our first date, and we've got six more weeks to do things together. We'll make some plans for the time we will have. Then when I do get to come home, we can really celebrate."

"Can we have more dates like this?"

"You bet we can…and, we can go to church together, and I can go to the mission and sit with you in chapel…"

Josie interrupted, "…And help me with my laundry duties?"

"Sure, why not?" Together, they laughed. "Seriously, Josie; I'd do almost anything to be with you more often, but laundry? That's a little much!"

"This was a wonderful dinner, Will."

"Yes, it was." Will raised his hand and motioned to the waiter who brought the check. He paid the bill, left a nice tip, and took her hand. "Let's go to the movies."

When the movie was finished, they walked outside into the darkness. Will had parked the car two blocks away so they could walk together. Josie put her arm around him and pulled him close as they walked. He put his arm over her shoulder, his fingers twirling her soft brown hair. Slowly, they walked...nothing was said. All their communication was in the emotional connection they each felt as their bodies were moving together.

When they got to the mission, Will parked the car under a light in front of the building. He got out and opened Josie's door. She took his hand and led him around to one of the back doors. "I have a key to a door where it's a little more private."

At the back door, she turned to face him. She put her hands on both sides of his face and looked up into his eyes. He put his arms around her waist and drew her close. Their lips met and locked in a passionate expression of love.

She pulled back slightly. "Will, this has been the most wonderful evening of my whole life. Thank you."

"I hope this is the first of many more evenings that will be special Josie."

She handed him the key, and he unlocked the door. Once more their lips met, "Good-night, Josie." He shut the door and walked away.

Very quietly, Josie found her way to the stairwell and walked slowly up the stairs. When she thought about the evening with Will, she couldn't help but think of all she had missed of her youth. Then she remembered Susan's prophecy on that last evening when they all had dinner together at Mort's and Susan's, "God will restore your seven years of loss and will bless you a hundred-fold."

"Tonight," She thought, "Was just the beginning of the hundred-fold."

Stevie was sleeping with his grandparents tonight, but out of habit, Josie quietly tip-toed into her room. As she slipped into bed, her mind was filled with thoughts and dreams of Will, and of the future. She closed her eyes and prayed. Sleep came almost immediately. Then, late in the night, the dream returned—the clumsy footsteps, the black hole sucking her into its depths, her inability to breathe or scream—she awoke sobbing. She quickly got out of bed and took a shower, as she always did when she had the dream. She lay awake thinking, "Where did the dream come from? She remembered it from a long time ago when it came frequently, and yet, for the seven years with Roger, the dream never came back, but why now? Why couldn't she remember? Every time she had the dream, her mood changed for several days, and then things would be okay again—until the dream returned. She felt as if she had to get to the bottom of it for the sake of her relationship with Will. "*I need to tell Will,*" She said to herself.

A week later, on their next real date, Will took her to a nice park where they could walk for a while before dinner. As they walked, they talked, mostly about Will's new future and what it would mean for their relationship. Will stopped and pulled her around to face him. He put his arms around her and drew her close, turned his head down and kissed her lightly.

"Josie," Will said, looking into her eyes, "I love you, and I want to marry you."

Josie's eyes got big as saucers, she smiled, but then suddenly, and unexpectedly, she felt herself in the grip of the cold hand of fear. She controlled her expression but she cried. She tightened her hold on him and didn't want to let go. She felt safe there; she felt she belonged. She felt Will could pull her out of the death-like grip of that black, whirlpool-like hole.

"Oh, Will, you can't possibly know how much I want that to happen. But..."

He broke off her thought, "I need to clear the air about my past, Josie."

She put two fingers to his lips, "I don't care about that."

He pulled her hand away from his mouth, "I have to tell you all about it. I don't ever want there to be anything between us." He took her hand, "Let's walk for a while."

As they walked, Josie could suppress her thoughts no longer. "Okay, Will. Let's start with the first question I asked you on our first date. What happened to your first marriage? If it's none of my business, just say so."

He turned to look into her eyes. In his face, she saw gentleness and understanding. She put her arm in his and they walked in silence for a few minutes.

"I don't mind you asking, Josie. It brings back a load of pain and guilt, but it reminds me of the wonderful grace of God." He paused for a few moments, and then continued. "We...." He stumbled for the right words. "I...broke some promises, Josie. I...uh violated my marriage vows. I had an affair with another woman."

Josie quickly took her arm from his. He looked down and continued. "I'd rather not talk about the details. They don't mean anything now. You see, I was stubborn, and selfish and wouldn't give it up. My wife left me and later filed for divorce. She was sick of me and my ways."

He laughed. "What a fool I was! Then, when I tried to go to the other woman, she didn't want me any more either. I can't say I blame her. How could she trust me? My life went into a downward spiral. I tried to relieve my pain and guilt by drinking and carousing even more."

Josie felt disappointed, betrayed. Now, she learns he isn't such a shining prince after all. "Will, it's hard for me to believe you were like that. You just don't seem like that kind of man. Somehow, I can't picture you in that role."

"Not now, Josie, but, it was all pretty bad. My wife remarried. That bothered me a lot at first. So I just drank more to drown my pain and tried to forget."

"But you're so different now, Will. What happened to change you?" Josie asked.

"Well," he said. "One night, I had gone out with some friends...drinking buddies. We were hanging out in a night club drinking and making passes at the women. Out of the blue, I felt sick, and I needed to get out of the smoke and sour beer smell into some fresh air. I was pretty drunk, and I stumbled outside and threw up. I tried to walk on down the street in what I thought was the direction of my apartment. My mind was soggy, and my thinking so blurred that I had no idea where I was—and I was thinking how easy it would be to end it all right there. I sat down on the curb and thought about the gun I had at home. I even thought how easy it would be, right there on the corner, to walk in front of the trucks in the street. I thought of every way possible to end my life. I didn't want to go on—I thought I had nothing worth living for."

He paused, trying to recollect more of what happened that night. "I walked for...I don't know...maybe a couple of hours, and I was sick of the life I was living. It was tearing me up inside, and the booze was eating away at my brain. I don't know how long I stumbled on, but I looked up and saw a church on the corner, and something...I can't explain it... drew me in. I opened the door and literally fell inside. I got up and stumbled on down the aisle, falling on the floor twice before I got to the altar rail."

"I could see only one person in the church, and she was in the front row. It was an old woman who was kneeling and praying by a picture of Jesus with his arms outstretched. There was a large crucifix behind the altar. When I got close and looked at her, I had to look twice, but I recognized her. It took my breath away, and I found myself gasping. I swear to God, Josie, it was my grandmother who died when I was twelve, and she looked exactly like she did then. Somehow, at that moment, I knew she was praying for me...from heaven she was praying for me. I knelt beside her and cried...I poured out my sin and pain to her and to God. Then I felt a warm hand on my shoulder. I looked up, and it was a man with a clerical collar, whom I guessed to be the pastor. I think he had seen me stumble into the church. He knelt beside me and called me by name as though he'd been expecting me. He told me about Jesus and how Jesus died for my sins. He helped me to receive Jesus into my life, and when he took his hand away, I felt a peace I had never felt before. I gave my life to Jesus that night."

Will turned and looked into Josie's eyes. Tears were rolling down his cheeks and tumbling off his chin. Josie pulled a tissue out of her pocket and gently wiped his chin and daubed his eyes. "I felt whole again, Josie," he sobbed. "The pain and the guilt were gone; I felt clean. When I turned to touch my grandmother, she was gone. I looked up at the picture of Jesus, and for the first time in my life, I knew what He had done for me on the cross, and I've never been the same since that night."

"The pastor asked me to his home next to the church, for some coffee. When I stood up to follow him, my mind was clear, and I was no longer drunk. As we drank coffee together, he told me how to grow in Jesus. He blessed me and prayed with me before I left and called a taxi to take me home."

Will laughed. "I'll never forget that taxi driver. He was some kind of Irishman. When he got to the church, he greeted the pastor like they knew each other very well, and had been through the same routine many times. His name was Lonnie, and while he was driving, he tried to sing, in an off-key way, some Christian tunes I recognized. When he got to my apartment, I pulled my wallet out to pay him, but he made me put it away. He told me that he and the reverend had some kind of deal, and it was all taken care of. He just got back in the cab and drove away."

The next day, I called my ex-wife and told her how sorry I was and asked for her forgiveness. She forgave me, and we've had no contact since that time. I decided I needed to go back to that church, so I retraced my steps from the bar. I found the church, but it was abandoned...hadn't been used for years. There was a faded sign in front that said, St. Peter's Church, Reverend Alonzo Pacheco, pastor. Then I knew that God had given me something very special, a kind of miracle that most people never experience. Of course, some would say that it was an apparition or that I dreamed it. I've never told anyone about that night...until now...because I don't want anyone to try to ridicule the experience or try to make me doubt that God took an old abandoned church and turned it into a miraculous cathedral just for me. After that, I moved here to Rock City and started a new life." (*See the story of Alonzo Pacheco in "Beyond These Walls" by the author*)

Josie was speechless. She stepped in front of Will, put her arms around him, and held him in a very tight embrace. "Oh, Will. After my experiences with John Brown and his angel, I'd be the last person on earth to doubt your miracle. I hope you hang onto that and never, ever, let it go. In God's timing, I believe you will tell that story, and many drunks are going to come to Christ."

Will smiled at her, bent his head down and kissed her, his wet cheeks blurring her makeup. "Let's walk down the street a bit and get ourselves some dinner."

"I'm with you."

When they got to the restaurant, she went immediately to the lady's room to fix her makeup. When she looked in the mirror, she took out the tissue she used to daub his eyes. "She daubed at her cheeks and put the tissue back in her pocket. *"Those are his tears on my cheeks,"* she said to herself. *"I'll keep them."* She finished fixing her cheeks and went to find Will."

He leaned over the table and took her hands in his. "Thanks for listening, Josie."

"Thanks for sharing, Will." Josie paused; something came to her mind and she pondered it for a few minutes. "Will, I want you to promise me something."

"What's that, Josie?"

"Your story, Will…it's the kind of story others need to hear…especially the kind of people who come to the mission. Many, if not all of them have been, or are now in, the kind of situation you were…"

"…I don't think I'm ready for a public audience, Josie. I'll have to think about it." He sounded adamant.

"No, Will! If you think about it, you'll find every reason and excuse not to do it. Promise me, right now, promise me."

Will looked into her loving and accepting eyes. "What did I ever do to deserve you, Josie? You're a gift from God." He paused, searching her eyes. "Yes, Josie, I promise you I will do it."

CHAPTER TWENTY-EIGHT

Josie went to bed that night thinking about Will and his telling her he wanted to marry her. She knew she loved him; she knew he loved her...yet she still feared. There was something unknown...something that had no voice, no image except for that dark, black hole...and it was keeping her from saying 'yes'.

During the night, she tossed and turned, waking several times thinking of marrying Will. Then she fell into a deep sleep during the wee hours of the morning. She dreamed about Will and a wedding. She saw a beautiful country church, the door was open, and a beautiful bright light was shining inside. She could see Will inside, waiting for her. She started running toward the open door, when without warning, the door shut just as she was about to go inside and take Will's hand. Then the familiar black hole returned and enveloped her, sweeping her away from the church, from the light, and from Will. She woke up crying. Turning over, she found Stevie standing beside her bed.

"What's the matter, Mama?"

"Nothing, Sweetheart...nothing at all."

"Why were you crying?"

She looked at him, like he was in another world. She brushed her face with the sleeve of her gown...it was wet. "I don't know, maybe I was happy?" Then predictably, she felt like she needed a shower. "Go back to sleep, Stevie."

She got up and went into the bathroom, turned on the water and climbed into the shower. When she finished, she went back to bed.

The next morning after breakfast, Josie was in the chapel praying when Isabelle came in and sat beside her. Isabelle read her Bible and took out a notebook where she kept lists of people and things she needed to pray about. Josie glanced at the notebook, *"I wonder if my name is in there?"* She thought to herself. As she was praying, she pleaded with God to help her understand the bad dream she had over and over again. As she meditated, God seemed to be saying, *"Talk to Isabelle."* She smiled and silently said, *"Yes, I'll talk to Isabelle."*

When Isabelle got up to leave, Josie followed her into the hallway. "Isabelle, may I talk to you for a few minutes?"

As if God was orchestrating things, Isabelle answered without hesitation. "Sure, Josie, come on to the office."

Josie followed Isabelle into her private office. "Mind if I shut the door, Isabelle?"

"Go ahead. What's on your mind?"

Josie hung her head, not knowing quite how to start."

Isabelle smiled. "Sit down on that old sofa. I've sensed something's been bothering you lately. Why don't we pray that the Holy Spirit will help you to speak and help me to find the answer to the issues that are eating you?"

They both bowed their heads while Isabelle took Josie's hands and prayed. "Father, your love for us is everlasting, your grace and mercy is without boundaries. I pray for Josie...by your Holy Spirit, enlighten her mind and body with your love that she may speak freely, and find healing for her troubled mind, AMEN."

When Isabelle looked up at Josie, she was crying quietly. "Where do I start, Isabelle?"

"Well, let's start at the present and maybe work backward. What is it you're experiencing that's so troubling? Does it have to do with Will Brent?"

Josie managed a slow, weak smile. "In a way, I guess it does." After a few minutes of thought, Josie continued. "Will told me he wants to marry me."

"That's wonderful, Josie. But I sense there's something troubling you about marriage," Isabelle responded.

"Everything within me says how blessed I am to have someone like Will. But, there's something blocking me from saying 'yes'. It's like I see a beautiful door off in the distance, but something holds me back from walking through that door. I want to walk to it, but when I try to say 'yes', something's standing in the way...keeping the door shut."

Isabelle waited as Josie was thinking. "There's something in your past, isn't there Josie? Not Roger...something else, maybe something so awful you've hidden it deep in some closet in your mind."

Josie was quiet for a few minutes. "I don't know, and if it's so awful, why can't I remember it? I keep having this horrible dream, actually nightmare would be a better word for it."

"Would you be comfortable describing that dream?"

"It's the same dream over and over again. When I was a child, I had it all the time. Then I met Roger and it stopped. Sometime after Roger's death, it started all over again. Since I met Will, the dream has intensified. It's like some unseen evil force won't let me be happy."

"Describe the dream for me, Josie."

Josie broke into sobs. She described the dream in all of its lurid detail. It was like an exploding volcano of emotion. At one point, she almost fainted. It took every ounce of energy she had to get it out.

Isabelle prayed silently for wisdom. "Have you ever mentioned this to your Mother?"

"No," Josie screamed. "I can't...she would never believe me. He said she'd never believe me. He told me if she found out, she'd never love me again. Oh, Isabelle, I feel so dirty. Every time I have the dream, I have to get up out of bed and shower. No matter how much I wash, I never feel clean. And now I'm afraid Will won't be able to love me if he knows..."

Isabelle got out of her chair and sat beside Josie on the old sofa. She put her arm around her and drew her into a tight embrace. Josie laid her head on Isabelle's shoulder and sobbed.

In the midst of sobbing, and without warning, she spat out something that came barging into her mind, "My brother, he..." She stopped herself in mid-sentence.

Isabelle felt a quiet move of the Holy Spirit. Her voice was very gentle, "Your brother...he raped you, Josie? Is that it?"

Josie slippped into a child voice, "Yes...NO!" She screamed. "I can't tell! They won't believe me! I mustn't tell Mama. He'll hurt me if I do."

"How old were you, Josie?"

Again Josie slipped into a child voice, "I'm nine years old."

Isabelle held Josie in a tight embrace for long minutes until the sobbing subsided and she seemed to relax. She knew that Josie was reliving an experience brought on by the trauma of the childhood rape.

Josie laid her head back on Isabelle's shoulder and relaxed. She seemed to be sleeping, so Isabelle got up, laid her out on the sofa, and went back to her desk. She resumed her work, periodically looking at Josie on the sofa.

After thirty minutes, Josie sat up and shook her head and looked around. "Oh, Isabelle, I must have fallen asleep. I'm sorry."

Again, Isabelle sat beside her on the sofa. "Josie, do you remember what we were talking about when you fell asleep?"

Josie thought for a few minutes. "I...I...I'm not sure." She looked down. "It was about the dream wasn't it, Isabelle?"

"Yes, Honey...the dream. You mentioned that your brother..."

"NO! Please, I feel so ashamed. I don't want to talk about it anymore. I need to get to my laundry duties."

At this point, Isabelle felt it best that she not push the issue any further. "Okay, Josie. Remember, I'm here for you. God doesn't want you to have to live with that pain and guilt."

"Thanks, Isabelle." She hurried out the door. She wanted to think about Will.

All day long as Josie worked, her mind periodically came back to her conversation with Isabelle and how she had fallen asleep. Her eyes began to water as she remembered. *"Josef,"* she whispered. *"Why...why did you do it?"* She hadn't been able to remember it until this very day. All the years gone by, and it lay buried deep in her mind. *"That's what the dream is telling me."*

Like an arrow through a target, suddenly an image of Will Brent shot through her mind. "I can't marry Will," She said aloud. Sheepishly, she looked around wondering if anybody heard her. She began to cry, looking up she pleaded, "Oh, God...what do I do now? How do I get that awful thing out of my mind? How do I tell Will?" Her soul was aching for relief. A very quiet voice from above seemed to whisper, *"Talk to Isabelle, she'll know what to do. Whatever she tells you, do it!"*

Her feet fairly flew out of the laundry straight to Isabelle's office. The door was open, she knocked quietly. "Come in, Josie."

"How'd you know it was me?"

Isabelle grinned, her white teeth showing like stars against an evening sky. "I didn't, but the Holy Spirit said you'd be coming back. Sit down."

Josie looked down at the floor. "I'm so ashamed, Isabelle. Now, you know...and I'm glad you know, but what do I do about Will? The Lord spoke to me in the laundry room and told me to talk to you and do whatever you say."

Isabelle was still smiling. "First, about Will, for the time being, just keep on loving him and allow him to love you. Find every good thing you can in your relationship. No matter what you think now, I'm confident God is going to bless the two of you. Second, I know someone who can help you with this issue from your past. He's a professional Christian counselor."

Josie stopped her. "Am I crazy, that I need to see a professional?"

"No, Josie. You're not crazy. Umm...did Will tell you about his past yet?"

"Yes, he did...and I love him even more for it."

"Then you really do love him, don't you?"

"Yes..."

"Okay, you don't have to do it immediately, but soon you'll need to tell him what happened to you when you were nine. If Will really loves you, he'll understand and love you in spite of it."

Isabelle flipped through her Rolodex and wrote down some information on a card. "Here's Doctor Hardt's phone number and address. It'll be up to you to make the appointment."

"Can Carla or Darlene go with me?"

"No, Josie. This is something you must do alone...its part of your growing up. Some things you have to do on your own. Now, remember what God told you in the laundry room. I've done my part, now you do yours!"

"I will, Isabelle. I promise!" She started to get up and leave.

"When?" Isabelle pushed her.

"Sometime soon, okay?"

"How about right now?" Isabelle picked up the phone and handed it to Josie.

Josie looked at the phone and then at Isabelle. She smiled, dialed the number, and made an appointment.

Isabelle smiled at her. "I'm proud of you, Josie. You've been obedient to the Lord and taken the first step in your healing."

"Thanks, Isabelle...back to the laundry!" Walking back to her duties, the dark mood seemed to lift.

"Josie's phone rang. "Hi, Josie. Guess what!"

"Let's see," She teased. "You're coming over to see me?"

"Well...uh...yes, but not exactly."

"What do you mean 'not exactly'?"

"What I mean is I'm going to speak at chapel this evening."

"Oh, Will...that's wonderful. I can't wait."

"Okay, see you this evening. Please pray for me. I've never done anything like this."

Josie felt good that Will was going to be the chapel speaker. In her heart and mind, she prayed for him all afternoon. Then with Stevie at her side, she found her way to the chapel. It was filled to capacity, the first time she'd seen so many people there.

Josie thought the music was better this evening for some reason. She felt the power of the Holy Spirit from the moment she walked through the door. After some singing, Isabelle introduced Will. A quiet gasp fell over many when she told

Josie's Gift

them Will works in the DA's office as an investigator. When Will stood to speak, he asked for everyone's prayers. Then he began and told the story just as he told it to Josie. When he finished, a hush fell over the chapel. The Holy Spirit was moving. Even before the invitation was given, a few men and women got out of their seats and made their way forward for prayer. While Will got off the stage to pray with those who were already in front, Isabelle continued praying and giving the invitation. It seemed as if a floodgate opened. The Holy Spirit moved mightily; large numbers of men and women headed for the front, some even running and falling on their knees at the altar rail.

Josie thanked God for such a powerful anointing on Will's testimony. She decided to go forward with other volunteers and help pray for those who were seeking healing for their own issues with drugs, alcohol, crime, and adultery. Stevie followed her and held her hand. He laid his little hands on those for whom Josie was praying. It was obvious that many were feeling the Holy Spirit's power. They began to shout and raise their hands. Some began to sing.

It looked like a revival was descending on the chapel with the power of a summer thunderstorm. People coming in from the streets, looking for something to eat or a place to sleep, were drawn to the power emanating from the chapel. God had made many hearts ready and was drawing people from blocks away, who like Will, found their selves hitting the bottom, and being drawn to the lights of the mission. The power of God was so pervasive that it was midnight before things subsided. Then, for five more evenings, the revival continued as many who had found Christ and healing for their lives wanted to testify. Will returned each evening to help out with the praying and counseling. Every night, the meetings went on 'til nearly midnight.

Quite unexpectedly, after the fifth night, like the quiet after a storm, things at the mission returned to normal.

Josie's Gift

Several days later, an article about the revival appeared in the religion section of the local paper. Will's picture was in the middle of it.

Josie, Moisés and Ruth Blandón, had never seen such a thing. It was totally unfamiliar to them. Carla helped them to understand what it was about. She reminded them of the story of Elijah, who prayed over an altar he had erected, challenging the prophets of Ba'al. She told them how the fire of God came down and consumed the sacrifices Elijah had prepared. All the false prophets were consumed and killed. She explained how Elijah's experience was a type of how God works, through the Holy Spirit, to purify the lives of those surrendered to Him, and how the fire of the Holy Spirit consumed the sin in many lives during the revival.

People whose lives had been changed were dispersing into many of the local churches. The entire Christian community in Rock City was feeling the effects of the Lighted Way Ministries revival. People were brought together across denominational lines to pray, raise money, and volunteer their time for the old mission on Third Street.

Josie's life was renewed. She never thought she would see miracles on the scale she had seen in the past five nights. She wrote letters to Becky, and to Mort and Susan, and Jerry in Littleville, enclosing copies of the news articles. She wrote to the Browns in Churchill, reminding them that she and Will, and the staff at the mission, loved them and were praying for them.

Josie's heart was swelling with love for Will. She admired him in so many ways. At the end of the week, they finally found time for another date. They drove to the familiar restaurant. Waiting for their food, she looked at Will, "I am so proud of you," She said.

"Honey, if it hadn't been for your insistence, I would never have given my testimony. God was directing you, and He certainly had His own plan for the outcome. To Him belongs the glory. But I'm glad you're proud of me; it makes me feel very good. And we can be proud to be in the Father's plan."

After they had eaten, Will drove to the park where they walked and talked. Josie felt like she needed to tell Will about her dream and about her brother.

Before she could say anything, Will spoke up, "Josie, remember last week when I told you I wanted to marry you?"

Josie stepped around in front of him. She looked up into his eyes and cocked her head slightly. She grinned, "You haven't changed your mind, have you?"

"Oh, NO...it's just that...well you haven't said anything, like, 'yes', or 'no'."

Josie's expression grew serious. She ran her fingers along the lines of his face, pulled his face down to meet her lips, then pulled her head back so she could talk. "Will Brent, I need to tell you something that's bothering me a lot. Actually," She paused. "Actually it's interfering with my willingness to say, 'yes'. I want to tell you all about it...then if you still love me, well..."

"Josie, I can't think of anything that would keep me from loving you and wanting you to marry me."

She put two fingers against his lips. Please don't say that until you've heard what I have to say. Let's sit down."

Will's anxiety level was growing, and he felt a cool chill with the lump in his throat as each word tumbled from her mouth. He wasn't sure what to expect, but afraid she was going to say, 'no'.

They sat on a park bench. Josie took his hand and stroked it, all the while looking only at his hand. For several minutes, she said nothing, nor did she look into his eyes. Her eyes began to drip tears...she still feared if she told him the story it might end their relationship. She prayed for strength. *"Maybe I can hide it, and he'll never need to know,"* She thought to herself. Then she heard Isabelle's voice, *"Will needs to know. If he still loves you afterward, then you'll know he loves you."*

She glanced up at Will's expectant expression. He could see and feel her unwillingness to tell him whatever it was she needed to get off her chest. He put his arm around her and drew her to him. With his hand he pushed her head over onto his shoulder. "My darling, Josie, my shoulder is big enough for your pain."

She continued stroking his hand. "Will, this is really difficult for me. Please be patient." She paused—after that she told him about her dream. She was surprised at how easy it was this time. It was much less emotional than when she told Isabelle. It inspired her to tell about Josef and his raping her.

Will listened. His eyes filled with tears as she described how painful it had been for her, having to live all her life with a dark memory she couldn't even bring into consciousness. As she was talking, he held her tighter. When she finished, he pulled her face around and kissed her forehead. "YES, Josie," he said. "YES, I want to marry you. I love you in spite of how you feel about yourself. You were an innocent victim of your brother's awful sin."

In between her sobs, Josie managed, "Oh, Will. I love you so much. I still have to sort things out regarding my family and how I deal with Josef. He's married now and has children of his own. I don't want to hurt my family, but I can't carry it alone anymore."

"Let Jesus help you carry this cross, Josie, and I'm here for you." Will paused, "After I gave my life to Jesus that night in the old church, I still carried a lot of pain. I had to have some help dealing with it, so I made an appointment with Doctor Hardt, a professional Christian counselor. He helped me deal with my emotional wounds."

Josie turned and looked at him. "Doctor Hardt, did you say? I have an appointment with him next week."

"That's great Josie. He'll help you deal with Josef, and with all the emotional wounds from the rape and the scars from your years with Roger."

"Emotional wounds?" Josie asked.

Will thought for a moment. "I learned that bad decisions I made during my drunken carousing left emotional wounds, not only in my own heart and mind, but also on the hearts and minds of others."

"Like?" Josie asked.

Will looked into Josie's questioning eyes. "Like my ex-wife, my mom and dad, and my brothers and sisters. I hurt people who love me, and I had to deal with it."

Josie seemed confused. "I still don't understand. I thought it was all over."

"You know, Josie," Will continued. "If you had surgery to remove a tumor or a diseased organ, there would be considerable pain. Both internal and external scars would be left on your body. The diseased organ is gone. The wound has healed. But the scar remains as evidence of the healing, and in some cases, you have to take medication for the rest of your life."

The two sat for several minutes in thoughtful silence. Will spoke, "I learned from Doctor Hardt, I needed healing for the wounds my bad decisions had inflicted. Like a physical wound, I've experienced healing, but memories remain as scars. I also learned that it's easy to suppress bad memories instead of dealing with the wounds."

Josie's eyes teared up. She spoke slowly. "What about the wounds that are caused by other people, like Josef or Roger?"

"Those, too, must be healed Josie," Will spoke decisively.

"Will you go to Doctor Hardt with me...for emotional support?" Josie asked.

"Not this time, Josie." Will answered. "It's best if you go alone. You need to deal with your wounds." He continued haltingly. "If at some time in the future, we both decide to marry, then we'll go together. We both carry baggage that could damage our relationship. We can deal with those things together with Doctor Hardt."

Josie arrived at Doctor Hardt's office for her appointment. In the office, the atmosphere was relaxed. She was anxious, and with the passing of each minute, felt like walking out, but her thoughts returned to Will. *"There's no way Will and I can enjoy a healthy relationship until I deal with my past. All of it,"* she said to herself.

Josie's introspection was interrupted by a friendly voice. "Doctor Hardt is ready for you. Just go to that door."

At the door, a friendly male voice greeted her, "I'm Doctor Hardt." He extended a hand to shake hers. Josie glanced around. The room looked more like somebody's living room than a doctor's office. Doctor Hardt spoke again. "Sit wherever you choose, Josie. I'll be sitting right here."

Josie sat down and looked around. A cross was hanging prominently on the wall to her left. An inviting picture of the Holy Family graced the wall to her right. A beautiful picture of a country church, surrounded by trees with colorful fall foliage, decorated the opposite wall. Josie couldn't take her eyes from the picture. A bright light inside the church, emanated from windows and a half-opened door. The light made a glow that seemed to dominate the scene. *"It's so inviting,"* she thought to herself. *"And so peaceful."*

"That's a beautiful picture isn't it, Josie," Doctor Hardt said, noting her gaze fixed on the picture.

"It looks like a place I had a dream about, and I want to go there!" Josie exclaimed.

"Everybody says that," Doctor Hardt responded. "It's because the picture represents a place of peace and wholeness, happiness and joy. It seems though everyone who comes here has a mental picture of a place like that...a place of healing. That's why it looks so familiar to you. One of the goals of our work together will be to find peace and healing for you."

Josie remained silent. She continued looking at the picture. She smiled. "Yes," she said. "I need that. Where do we start?"

Doctor Hardt responded. "On the form you filled out for me, you mentioned something about your past, about some kind of baggage you carry."

Josie looked at the floor. "Does anybody else know what we talk about in here?" She asked.

"Only the three of us, Josie," Doctor Hardt answered, "You and I, and God. Once, a very wise man said, 'The eyes of the Lord are ten thousand times brighter than the sun. He sees every step you take and sees into the hidden corners of your life. He knows every step before you make it and still knows them after they are made'." (Ecclesiasticus 23:19, 20)

Josie began to relax. They talked as if they were having a friendly conversation, but she was still reluctant to talk about the dream and about Josef. It was much easier to talk about her life with Roger, and the nightmare kept coming back.

Josie continued to see Doctor Hardt twice a week. She was feeling better about herself, and yet she knew she hadn't dealt with the most important issue of her childhood. This time, she entered the office with a sense of anticipation. She had a very strong feeling that this would be the time to talk about the rape and the dream. She was awash with anticipation and worry. She was nervous and anxious. She silently prayed that the Holy Spirit would help her and walk this difficult journey beside her.

Doctor Hardt began the session with a short prayer and a summary of the previous counseling sessions. Then he was quiet for a few minutes as if waiting for Josie to begin talking. Josie was uncomfortable with the silence. Finally, Doctor Hardt spoke.

"Josie, you've been coming for counseling for nearly three weeks. I'm really pleased with the progress you're making. You seem to be in a more upbeat mood than before."

Doctor Hardt continued. "You've looked at the whole episode with Roger in a very rational way, and you've reconciled that part of your past with your present circumstances. You've shown a very important element of spiritual and personal wholeness; you've developed a mature willingness to accept responsibility for your past decisions without blaming others. Though it was a struggle, you've been able to forgive Roger."

"I know," Josie replied. "And I feel better about myself. And yet..." She stopped as if something couldn't come out in words.

"And yet, what, Josie?" Doctor Hardt asked. "There's a piece of this picture that's still missing isn't there?"

Josie looked up at the picture of the church. "That open door," she said. "It's like, every time I get to it, the door shuts, and I can't get in. There seems to be some evil force, some kind of darkness that forces out the light." She hung her head, "And the dream...it keeps coming back."

Words choked in her throat and tears formed in her eyes. She tried, but couldn't speak. She closed her eyes. Dark memories from long ago flooded her mind, joining the flood of tears in her eyes. Josie put her head down into her hands, her elbows resting on her knees, and she sobbed uncontrollably.

Josie could see the shadowy figure standing in front of her. It moved closer. She started to scream, but a hand covered her mouth. Then without invitation the figure completely covered her. She struggled to breathe, but no breath came to her hurting lungs. She struggled to scream, but no sound came from her parched throat. She felt sharp pain and heard heavy breathing.

Her body shook, and the scream finally came. "No, Josef! Please, no!" She sobbed.

Doctor Hardt recognized immediately what she was experiencing and spoke quietly. "It's all right, Josie. You're safe here."

Josie's sobbing continued for what seemed an eternity. Finally, she relaxed and looked up again at the picture. Doctor Hardt followed her gaze. "We're going to walk through that door, Josie," he said. "This time, no evil force will close it. Jesus' love is the light, and His love will illuminate the dark corner of your life where your secret's been hidden."

Josie's mind was racing. She slumped into the chair, her head in her hands. The secret she carried alone for the past fifteen years was out in the daylight. She felt drained. Her breathing was in short gasps, half sobs.

Doctor Hardt remained silent and prayerful. Finally he spoke. "God is here Josie and he loves you. He wants to heal your wounds."

As if she didn't hear what Doctor Hardt had said, Josie looked at the picture of the Holy Family and then back at the floor. "I feel so ashamed," she said. "I feel dirty and ugly. How could anybody love me?"

Doctor Hardt spoke again. "Josie, listen to me."

Josie turned her head and looked into his eyes. She saw warmth and understanding. Her mind drifted back in time. She was eight. A puppy that the family adopted was playing in the yard. Suddenly the puppy saw something across the street; and ran. She heard the screeching of tires. A scream rose in her throat, and she started to run. She felt strong arms sweep her up and carry her in the direction of the house. She put her arms around Papa's neck and cried. His warmth and strength brought her comfort and peace. She looked up at Doctor Hardt again. "He's so much like Papa," she said to herself. "I can trust him."

Doctor Hardt looked straight into her eyes as he spoke. "Don't ever forget how much you are loved, Josie. Not only are you loved by God, but also by your wonderful Jewish family. And, you have a wonderful friend in Will, who loves you too."

"I know all that," she said. "I can put on a good act, but my heart's broken in pieces."

Doctor Hardt spoke softly and lovingly. "God's going to bring all those pieces together and heal each one. Today and over the next several counseling sessions, we're going to talk about each piece. We'll talk about Josef, and you must remember it was his sin, so long ago, that caused you this pain and changed the course of your life. It wasn't by any choice of yours that you were violently assaulted when you were nine. However, now that this horrible incident's out in the open, you can choose what you do about it from this point on. You can't change it or make it go away, but you can choose what you do with it from this day forward."

Josie looked at him with question written into her expression. "Choose?" She asked.

"Yes, Josie you can choose. You can choose to continue to live with your pain, or you can choose to do something about your pain. Which plan do you want to follow from now on?"

Josie looked at the picture of the church. "Yes, I can choose." She said it with determination, as if it was a fresh discovery. "I want to put the pieces back together."

CHAPTER TWENTY-NINE

Over several weeks of counseling, Josie was able to face the issue of having been raped by her brother. With Doctor Hardt's help, she came to understand that she would always have the memories, but with God's help and the healing power of the Holy Spirit, she was looking forward instead of backward. She had even been able to forgive Josef, who had victimized her.

Still, she needed answers to some pressing questions. She sat silently, thinking to herself. Doctor Hardt was patient. Finally he said, "Josie, I've learned when you're silent and have that look in your eyes, you're seeing something far, far away. Your mind's on something important. Want to talk about it?"

"Doctor Hardt, sometimes I think you can read my mind!" She chuckled.

"No, I don't read minds, but I've learned to know when you have something important you need to talk about." He smiled. "And it's good to see you more relaxed when you're thinking about some of your major issues."

Josie looked into Doctor Hardt's eyes. She saw understanding and patience. "Why," she said hesitantly. "Why didn't I tell my parents when it was happening? Then it would have stopped!"

"You have the answer to that, Josie." Doctor Hardt replied.

Josie was thoughtful. "You know," she began. "My family is so strong in their faith as believers, and in their Jewish traditions, they probably would never think something like that could happen to their own children."

"That's true, Josie. You're on the right track." Doctor Hardt said.

Josie continued. "I guess it was hard for me as a nine-year-old, to believe my mom and dad would still love me after what happened. Josef told me they would blame me."

"Yes, that's the key. Why do you think you believed that, Josie?" Doctor Hardt asked.

Josie paused for a few moments. "Because...I...uh...felt guilty, I felt ugly, and I felt dirty. After each time, I ran to the bathroom and took a shower. I tried to make myself clean." Tears filled her eyes. "I felt like my parents would reject me if they knew. Josef told me nobody would believe me, and if I told Mama or Papa, he'd hurt me."

"So you bore that awful secret all alone?" Doctor Hardt asked.

Josie smiled through her tears. "Now, I know," she said. "That I wasn't really alone. Jesus was there all the time reaching out to me." She lowered her head. "But I didn't take his hand. I could have, but didn't."

Josie's gaze once again turned up to look at the picture on the wall. "That open door," she said. "I can't get it out of my mind. She was silent and thoughtful. Doctor Hardt waited.

"I know," Josie finally said emphatically. "I know Jesus was there in my suffering. I know it was me that wouldn't take his hand and go on to healing and strength to do what was right."

Josie's eyes filled with more tears. "There were times when I hurt so bad, I even thought it would be better to die.

I hated everybody, especially myself. I even hated God for allowing it to happen."

Josie looked at Doctor Hardt. "I was praying yesterday and I realized something important."

"What was that?" Doctor Hardt asked.

Josie smiled. "Jesus suffered and died because of the actions of evil and sinful people."

"And you, Josie?" Doctor Hardt asked.

"Me," she answered. "I too suffered because of the actions of one evil and sinful person." She paused thoughtfully, "And in some ways, I too, died...my pride and self-esteem died...my purity died...my childhood died. At times even my will to live, died." She continued...her words were measured and careful, "All because of one very evil person." She felt anger making its way into her mind.

"Was there any meaningfulness in Jesus' suffering and death, Josie?" Doctor Hardt asked.

Josie looked again at the picture. "It was His suffering and death that paved the way to heaven for me." She said.

"Without that, His suffering and death would have been meaningless, wouldn't it, Josie?" Doctor Hardt asked.

"Yes," she answered.

Doctor Hardt continued. "Some years ago, a very wise Jewish psychiatrist, Doctor Viktor Frankl, a survivor of the Auschwitz prison camp during World War Two (see Frankl's book, *Man's Search for Meaning*), said that finding meaning in suffering is the greatest capacity of the human spirit. He taught that we can find meaning even in the midst of our suffering. Think about it, Josie, this very moment, Jesus is glorified in heaven. He is not sad and depressed from His suffering and death. Nor is he angry. All of heaven is full of His joy."

"How can I find any meaning in what an evil person did to me fifteen years ago?" Josie asked. "What kind of joy can there be in such pain?"

"Right now, Josie," Doctor Hardt began. "You're absorbed by the pain of your past. You locked up the rape and an evil man in the far recesses of your mind until recently when Will came into the picture. He offers you a healthy Christian relationship, and it's difficult for you to reconcile that relationship with the ugliness of your past. Now that things are out in the open, it's difficult for you to overcome your anger."

Josie looked at Doctor Hardt. Something clicked in her mind. A new light came on in her understanding. She smiled. "Deep down inside I still look at myself as dirty and ugly. I'm still an angry little girl. I don't see myself as worthy of a Christian man like Will," she said.

"You know, Josie," Dr Hardt said. "We tend to confirm our feelings about ourselves in our relationships."

Josie interrupted. "That's why I was so attracted to Roger, wasn't it? I felt dirty, ugly, and angry, so I looked for someone who would be as bad as I thought I was." She smiled and laughed. "Mama said that Roger was an ugly frog in a slimy pond. I thought that I could kiss him, and he would become a handsome prince who could rescue me from all my pain." She laughed some more. "We both ended up in the slimy pond."

Doctor Hardt smiled with understanding, "Doctor Frankl also said that guilt, pain, and death are the tragic triad of human suffering. When you were raped, you experienced death, pain and guilt. In the decisions that came out of your struggles with guilt, pain, and death, you decided who you were, you decided what you ought to do, and you decided on what you could base your hopes. Roger came along and you thought you had the answers."

Doctor Hardt continued. "You really want to put your heart into a relationship with Will, but it contradicts what you've believed about yourself, doesn't it?"

Josie's conversation with Doctor Hardt was gaining momentum. It was as if missing pieces of a puzzle were suddenly available to complete the picture of her life. Josie looked again at the picture of the church. She paused, her mind deep in thought. As if talking to herself, she said softly, "The door is open. The light is there. There's so much peace and joy inside."

Still looking at the picture of the church, Josie's eyes filled with tears. "Will's in there isn't he?"

"I don't know," Doctor Hardt answered. "The door's open. You must take a chance and walk in and find out for yourself, who's in there. But there're no ugly frogs to kiss, and the slimy pond's in the past to stay. The memory's there, and the scar's there, but the wound has healed. You've only one thing left to do."

"What's that?" Josie asked drying her eyes.

"Reconcile the past to your present relationship with Will," Doctor Hardt answered.

"What do I have to do?" Josie asked.

"Most of it, you've already done," Doctor Hardt answered.

Josie looked surprised. Doctor Hardt continued. "Remember the tragic triad of suffering that we talked about a few minutes ago?"

Josie nodded her head.

"In response to your guilt, pain, and death, you made some bad decisions. But, you also made some good decisions, Josie. Let's talk about them.

"First, you agreed with Judge Jacobson to go with Reverend Isabelle and live at the mission instead of living on the street. Reverend Isabelle opened the door to a transformed life for you. One more thing; remember we talked about meaning in your suffering. You found your meaning in your son, Steve. You distanced yourself from your own pain over the past years by devoting your life to him."

Josie was speechless. Tears again filled her eyes. "I never thought of it that way," she said.

Doctor Hardt continued. "Your relationship with Jesus has given you a new identity. St. Paul declares, 'Whoever is in Christ is a new creation: the old things have passed away,' (2 Corinthians 5:17). A very long time ago, there was a little girl of nine named Josie. She was alive and as pure as the morning dew. Then a violent act took away her purity and her hopes and dreams for life. It left her empty and angry. Now, Josie, God has brought you back to life in a beautiful and powerful resurrection. And He has a wonderful plan for your life. Today, right this moment, is the first day of that new resurrected life."

Josie thought about the prophecy Susan had given her in Littleville. "Does His plan include Will?" Josie asked.

Doctor Hardt smiled. "I can't answer that for you, Josie. What do you think?"

Josie looked at Doctor Hardt and smiled. "Yes," she said. "I think it does!" For several minutes, she looked thoughtfully at the picture. "Doctor Hardt, what do I do about Josef? He's my brother, and I can't avoid him forever. I won't be free to go through that door until I do something about him."

"You're right, Josie, you have a chain of pain that still connects you to Josef." Looking at his watch, "Our time's up for today. Between now and next week, I want you to talk that issue over with Will and come up with a plan. He knows the legal issues involved. Then when you come in next week, we'll talk about it."

During the time Josie was seeing Doctor Hardt, she and Will spent most evenings together at the mission. Will was an asset in helping to counsel and pray with the men. Each weekend, they had their own time together on their regular date. Josie couldn't wait for the weekend so she could tell

Will how good she was feeling and what Doctor Hardt had said about talking to him about Josef.

After dinner at their favorite restaurant, Josie and Will walked in the park. Josie turned to Will, "Remember me telling you about my brother raping me?"

"I remember. How's it going with Doctor Hardt?"

"I have to make some decisions about Josef and my family."

"I figured as much."

"Doctor Hardt asked me to talk this issue over with you before my next counseling session. He said you would know about all the legal stuff involved."

Will took a deep breath and sighed. "Let's sit down." After finding a park bench, Will responded to her statement. "Josie, this is a very serious legal matter. But what I think is even more serious is what this is going to do to your family if you bring it out in the open. You have to ask yourself, 'Am I ready to face the fallout that's going to come?'"

"I know, Will, and I'm worried. Somehow I have to get it out and face it. I have to do something about it!" Josie thought for several minutes. "Can he still be prosecuted?"

"The statute of limitations has changed in regard to sex crimes, and yes, he can be prosecuted if that's the route you want to take."

"The tone of your voice says there are obstacles to that."

"Yes! If you do press charges, there are a couple of things you should consider. First, your chances of getting a conviction are probably very slim to none. In court, it'll turn into a 'she says'...'he says' situation. If he's married and has children, you can bet he'll never confess it outright. For sure, he'll deny it ever happened. There are no witnesses, and there's no residue DNA for testing...so you're left with a very slim chance of getting a conviction."

Josie began to cry softly. "I thought you were on my side, Will Brent!"

"I am on your side, Sweetheart, but I have to be honest. I've had some experience in these kinds of cases, and I can tell you for sure, that going to court with no evidence is something no DA wants to tackle."

"But I'm not lying, Will. Won't the judge believe me?"

"Honey, the judge has to look at facts, and I hate to say it, but from his perspective, your claim doesn't make it a fact—especially in light of it being so long ago. You know it's a fact, I believe it's a fact, but that's only because you experienced it, and because I love you. That's just the reality of things."

Josie felt like she had to resign herself to another course of action. "So, where does that leave me? What are my options?"

"I can tell you what I would do, Josie, but the decision is yours to make, not mine."

"Okay, so what would you do?"

Will looked at her for several long moments. "I'll tell you what I'd like to do! I'd like to go face him, and beat the crap out of him. While I was doing it, I would tell him what a low life he is and how much I'd like to see him burn in hell for what he did." Will's voice was becoming angry and bitter.

Josie got a worried look on her face. "Would you really do that, Will?"

"Will's face took on a sheepish look. He hung his head. "No, not really! I said that's what I'd like to do, but I wouldn't really do it. I have to work on forgiving him for what he did to you."

"Seriously, what would you do, Will?"

For a few moments, Will was thoughtful. "Would you consider the possibility of confronting him in person, just the two of you? Maybe you could resolve it, and then it wouldn't have to come out in the open with your family."

Josie searched his eyes. "I think that would be scary. I'm not sure I could do it."

"I have the feeling that Josef has done some worrying of his own through the years, worrying that someday you'd show up at his doorstep and face him with it. Surely, he's felt guilty about it."

Josie was silent. Finally she spoke. "Will, Josef has a daughter who's nine. I hate to think he might be doing it to her, or to someone else, like one of her friends."

"That's a worrisome thought...but, altogether possible. When a man does that once, he's very likely to do it again. I hate to think of that."

"Can I do anything about that?"

"Probably not! This is one of those situations where there're no winners. Unfortunately the law can't step in 'til something disastrous happens. The only power you have now, is to confront him, and let him know if anything happens in the future, you'll tell all and live to see him hang, so to speak."

"So," Josie said. "What I have to do now is make a plan to confront Josef without my parents knowing about it... and without his family finding out." Josie's adrenaline levels were rising. She was feeling fear and then anger rise up in her mind, "It's not fair, Will. Josef gets by with ruining my life, but I can't do anything to ruin his life."

"I don't blame you for feeling that way, Josie. You have every right to feel disappointed because, at least for the time being, he goes unpunished." Will thought for several moments, then added, "We have to pray that if he repeats with another little girl, she'll have the courage to go to a trusted adult and talk about it."

Josie sighed, "Of course, I know you're right, but I don't like it, and it'll be difficult for me to work through it."

"Let Doctor Hardt know what you decide, and talk it through with him."

Josie spent the next several days planning her next move in confronting Josef. She believed she needed to plan it very carefully, even to the extent of writing a script for her first telephone call. At her next counseling session, she told Doctor Hardt of her plan and her discussion with Will. Doctor Hardt agreed that the idea of confrontation would probably be best if it could end in forgiveness and reconciliation.

Josie spoke with Isabelle and was more confident of what she wanted to say to Josef. She got the addresses and phone numbers of both of her brothers from her mom. Her plan was to call Josef and set up a time and place to meet privately. It would be during the private meeting that she would confront him with what she wanted to say. "*What if he refused a private meeting?*" She asked herself. "*I'll have to be clever and tell him that I've talked to someone in the D.A,'s office, which is true.*" She smiled at her thoughts of what he would say and do.

"Hi, Sharon, this is Josie. Is Josef home, and can I talk to him please?"

"Hi, Josie!" Sharon's surprise was evident in her tone of voice. "Uh...how're you doing? We've read about you and Roger in the newspaper." There was an awkward silence. "Well...I'll get Josef for you, just hang on. Uh...it's good to hear from you, Josie."

Josie could hear Josef in the background asking who was on the phone. She imagined how nervous he must be at hearing she wanted to talk to him.

"Hi, Josie! How are you? It's been a very long time since we've seen each other." His voice began to sound nervous. "Uh...what's up? Are you okay? Are Mom and Dad okay?"

"We're all okay, Josef. Uh...there's something very important I need to talk to you about. I need to meet with you privately. You name the time and the place."

"I can't really think of anything we need to talk about privately, Josie. You're welcome to come here anytime you want to visit." He glanced at Sharon who was listening and getting curious about what was going on.

"Josef, I can guarantee, you won't want the things I need to discuss, to be brought up in your home with your wife and children present."

"Look, Josie..."

In the background Josie heard Sharon ask him what was wrong. It was obvious he was worried and nervous.

"...Nothing Sharon, everything's okay. Uh...Josie, give me your phone number, and I'll call you tomorrow."

Josie gave him the number, which he wrote down.

Josef called as he promised. "What's this all about, Josie?"

"Give me a time and place, Josef. We'll meet face to face and talk about it."

"Okay, I'm going to be near Rock City on business, day after tomorrow. Give me a time and place convenient for you."

"Ask for directions to Memorial Park. I'll be standing on the northwest corner of the park at ten in the morning. We'll find a bench where we can sit and talk in private."

"Josie, I don't see why all the secrecy. Can't you give me some clue what this is about?"

"Okay, Josef! This is about your future. Goodbye." Josie hung up and smiled, inwardly satisfied by how she handled things and how worried he must be. "*Well,*" she thought to herself, "*he can just stew over it for another day.*"

That night she told Will all about her phone conversation. "What do you think, Will?"

"I think that was the right thing to do. I'll drive you over there and sit in my car parked near the northwest corner to watch and make sure everything goes okay. I'm going to talk to Sandy and see if his guys can fix you up with a wire. Do you mind if I tell him what this is all about?"

"A wire?"

"Yeah, it's a small transmitting device that you can wear under your blouse that will send a signal to a recording device I'll have in my car. We'll need Judge Jacobson's approval but I think he'll go along with it."

Josie thought for a few moments. She was hesitant about Sandy knowing about Josef, but decided the wire would be a good thing. "Thank you, Will...yes, you may talk to Sandy."

"If he admits his assaults, it'll be on the recorder. Also, if he gets violent, I'll know about it."

Josie waited at the designated corner. She was nervous, but wanted to get the meeting over with. *"I wish I'd asked Josef what kind of car he'd be driving"*, she thought to herself. After she'd been there about ten minutes, a car slowly drove by. She made eye contact with the driver; it was Josef. She watched him park and walk toward her. He approached and tried to draw her into an embrace as if they were loving brother and sister, but she brusquely pushed him away. She pointed to a bench and started walking in that direction. He reluctantly followed, nervously looking around.

Josie sat down. She looked in the direction of the street where she saw Will's car. He could see her and Josef. Josef stayed on his feet. He paced nervously back and forth in front of Josie and the bench. Josie could see that he was both angry and afraid.

"What's this all about, Josie?" His voice was gruff, with a tone of threat.

"Sit down, Josef," Josie directed.

He gave her a detached look and then sat down. "Okay, now what?"

She turned to face him. She looked directly into his eyes. "I was nine years old, Josef...just nine years old. I have only one question: why did you do it?"

His eyes flashed fire. "I don't know what you're talking about!"

Josie remained calm. "You know exactly what I'm talking about, Josef!" Her voice rising a little.

He stood up and walked around the bench. He stood in front of her...she felt threatened but held her ground. "Why did you do it, Josef?" She pressed.

He leaned down into her face. He glared into her eyes. He pointed his finger directly into her face just inches away. "Because you wanted it; you were asking for it. The way you acted...the way you dressed...the way you looked at me... do you hear me Josie? You were asking for it." His voice was rising, and he anxiously looked around.

Josie smiled and laughed. "My counselor told me you would say that. You want to blame me. You want to make me the perpetrator, don't you? Well, I'm not buying that any more, Josef. My counselor told me that's what all child sex abusers do."

Josef's demeanor changed suddenly. Now he began to look scared. "You...uh...you've seen a counselor?"

"Yes, I've seen a counselor and you know what? The D.A.'s office told me the same thing." She glared at him and waited for his response.

"Are...uh...are you going to follow through with charges?" Now he was really afraid, and he showed it. He stood up again and paced back and forth. He couldn't think of anything more to say.

"Whether I press charges will depend on you, Josef."

"You can't prove a thing, Josie, and you know it. What do you want? You want money...what?"

She looked at him and felt a twinge of pity. "I want...I want to forgive you, Josef."

Josie's Gift

He seemed to breathe a sigh of relief. "Okay, do it, and let's forget it!"

"It's not that easy, you see, you have to ask me for forgiveness and admit what you did and what's more, you must promise me that it will never happen again."

He hung his head, and looked at her. He was defiant, "Okay, I did it...you hear...I did it. Dammit...I did it. I'm sorry; please forgive me. It will never happen again. I'll never bother you again." His words sounded hollow. He was in a hurry to end their conversation.

Josie was calm. She looked him in the eye. "Josef, I forgive you for what you did to me, but your promise not to do it again is insincere. You have a nine-year-old daughter...she has friends who are nine-years-old. You have access to nine-year-old girls. My counselor and the D.A.'s office tell me that it's highly likely you would repeat the offense. Promise me, Josef!"

He was visibly shaken. His hands trembled, his eyes were wet...his mouth was dry. "Yes, yes, I promise." He dropped his head and rested it on his hands, his elbows on his knees. He looked up at her. "Do you know what this will do, Josie? This will ruin my life if it gets out. I can't let that happen."

"Josef, listen to me." Her words were slow and deliberate. "This doesn't have to get out. It should be private between the two of us and God. But, Josef, if I ever hear of you doing that to any other child, I'll tell the whole world about you."

"Nobody will believe..."

Josie interrupted him. She smiled in his face. "That's what you told me wasn't it? Well, Josef, when I tell it, they will believe me. You can be sure of it! You need to go to God and ask for forgiveness. You need to ask Him to change your life. I wish I could help you with that, but I'm too involved. You need to find somebody who knows Jesus and ask for help."

Josef was silent and unexpressive. He gave her a cold look.

Josie stood and moved in front of him. "Good bye, Josef. God loves you and wants to heal your heart and forgive your sins. Remember this day, Josef." She turned and walked toward Will's car.

Josef looked at her back as she walked away. Abruptly, he leaped to his feet, pulled a knife from his pocket, and lunged in her direction. "I'm not going to allow you to ruin my life," he screamed as he lashed out at her head with the knife.

When Will saw Josef raise the knife and was about to plunge it into Josie's neck, he was out of his car and rushing to her aid. Before he got to her, Josef had stabbed her in the back of her neck and was on top of her on the ground. Before he could plunge the knife into Josie's back again, he felt the cold steel of a gun barrel against his left temple.

"Drop the knife, Josef. If you move that knife one inch toward Josie, I'll blow your brains out."

Josef began screaming. "She's a slut, I tell you...nothing but a cheap slut."

When Josef failed to drop the knife, Will drew his fist back and hit him as hard as he could on the side of his head. Josef rolled over on his side clutching his head. Will stood over him, his gun pointed at his head.

"Put your hands behind your back and roll onto your stomach. **NOW**, Josef." Will leaned close to his face, "I should kill you, Josef; but better that you face the consequences through the legal processes."

A uniformed officer got there just as Will placed handcuffs on Josef. "You okay, Mister Brent?"

"Yeah, call for an ambulance here." He turned toward Josie who lay unconscious on her stomach in the grass. He fell on his knees beside her. "Don't move, Josie. You're going to be okay." With one hand he put his handkerchief

Josie's Gift

over her wound. With his other hand he stroked her hair, and with tears in his eyes he cried out to God for help.

"What do I charge this guy with, Mister Brent?" The officer asked.

Will looked up. There was anger in his voice. "Book him for assault with a deadly weapon with intent to commit murder."

"Yes, Sir!" The officer dragged Josef to his feet. After pushing him into the back seat of his patrol car, he retrieved the knife and carefully placed it into a plastic evidence bag.

The EMS arrived and immediately got to work on Josie. Will got his camera from the car and took several pictures. The med techs stopped the bleeding, got her neck braced, and prepped her for transport.

Will's thoughts now were on Josie's family and how they would react to this. "No matter," he thought. "I've got to get to the hospital and be with Josie."

On the way to the hospital, Will called Isabelle. He was still pumped up with adrenaline and shaking. "Hi, Isabelle, Josie's in the hospital. I'll tell you the story later. Get her family together and get there as fast as you can, will you?"

"Okay, Will. I'm on the way."

CHAPTER THIRTY

By the time Will arrived at the hospital, Josie was already in surgery. As soon as Sandy arrived, Will told him what had happened and gave him the recording equipment.

Sandy reached for the recorder and put his other hand on Will's shoulder. "I'm sorry about this, Will. I thought there could be a remote possibility something like this might happen so I had the uniformed officer nearby as a precaution."

Will pressed his hand on top of Sandy's hand still on his shoulder. "Pray for me, Sandy. I've got to talk to the family. This is going to be tough—I'm still pumped up with adrenaline. They'll need to know the whole story now. We all wanted to prevent something like this, but people like Josef are unpredictable. I'm assuming you'll contact his wife and let her know her husband's in custody."

Sandy sighed. "Yeah, I'll contact her. If she decides to come here to see her husband, I'll help her find accommodations. She'll have to get him a lawyer, and if she expects to have him released pending a hearing and trial, she'll also have to make arrangements for a bond. As we build the case, I'm going to suggest to the D.A. that we have him evaluated by a psychiatrist as soon as possible. I think he's got some furniture missing in the upstairs apartment."

Will turned and looked at Sandy, his voice a little broken. "He must have been crazed with fear and seething with anger to attempt such a thing in public...in broad daylight. Maybe a psychiatrist can make some sense out of it."

The two men turned as Isabelle arrived with Josie's family. Will ushered them toward a private conference room.

"Mind if I tag along, Will?" Sandy asked.

"No, Sandy. I'll feel better with you there to help answer questions."

When all were seated at the large conference table, everyone looked expectantly at Will. Ruth had tears in her eyes, and Moisés held her hand. Stevie was sitting on Isabelle's lap and looked very sad. Will looked around the table, made eye contact one by one, took a deep breath and began.

"I truly wish things had not turned out this way; but for reasons known only to God, they did. First of all, indications are that Josie will survive despite a deep stab wound at the base of her neck. She's still in surgery at this time. The surgeon will come here and let us know when the surgery is over and what her condition is at that time." He paused and made eye contact with each person again. "That said; I know each one of you wants to know, how this happened." He paused again, looked around, then continued. "The person who attacked her...was um...her brother, Josef." There were gasps from everyone. They looked at each other. Will continued, "Josef is in police custody at this time and is being booked on the charge of attempted murder."

When Ruth heard that news, she burst into uncontrollable sobs. Moisés cradled her in his arms. He looked stern, his eyes narrowed, he spoke decisively. "Señor Will, that could not be my son...he would **never** attack his own sister."

"I understand your feelings, Moisés. Unfortunately it is true. We have witnesses, including me. In addition, we have a recording of the conversation that led to the attack. With all my heart, I wish it were not true. Our lives are all going to change from this day forward. We must pray for his family and reach out to them. I expect Sharon will arrive sometime this evening or perhaps tomorrow. She will take this very hard. Her life and the lives of her children will never be the same."

Isabelle looked around at everybody then turned to Will. "What motivated Josef to do such a thing, Will?"

Will turned and looked at Sandy. Sandy knew what he was thinking, and took Stevie's hand. "Let's you and me go get some ice cream, Stevie." Stevie looked at Sandy and seemed to understand that what was to follow would be for adults only.

After Sandy left the room with Stevie, Will attempted to explain what had happened when Josie was nine years old. He also mentioned Josie's counseling sessions with Doctor Hardt. The room was quiet and no one spoke. Will continued. "Unknown to any of you, Josie's been carrying a very painful memory since she was nine years old. She finally mustered the courage to face it. As part of her healing process, she felt she needed to face her abuser."

After a long silence, with a tone of resignation in his voice, Moisés asked, "What will happen now, to Josef?"

"The judge will set a hearing and make the determination as to the amount of bond for his release. My guess is, under these circumstances the bond will be set so high, it will be impossible to cover…that may be best. At some point in the near future, he'll be evaluated by a psychiatrist. From then on, justice will take its course. In any case, he's looking at a long period of time in prison or in a psychiatric hospital or some combination of both. I will say this, when Sharon gets here, she's going to need all the love and acceptance you can give her. Remember, she's an innocent person in this tragedy. And, don't forget Josef, he'll need your support, not to approve of his actions, but because he is your son, and he needs Jesus in his life."

Moisés spoke for the family. "You are very wise, Señor Will. We will do as you say. Now we shall await the outcome of Josie's surgery and pray together for her healing."

The whole family, including Will stood and held hands. Isabelle led them in a prayer for healing of Josie and comfort and strength for Sharon.

Several hours later, the surgeon came to the room and greeted them. "The surgery went well," he said. "She's doing just fine. Fortunately there was no damage to major arteries or to any of the vertebra in her neck. The knife blade narrowly missed her esophagus and one carotid artery. Injuries consisted of cut muscle and neck tendons, which we repaired. We think, with time and some rehabilitation, she'll recover without residual damage, except for a small scar of course. From the wound, it appeared the knife that was used in the stabbing was a folding knife with a relatively narrow blade maybe four to six inches in length."

"When can we see her?" Will asked.

"As soon as they have her cleaned up and into recovery, I think it will be okay for all of you to go to her bedside, one at a time for just a few moments each. Just remember, she'll still be under the anesthetic, but may be able to hear, and may be aware of your presence. You can come back tomorrow, and she should be awake. She'll be wearing a neck brace that will restrict her head movements, so be very careful with the hugs. As soon as she's awake and we know she's stable, we'll move her to the intensive care ward."

"I'm her mother, Doctor. May I stay with her through the night?" Ruth asked.

"I'll tell the intensive care nurse to allow you to be there."

"Thank you, Doctor," all said, almost in unison.

Will decided he'd go to the police station and check with Sandy about Josef. When he got there, he found Josef in a holding cell, lying on the cot with his eyes closed. When the keys clinked in the door, he expectantly sat up. When he saw Will, he closed his eyes, sighed, and lay back down.

"Whatta you doin here?" he mumbled.

"Just thought I'd visit for a minute or two and let you know about Josie and your family."

"Should I care?" Josef muttered defiantly.

"Yes, Josef, you should care!" Will felt his adrenaline rising, and his response was forceful. "You should be thankful that Josie made it through surgery just fine, and she'll be okay. Your mom and dad are very concerned for you. They love you in spite of what you've done."

Josef looked up at Will. "Why did she have to do it?" He asked heatedly.

"You should ask that question of yourself, Josef. Look back fifteen years and ask yourself why you did what you did. It was your decision then...and now this is the consequence of that very unfortunate choice."

Josef was silent. He just looked at Will...his blank expression said he neither understood, nor accepted what Will was saying. Will turned around to leave.

Josef spoke. His tone was acquiescent. "I guess this means I'll be in prison for a long time, doesn't it?"

"Yes, Josef...a long, long, time! You may be eligible to apply for parole in five to ten years. You'll remember the choice you made fifteen years ago for the rest of your life. You can be forgiven, but you won't forget...nor will you forget that you tried to kill your sister."

Josef broke into tears. His voice was pleading. "Mister Brent, I didn't want to kill her, I just wanted to hurt her...to punish her for ruining my life."

"You made your choices, Josef. Now you'll live with them. Josie didn't ruin your life...you did! Right up until the moment you rushed after her with that knife, you could have changed the course of your whole life. Had you acted rationally, you and Josie could have been reconciled as brother and sister, and it would have been over with." Will's eyes were piercing when he looked at Josef. As he turned to leave, he spoke with a tone of finality in his voice. "Somehow, Josef, I can't feel sorry for you. I pray for you to find Jesus... but, I can't feel sorry for you. While you're thinking about your own life being ruined; think about Sharon and your kids, and about Moisés and Ruth. How many lives have you ruined, Josef? One unfortunate and unwise choice...one loss of control, yielding to your lust...how many lives are ruined now, Josef?"

Sharon didn't arrive until the next afternoon. She checked into a motel and then went to the police station to talk to whoever was in charge of the case. She was allowed to see Josef and arrange for an attorney to represent him. Sandy met her at the holding cell and introduced himself. He invited her to follow him into a private conference room where they could talk.
"I know this is very difficult for you, Missus Blandón. I need to tell you exactly what happened. If you'd rather wait until the attorney gets here, we can do that."
"No, detective, I'd like to hear it from you in private. First, I need to tell you something that happened just before I left home. It's why I was delayed in getting here until today." Sharon hung her head and wiped tears from her eyes.
Sandy was patient and waited.
Sharon looked up and continued. "It's...uh...very depressing, and it's difficult for me to talk about. It was...a total shock."
"You mean, what Josef did to Josie?"
"Well, that too."
"There's something else?"
"Yes, you see our daughter, Sandra is nine years old. Last night she brought one of her friends, Lilly, to talk to

me about Josef. Lilly said he had been fondling her inappropriately for several months. I asked Sandra if it had been happening to her. She was very reluctant, but said it was. I asked why they just now brought it to light. They both told me; that since he was in jail now, they didn't have to worry about him hurting them."

Sandy shook his head. "I'm very sorry, Missus Blandón. This must be very hard on you."

Sharon dabbed at her eyes with a tissue Sandy offered. "This morning before I left, I took the girls, along with Lilly's parents, to the police station to be interviewed. They set up something with a social worker for tomorrow, so I have to go back in the morning. As soon as the interviews are over, Sandra will stay with Lilly at her house, and I'll be back. I need to talk to Josie and to the Blandón's as soon as I can."

"This will be a very difficult time for you, Missus Blandón. I can assure you that my prayers and the prayers of many others are with you. Josie and her parents are living at the old mission on Third Street. I'll see that you get directions so you'll know how to find it. Reverend Isabelle Jefferson, the pastor, will comfort you and assist you. Will Brent works at the DA's office, and he'll be able to keep you abreast of what will happen in your husband's case."

Sandy looked around. "I believe the attorney is here and will need to talk with you. Come, I'll introduce you. If you need anything, I'll be in my office."

By the second day after surgery, Josie was much improved and they had moved her to a private room. She was taking pain medication so her mind was a little fuzzy at times and her speech a little slurred. The surgeon said she should be off the medication within a day or two but would still get antibiotics intravenously. As soon as she could swallow properly, she could take the antibiotics orally. Ruth stayed with her daughter at the hospital. When she needed to go out to take a shower or change clothes, Moisés picked her up and drove her to the mission. Both Moisés and Will stayed in the room for several hours each evening.

After the children's interviews with the social worker, Sharon returned to Rock City. By the time Sharon visited Josie, she had been in the hospital for four days. It was awkward, neither woman knowing quite what to say. Josie was sitting up in a chair. Nurses were preparing her to be released.

"Hi, Josie, looks like you're doing okay." Sharon was nervous and apprehensive.

Josie took her hand. "Sharon, I'm so, so, sorry this had to happen."

Both women broke into tears. Sharon leaned over and gently hugged Josie. "I don't know what to say, Josie, except I'm sorry too. I know you've been through a lot, and this doesn't help any."

"Sharon, Sandy told me about your daughter and her friend. Right now, your pain is far worse than mine. I've already grieved my loss, so now my pain is only physical. You and the girls have yet to grieve your losses. I'm sure you're at the confusion and denial stage and wondering how this could possibly have happened."

"You're right, Josie. I can't seem to get my mind wrapped around it. It's uh...hard for me to admit that something like this could happen in my own family...um...between my own husband and his own daughter."

"I'm scheduled to be released in just a little while. The nurses will be here shortly to change the dressing on my wound. They'll fit me with a more comfortable neck brace, and I'll be good to go. Papa and Mama will be here to pick me up. Mama is still at the stage of denial and confusion you're in. Take time to share your feelings and allow her to share hers. Papa is stiff and strong, but he's very angry. Josef is his oldest son, and you know what that means to a Jew. He grieves inside, silently and alone. His disappointment is overwhelming, and he faces a very difficult decision: whether or not to disown Josef. They haven't been to the jail to visit him yet, so please ask them to go with you when you go. Help them to understand that I can't go, because as the victim, I can't be in contact with my assailant."

"I will, Josie...I will!"

Josie held onto the arms of the chair and slowly stood to face Sharon. She reached out and put her arms around her sister-in-law's neck, and they embraced in a clumsy hug. "We can only pray, Sharon, for Josef to find a relationship with Yeshua, and be open to the power of Ruach-HaKodesh to change his whole life."

It would be several days before Josef could be arraigned and six more weeks before he would face trial. Because of Will's role in the arrest and his witnessing of the crime, his appointment to the U.S. Marshall's Academy had to be postponed. That meant at least another month or perhaps two before he could leave for Glynco, Georgia. Will and Josie turned their attention to marriage.

CHAPTER THIRTY-ONE

Will was very careful to speak to Moisés about his desire to marry Josie. Moisés had grown very fond of Will and knew he would sooner or later ask for her in marriage. On the one hand, he was happy for Josie and welcomed Will into his family, but on the other hand he was bothered that Will had no Jewish ancestry. Will reminded Moisés of the Apostle Paul, who was very fond of the young man Timothy, whose mother was Jewish, but his father was Greek...a gentile. Moisés reminded Will that because Josie was an ethnic Jew, their children would also be considered ethnic Jews. The two men reached agreement, and Moisés welcomed Will into his family. The next event that must happen was for Will's family and Josie's family to meet together. Will was to make the arrangements. After that meeting, and if everything was agreeable between them, Will and Josie, according to Jewish custom, would be officially engaged.

Despite the turbulent events surrounding Josef, Josie and Will set a date for their wedding to occur sometime after the trial but before Will had to report to the Academy. As soon as the trial date was set, they would set the date for their wedding. The events surrounding Josef put a damper on the joy everybody felt about the wedding, but Will convinced them all that he and Josie had to move on with their plans and with their lives.

As things moved forward, Will's family and Josie's family met formally and ceremoniously accepted each other to become, what in Spanish is called, *compadres*. While such things did not seem so terribly significant to the Brent family; to the Blandón's, the traditions were most essential and were considered a vital foundation of the marriage. During a grand dinner at a downtown hotel, with their families and many friends present, Will made the announcement that he and Josie were engaged to be married, and he very ceremoniously presented her with a ring. He then lifted a large china plate and dropped it on the floor, where it broke into hundreds of little pieces. As breaking of the plate is irreversible, so the engagement of Will and Josie is also considered irreversible. Josie then became what in Hebrew is called the *Kallah* and Will, the *Chosen,* a Jewish term meaning the bridegroom.

Over the next several weeks, the couple was busy getting things arranged so the two of them could live at Will's house. They had to take care of legal papers, get a marriage license, write invitations, arrange for a reception, and a hundred other things. It was easy for both Josie and Will to get stressed out over trying to agree on the many arrangements that had to be made. They asked Isabelle if she and Carla could perform the ceremony and if they could be married in the Mission Chapel. Isabelle agreed and made the necessary arrangements. The wedding would be a mixture of cultures and religious traditions.

The day of the wedding finally arrived. In keeping with Jewish custom, Josie stood alone in the back of the chapel. What was about to happen, was an old Jewish tradition that brought remembrance of the Patriarch Isaac and his marriage to Rebekah when she covered her head upon seeing Isaac in the field. Will walked up the aisle toward the back of the church. He was followed by his and Josie's family and their friends. Upon meeting Josie, he lifted the veil to verify her identity. The veil would symbolize the modesty, dignity and chastity that would characterize her new life as a virtuous Jewish woman. Following Jewish tradition, Will turned around and walked toward Reverend Isabelle and Carla, followed by his father and Moisés. Upon nearing the altar, they stopped. Josie walked down the aisle toward Will, followed by her mother, Will's mother, and other women. Upon reaching Will, they processed around him seven times. In Jewish tradition, this symbolizes the earth's rotating on its axis seven times during the seven days of creation.

After the seven circles, Josie took her place at Will's right hand, and they faced the altar. According to tradition, they both signed the *Kesubah* or contract which stipulates the conditions of the marriage in great detail. Then Reverend Isabelle proceeded with the vows. They exchanged rings, and Carla read the seven blessings in the Messianic tradition and then gave the final blessing. Isabelle gave Josie and Will each a candle. Will lit his first, then turned to Josie and lit hers from his. Together they lit a single candle on the altar. The candles symbolized the two lives becoming one. Reverend Isabelle's voice boomed. "In as much as Josie Blandón Brown and William Colin Brent have consented to the estate of holy matrimony, and have witnessed the same before God and here before His congregation, I now pronounce them to be man and wife."

The reception at a downtown hotel was jovial. All eyes were upon the bride and groom as they each took a drink from a common wine glass. Will then laid the glass on the floor and broke it with his foot symbolizing the fragility of human happiness and joy.

Then the happy festivities began. They enjoyed a sumptuous meal, and the adults talked, and happy children played with each other. After the meal, the dance began. As Will took Josie into his arms and began the slow movement to the center of the floor, he whispered, "Now, I pray God to bless us, as we begin our life as one in him!"

Josie whispered, "And, my husband, you are God's gift to me, to be my love forever."

After Josie's dad and Will's Dad, her brothers and his brothers had all danced with Josie, Sandy made his way onto the floor. As he took Josie's hand, he remarked, "This ole cop isn't much at dancin', but this is one I couldn't pass up."

Josie looked up into his brown eyes, "Sandy, I can't tell you how grateful I am to Adonai for bringing you into my life. I know you don't do all you did for me, for all your... er...criminals, so it was surely a gracious gift of our Lord, that brought you to my case instead of some other cop."

With no appropriate response, Sandy looked at her again. "You've become quite a lady, Josie. I know God is going to bless you and Will." He paused, and then continued, "There's an old Mexican proverb that says, 'A house does not rest upon the ground, but upon a woman'."

He gave her a hug and gave her back to her husband.

*Sameach TeSmach Re'lim, KeSamechacha
Yetsircha BeGan Eden MiKedem. Baruch at
Adonai, MeSame'ach Chatan VeKalah
(Let the loving couple be very happy, just as You
made Your creation happy in the garden of Eden,
so long ago. You are blessed, Lord, who makes the
bridegroom and the bride happy)
From Shevah Berachot, The Fifth Blessing*

EPILOGUE

Josef Blandón's trial came and went before the wedding. He was sentenced to twenty years in state prison and was quickly extradited to Churchill where he faced charges of molesting his daughter and her friend, Lily. Josie would never see her brother again. After serving just five years, he was murdered in prison by a Muslim gang member, who found out Josef was a Jew and a child molester. It happened just two years before he was eligible for a parole hearing. Sharon remarried two years after his death. Her husband adopted her two children and changed their names.

Josie Brent became pregnant before **Will** left for the U.S. Marshal's Academy. When he returned, he was assigned to the Central Texas District and headquartered in San Antonio. The family moved to San Antonio and established a new life. Will legally adopted Stevie and changed his name to Brent. Stevie was entering second grade when their son Moisés was born and named for his grandfather. Two years later, she gave birth to Levi. After Levi, they had no more children. In spite of the doctors telling her to have no more children before Moisés, she and Will made the decision to have at least two children and trust God for the results. God answered their prayers, and both Levi and Moisés were healthy and there were no birth complications.

After her children were in school, Josie worked tirelessly to set up Christian shelters around the state patterned after the Lighted Way Ministries. She traveled and gave speeches whenever possible in support of her dream. She became somewhat of a celebrity and appeared on television and radio many times. Ultimately, she had to curtail her traveling until all her sons were out of school and in college. Will served a long and distinguished career in the U.S. Marshall's service.

Israel Blandón, Josie's next oldest brother, was in attendance at the wedding, and visited Josie and Will frequently. He and his wife, Rachel, assumed the care of his mother Ruth, after his father's death. He carried on the family patriarchal Jewish traditions of his father.

Steven Richard Brent, Josie's first son by Roger Brown, majored in history and languages in college, specializing in Arabic and Spanish. During his childhood, he learned Hebrew from his grandfather. Following graduation, he enlisted in the Army and was immediately sent to Fort Benning, Georgia to the Infantry Officer Candidate School. After graduation as a second lieutenant, he was deployed to Iraq during the Iraq War. He applied for Military Intelligence School and was accepted. After graduating, he was accepted in the Delta Force Training Center at Fort Bragg, North Carolina. By the time he graduated, he was a Captain. After that, he was sent on secret missions into the Middle East. His family never knew where he was or what he was doing. Occasionally, he showed up at home unannounced, stayed for several days or weeks and then was off again. He remained unmarried until the end of his military career. He retired as Brigadier General.

Moisés Brent, Josie's oldest son by Will Brent, studied Engineering in college and after graduation, took a job with a military contractor making secret weapons and munitions for the Department of Defense. He married, and he and his wife moved to the West Coast. They had four children.

Levi Brent, Josie's youngest son, majored in criminal justice in college, went on to law school and followed his father as a District Attorney Investigator. He then entered the U.S. Marshal's Service. He married and was assigned to El Paso. He and his wife had three children.

Reverend Isabelle Jefferson retired after serving the Lighted Way Ministries for forty-two years. She was in poor health but lived in the mission for two more years before her death. During the two years after retiring, she gave herself to prayer, bible study and writing. She was buried beside her mother, Rosie.

Carla Schmid took over Isabelle's position at the Mission and **Darlene Goodnow** assumed Carla's position as director of the Women's Division.

Detective Randall Sandoval worked with Sheriff Paul Mortenson and others on a Multi-State Task Force assigned to investigate and locate drugs and cartel members in the U.S. Border area. After Sandy's retirement, he and Susan moved to the mountains of west Texas and bought a small ranch. They lived the rest of their lives in the mountains northeast of El Paso. Every fall they entertained U. S. Marshall Levi Brent and his family. Sandy and Levi enjoyed elk hunting in the mountains of New Mexico. Occasionally, when he had assignments at Fort Bliss, Major Steven R. Brent showed up unexpectedly and was always welcomed. Major Brent enjoyed the quiet and tranquil life in the mountains.

Josie's Gift

Sheriff Paul Mortenson resigned from his office as sheriff and spent the rest of his career working on the Drug Task Force. **Susan** raised funds and was successful in establishing a mission in Littleville patterned after the Lighted Way Ministries in Rock City. After his retirement, Mort and Susan moved to west Texas to be near Sandy and Joann.

Deputy Jerry Walker was elected to the sheriff's job and took over after Mort left. He served for twenty-two more years before he retired.

Becky Hall worked with Susan Mortenson to establish the mission in Littleville. She entered a local college and earned a degree in alcohol and drug abuse counseling. She assumed the job of Director when Susan left for west Texas with Mort. Becky lived and served at the mission for the next thirty years. She visited Will and Josie often and Josie was a frequent speaker at the Littleville mission. She never married.

John and Doris Brown worked tirelessly in Churchill to establish a mission ministry patterned after the Lighted Way Ministries in Rock City. Joe Richard and his family moved to Churchill, to be near his parents. His wife was a faithful volunteer at the mission. On one occasion, David Lee and his family attended a mission service where his father, John was speaking. Both David Lee and his wife gave their lives to Christ and became active members of a community church in their town. John was often invited to preach there. Joe Richard became an author and published fourteen best-selling Christian novels during his lifetime. His life was tragically cut short in a subway explosion in Chicago carried out by Islamic jihadists.

Juanita Talamantes and her brother **Enrique,** were instrumental in the investigation of the Salazar businesses of drugs and guns. Unfortunately they were denied permanent resident alien status and deported back to Mexico. U.S. Marshall Will Brent and the border drug task force were able to recruit both Enrique and Juanita into a secret network funded by the U. S. Government that provided intelligence and assistance to agents operating in Mexico. They were given new identities and set up in a "front" business to legitimize their activities. After the collapse of the Mexican government in 2015, Juanita and Enrique were to come into contact with Colonel Steven Brent who was sent on a top secret mission inside Mexico.

> *"Oh Lord have mercy on Your people, fill the world with Your light so that heaven and earth will be filled with Your glory and Your praise, amen, amen.*
> *Dated in Purgatory, the fifth month of the year five thousand and fifty seven of our creation. Luis de Carvajal, el mozo, Joseph Lumbroso (the enlightened) 1567-December 8, 1596 [burned at the stake, in Mexico City], his memory is a blessing."*
> *From his extensive writings during a period of penance [imprisonment for his faith], translated by Seymour B. Liebman.*